BAPTISED BY ICE

BAPTISED BY ICE

Book 2 in 'The Hand of God' series

HARRY A. DOBSON

For permission requests, please contact: harryadobson@gmail.com

Find out more about the author and upcoming books online at
www.harrydobson.co.uk
Facebook: Harry A. Dobson – Author https://www.facebook.com/profile.
php?id=100083339500392

Produced in United Kingdom.

Editorial services by www.bookeditingservices.co.uk

CONTENTS

Chapter 1: The Papal States—June 1253.....................1
Chapter 2: Gascony.....................18
Chapter 3: Twelve years ago.....................30
Chapter 4: Gascony.....................47
Chapter 5: Twelve years ago.....................56
Chapter 6: Gascony.....................71
Chapter 7: Twelve years ago.....................85
Chapter 8: Twelve years ago.....................98
Chapter 9: Gascony.....................115
Chapter 10: Twelve years ago.....................124
Chapter 11: Twelve years ago.....................133
Chapter 12: Gascony.....................144
Chapter 13: Twelve years ago.....................156
Chapter 14: Gascony.....................168
Chapter 15: Twelve years ago.....................182
Chapter 16: Gascony.....................198
Chapter 17: Twelve years ago.....................211
Chapter 18: Gascony.....................229
Chapter 19: Twelve years ago.....................244
Chapter 20: Gascony.....................260
Chapter 21: Gascony.....................286
Chapter 22: Twelve years ago.....................296
Chapter 23: Gascony.....................353
Chapter 24: Gascony.....................368

Chapter 1

THE PAPAL STATES—
JUNE 1253

Leonardo sighed in frustration. He threw his quill down on the desk and leant back in his chair, rubbing an ink-blackened thumb and forefinger into his eyes. When he opened them, the flickering orange glow from the candlelight illuminated the mountain of paper that covered the desk's surface. There were lists, accounts, charters, deeds, complaints and a myriad of other documents that Leonardo had to read and sign off. It was all he could do to keep up with the constant flow of it.

There was a knock on the door of his office. The door opened and a young monk peered cautiously around it.

'Father Leonardo? I have the last of it for the day.' He held up another stack of paper. Leonardo tutted tersely and shook his head. There was more! Of course there was.

'Yes, yes, set it down here with the rest of it,' he replied, indicating to the end of his desk. He watched as the monk walked in, stopped at the desk and hesitated for a moment, searching for some free space to deposit his delivery. He then gingerly placed the sheets of paper down on the least covered corner before stepping back.

'Thank you.'

The monk bowed and hesitated once more, before adding tentatively, 'Um, the evening meal will be served in a quarter hour, should you care to join us.'

Leonardo dipped his head in acknowledgement. 'Very well. That will be all.' The young monk took his cue and hurried out, disappearing into the corridor.

Leonardo sighed once more. He knew the other monks, priests and friars were still unsure of him, even after so many months. But that was the way he preferred it. He stood and walked to the window, looking through the glass out to the main courtyard of the cloister beyond. The sun had just set, but there was enough light to make out the vast stone buildings that formed a neat square, as well as the rooftops of others beyond.

It was the largest abbey outside Rome itself and Leonardo, much to his surprise, was the abbot. His predecessor had run the abbey's various sources of income into the ground and then died under mysterious circumstances. Then, a cardinal had ridden from the Vatican itself to appoint a new abbot. The cardinal's name was Emilio Di Volterra and, in the circles in which he was known, he was feared. What the Cardinal Emilio wanted, the Cardinal Emilio always got. And he wanted Leonardo to be the new abbot.

No one would challenge him on that, for no one dared; not even the Pope himself. It didn't matter that the abbey was one of the most significant in the entirety of the Papal States, or that Leonardo was hardly qualified for the job, at least on paper.

The other churchmen at the abbey had begrudgingly accepted him at the beginning, but when it became clear that Leonardo was a fair and capable leader, they had no cause for complaint. Under the leadership of the tall, green-eyed young priest, the abbey was soon turning a profit from wool and wine production and bringing in a decent harvest each year. No one could deny that Leonardo was not efficient. In fact, he had proven that he could be quite adept at handling some of the more delicate situations that arose around the abbey every now and again.

When disagreements between two parties broke out, Leonardo had adjudicated by hearing both sides and passing a fair judgement, usually a compromise that saw the concerned parties happy. Once, when accusations of sodomy met his ears between two monks, he simply had one sent to another abbey on a permanent posting under the guise that the abbey needed the extra manpower. As a result, he managed to avert a long and embarrassing trial.

Nor had Leonardo given anyone reason to dislike him by lording over them unnecessarily. Although, at the same time, it was also true that there were few there who would jump to their feet and sing his praises, for how could they? Leonardo was a man who kept very much to himself and spoke only to the others when he had to. He was still very much an enigma to them. And that was fine with him.

Leonardo was good at his job, he knew. But then, he was good at most things. If only he had known how much paperwork there would be... It was not at all the sort of work he was used to. Leonardo's previous role had been rather more... active. He glanced back at the drawer of his desk, where his twin daggers were tucked away safely. Every now and again, he would take them out and inspect them, give them a quick polish, and re-apply some oil to the steel. Sometimes, it felt as though they called to him, as if they begged to be used again.

He had missed the way his heart thudded in his chest when he hunted down a target, when he had stalked his prey, licking his lips in anticipation as he slowly pulled the daggers from their sheaths before he pounced on whomever it was the Order needed eliminating. He knew he shouldn't, but he even missed the way the blade felt as he plunged it into a body, the way the flesh created resistance for the blade for a moment before it sank in deep.

Damn it! he thought. *What is wrong with me?* Leonardo knew he would have to punish himself for such ungodly thoughts later. He shook his head in disgust. What had he become? Perhaps it was best that he was here, in such a peaceful environment where his work kept him busy and distracted, and it was easy to keep the darkness within at bay. Leonardo somehow knew that he would always be plagued by dark thoughts and emotions, but at least here they could be supressed to a certain degree. And he could still serve the Order, albeit not in a manner that best utilised his training.

The Order, he thought. The Order of The Hand of God was Leonardo's cornerstone, his anchor, his linchpin. It had been, ever since Emilio had taken him in all those years ago. It had given him a home, fed him, clothed him, taught him. But, most importantly of all, it had given his life a direction, a purpose. It had given him meaning. It had been his life for so long now that he didn't know what he would do without it. Nor did he ever bother to imagine another life for himself. For, what would that look like for a man such as him?

No, the Order was the only place Leonardo could fit in. To a certain extent, he needed it. Even despite the fact it was a cold and indifferent organisation, there could be no room for treachery, doubt or incompetence within its ranks. Any agents, members or other associates who manifested such symptoms were sure to meet a sticky end. Moreover, the Order demanded much from its servants; upon taking the oath, one was always expected to put the Order first and sacrifice a great deal, not least of all maintaining the secrecy in which the Order shrouded itself.

Despite being the wealthiest branch of the Catholic Church, most people didn't even know that the Order of The Hand of God existed at all. Indeed, its discovery alone was enough reason to warrant the execution of a layman. Even people at the highest levels of European society had no idea that, moving silently within their courts, royal houses and castles, were deadly agents and spies dressed as men of the cloth. Keeping the Order secret was a challenge within itself. Nor was it advisable to have a family – or roots of any kind, for that matter. Who knew where the Order would send you next? It was impossible to predict what political turmoil or global events would constitute intervention from the Order of The Hand of God.

But, despite all the sacrifices and the hardships, the Order was Leonardo's home. It was the only one he had ever really known. He took comfort in knowing that the organisation would always have a use for someone like him. So long as God's balance needed to be restored, the Order would need him.

Leonardo sighed. He wished he could just be more active. The abbey could feel claustrophobic at times. It was a bubble, a little world of its own tucked away where nothing much happened. Leonardo had been there over a year and, so far, the most interesting thing that had happened was the scandal of sodomy between the two young monks. Gone were the days of him gallivanting around the continent on horseback with only a name, an address and an order to kill. Now, his life was very much the opposite. He felt as though he were stagnating.

Sometimes, Leonardo wondered why Emilio had put him there. Emilio knew full well that Leonardo's talents lay elsewhere and, while he was perfectly capable of running the abbey, Emilio had to know that Leonardo could be more effective in a different role. Somehow, that didn't matter to Emilio; he seemed to have a different vision for Leonardo. He kept hinting at greater things to come, that Leonardo might rise high in the Order, especially now that his name was known amongst its ranks.

Emilio had failed to see that it was not something Leonardo himself cared for. He was perfectly happy with a simpler life. Still, he would suffer it, nonetheless. If the Order needed Leonardo to be the abbot, then that was exactly who he would be. Leonardo nodded to himself. So be it.

At least he had something to look forward to that night. He strode from his office, forgetting the paperwork for the time being, and made his way to the yard where his horse was stabled. That particular night, Emilio had requested his presence in the Vatican to deal with a rival cardinal that had foolishly been stepping on his toes in matters of ruling the Papal States.

When Leonardo got to the stables, his horse had already been saddled in preparation as he had requested, and all he had to do was leap up onto its back and dig in his heels. Leonardo had a long ride to complete, complicated slightly by the darkness of the night. He didn't mind; he felt at home in the shadows.

As he rode towards the eternal city, he felt some of the claustrophobia leave him like a weight being lifted from his back. He sucked in the cool, night air and almost smiled. Soon, he had already travelled as far from the abbey as he had in a season. Behind him, he left some of the pressures of his new responsibilities and could breathe a sigh of relief.

After riding fast and hard for several hours, both Leonardo and his horse were sweating as they skidded through the walls of the great city and into the compact metropolis of sprawling houses and buildings, lit by the feeble light of the moon.

Here and there, braziers burnt, and the odd constable patrolled the streets to ensure that the peace was kept. Apart from that, the city was empty, its inhabitants asleep. Leonardo pressed on to the Vatican. Here, the architecture became increasingly more grand, as the last surviving remnants of the once-great Roman empire rose from the earth in the form of magnificent columns and arches that modern masons were only just beginning to be able to emulate.

Before long, Leonardo found himself in the heart of Catholicism in Europe. Ahead, there was a checkpoint he would need to pass through to gain access to the Vatican. Two guards stood at a gate brandishing polearms. They stopped him as he approached.

Wordlessly, Leonardo produced a sealed piece of parchment from his robes and handed it down to the nearest guard. The guard held it up in such a way that the light from a nearby brazier illuminated the symbol upon it. The man grunted, handing it back up to Leonardo before nodding to his companion. The gates swung open, and Leonardo trotted inside.

Leaving his horse tethered nearby, he strode toward the designated meeting point. He made his way silently through great courtyards floored with neat, marble flagstones and busts or statues in their centre. Fountains trickled here and there, and Leonardo had to restrain himself from stopping at one and taking a long drink. He was still breathing heavily from the ride and wondered if he had become unfit.

His ever-watchful eyes picked up movement in the shadows ahead. Two large, cloaked figures stepped out into the moonlight as he approached. Leonardo recognised the two men; they were Emilio's bodyguards. Each was as tall and broad as the other and both seemed to display a constant glower on their faces.

'Stop there,' one of them grunted in a deep voice, holding up a meaty palm to Leonardo as he walked over. Leonardo stopped and lifted the hood from his head, raising an eyebrow at the man.

'Now, now, Brutus,' came a voice from the shadows. 'Leonardo is a friend. A good one, at that.' Emilio Di Volterra sidled out of the darkness. He was wearing immaculate crimson robes, likely worth as much as Leonardo's horse, and put an arm on his henchman's shoulder.

'Let us not forget our manners.' Emilio's lips curved up into a smile from beneath a neatly trimmed, but greying, beard and he held out his hand. Leonardo bowed deeply and took the hand in his, kissing the fat signet ring on the forefinger before straightening.

'Father, good evening,' he said, looking at Emilio with his bright green eyes. The face he looked into had gained a few extra lines over the last few years and, for the moment, wore a welcoming expression, though Leonardo knew exactly how fast it could change.

'Apologies, my son,' Emilio replied, gesturing at his bodyguard. 'One can never be too careful these days. Come, let us walk.'

Leonardo gave the man Brutus and the other a hard look, before he and Emilio made their way through the sprawl of church buildings. He was confident he could have taken them both.

'Now,' Emilio went on. 'I thought it would be a good idea for you to be present this evening. It is high time more of the clergy began to learn of you, Leonardo. If, one day, you are to hold a position of power, you will need to be known. You must start to build a network.' Emilio's mouth twitched. 'Perhaps the young Cardinal Geragio can be among the first.'

'As you wish, Father,' Leonardo replied as they walked quietly in the night, the bodyguards in tow. 'Does the Cardinal know of our existence?'

'No.' Emilio allowed himself a smirk. 'But the arrogant little wretch is about to learn.'

A minute later, the party had arrived at a set of rich apartments located on the outskirts of the walled cloister. Emilio's men produced a torch each and lit them on nearby braziers.

7

'There, the second door,' Emilio said, directing his henchmen to one of the lavish apartments, each two storeys of white stone. One of the men knelt to inspect the locking mechanism, squinting in the torchlight at the small keyhole, before straightening and giving the other man a nod.

Then he took a step back from the door, inhaled a deep breath and delivered a mighty kick, slamming a huge boot onto the timber and causing a great 'bang'. This was followed by a thud as the door splintered open and flew inwards, bouncing off the hinges as it hit the interior wall.

Emilio's men were already shouldering their way inside before the dust had settled, brandishing their torches and looking around for signs of life.

'Upstairs,' Emilio ordered as he and Leonardo followed the two guards closely behind. Leonardo could make out muffled cries of confusion as someone was stirring above them. Emilio's men were thudding up the stairs and disappeared from sight for a moment. The night was suddenly pierced with a cry of alarm, followed by a scuffle and several thuds as whoever was upstairs was subdued and gave an effeminate shriek.

Leonardo and Emilio exchanged a glance, the latter giving the former a smirk and a wink before the pair headed up to see what was going on.

Emilio climbed the stairs leisurely, as if he had all the time in the world, hiking up his long, elegant robes as he went. On the landing, the space opened up to a large bedroom with a four-poster bed along one wall and various other expensive items of furniture such as a cushioned settee and an armchair, now knocked over in the struggle that had taken place a moment before. One of Emilio's henchmen was kneeling on the back of a thin, naked man in his thirties, while the other was brandishing a torch in the direction of a naked youth, huddled in one corner of the room, hugging his knees and quite clearly terrified by the intruders.

The man was struggling pitifully under the weight of the henchman, who must have weighed half as much again as the young cardinal.

'Please!' he pleaded. 'Take what you want, but don't kill me!' He struggled some more, deciding to try a different tac and appeal to his intruder's Christian sympathies. 'You can't kill me. I'm a cardinal of Rome, damn you! Get off me!'

Emilio let out a chuckle at the sight of Cardinal Geragio in distress and couldn't resist the opportunity to gloat. 'Ah, Geragio, I almost didn't recognise you without your cassock.'

Geragio turned his head, with more than a little difficulty as there was a large knee pressed into his upper back. He looked up at the intruder, his features displaying at first shock, then anger.

'You! What in God's name do you think you're doing? I'll have you thrown out of the Vatican for this!' He redoubled his efforts to escape, but to no avail. When Emilio gave his man a nod, a fist was promptly thumped into the back of Geragio's head, which bounced from the floorboards and persuaded him to cease.

Emilio tutted. 'It's about time you learnt when to hold your tongue. And you'll accuse me of nothing, lest you want to be condemned for crimes against nature.' Emilio nodded at the boy in the corner.

As Geragio followed his gaze and saw what he was getting at, he spluttered, 'He's... he's just my assistant. Nothing was happening here. You have proof of nothing! And, anyway, I'm not the only one who—' He stopped abruptly.

Emilio scoffed at that. 'What was that? Oh, Geragio, soon you will learn that I am not a man who needs proof for his accusations to stick.' He looked up at his other bodyguard, and then to the boy. 'Let him go, we have no need of him now. Besides, banishment from the Church is the least of your worries, Geragio.'

The bodyguard stood back and the wide, terrified eyes of the adolescent flicked from Emilio to the bodyguard to Geragio. He then leapt to his feet and darted for a bundle of clothing to hide his modesty, before sprinting for the stairs.

Leonardo stepped aside as the boy barrelled past him, keen to be as far away as possible from the menacing group of intruders. A moment later, he had thudded down the stairs and out of the apartment, disappearing into the night.

Emilio turned his attention back to Cardinal Geragio.

'Stand him up!' he commanded. The henchman hauled the churchman to his feet and gripped his arms behind him, shoving him forward so he was facing Emilio. Geragio whimpered, as the henchman grabbed a fistful of his hair and tugged his head back for good measure, his manhood flopping around in the torchlight comically.

Geragio gasped from the pain. 'You can't treat me like this!'

'But I am,' Emilio said simply with a smirk. However, when he spoke next, the playfulness in his voice had vanished and was replaced by a hard, steely tone. 'Now, you will listen to me. I suggest you drink in every word, for this will be your only warning.'

Emilio stepped forward and produced a coin from his pocket. Upon it, the symbol of the Order of The Hand of God was stamped into the silver, an outstretched arm holding Christ's cross aloft. Emilio held it under Geragio's nose for him to see, and the young cardinal's brow creased as he gazed upon it as the silver caught the torchlight.

'Do you know what this is?' asked Emilio.

Geragio licked his lips and squinted. 'Yes, but… it does not exist. It is a rumour, a myth…'

Emilio's smile was a cold, thin line on his face. 'Wrong!' he mocked. 'Doubt me, and I'll show you just how real it is…'

Leonardo watched as Geragio's eyes flickered back and forth in the dim light. 'You're lying…' he said, but there was plenty of doubt in his expression.

'Am I?' Emilio smirked, clearly enjoying himself. 'I'd be willing to bet that, of the multitude of rumours you have undoubtedly heard about my organisation, most are true.'

'Impossible, the Pope would never allow it!'

Emilio had to chuckle. 'Fool! How do you think Innocent became Pope in the first place? Because I wanted it so! My reach extends further and deeper than you know, and you'd do well to take heed. Get in my way again and I will unleash the full wrath of my Order upon you!' Emilio's voice cut the air and his dark eyes burnt into Geragio's, who had to look away.

'Get in your way? I don't know what you mean…' he mumbled.

Emilio tutted. 'Do not be so careless to think that I do not know! You will stop whatever it is you are plotting in Milan with the Visconti. I have my own plans for that city... Oh yes, I know!' He nodded as Geragio looked up in shock at the mention of the plot.

'And that is not all I know,' continued Emilio. 'I know about the grave in a little village outside of Ancona. I know what and who is buried there, and I also know several witnesses who will swear on the book before a court as to exactly how the contents of that grave ended up there!' At that, Geragio paled, his mouth hanging open in shock as he realised he was beaten.

'How?' was all he managed to whimper.

'How? Because I have eyes everywhere!' said Emilio. 'And the moment that I get so much as a whiff of you fiddling with my business again, I will turn your life upside down before you can even wonder where it all went wrong.' His nostrils flared and he stepped back for a moment, pausing for effect to let his words sink in.

Cardinal Geragio looked despondent. His bare shoulders seemed to sag. It seemed as though the only thing stopping him from collapsing into a helpless heap on the floor were the meaty hands clamped around his biceps.

'Good,' said Emilio. 'You appear to have understood the gravity of your situation. Now, there is someone I would like you to meet.' He turned. 'Leonardo? Step forward, if you would.'

Leonardo did as he was bid, taking two paces into the centre of the room and removing his hood. Geragio looked up and recoiled in shock, or as much as he could in the henchman's vice-like grip, as he had apparently not realised that the dark corner of the room had been occupied.

In the torchlight, Geragio's eyes found a tall, athletic man with very short, fair hair, and high cheekbones built into an elegant face, whose chin was neatly shaved. A pair of bright green eyes bore into his and seemed not only to reflect the light, but to project a glow of their own.

'This is Leonardo. He is a servant of mine. In the coming years, you will see him appear more frequently in the politics of the Papacy.

You will not oppose him, nor stand in his way, Geragio. Is that clear?' Emilio raised his eyebrows expectantly.

The young cardinal nodded dejectedly.

'In fact,' continued Emilio, 'should he request it, you will offer him your assistance and hold back none of your abilities, limited though they may be.'

Geragio looked up at Emilio, clenching his jaw and summoned up the courage to speak. 'What are you planning? What do you need me and… him for?' He nodded toward Leonardo.

Emilio gave an impatient 'Tssk!' and gestured to the bodyguard who stood holding the torch. The guard took a step forward and, with his free hand, delivered a balled fist to Geragio's exposed flank. The cardinal let out a cry of pain and sank to his knees, him arms unable to shield him as they were still firmly clasped behind his back.

'That is the last time you will question me,' said Emilio. 'The pain I will cause you next time will be far greater and far more permanent. What I do from now on is no longer your concern. As for yourself, Geragio, you will cease all your… extracurricular activities and be content with the position you currently hold. And, if you want to keep it, then I suggest you do whatever I ask of you, as soon as I ask it!'

Emilio's eyes burnt into the younger man's, who again had to look away. Leonardo almost felt sorry for him. Elevated to such a lofty position, whether through merit or otherwise, was no small thing. Yet, now, Geragio was beginning to realise that he had wildly underestimated his political opposition and was as helpless as a crying babe on the forest floor.

The older and far more experienced Cardinal Emilio Di Volterra was the fiercest and hungriest of all the wolves; he had been a player in the game for decades, before any of the other men present in the room had even been born. Poor Geragio had never stood a chance.

Leonardo watched his master glare down at the naked churchman. There was no expression of triumph to be found on his face; for Emilio, the younger man, was nothing more than a nuisance. What was one more cardinal when Emilio had practically all the might of the Catholic Church under his thumb? Even the Pope himself.

Leonardo knew that the truth was that Emilio's power was far greater than he was letting on, as was the reach of their organisation.

The Order of The Hand of God stretched across all of Christendom. It dictated whether nations rose or fell; it thwarted kings and crowned them. The Order steered the politics of the land in whichever direction it saw fit, and it did it all in secrecy – or, at least, until those rare occasions when it wanted to reveal itself.

Emilio straightened and glanced at Leonardo. 'I think it's time we took our leave and let our friend Geragio mull things over. What say you, my boy?'

'As you wish, Father,' Leonardo said simply.

'Very good.' Emilio took one last, long look at his distressed former adversary. 'I shall see you at consistory, Geragio. Until then, do give the novitiates' backsides a rest, won't you?' With that, he turned and made a gesture with his hand as he headed down the stairs. The big man gripping Geragio tossed him to the floor unceremoniously and Geragio let out an 'oof!' of surprise.

As the second bodyguard followed Emilio down the stairs to leave, he delivered the cardinal a nasty kick to the ribs for good measure that made the man cry out in pain, clutching his sides. Leonardo followed, leaving the humbled cardinal groaning and naked on the floorboards.

Outside, the first light of the morning sun was beginning to show and a new day was dawning. Emilio stood in the street, flanked once more by his guards. His deep, crimson robes looked all the more regal now that Leonardo could see him better. His sharp features, neatly trimmed hair and the various golden rings adorning his fingers gave him a kingly appearance. Leonardo knew that it had not always been so; his master seemed to have acquired a taste for the finer things in life these past few years.

'Come, Leonardo,' Emilio commanded. 'Walk with me.' The pair strolled along in silence for a while, through the deserted streets of the ecclesial district of Rome, before the city had woken, the omnipresent guards in tow several paces behind.

The air was clean and fresh and the first of the day's birdsong met their ears as Leonardo thought best how to broach a subject. After several minutes, they rounded a corner to see the Basilica di Santa Maria looming ahead of them, a structure Leonardo was particularly fond of and had not yet managed to do justice in his sketches.

He took a breath and spoke. 'Father, why is it you are so determined to have me enter your world of politics? Don't you think my talents are better suited elsewhere?' Leonardo turned to look at his adoptive father, who stopped.

Emilio raised an eyebrow. 'You are unhappy?' It was half question, half statement.

Leonardo looked down, grinding his teeth and searching for an answer. 'My happiness has nothing to do with it, Father. I just feel that I could be of more use to the Order in a different role.'

'But you have done well at the abbey, you are good at this,' Emilio assured him.

'But not as good as I am at… eliminating threats,' Leonardo countered.

'Yes, but now the threats you face are of a different nature.' Emilio sighed. 'You and I both know that you are quite capable of doing whatever you set your mind to. Doing and thriving, I might add.' Emilio gripped Leonardo's shoulder, then and gave him an earnest look. 'The reason I want you involved here is because I need people I can trust by my side. Though the Order employs many under its name, especially here in Rome, I still have very few that I would rely upon.'

Emilio sighed again and looked around at some of the most magnificent buildings in Europe that represented the power of the Western world. 'God knows I need men I can trust in these uncertain times.' He paused, his back to Leonardo, as he drank in the splendour of the basilica.

Leonardo broke the silence a moment later and said in a soft voice, 'If politics is the best way I can serve the Order, then that is what I shall do, Father.' He bowed his head humbly as Emilio turned and smiled.

'Ah! There he is,' he replied. 'God's greatest champion! Yes, I believe that politics is your destiny, Leonardo. However, I know you are fond of tasks that take a more practical nature. So, if you do this for me, then I shall reward you from time to time with something a little more… engaging.'

At that, Leonardo looked up, his focus now on Emilio as he watched him closely, the older man's mouth curving up into a smile.

'In fact, I think I will have something for you to sink your teeth into later this year…' Emilio trailed off and his smile broadened as he watched the bright green eyes fill with interest.

'And what is it that you need done, Father?' asked Leonardo. 'Set me upon it and I will see it through.'

Emilio laughed. 'Ha! I do not doubt it, my boy! Very well, let us sit and I shall explain.' He indicated the steps of the basilica, where they sat and watched a pair of monks cross the far side of the courtyard, no doubt preparing for matins. Emilio's guards positioned themselves on either side, looking outward for any sign of a threat, regardless that the day was quiet and peaceful.

Emilio lowered himself down and brushed off his robes before he turned to Leonardo, who was watching him expectantly.

'During my latest correspondences with my colleague, the Nordic Finger, I have been updated with the news of the English king, Henry III.'

Leonardo listened carefully. The Order of The Hand of God divided Catholic Europe into roughly five parts, each controlled by a particularly powerful individual known as a 'Finger'. Emilio, for example, was the Papal Finger.

The Nordic Finger was responsible for the countries in Britain and Scandinavia, and would normally hold a seat in the royal court of one of the kingdoms under their charge, their true identities revealed only to those within their inner circle. Leonardo, as a result, though he held a prestigious position within the ranks of the Order, was not privy to the names of the other Fingers.

'What news, Father?'

'Trouble in Gascony. It seems the English king has been struggling to retain control of his last remaining territory on the mainland. My colleague fears that, should it fall into the hands of France or Castile, the balance of power would be upset. In this instance, I feel he is correct.'

'How can I help the situation?' Leonardo asked.

Emilio stroked his beard for a moment. 'There is someone I want you to make contact with,' he replied. 'Someone I think you will remember.'

'Who?'

'The huntsman of the Nordic Finger. His best agent. He is to my colleague what you are to me.'

Emilio paused and watched as Leonardo's brow furrowed.

'His name is Sebastien.'

Hearing the name, Leonardo stiffened, his gaze fixed on the cloister ahead. He kept the emotion from his face, but Emilio couldn't help but notice a tendon in his neck twitch.

'Ah, you do remember, of course you do. Good.' Emilio produced a folded letter from his pocket and handed it over to his charge. 'The details of your meeting are in this letter. Head to Bordeaux. There, you will find your old comrade. Together, you will ensure that Gascony remains in English hands, at least for the time being.'

Leonardo looked from the letter to Emilio. 'You were going to give me this task anyway, weren't you?'

The corner of Emilio's mouth twitched, and he gave a curt nod. 'Yes. I was.'

Leonardo nodded thoughtfully.

'One more thing, Leonardo,' said Emilio. 'Gascony is under threat from Castilian invasion. I want to know just how independent a thinker King Alfonso of Castile is, or whether his designs on Gascony are the suggestion of another – more specifically, the Iberian Finger. Do you understand?'

Leonardo raised his eyebrows in surprise at that, then nodded earnestly. *Now, that is interesting*, he thought. Leonardo had never heard of any of the Fingers acting against one another intentionally. If it was true that the Iberian Finger and the Nordic Finger had opposing agendas, then he could very much understand why Emilio would want to be aware, and why he would send someone he trusted to find out.

'I understand, Father,' he stated assuredly. 'I will find out what I can.'

'Excellent,' said Emilio. 'Then go and meet with Sebastien, the pair of you will be working closely on this.

'As you wish, Father,' Leonardo replied, dipping his head.

Emilio patted Leonardo's arm and made to stand. Leonardo leapt up and helped his master.

'Thank you, my boy.' Emilio looked toward the dawn. 'The day is young and the pair of us have work to do. Let us be about it! Good luck.' With a snap of his fingers, he turned and his guards fell into step on either side once more, leaving Leonardo standing alone in the square before the basilica.

Leonardo watched Emilio stride away. He was very much looking forward to being able to stretch his legs, so to speak. It had been too long since he had left the country, and longer still since he had had any real action.

However, what he was *not* looking forward to were the bitter memories of the past, which the agent he was required to rendezvous with in Bordeaux was sure to bring flooding back. It had been over a decade since they had last crossed paths. A shadow flickered over Leonardo's face as he remembered the circumstances in which they had parted ways, and he ground his teeth in frustration. *No matter*, he thought. He would have to put it behind him, for the Order's needs outweighed his own, as they always did.

Chapter 2

GASCONY

Leonardo's journey had been, thus far, quite pleasant. The days were hot, perhaps sometimes a little too hot, but there was usually shade to be found around midday. He had made good time sailing from Italy to Marseille over the calm waters of the Mediterranean, docking in Frankia, where the language changed and the customs were refreshingly dissimilar.

Then, he had hired a horse and ridden to Toulouse, a bustling city where he could lose himself as well as he could when back in the streets of Rome. He had not stopped. Next, the quickest way to Bordeaux was to hop on one of the many barges that sailed down the Garonne, the great river that cut north and west over Gascony and took water from the foothills of the Pyrenees, all the way to the Bay of Biscay and the ocean beyond.

Of the mountains themselves, Leonardo had had but a glimpse of snowy peaks many miles in the distance, obscured by the summer haze in the air. They were familiar to him, those peaks. Once again, he found the swirl of blurry images, over a decade old, flash before his eyes, half-forgotten memories of trials, tests and suffering. Stormy winter nights, hunger and pain and the cold. The kind of cold that seemed to penetrate deep into his bones and made him shiver, even as he warmed himself by the fire. But there, he remembered, he had experienced much worse than the cold.

He shook his head and dismissed the intrusion from the past and focused on what was happening in the present. He stood upon the bow of a trading vessel, enjoying the way its prow cut gently through the meandering Garonne. It was a beautiful day with not a cloud in the sky. To either side of the river were gently sloping hills that rose to form the edges of the shallow valley, rolling away into the distance. Peasants tilled fertile pastures that, in this part of the world, grew fast and reliably.

Leonardo watched as a shirtless group of men hacked away at the earth with shovels, digging a trench for the rainwater to drain, their skin bronzed from the exposure to the sun. One of them paused and straightened, glancing over at Leonardo's barge, before adjusting a straw hat and taking another swing with his pick.

Women in plain skirts of browns and beiges chatted as they picked at vineyards on the other side of the river, plucking away at the grapes and collecting them in wicker baskets held in the crooks of their arms.

There was a gentle breeze that made the trees stir slightly and show off their leaves in the afternoon sunlight that, when it shone through them, seemed to fracture into golden rays.

Closer to the boat, wildflowers grew by the water's edge, pollenated by bumblebees and butterflies. Geese swam out of the way with their babies chirping in tow, taking shelter in the reeds that they shared with the otters.

Leonardo reflected on how beautiful the land of Gascony was. He found it difficult to imagine, seeing such a peaceful presentation, that much of the province was currently in open rebellion. From what he had learnt during his travels, some parts had been affected worse than others. Crops had been burnt, vineyards destroyed, and castles raised. Yet, none of this had been done by the rebel nobles; no, the land was their livelihood. They would never destroy what was so lucrative.

Instead, it had been the iron-handed regent that the King of the English, Henry III, had placed in command of the province. Over the last three years, a name had played upon the lips of the Gascon nobles and, for many, it was bitter tasting. Simon de Montfort, Earl of Leicester, was a capable military commander and his response to the minor rebel insurrections had been swift and brutal. With the outrage he had caused, Leonardo suspected that, whatever grievances the nobility had against the English king, they had now been eclipsed with fresh injustices. He supposed he would learn more once he arrived at Bordeaux.

'Not long now, Father. Another hour or so.' The driver at the rudder, behind Leonardo, broke the silence. Leonardo gave him a nod to show that he had heard, adjusting his black priests' robes so that the back of his neck was a little better protected from the sun.

Soon after, the ship rounded another meandering curve in the river and there, ahead, was the city of Bordeaux. The first things Leonardo saw were the spires of the cathedral and churches, towers of pale stone that pierced the sky and could be seen for miles around. Then, as they approached and the river widened, the houses came into view. Facades of buildings, permeated with small, shuttered windows and orange-tiled roofs, lined the banks of the river on either side.

Countless ships and barges travelled the river, some having arrived by way of the sea beyond, to transport goods that would then be sold in one of Bordeaux's many great markets to supply the region.

As the buildings on either side of them grew closer, Leonardo could see that many of the warehouses by the river were dedicated solely to Gascony's major export: wine. Tens of thousands of gallons would be brought from the surrounding countryside each year to be sold to the rest of Europe. A small portion would come from the King's own lands, but all of the rest would be taxed. As Leonardo watched, the barrels were being rolled up the wooden walkways onto waiting ships. That was one way the rebels could make the English king suffer – deprive him of his wine.

They neared a dock and the driver gave the men on the shore a wave.

'Here we are then, Father,' the driver said, letting out a grunt as the boat bumped into the wooden posts so that it could be tied to the dock.

'My thanks.' Leonardo gave the man a nod and tossed him a coin. Stepping off the boat and onto the docks, he sidestepped the waiting men with their cargo ready to be loaded onto the barge and, from there, to be transported upriver, and he strode onwards into the city. His destination was the cathedral, a difficult target to miss, for its steeple dominated the skyline and was rarely out of view.

Bordeaux was a large city and had a population to match. Here in its heart, it was easy to see how one from the countryside could become overwhelmed in the crowds; but it was exactly the kind of environment in which Leonardo thrived. Donned in the garb of a priest, he could pass practically unseen by the common folk. Perhaps he would receive a respectful nod from a particularly pious passer-by, but that was all; for churchmen were as common as grains of sand on a beach. No one bothered to pay him any attention; no one knew who, or what, he really was. He had found over the years that that was something that excited him.

Leonardo swept past several market stalls on his way to the main square. A plethora of sounds, sights and smells met his senses as he made his way through the fish markets, sidestepping customers and vendors alike, waving away the hottest deals on fresh salmon, before he had broken through and was passing into a narrow street with buildings rising on either side. After a few hundred yards, the road made a dog's leg. The street opened up to the city's main square and there, in front of him, was the cathedral of Bordeaux in all its magnificence.

Leonardo paused for a moment, looking up at the building silhouetted against the glaring sun. He gazed up at the intricately carved stonework, the flying buttresses, the perfectly proportioned archways, the layers, the levels, the scale! Everything, from the great oak doors to the hand-carved gargoyles, was a fantastic work of art in his eyes.

Still, there would be time to appreciate that later. Leonardo headed for the doors that were open to the public. As soon as he had stepped across the threshold, the atmosphere changed. The hubbub of the outside world lessened to a murmur and the air was cool and still. The interior was no less magnificent than the exterior, Leonardo mused.

Monks walked here and there, or otherwise sat praying in silent contemplation, and a group of nuns huddled in one corner of the great hall talking in low whispers. Leonardo passed them, heading for the room next to the chapel that he knew would be at the rear of the great church. He found it and tapped softly on the door, hoping that what he sought lay within. The door opened a crack and a face peered out.

'You are not from here,' the face stated after looking him up and down briefly.

'No. I am a traveller and I have come to collect my tithe.' Leonardo held up a signet ring with the symbol of his Order imprinted onto the silver. The face squinted down at it, then back up at Leonardo, and then back down again.

'Wait here,' it said.

Leonardo waited. A moment later, the face was back at the crack in the door and its owner pushed a small, leather sack through the gap and dropped it into Leonardo's outstretched palm. *That should do*, he thought. He gave a nod and turned on his heel, already striding for the exit.

The Order was nothing if not efficient. And well funded. The sack of gold he had just collected was more money than most people ever saw in a lifetime, and would certainly help him grease whatever wheels he needed over the coming months. He tied the leather sack carefully to his belt before re-emerging into the sun.

Outside, something had changed. The activity in the square in front of the cathedral had ground to a halt. Passers-by had stopped to stare, in anxious interest, at the group of young men swaggering into the centre. They were finely dressed in colourful tunics, knee-high boots of thick leather, embroidered trousers buckled around the waist with ornate belts, and were armed with daggers or clubs.

They numbered half a dozen and seemed to be led by one a little older than the rest, his tunic the best fitting and most expensive looking. He was handsome, with a square jaw and a head of full, fair hair. The only blemish Leonardo could see was a red birthmark that ran up the man's neck and to just below his left ear. His thumbs were hooked into his belt, and he glared around at the townsfolk as if they had somehow wronged him.

A young lady, carrying a wicker basket full of apples for the market, tried to give them a wide berth, but did not step far enough away. One of the other youths had tapped his friend on the shoulder and pointed. They had both jogged over to corner the girl, helping themselves to the apples and tossing them over to their comrades, who laughed in delight. The girl, clearly uncomfortable, managed to make good her escape, but not before half her cargo had gone spilling out onto the packed earth.

Leonardo watched the display with interest, noting how no one seemed to be doing anything to stop the youths, which made him wonder who they were exactly. Regular street thugs seldom wore such fine garb.

Their leader continued to glare at the folks lining the square as they went about their business, as if daring them to challenge him. When none did, the group sidled over to the stalls lining the square and seemed to get a kick from the way the merchants took a nervous step back as they approached.

'What are you looking at?' one youth shouted at a cloth merchant, and sniggered at the way the man recoiled in shock when the youth took a lunge forward, as if to strike at him.

Glancing around, Leonardo could see that the crowds in the square, numerous only minutes ago, had now evaporated and he found himself standing alone before the cathedral, with the group of young men heading his way. He decided he would remain where he stood. Perhaps it would be a good test for the youths – would they be so bold as to disturb a man of God?

Their birthmarked leader was continuing to stalk about, searching for a target. There were none who would meet his eye and that seemed to aggravate him all the more. *An angry young man indeed*, Leonardo mused.

Just as that thought crossed his mind, those angry eyes locked onto his own and narrowed menacingly. The young man headed toward him, the dagger he wore on his hip clearly visible.

'Don't you have some praying to be getting on with, priest? Why are you standing there gawking at me? Move along!' The young man spoke in a tone that conveyed he was used to being obeyed. At the sound of their leader giving an order, the youth's cronies stopped their chortling and fell silent to watch with interest, evidently waiting for Leonardo to obey.

Yet, Leonardo did not. Instead, he held the gaze calmly, his bright green eyes unblinking. He could sense the rest of the townsfolk around him had stopped what they were doing to watch, curious to see what would happen next. The square had fallen deathly silent, and no one moved nor spoke.

'I have already made my peace with God. Now I wish to enjoy the afternoon,' Leonardo said in reply.

The young man sneered as he looked Leonardo up and down, who stood unthreateningly with his arms hanging by his sides. 'Enjoy it somewhere else then, you nuisance. Your presence is irking me.'

He half turned away, clearly expecting Leonardo to hurry along and be on his way, but turned back when Leonardo responded.

'No. I think I will enjoy the cathedral a little longer.'

The young man before him raised his eyebrows incredulously. 'No? Did you just tell me no?' He scoffed in disbelief. 'You must be a simpleton.'

Leonardo sighed. 'I am not,' was all he could be bothered to offer in reply.

The youth bristled. His companions, seeing their leader was agitated, fanned out slightly and formed a loose half-circle around the pair.

'You're obviously not from here,' he said. 'You don't seem to know who I am.' The youth smiled nastily, as if the utterance of his own name would be his ace in the hole.

'I do not know who you are, though I'm sure you'll tell me,' Leonardo said. He remained as still as a post, but could feel the pace of his heart quickening as it pumped blood and adrenaline around his body, feeding his muscles and preparing them for action.

'I am Gaillard Solers,' said the young man. 'You will have heard the name. I am the head of my family, and we are the blood of this city!' He stuck out his chin triumphantly, as if he had gotten one over on Leonardo. Truthfully, Leonardo had heard the name before; the Solers clan and their supporters dominated half the wine trade of the area and were supposed to be quite wealthy. Yet, Leonardo decided not to give the young Gaillard the satisfaction.

'I see. And what concern is that of mine, Master Solers?' Leonardo asked with an infuriating calmness.

Gaillard's nostrils flared. 'It means you should show me some respect and move along!'

Leonardo must have been the young man's senior by ten years or so and did not care to be ordered around by someone so pompous. Yet, he was an expert in mastering his emotions. He gave no response to Gaillard's command and simply stood, cocking his head to one side, waiting for Gaillard's reaction.

The latter was beginning to redden with rage, for it was seldom that he didn't get what he wanted. He took several paces toward the silent priest until their faces were inches apart.

'Fine. If you won't move, then I will move you!'

Leonardo felt the breath on his face and watched as Gaillard stepped back, bringing up his hands ready to shove Leonardo, who watched, as if it were happening in slow motion.

He almost had time to smile, for the young man was much too slow. Leonardo's movement, on the other hand, was the polar opposite. For the folks standing watching, it was like watching a lightning flash. Before Gaillard had even thought about shoving the priest, Leonardo was already moving, sidestepping outside his opponent's guard, and brought up his left hand to smack Gaillard's cheek with an open palm.

The blow connected perfectly. There was a sharp intake of breath from the onlookers as the crack of Leonardo's hand hitting the young nobleman's face echoed off the walls of the cathedral and resounded in the square.

Gaillard stumbled from the force of the blow, his mouth wide open in shock as he brought his hand up to feel his cheek. His companions, equally surprised, seemed frozen to the spot, not knowing whether to help their leader or attack Leonardo.

However, they were spared the choice, for, just then, three armed knights on horseback rode at a gallop into the square. The sound of the horses' hooves, smacking the packed earth, filled the tense silence.

'Solers!' the rider at the fore cried, as he brought his mount skidding to a halt several yards away. 'You know the rules. Weapons for civilians have been outlawed within the defences of the city! Disarm at once!'

Gaillard Solers and his companions had turned at the sound of the arrival of the newcomers. Leonardo watched as the young man's face twisted into a mask of mocking dislike, the priest behind him forgotten for the time being.

'Look!' he said to his fellows. 'Drogo de Barentin, the idiot King's lapdog!'

There was a ripple of laughter amongst the young noblemen. However, although they were seven and the riders only three, Leonardo could detect a hint of nervousness about them, for the riders were well armed and the man Gaillard had addressed as Drogo de Barentin did not look like a pushover. He was in his forties, bald, bearded and broad. He had a slab of a nose and a scar that passed from one cheek, over both lips and down to his chin.

'What will you and your fifteen knights do?' Gaillard continued to taunt. 'Tickle me to death?' There was more laughter.

Drogo narrowed his eyes. 'You will keep the King's peace. And the next time I see you, you'd better not be armed.'

'Tssk!' Gaillard hawked and spat into the earth. 'That's what I think of your King and his peace!' He turned back to Leonardo and glared hatefully, the muscles in his jaw taught. 'You should hope that we don't happen to meet again, priest. Next time, there may be no King's men to save you! Come on, boys. Let's leave the English fools to play with themselves!'

There was a snigger and they all turned and followed Gaillard Solers, who strode away, his chin still stuck in the air as if the city and everything in it were his. Once he was out of sight, it was as though the other townsfolk breathed a sigh of relief, and a veil of tension was lifted. They continued about their business, everything back to how it had been several minutes before.

'And how did you manage to upset young Master Solers, Father?' Drogo de Barentin squeezed his legs together, so that his horse advanced several paces.

Leonardo smiled. 'I was in the wrong place at the wrong time, sir knight.'

'Hmm.' Drogo grunted as he looked about for any signs of a further threat. Satisfied, he swung from his horse with a 'clink' as the buckles of his sword belt hit his maille hauberk. 'It seems that's all it takes these days. He didn't harm you, did he? I can tell from your accent you're not from around here. Maybe you don't know the situation here in Gascony, but things of late have been volatile, at best.'

'He didn't touch me,' Leonardo said, feeling it best not to mention the part about him slapping the young nobleman. 'Volatile, you say. How so?'

'You must have heard of the war?' replied Drogo. 'Half of the nobles are in open rebellion. Every week that goes by, another town falls into their hands.' He sighed and patted his horse's muzzle. 'It didn't help, either, that the leader of the rebels was here in Bordeaux. Rostand Solers, the late father of your new friend.' He nodded in the direction Gaillard Solers had gone. 'He died in captivity under Montfort's rule a couple of years ago. It may only be a matter of time before Gascony falls for good.'

'And where is the King?' asked Leonardo. 'I cannot imagine he would allow that to happen so easily.'

Drogo rolled his eyes. 'The King's mind is occupied with other matters. For now, he is still at Westminster. I am acting on his behalf as Seneschal of Gascony. Me and my fourteen men.' Drogo chewed the last words bitterly.

'Ah, so that's what Master Solers meant,' said Leonardo, nodding his head. 'Fifteen knights seems a little inadequate.'

Drogo snorted. 'It's a joke! And an insult to the loyalists. It means my hands are tied. There is only so much I can do to deal with brats like Solers. I fear the time when he finds the balls to muster the rebels in the countryside and attempts to take Bordeaux. The whole city saw the King's reactive force arrive on just one ship!' He sighed again, and rubbed a thumb and forefinger into tired eyes, suddenly looking as though he had aged several years. 'Forgive me, foreigners are rare these days. Under different circumstances, you would have received a better welcome.'

Leonardo shrugged. 'It was not altogether unpleasant,' he replied.

Drogo grunted once more, giving the priest a thoughtful look, before clambering back up into the saddle. His fellow knights had been waited patiently.

'Take care, Father,' he called, before wheeling his mount around and cantering off back the way he had come, leaving Leonardo alone again.

Leonardo pursed his lips, thinking on what he had heard. Then, it occurred to him to check that he had not lost his gold-filled purse in the excitement. He put a hand to his belt. He had not. He breathed a sigh of relief.

Just as he did so, his ears pricked up and the senses at the back of his head tingled. He stiffened. He had the same feeling whenever he felt eyes watching him. Slowly, Leonardo turned to see a cloaked and hooded figure standing watching him from an alleyway, at the far end of the square, hidden away in the shadows between two buildings.

He squinted. The figure was too distant to properly identify. How long had they been watching him? Something about the way the figure stood stock still, the plain brown robes, the way the hands were clasped at the waist in front of them screamed familiarity...

And then it clicked. Leonardo walked toward the figure. As he approached, he began to make out the features under the hood that slowly came into focus. A square, shaven jaw, a smattering of freckles over pale skin, short and neatly trimmed chestnut hair and a pair of intelligent brown eyes.

Leonardo came to a stop before the man. There was a moment of silence as he held the cold gaze of the keen brown eyes. Those seconds allowed him to process the changes in the appearance of the man before him. After over a decade apart, the only differences were a few extra lines around the eyes and mouth, as far as Leonardo could tell.

'Sebastien,' he said.

'Leonardo,' Sebastien croaked back. Neither offered their hand in greeting, nor made any attempt to close the distance between them, be it literally or otherwise. As the silence drew on, so did the stalemate.

'So,' Leonardo said eventually. 'It seems we will be working together for a time.'

'Yes.' For a moment, it seemed as though Sebastien was about to grimace, but managed to control himself. To anyone else, it would have been imperceptible, but Leonardo knew the man particularly well. 'It would appear so.'

Chapter 3

TWELVE YEARS AGO

Leonardo was nineteen years old. He gazed upward with more than a little trepidation. The great mountains of the Pyrenees rose up ominously before him, their mysterious peaks wreathed in cloud. The cart he had caught a lift on trundled away down the fork in the road, the sound of the peasant farmer driving the oxen and whistling to himself nonchalantly quickly fading away until Leonardo was completely alone.

His path took him upwards, but to where, he was not entirely certain. Over his shoulder, a sack was slung with everything he owned in the world and, in his hand, he clutched the letter of instruction. He opened it and peered at the words written there for the hundredth time. 'Travel to Toulouse, then take the southern road and climb into the mountains until you come to the town of Arreau. Then, climb further still on the south-easterly road. At the end of it, you will find the monastery.'

He frowned. *The instructions could have been more detailed,* he mused. It had taken him half of the previous day to get from the foothills to Arreau alone; who knew where this south-easterly road ended? It could be anywhere. Leonardo had already come to learn that the mountains were vast, stretching from one sea to the other; to say that they were a formidable obstacle would be a gross understatement.

They stood before him, dominating the landscape; ancient monoliths, bult by God himself, that could keep even the sun from piercing into the valley floor. Impossibly vast, craggy masses of undulating rock formed their random bulk, their lower surfaces blanketed by an army of uniform evergreens, as though standing guard. Even though it was June, Leonardo could still see snow higher up and the air carried the slightest of chills. He dreaded to think what climate the winter months would bring.

He turned his attention to the crossroads, where the south-easterly road wound upwards into the distance, away from the scant civilisation that managed to survive this high up in the wilderness. Truth be told, it looked less like a road and more like a path. *Was there really a fortified monastery waiting up there?* he wondered. Leonardo checked the letter once more, just to be absolutely certain there were no details he had missed. There were not.

He took a deep breath and readjusted the sack on his back, taking the first step upward and into the unknown.

The going was tough. It was clear that no cart had passed this way for a long time. In places, the road was completely covered by landslides, where great slabs of rock had detached themselves from the cliff face and cascaded down to obstruct the road, along with heaps of scree. Panting, Leonardo had to clamber over them, already sweating from the effort of the long, upward slog.

Every now and again, he had to wipe his brow and pause for rest. It was almost as though the air were thinner; for, no matter how much of it he sucked into his lungs, he still felt out of breath. He pressed on, forever craning his neck to look ahead for any signs of life.

Over the next ridge, Leonardo kept promising himself. *Over the next one.* But they were deceiving; just when he thought he must run out of mountain at any moment, he stumbled over yet another hillock, to be greeted by a great expanse of grassy, snowy and craggy mass above him.

After several hours, the snow that covered the ground sporadically became more common, and more of a nuisance. Leonardo's thin, leather boots were damp and offered little support. He cursed every other minute as he slipped and slid on the uneven ground.

Once, there was a break in the terrain that allowed him to look back down and see the way he had come. *Was that tiny collection of buildings Arreau?* he thought incredulously. He had come so far!

Leonardo had never been so high up, and felt a wave of dizziness wash over him as he gazed out at the land thousands of feet below. Suddenly, he was gripped by a jolt of fear, as the thought occurred to him that he might run out of sky, too, and tumble into whatever lay beyond. Perhaps that was heaven? As soon as he had thought it, he shook it from his head. *Nonsense.* He was on a mountain and that was real enough.

He continued on, following the road that, at this point, seemed fit only for goats and certainly not for men. There was a niggling doubt in the back of his mind that he had chosen the wrong path and had, somehow, made a mistake at the bottom. What if he had been climbing the wrong mountain? What if the road that led up to the monastery had branched from a different crossroads? Leonardo did not like the idea of spending the night on the mountainside so exposed. He hesitated, wondering if he should go back down.

No, he thought. *So long as there is a path to tread, I have to see it through.* So, upwards he went. He was glad that was the decision he made, for, half an hour later, he saw the first signs of life. There, by a bent pine tree, was a neat pile of rocks that someone must have placed, as if they were a marker of sorts. Leonardo scrambled up to them and ran his fingers over their rough surface and grinned. Surely, that had to be a sign.

Invigorated with a new energy, he pressed on, climbing quicker than before. Then, after another short climb, he crested the ridge and saw it; the monastery!

His breath caught in his lungs for a moment as he drank in the scene that lay before him. Here, he really was near the top, for the ridge he now stood upon enabled him to see down into a whole new valley, long and deep. Its sides were impossibly sheer, permeated here and there by little waterfalls that brought the trickling meltwater down to the valley floor.

The path on which Leonardo stood curved away to the left, following the south-facing wall of the valley where, several hundred yards away, a natural cleft had formed that created a sort of flat plateau that followed the valley's curve. It was shaped a bit like a banana, the tip ending in a sheer cliff face and the stalk being the entry road and, therefore, the only way in.

And there, built into the cleft, was a large, squat, stone building made of roughly carved, bulky grey stones. Though the design was simple, with small windows breaking up the plain facade here and there, and a timber roof built onto the second storey, it was nonetheless a marvel. How in the world had someone managed to build something like that so high up? And so close to the edge!

The front face of the building was so close to the sheer cliff that dropped away beneath it that, in order to skirt around it, it appeared one would have to have their back to the stone wall and edge gingerly along the cliff so as not to fall to their death. Around it, there was a collection of other buildings, some built into the back of the cliff, which rose up above the compound and terminated a hundred feet above it, the true top of the mountain.

They were all simple utilitarian designs, rugged and sturdy. Half-melted snow trickled down the wooden shingles to drip from opaque icicles, which decorated the building's edge. Rags hanging from a rusted weathervane were tugged at by a gentle breeze.

Leonardo gazed in wonder at his discovery and had no idea what he would find there, nor what to expect. The wind picked up and whipped at his cloak, made cool by the altitude as it pinched his skin, and he found he was more than a little apprehensive.

Still, it was not as if he could stand here forever. He sucked in a deep breath and walked toward the great slab of a wooden door that was the entrance to the large, stone hall. However, when he was not ten paces away, it was almost as if he had set off some kind of alarm, for the door burst open, and a man stood staring at him from the entrance.

His black robes billowed in the wind, a stark contrast to his bone-white hair and beard, that were both long and covered half his face, though not so much that Leonardo could not see he was older, perhaps fifty or sixty. The face was lined and weathered, the features so hard they looked as though they had been hacked from oak. A pair of shrewd, calculating eyes regarded Leonardo silently for a moment.

As the silence lengthened, Leonardo felt quite uncomfortable and decided he would break it first. He cleared his throat.

'Greetings. I am sent from the Papal States. My name is—'

'I know who you are!' A harsh voice cut through the air. 'Emilio's boy.' The bearded man still blocked Leonardo's entry. He had a sudden pang of fear that he would be turned away; that, for whatever reason, this man had decided he would not make the cut.

A moment later, the man spoke again. 'I am Magnus. You had better come in.' He then moved aside to allow Leonardo to enter.

Leonardo licked his lips nervously before stepping over the threshold. The interior was gloomy, and his eyes took a moment to adjust. The first thing he noticed was the size of the hall in which he found himself. It was long and spacious, and a fire burnt in an enormous hearth built into one side. Sconces lined the rest of the bare, stone walls. The further half of the room was filled with crude pine tables and chairs, with the fore clear of furniture, creating a wide, open space.

The hall was without decoration or colour and had a minimalistic feel, as though everything in it had earned a place for a reason. Sitting at one of the tables, poring over a book, was another man. He looked up as Leonardo entered, gazing at him with interest.

Magnus's harsh voice barked behind Leonardo. 'See here, Antonio. We have our first visitor of the season. He is also Italian.'

As Magnus closed the door, Antonio stood and walked over to Leonardo, who was waiting nervously for any kind of instruction. Antonio was of average height and had a slight build, tanned skin and medium-length black hair that was oiled back over his head. Like Magnus, he sported a beard, though Antonio's was much shorter and neatly trimmed. He was younger than Magnus, too, somewhere in his thirties, Leonardo guessed. He sidled silently over, his expression unreadable.

He stopped before Leonardo without saying a word and gave a short bow. Leonardo hesitated for a moment, then returned the bow awkwardly.

'Greetings, I am Leonardo. From where in Italy do you hail?' he asked politely.

Antonio said nothing. He simply maintained the blank expression, his dark eyes unblinking. Magnus came to stand beside them.

'Antonio does not speak,' he said, tucking his thumbs into his belt.

'Ah, he has taken a vow of silence?' Leonardo asked, glancing at Magnus.

'No,' Magnus said. 'He has no tongue.'

'Oh.'

There was another uncomfortable silence as Leonardo felt the two men looking him up and down with scrutiny, as if assessing him.

Finally, Magnus spoke again. 'Welcome to the monastery. This will be your home for the next year and a half. That is, should you survive the trials ahead.'

Leonardo thought for a moment that the man was joking, but his expression showed not a hint of amusement.

'Trials?' he asked.

'You will see,' replied Magnus. 'Once the other students arrive, I will explain. For now, all you need to know is that we,' he added, indicated himself and Antonio, 'will be your teachers. You will refer to us as such, understood?'

'Yes, Teacher,' Leonardo answered quickly.

'Good. We number four in total,' Magnus's harsh, gruff voice went on. 'The other two are out on the hunt at present. They will be back before dark. In a fortnight, the training will begin. Until then, familiarise yourself with the compound. You will be staying in the bunkhouse. Antonio will show you where. Tomorrow, you will rise at first light and be ready to work.'

'What sort of work?' Leonardo asked, his curiosity getting the better of him. However, he regretted the question as soon as it had left his mouth, for Magnus bristled with annoyance.

Narrowing his eyes, Magnus said, 'I don't want to hear you speak unless I ask you a question. You would do well to learn that, boy. Keeping your mouth shut will make your life easier here. You will work and train, however and whenever we ask it of you, and you will obey! Defy any one of us, and I will throw you down the mountain and you can crawl back to Emilio to tell him you have failed. I'm sure you know that Emilio is not a man who takes it lightly when his subjects embarrass him. Do I make myself clear?' His hard features moulded into a frown.

Leonardo nodded. 'Err, yes, Teacher,' he added hastily, his cheeks turning a shade of pink at the rebuke.

'Better,' said Magnus. 'Go then, to the bunkhouse. Be back here in the evening for supper. That is all.' He had already turned away, heading to a staircase at the far end of the hall that led to the second floor, where Leonardo guessed the 'teachers' lived.

Antonio tapped Leonardo on the shoulder and beckoned him to follow. The pair were soon back outside in the sun, which seemed especially bright in comparison to the dimness of the hall. Leonardo followed Antonio across the large, open courtyard that was not quite flat, as the bedrock protruded from the earth here and there. They headed in silence to the collection of other, smaller stone buildings that were built up against the mountainside.

They were all built in the same style as the great hall; large, irregular blocks of stone bound together with lime mortar to form very plain, but practical, shapes. It was a far cry from the exquisitely detailed architecture of Rome, but it did the job, nonetheless.

Suddenly, Antonio stopped before one of the buildings, pointing at the nearest of them. He then put both his hands together next to his head, which he tilted to one side and shut his eyes to represent sleep.

'Ah, that's the bunkhouse?' Leonardo asked.

Antonio nodded, then pointed at the next, putting his hands together as if to pray.

'The chapel?'

Another nod. Next, Antonio made a square shape with his hands and then put them to his head to make horns with his fingers, pointing at the last two buildings.

'A storehouse and a barn?'

Antonio gave a thumbs up, then pointed at Leonardo and then to the bunkhouse.

'Yes, I understand, Teacher.'

Leonardo walked over to try the door of the bunkhouse, lifted the latch and pushed it open with a creak. Inside, the room was dark, but he could make out a dozen beds as well as a large, empty fireplace built into one wall. Like the great hall, the bunkhouse seemed sparse and unpretentious. It was everything it needed to be and nothing it didn't.

Leonardo thought of something and turned to ask Antonio. 'Where might I find some firewood…' But Antonio had gone, disappeared without a sound, and Leonardo was alone.

'Huh,' he muttered at Antonio's vanishing act.

Leonardo turned back to the bunkhouse and stepped inside, leaving the door open so he would have some light. The simple wooden beds were set out at intervals along either wall, each with a mattress of straw covered by a linen sheet. On top of that, lay a couple of neatly folded thick, woollen blankets and, at the foot of each bed, was a chest and a chamber pot. Sconces in the walls held candles that were unlit, and Leonardo squinted into the shadows of the room to see a neatly stacked pile of logs.

Good, he thought. He could light the fire then, for he was sure that, even in June, the nights at such an altitude were bound to be cold. He put his meagre belongings down onto the bed nearest the hearth and set about the task. Once it was done, he looked into the chest at the foot of his bed to find what looked like piles of linen bandages. He guessed they were used to wrap around his limbs during the colder weather and wondered, once more, what winter would be like, concluding that he was in no rush to find out.

Then, Leonardo stepped outside into the chilly afternoon air to explore a little more of his new home. The chapel was much the same as the rest of the buildings on the inside – boxy, with bare stone walls, some simple wooden pews and an altar at the far end. Lit candles illuminated the room and, interestingly, secured to the rear wall by two iron pins, was an enormous, gilded cross that looked quite out of place. It was constructed from oak and coated with decorative silver sheets that were riveted to the wood and polished to a sheen, reflecting the candlelight. Here and there, rubies were recessed into the surface, and they glinted prettily in the dim light. So far, it was the only clue Leonardo had seen that hinted at the enormous wealth he knew the Order possessed.

Outside, Leonardo found that the door to the storeroom was locked. *Perhaps there was something in there worth guarding,* Leonardo decided. From whom, he didn't know, for he imagined that there were seldom pilgrims arriving at the monastery.

Leonardo moved on to the barn, where the sound and smell of a score of goats assaulted his senses. They were trapped inside a fenced enclosure, in front of the tall, double doors of the barn. However, they seemed content enough to munch on bales of hay and hop amongst each other, braying and knocking horns together in play. *Amusing creatures,* he thought, and stood watching them for a while, before he turned his attention to the valley and the epic scenery that surrounded the monastery.

He sucked in a lungful of air and thought that it was truly the land of the divine. The way the enormous snowy peaks erupted from the earth and pierced the sky! If it was possible for the living to bridge the gap between the mortal realm and Elysium, the gateway was surely here.

After some more exploring of the far end of the cleft, in which the monastery sat, Leonardo turned away and headed back to the great hall, wondering if supper was ready and what that might entail.

When he pushed the door open, the sound of a great booming laugh met his ears and he saw two men standing around the hearth over a cooking pot, a pair of freshly killed and skinned hares in the process of being prepared on the table beside them. Leonardo guessed the men must have been the last of the two teachers. At the sound of his entry, they looked up.

The first was perhaps the most muscular man Leonardo had ever seen. He wore a linen shirt and trousers, the sleeves of the shirt rolled up to reveal massive forearms, and a chest that looked as though it threatened to split the material. He was tanned and fair, with long, straw-coloured hair that fell to his shoulders, and an enormous moustache that stretched from one side of his face to the other and covered his mouth.

The second man was dressed similarly, but also wore a black jacket. He had a bow and a sheaf of arrows slung over one shoulder. He was tall and thin, his head and features seemingly stretched to the point that they gave his shaven face a haunting, gaunt look.

They stopped their conversation to stare at Leonardo. Magnus spoke up from the back of the room.

'Come forward, boy. Meet Drogoradz,' he said, indicating the muscular moustached one, 'and Walter.' He was the other, taller man.

Leonardo closed the door behind him and walked toward the fire. 'Greetings, Teacher,' he said to each of the new faces in turn, giving a polite bow as Antonio had done.

'Ha!' Drogoradz boomed. 'You haven't wasted any time beginning the lessons, then, Magnus!' he said in heavily accented Frankish. He sounded as though he had come from Eastern Europe, perhaps the far corners of the Holy Roman Empire or even further afield.

He looked at Leonardo. 'Well, don't just stand there, boy. Make yourself useful! Get the meat off those bones and into the pot.' He indicated to the hares on the table. Walter gave Leonardo the same long, hard look Antonio and Magnus had when he had first entered the hall, but didn't seem particularly impressed with what he saw and soon turned back to the fire.

Leonardo rolled up his sleeves and, doing as he was bid, took up a knife lying on the table and began to prepare the meat. A moment later, his instructors continued the conversation he had interrupted.

'I met one myself, once,' Drogoradz boomed over his shoulder to Magnus as he stirred the pot. He had one of those voices that dominated any room. 'Sweet little thing, she was. I would have had no idea that she was a killer, had I not seen her poison that chalice with my own two eyes... She didn't even bat an eyelid, and had that same harmless smile on her pretty lips the whole time! I'm glad that I was not her intended victim, for I would never have seen her coming!' He shook his head with a rueful smile.

'Women!' Magnus barked from the back of the hall. 'They can be twice as ruthless as men under the right circumstances.'

'Aye,' said Drogoradz. 'I suppose that's why the Order employs them.'

Leonardo's ears pricked up at that. 'Wait, the Order employs female agents?' he burst out.

'Quiet!' Walter spoke up for the first time, using a scathing tone. 'Did we ask for your input, boy? Hold your tongue!' Walter glared at him and Leonardo averted his gaze.

Drogoradz chuckled. 'That's right, the Order does employ women to kill. Why wouldn't it? No one ever suspects them. They'll slip into bed with you at night, and feed you a concoction of nightshade mixed into your wine and you'll never see the morning! Not a bad way to go, truth be told. Is it honourable? No. But effective? Absolutely!' He gave another chuckle and added a handful of herbs to the pot.

How interesting, Leonardo thought. There was so much he didn't know about the organisation he had recently pledged a life of servitude to. It had only been a few months since he had taken the oath, for Emilio had told him that he could not begin his training in earnest before he had done so. The Order of The Hand of God demanded total loyalty so that it might guard its secrets; secrets that were, apparently, just as well guarded to those within its ranks as those without. What else would Leonardo learn over the coming months?

'Hmm,' replied Walter. 'Honour is of little consequence next to the results. If a method works, why should we not use it to achieve our goals?' He looked at Drogoradz and then Magnus. 'Is that not why, after all, us agents are anointed with the second baptism?'

That was another thing Leonardo was yet to learn about – 'the second baptism', as it was known in the Order. It was a special ritual given only to the most capable members. Supposedly, were he successful here in his training, Leonardo would be blessed with it before he returned to Emilio. That was, if he survived. As to what the ritual involved, he was unsure, only that it was supposed to protect their souls and allowed them to commit sins that other men could not, or would not.

'Of course,' Drogoradz allowed. 'The mission comes first, no matter the method. But, given the option, I always prefer to give a man a fighting chance before I kill him...' His eyes met Leonardo's then, and Drogoradz flashed him a wicked grin. Leonardo gulped.

After that, the conversation turned to the patterns of the weather on the mountain and how unpredictable it could be. Leonardo finished cutting the meat and tossed it into the pot at Walter's instruction. He listened to the men talk, taking in every word, for it was the first time he had been properly exposed to the other men of the Order save Emilio.

A few minutes later, the stew was ready and Drogoradz called them to the table. The instructors made for the table closest to the fire and Leonardo hesitated, unsure where to sit. Antonio seemed to materialise out of thin air; when Leonardo turned around there he was, sitting silently, watching him. The effect was more than a little eerie.

'Back there,' Drogoradz said, indicating to one of the furthest tables from the light. 'Initiates eat together in silence. There are bowls and spoons on the shelf. Help yourself.'

Leonardo did so, after his superiors had taken their fill, and made his way to the back of the room with a steaming bowl of stew, glad to be out of the spotlight. He ate greedily, for the climb had been long and hard and the stew was rich. Once he was done, he was content enough to wait for his new masters to finish and, before long, they had.

They stood in unison. Walter turned to Leonardo, snapping his fingers and pointing at their empty bowls.

'You, clean this up. Be outside at dawn, ready to work.'

'Yes, Teacher,' Leonardo obeyed, setting to his task as the others took the stairs at the far end of the hall in single file. Once he was alone, he could breathe a sigh of relief. He found a pail of water in a cupboard by the fire, where a plethora of spices were kept for cooking and, as he cleaned, wondered what exactly he had let himself in for.

His teachers struck him as being very tough men, and what was it that the big, Eastern European Drogoradz had said? That he preferred to kill men face to face? Leonardo had no doubt that the four of them, being the Order's elite holy warriors, were no strangers to a fight, and death was undoubtedly as much a part of their lives as all the other mundane tasks of the day. The realisation made Leonardo's stomach knot with anxiety.

But then, Leonardo reasoned, he himself was only nineteen and he had already killed. Yet, as soon as he'd thought it, he realised the difference between himself and his teachers. The look in their eyes told him there was something missing entirely – empathy.

Leonardo sighed. Some of the things he had done with his own hands sickened him. Could he do it again?

He shook the question from his mind, leaving it unanswered, and made his way from the hall and out into the night. With the sun behind the mountains, it was gloomy, yet there was still light to see. Leonardo scooped snow into a pot with his hands from a snowbank that had built up against the side of the bunkhouse; then, he made his way inside, ensuring the door was firmly shut before taking the pot to the fire. *At least I will have water in the morning*, he thought.

After he'd thrown a couple more logs onto the fire, he stretched himself out on one of the beds with a groan. As his aching body drifted off to sleep, he wondered what the other 'initiates' would be like, and whether they would become friends.

Leonardo shovelled another load of shit into the barrow as Walter watched him like a hawk. They were in the goat enclosure, having shut the animals into the barn.

'Over there, to the left. Don't miss that corner out!' Walter seemed to take pleasure in barking orders at Leonardo, who found that he was beginning to struggle to keep the bitterness out of his voice with each 'Yes, Teacher' that he uttered.

The charade had gone on for several hours already, with no hint of it stopping, and Leonardo began to wonder when or if they would break for lunch.

'That's it, then we'll start on sweeping the yard,' said Walter.

Leonardo sighed as his barrow filled once more and he heaved on its handles to go and dump it. He hadn't known what the training would involve, but didn't see how shovelling shit would help him become an elite warrior.

He gritted his teeth. It was the first day and he could hardly give up. Nor was he entirely sure if giving up was an option.

Just then, Drogoradz called them in for food and Leonardo breathed a sigh of relief. He ate in silence as he had the night before, listening to the conversation of his superiors. Once they had eaten, he repeated the same procedure of cleaning up after everyone, before Walter summoned him out into the yard yet again without so much as a pause.

Leonardo trudged after him, mentally preparing himself for the mundane tasks to come.

'Pick your feet up, boy!' Walter growled. 'You'll find the broom over th—' Before he could finish the sentence, his head turned to look at something to their left. Leonardo followed his gaze and heard whatever it was before he saw it. Was that panting?

A moment later, a figure had stumbled into view, climbing his way up the steep track to where it levelled out. He was dressed in a worn-looking woollen cloak, a cheap pair of trousers and shirt, and had a sack of affairs slung over his shoulder, much like Leonardo had upon his arrival the previous day. He had a young face, and could not have been much more than twenty. The young man was of average height and build, pale, freckled skin with a healthy, red glow to the cheeks. His short, chestnut hair was a little damp with sweat.

He looked up and spotted Leonardo and Walter, and gave them both an uncertain smile.

'You. Name yourself, boy!' Walter barked rudely.

The smile faltered. 'I… I am sent by the Nordic Finger. My name is Sebastien.' He approached and stuck out a hand for Walter to shake. It was ignored.

43

'You will address me as Teacher, understood?' Walter glared at him.

'Erm… yes, Teacher.' Sebastien glanced at Leonardo, clearly trying to decide if he was master or student. However, Walter made sure that was cleared up, for he pointed at the bunkhouse and said, 'Drop your things in there and return here immediately. You can help the other initiate sweep the yard.'

'Yes, Teacher!'

A minute later, Leonardo and Sebastien were working side by side, under the watchful gaze of Walter, who seemed to have made it his mission to find the pair of them the most menial tasks he could. Sebastien flashed Leonardo a grin, which was returned, the pair of them grateful to have another in the same boat.

'So, where are you from?' Sebastien asked as they brushed pine needles from the rocky ground.

Leonardo opened his mouth to reply, but was cut off.

'Quiet!' Walter's voice rang out behind them. 'I said work, did I not? I don't recall asking you to natter!'

Sebastien gave a smirk and a roll of the eyes, and Leonardo had to stifle a laugh. Suddenly, sweeping the yard didn't seem like such an awful task, after all.

And so the afternoon went on, passing much quicker than the morning had, and before either of them knew it, it was time for supper. Leonardo made sure Sebastien knew the drill by tugging at his sleeve and indicating the rearmost table, away from the four seasoned agents by the fire. Once the other men had had a good look at the newcomer and taken their fill of the food in the pot, the initiates were allowed to eat. They sat alone, not daring to speak lest they be reprimanded. Then, once their superiors had finished, Leonardo showed his new companion how to clean up after them.

When it was done, they left the hall and were, for the first time that day, alone.

'Rome,' Leonardo said as they walked back to the bunkhouse together.

'What?'

'You asked me where I'm from. It's Rome.'

'Ah, I see. I'm from England.' Sebastien stopped and stuck out his hand. 'My name is Sebastien,' he said for the second time that day.

Leonardo took the hand in his. 'Leonardo,' he replied, shaking it.

'Pleasure to meet you!' said Sebastien. 'Hey, what say we get that fire going, eh? I can feel it getting chilly out here already.'

'Yes, let's.'

They walked to the bunkhouse and Leonardo pulled the door open, holding it for his new friend.

'So, when did you get here?' asked Sebastien.

'Only yesterday.' The door banged shut behind them and Leonardo made for the hearth.

'By God, it's a long way up!' said Sebastien. 'I don't think I've ever been so high before!'

'Nor me,' replied Leonardo. 'There is snow here all year round, too.'

'Aye, I bet!'

There was a moment of silence as Leonardo knelt by the hearth with a flint and steel to light a pile of kindling.

'So,' Sebastien continued, hands on hips as he gazed around at the bunkhouse. 'I can't honestly say I know what we are going to be learning up here. Have they told you?'

'They've told me next to nothing,' replied Leonardo. 'Our leader, Magnus, the one with the long white beard, will explain when we are all present.'

Sebastien frowned. 'Right, so when will that be? And how many others are there? Do you know where they're all from?'

As a small flame began to lick at the pile of kindling, Leonardo straightened and turned to look at the other youth. Shaking his head with a grin, he shrugged.

'No idea. Only that we begin in earnest within a fortnight.'

'Huh. So, I guess we'll be sweeping up until then.'

'It looks that way, yes.'

'Who would have thought that eternal salvation could be won through the use of a common broomstick!' Sebastien laughed good-naturedly, as he lowered himself down onto the bed opposite Leonardo's.

45

Leonardo smiled. 'With any luck, some of the lessons will be more interesting than that. I know that the skills we learn here we will need to use if we ever become agents ourselves.'

Sebastien's smile faded and his face became serious. 'You know, I heard rumours that some of the men sent up this mountain never come back down.'

There was a moment's silence as the fire crackled.

'That's probably true enough,' Leonardo admitted, as he stared solemnly at the flames.

'Look,' Sebastien said, standing once more and walking to the fire to face Leonardo. 'I don't know what will happen over the next year, what trials we will face or what we will have to do, but I'm sure none of it will be easy. And I'm sure that most of it will likely be dangerous.' He looked Leonardo up and down before continuing. 'You look fit enough, and you don't strike me as a fool, either. What say you, that we look out for one another? With the perils to come, it would be a blessing to have a friend at your back, hey?'

Leonardo looked at Sebastien, thinking carefully before nodding. 'I think that would be a good idea.'

And, as the flames burnt hot in the hearth between them, they clasped hands once more. A friendship was born.

Chapter 4

GASCONY

The centre of parliament in Bordeaux was unmissable; a collection of fortified buildings that were as much works of art as they were practical defences. Hewn from blocks of limestone, their surfaces pale, flat and untarnished by the weather, they seemed to glow. Generous towers demonstrated the master builder's precision. Their roofs curved upwards, forming a tapering spire that, while difficult to execute, made a very pleasant shape for the eye to behold.

The whole thing sat in a square opposite the great bell tower and was relatively new, paid for by the profits from Gascony's various exports, chiefly wine. It was no wonder that the English king wanted to hold on to the region.

However, the times of peace needed to construct such wonders of engineering had drawn to a close. The loyalists were few and far between, and those disgruntled nobles that sought an end to the old regime were leaving the city to go south and east to join the growing opposition to the King.

The atmosphere within the parliamentary buildings was quiet and cowed. As Leonardo allowed Sebastien to lead him through the halls, he couldn't help but notice how few people inhabited the space. Every now and again, a finely dressed clerk would cross their path and disappear through a door, the only sign of life that the building was not completely deserted save for the guards.

The pair of them had barely said a word since they'd met by the cathedral. Sebastien had gestured for him to follow, and Leonardo had done so and they had walked through the streets in silence, neither wanting to be the first to break it. Yet, that had to come to an end, for they had reached a door guarded by two burly men-at-arms, and Leonardo suspected that whoever was within must have been Sebastien's contact.

The latter suddenly stopped several paces from the door and turned to Leonardo, his eyes hard.

'Now, you listen,' he said. 'Just because we have to work together, doesn't mean I have to like it. What it does mean is that you will do what I tell you and follow my lead. Of the two of us, the English court is my domain, and I am known to it. So far as I understand it, you were sent by our masters to assist me in the matter of the redirection of the events in Gascony as they unfold. Personally, I don't see the necessity of that. However, such is the way of things. Just do as I do, understood?' Sebastien stared questioningly at Leonardo, as if daring him to disagree. Clearly, he had not forgotten the manner in which they had parted ways twelve years ago.

After a moment, Leonardo conceded, his expression blank. 'As you wish,' he replied with a dip of the head.

Sebastien blew the air from his cheeks. 'Good. Now, let's go in. Be aware, she's a clever woman.'

She? Leonardo thought. *Interesting.*

The men-at-arms clearly knew Sebastien and gave him a nod, allowing him to knock thrice on the door. It was opened and, in the doorway, stood a burly knight. He gave the pair of them a long look before opening the door fully and stepping aside to let them in with a mutter of, 'Afternoon, Father Sebastien.'

'To you, as well.'

Within, the room was large and dominated by a table that was acting as a desk at present. It was covered with papers and maps and, behind it, stood two people. One was a short, ageing nobleman with greying hair and wearing well-made, but plain, clothes.

48

The other person was far more remarkable, however. She was a tall woman, dressed in a wonderful green velvet gown with intricate frills at the cuffs, and was tied at the waist with a belt. Jewels glittered around her slim neck, accentuated by the way her hair was tied behind her head in a neat bun. She was young, attractive and clearly someone with a good deal of power, for she spoke to the older man authoritatively.

As Leonardo and Sebastien entered, the couple looked up to see the newcomers. Sebastien bowed deeply and Leonardo followed suit. When they straightened, the woman smiled warmly.

'Ah, Father Sebastien!' she exclaimed. 'You have returned. And who is this you have brought me?'

Sebastien returned the smile and Leonardo knew him enough to know it was genuine.

'Your Highness, the pleasure is mine.'

Your Highness? Leonardo thought, as his old comrade exchanged familiar pleasantries with the woman. *Did that mean...*

'Your Highness, this is Brother Leonardo, a colleague from the Vatican. Leonardo, I present Lady Eleanor of Provence, Queen of England.'

Leonardo had to work hard not to raise his eyebrows in surprise. Instead, he bowed again and said, 'I am at your service, Your Highness.'

'Wonderful!' she replied. 'A friend of Sebastien's is a friend of mine.' At the mention of the word 'friend', Leonardo felt Sebastien bristle at his side. 'Come, gentlemen. Sit. Roger de Ros and I were just finishing up.'

'Greetings.' Roger de Ros, the small nobleman standing with the Queen, gave them both a nod as they approached the desk. Leonardo would later find out that Roger de Ros was in charge of 'the great wardrobe', a vast store of cloths and other goods that was the financial centre of the King's resistance.

Roger turned back to the Queen and continued his conversation from where he had apparently left off.

'Yes, so, in conclusion, Your Highness, there is not enough cash at our disposal for your husband to field an army for two months, let alone an entire campaigning season. What would you like me to do?' Roger looked at her, waiting, clearly expecting Lady Eleanor to provide him with a solution.

Which she promptly did. Speaking clearly and confidently, she began, 'I want you to sell everything. Offer good prices – neigh, the best prices; we need that money fast. However, I suspect that alone will not be enough. Take out loans to buy more wine and have it shipped back to England. Double the current rate, if you can. I know the merchants have been muttering about the rebellion having had an effect on prices and tax; assure them that it is not the case. As far as they are concerned, things will continue as normal, and the crown has a firm grasp of the situation here. If that is still not enough, then my husband will have to capture what wealth he does not currently possess from his opponents. When he finally arrives, that is.' She gave Roger de Ros a knowing look.

Roger smiled and nodded. 'I will see it is done at once, Your Highness. I shall return the day after tomorrow to update you of my progress.'

He bowed, turned, nodded to Leonardo and Sebastien, and left. The knight at the entrance opened the door for him. Roger was apparently a permanent fixture around the Queen.

Once he had gone, the Queen sighed and rubbed her forehead wearily, glancing down at all the documents covering her desk, before looking up at Sebastien.

'I didn't expect it to be this hard, Sebastien,' she said. 'It turns out we are not nearly as popular here as I thought. God, I hope my husband appreciates the urgency of my letters. Now that de Montfort has gone, we need his men here now.'

She frowned at the map of Gascony on the table, pins stuck in several places that indicated locations of strategic importance.

'Do you have any idea when he is set to arrive, Your Highness?' Sebastien asked.

'In a month or so. His replies have been vague. His heart is still set on crusade. Yet, I hope that, by now, the uprising will have impressed upon him the need to act here in Gascony. Lest we lose the territory altogether…'

King Henry III of England was just as pious as his French counterpart, Louis XI of France. When Louis' crusade to the Holy Land two years prior had ended in disaster, it only bolstered Henry's crusading fervour – though, supposedly not out of any sense of competition. It was said that Henry actually admired Louis and had taken the cross in light of his defeat. Henry had even gone so far as to persuade the Pope to allow him to levy a tax of one tenth of all ecclesiastical revenues from the Church to fund his endeavour, now that he had made a formal pledge.

However, Henry's enthusiasm was not shared by his nobles. They were loath to lend him money and, earlier that year, Henry had stormed out of parliament at Westminster when an increase of general tax had been denied to him.

Gascony was yet another hurdle that seemed to bar his path east, for the unrest was draining his coffers of the money saved for his pilgrimage. That, and the threat of invasion from the King of Castile, Alfonso X, meant that he had to postpone the venture to manage his domestic affairs.

Presently, Sebastien spoke up. 'Perhaps there is something we can do to alleviate the burden.'

The Queen looked at him thoughtfully, then spoke directly to Leonardo. 'What do you know of the situation here, Father?'

'Only what I have learnt on my journey, Your Highness,' Leonardo replied. 'The nobles of Gascony have taken up arms at their supposed mistreatment at the hands of Simon de Montfort.'

'Yes, that is essentially the gist of it,' said the Queen. 'De Montfort did exactly what Henry asked of him, when he was sent here as regent several years ago. It's just the way he did it that was perhaps inadvisable. You see, de Montfort has always been a capable man, and a sound military leader. However, he treated the pacification of Gascony as though it were a military campaign in hostile territory. In a year, there were no rebels who would dare to stand against him, for he had either killed them, imprisoned them or destroyed their crops and vineyards.' She pursed her lips distastefully; she knew, as well as any, that one could not get away with persecuting the high nobility as they might with the common man.

'Then there was the debacle with Rostand Solers in 1249.' Leonardo remembered the youth, Gaillard, in the square before the cathedral.

Queen Eleanor shook her head sadly. 'De Montfort seemed to have forgotten that Gascony is a part of the King's land, and that you can't go around killing your nobles the moment they disagree with you, if you hope for the others to remain loyal. It looks bad.'

She paused for a moment and sighed once more. 'Of course, de Montfort was tried last year for misconduct at Westminster – and found not guilty, by the way, for he had technically only done what was asked of him. He and the King have been at odds ever since, and now here I am in the King's place.'

Leonardo looked her up and down carefully. She exuded an air of competence, and while her mind was sharp and she was clearly a capable and intelligent woman, she did not seem unkind, and Leonardo found that he rather liked her.

Evidently, so too did Sebastien, for he gave the Queen a rueful grin and said, 'Well, I suppose it's up to us to clean up the mess, then!'

'Ha! We can try.' Then the Queen turned to Leonardo again. 'So, Father Leonardo, just what is it exactly that you do for the Church?' Her tone had turned serious, and she gave him a shrewd look.

What was she getting at? Leonardo thought. *Did she know about the Order?* He glanced at Sebastien from the corner of his eye. Sebastien gave him an almost imperceptible nod. Then Leonardo remembered that there was a knight sitting by the door and he gave a dip of the head in his direction, followed by a questioning look at Sebastien.

'Don't worry about Sir Derek,' Sebastien said coolly. 'He's a loyal man. Speak freely, Leonardo.' Both he and the Queen watched Leonardo expectantly, as he tried to ascertain what she knew. Leonardo decided to play it safe.

'I possess a similar set of skills to that of Sebastien, Your Highness.' Leonardo kept his face blank, giving nothing more away.

'Hmm. Then you must be equally as talented.' The Queen looked him up and down, as if seeing him in a new light.

That, Leonardo thought, *was intriguing.* He could guess that she wasn't talking about Sebastien's scroll work, for Leonardo knew he had never had the patience for it. No, the Queen seemed to be well aware what Sebastien was. That made her all the more of a mystery.

The Nordic Finger had seen fit to entrust her with one of the Order's rare and precious agents – which, by extension, meant that Leonardo trusted her with the knowledge of the existence of the Order itself. That was a good deal of responsibility.

'Well,' the Queen went on. 'Let us talk about the opposition, shall we? Perhaps we can set the two of you to task with something practical. Let's see now...' Her full, red lips pursed as she leant onto the table and began to study the map.

'See here,' she pointed, 'the rebels have seized Bazas and La Reole. Before my husband arrives in a month, I want to have the groundwork ready so that the siege of those cities can begin as soon as Henry lands with his army.' Sebastien and Leonardo leant in with interest.

'The rebels in Bazas are led by Amaneus d'Albret, William de Pins and Bernard de Bouville, to name just a few,' the Queen continued. 'To that end, we will need to retake the town of Langon to serve as a base of operations from which we can attack both cities.'

The Queen paused and held up her hands. 'However, that will have to take a backseat for the moment, as the biggest thorn in our side is, of course, Gaston de Bearn. He claims overlordship over Sault-de-Navailles and Lados, yet we know that he has designs on all of Gascony. He would, if he had the power, take it all for himself.

'Gaston has done much to fuel the fire of the rebels, and now my spies have told me he has even opened up a line of communication with the King of Castile. Alfonso is sending Gaston gold, weapons and other supplies from the far side of the Pyrenees. This must stop. That is what I want the pair of you to focus on, at least for the time being.'

Sebastien rubbed his shaven chin thoughtfully. 'I'm assuming he carts everything across Aragon, over the mountains through this pass, and up to Pau?' He pointed to the map.

'Why wouldn't he transport it by sea?' Leonardo asked. 'Surely, it would be easier?'

'Yes,' the Queen allowed. 'But it would then have to pass through Bayonne, and there are loyalists there who might confiscate the goods.'

'I see,' replied Leonardo. 'So, from Pau, Gaston distributes the contraband northwards to the rebels. These convoys will not be easy to stop, Your Highness. One would not risk leaving them undefended.'

'True. But Gaston is overconfident, he will not expect a raid into his own land. Besides, from what I know about Sebastien, it should be straightforward enough.' She gave a sly, conspiratorial smile to Sebastien, who returned it with a wink.

Leonardo frowned, observing how the two of them were very comfortable around one another. Just how long had they been working together?

Just then, Sebastien turned to Leonardo and, in an instant, the warmth from his expression had faded. 'It is not outside the realm of possibility for two of us. That is, not unless you have lost your touch...'

Leonardo narrowed his eyes, returning the gaze. 'I have not.'

'Good. Then we will leave tonight.'

'Very well,' the Queen said, straightening. 'I will fill you in on the details later, Sebastien. Father Leonardo, it was a pleasure to meet you. Now, if you wouldn't mind leaving Sebastien and I. We have several other matters to discuss alone.'

Leonardo looked from one to the other silently. Then he gave another deep bow. 'As you wish, Your Highness.' He felt their eyes on his back as he turned to leave, waiting by the door as the mean-looking Sir Derek stood to open it for him. A moment later, Leonardo was out in the corridor again and the door was shut with a thud.

He walked down the corridor deep in thought. The Queen was formidable, he recognised, and she knew about the Order. It seemed that, while her husband was not present, she had been entrusted to spearhead the resistance. Leonardo could see why.

What he did not fully understand was the relationship Sebastien had with her. Was he merely on loan from the Nordic Finger? Or did he always work for the Queen back in England? They seemed familiar enough. Did that mean Sebastien was the Queen's man? Or was it something else?

It was probably nothing, Leonardo decided. Sebastien had always been the charming one. Needless to say, the attack on Gaston de Bearn's supply line seemed as good a place to start as any, though Leonardo was unsure how he was going to find out just how involved the Iberian Finger was in the demise of Gascony and the English crown. He hoped an opportunity would present itself, for he saw no clear solution to that problem.

Just then, he was awoken from his reverie as a trio of young ladies, all dressed in a similar fashion to the Queen, passed him in the hallway. He caught the eye of the middle lady, whose bright red hair flowed around her pretty face and down her back. She smiled at him as she walked past, and Leonardo turned to watch as the three of them reached the end of the hall to knock on the door he had just exited.

Sir Derek's face appeared, and he let them in, closing the door after them. *They must be the Queen's ladies-in-waiting, her royal attendees*, Leonardo thought. He guessed she must keep them close, for they would have been something familiar in what, for the Queen, was a strange and foreign place.

Of all people, Leonardo could relate to what it was like to be an outsider, for that is what he had always been.

Chapter 5

Twelve years ago

Magnus's bone-white hair blew around his face in the wind, making him look like a wild thing. His hard, icy blue eyes matched the clear morning sky behind him as they glared out from beneath long, pale locks. The day was just beginning, but it was no ordinary day. No, it was a particularly ostentatious day. It was the day Leonardo and the other six would begin their training.

The other six initiates included Sebastien, with whom Leonardo had become quite familiar over the last couple of weeks. They had endured the menial work that had kept them busy from dawn until dusk and, as they found themselves on the receiving end of their superiors' criticisms when they were scolded for doing something they shouldn't, it only brought them closer.

Once the sun had set, they were allowed to retreat to the bunkhouse, where the first thing they would do was to light a fire. Before they drifted off to sleep, they would talk and share their stories.

Sebastien was an orphan from Wessex and had been surviving in the forests of the English countryside with a group of other vagabonds for as long as he could remember. Then, in his teens, he had been caught by a local lord trapping deer, and would have lost his hand to the lord's axe as punishment were it not for a friar who persuaded the lord that Sebastien could be more useful to the Church with all four limbs intact.

Out of gratitude to his saviour, Sebastien had given the ecclesiastical life a go, but it had soon become clear he was far too restless to be cooped up indoors all day learning to read and write. From there, he was sent to London to join one of England's largest monastic farms to till the earth.

But Sebastien had had other ideas and, at seventeen, had gotten into a fight with two other monks, beating them quite badly. Everything pointed to him being expelled from the Church, when, in a bizarre turn of events, a shadowy figure had arrived just in time to whisk him away to a private residence outside the city.

That had been the Nordic Finger's man, and Sebastien had soon met the powerful churchman himself, once he had taken the oath after being given an offer of a life that was altogether more exciting than psalms, matins, ink pots, parchment and prayer. Exciting, but dangerous.

Sebastien, just like Leonardo, had been groomed for this training by his master ever since. And now, here he stood.

The other five had similar stories. They came from every corner of Christendom and, though in appearance they may have been polar opposites, what they all had in common was that they were outcasts and misfits; were they to disappear from the face of the earth, no one would miss them. A life of service to the Order of The Hand of God was likely to be the best opportunity they would ever get.

Leonardo and Sebastien had met the next of their number, Njal, several days after their arrival. Njal was a Norwegian, fair and muscular. He was a good hand taller than the pair of them and didn't say much, but was always quick with a smile and often found himself in trouble with Walter and Drogoradz for laughing too loudly at one of Sebastien's jokes, for Sebastien was often cracking them.

Then, there was Alof. He was fair and Germanic and quick to question the 'why' of everything they were doing, which Leonardo had found rather annoying. Next was Ebel, who hailed from the Far East. It was clear that he came from the very fringes of the lands of Christ, for his skin and hair were dark, and he could have been

Turkish or Greek. From the moment he met him, Leonardo had gotten the impression that Ebel was very sharp witted; there was not much that escaped his quiet gaze, and Leonardo learnt that Ebel could speak five different languages. Yet, Ebel was very slight and lacked any great degree of physical fortitude.

The second to last was Gabriel, Portuguese and almost as dark in complexion as Ebel. He had a very serious look about him, and from the moment he had entered the bunkhouse with his chin jutted in the air, his arrogance had been self-evident. No matter, the daily chore of picking at the tenacious weeds that had managed to grow between the rocks in the yard had humbled him somewhat and he had soon fallen into line with the rest of them, though with more than a little grumbling.

Finally, there was Sigbald, a Dane. Sigbald had been the last to arrive, a couple of days prior, but it had only taken twenty-four hours for the stocky young man to banter with Sebastien. He was a likeable fellow, someone whose presence could not be forgotten, for he was always chatting about this and that or joking around with the other initiates.

Though yet a little unsure of one another, they all quickly realised they would be on the same side against the older and much more experienced agents of the Order that were to be their tutors. The atmosphere in the bunkhouse the previous night had been one of nerves, anxiety, trepidation, fear and at least a little excitement. The seven of them, none older than twenty-two years of age, had sat on their bunks and discussed, in their common language of Frankish, what the future held for them.

None of them knew for sure, and they had eventually fallen into a fitful sleep as their minds imagined what trials awaited. With any luck, the morning would bring answers.

They did not have to wait long. Once the day had begun and they had found themselves in the yard, Magnus was striding from the great hall with Walter, Antonio and Drogoradz in tow, barking at the seven of them to form a line before him.

'Right then!' he declared, pacing before the array of youths before him and staring each one in the eye in turn. 'Right then,' he said again, as more of a growl this time. There was an uncomfortable silence as his piercing blue eyes bore into them.

'Seven of you. A good enough number.' He nodded to himself and took a couple of paces back so he could see them all, then clasped his hands behind his back. Antonio, Walter and Drogoradz stood behind him. Drogoradz had taken an apple from his pocket and was shaving chunks from it with an enormous dagger that was more of a short sword, popping the chunks into his mouth intermittently.

They waited for Magnus to go on.

'So, you are all here because you are the young men of the Order with the most potential.' He looked the slight Ebel up and down and continued. 'Personally, I don't see it, but I'm willing to give you the benefit of the doubt.'

Walter folded his arms and gave them a look of disdain, as Magnus continued to pace back and forth.

'This is the monastery.' Magnus spread his arms and indicated the humble collection of buildings around them. 'This is where you will undergo your training to become agents of the Order of The Hand of God. This is where you will suffer.'

At that, the silent Antonio had cocked his head to one side, the hint of a smile playing at his lips. Leonardo felt Sigbald shift his weight uncomfortably next to him.

'Should you manage to endure the duration and, of course, meet our standards, then in March the year after next you will receive the second baptism and become one of us. The next time you leave the Pyrenees, you will either have failed, or you will be agents. And there are some amongst you who will likely never leave these mountains altogether.' Magnus paused for effect, glaring around at them.

'Of all the types of wild terrain such as moors, jungles and deserts, it is the mountains that will kill you the fastest, so listen to us. Do as we command, and you will survive. Ignore us, and you will perish.'

He paused and glared at the seven initiates again for a moment.

'My name is Magnus. Behind me are Antonio, Walter and Drogoradz.' Magnus pointed to each of the masters in turn. 'You will only speak when spoken to and will refer to us as Teacher. You will respect that we know what we are talking about and, if you wish to learn, you will be attentive, you will give all of your efforts to the tasks we set you, and you will keep your mouths shut. Those of you who display a poor attitude... well, let's just say the mountain isn't the only thing that can cause harm up here...'

To Leonardo's left, Sebastien gulped audibly.

Magnus continued. 'Some of the skills you will learn here will include wrestling, swordplay, tracking, stealth, concoctions, espionage, disguise and camouflage to name but a few. Undoubtedly, you will be better at some than others. What we ask of you is not that you excel in any one aspect, but that you have a healthy grasp of each. Neglect any one of the disciplines and you are sure to fail. We will test you; the challenges ahead will be hard, the hardest of your lives! But know this – survive, succeed, and you will leave here different men. This mountain is a crucible and, for the time being, you are heaps of ore. It is you who will decide what it will produce from you. Precious metal? Or slag!'

The wind blew another gust in the silence that followed and seemed to howl around the mountainside forebodingly.

'Questions?'

After a moment, Gabriel raised his hand.

'Speak, boy,' Magnus barked at him.

Gabriel cleared his throat. 'Um, what happens if we fail, or if we find that the training is not for us?'

Walter scoffed behind Magnus, who had closed his eyes in irritation, allowing the question to hang stupidly in the air for a moment. When he opened them, he gave Gabriel a look of disdain.

'You have all given oaths. There will be no going back. Success is your only option. Well, the only viable one.'

Gabriel reddened and looked at his feet.

'Anyone else?' barked Magnus. After that, no one else had any questions. Or, at least, none they dared to ask.

'Very well!' Magnus smacked his hands together. 'Let us begin!'

And so Leonardo's journey within the Order of The Hand of God began in earnest. He found himself being shepherded along with the others to the storehouse, which was promptly unlocked and a set of equipment distributed to each of them, including a pair of wicker platforms that were to be strapped around the feet with leather chords.

'What are these for?' Sebastien had asked no one in particular, his curiosity rewarded by a smack around the side of the head by Drogoradz as he passed them. Sebastien soon learnt to keep his thoughts to himself.

It seemed that all eleven of the men inhabiting the monastery were to sally out that day for an incursion into the surrounding mountains. Leonardo soon found himself panting in the wake of Magnus and Antonio, the former being more than twice his age, as they ploughed up a nearby mountain relentlessly.

The going was tough, and Leonardo was soon sucking air into his lungs in great gulps, hoping he would reach the top soon. The initiates quickly realised what the wicker platforms were for, as, once they reached a snow-covered stretch of land that seemed to blanket the higher slopes of the mountain from there on, the seven initiates watched as their teachers stopped to strap the things on silently, no word of instruction given.

They all hastily bent to do the same, tying the cumbersome things around their feet, and discovered that the platforms allowed them to walk across the surface of the snow without sinking into it. A moment later, they were off again.

Before long, they were stretched out in a ragged line, with Leonardo and Sebastien at the fore, barely keeping up with Magnus and Antonio as they climbed ever higher. Turning back to look down at the steep slope once, Leonardo could see that the cleft in which the monastery sat was now out of sight, seemingly far below. He heard the harsh words of Walter as Ebel and Alof were beginning to slow, their hunched forms trudging up, one step at a time, as Walter shouted at them.

'Come on, pick up the pace or we'll be here all day!'

An hour later, Leonardo and Sebastien had stopped again as Antonio had begun to wrap his head and face with a kind of shawl. He saw the pair of them watching him and gestured to the leather satchels they had been given, and then pointed up at the sun.

Leonardo had quickly understood that the shawl was meant to protect their skin from the rays of the sun, for it was a bright and cloudless day and they had already noted the way in which the snow reflected the light into their eyes, and he could imagine how it would burn them. They wrapped themselves as best they could. Once it was done, Gabriel slogged up to their position and planted both hands on his knees, gasping for air.

'By St Dominic's beard!' he exclaimed. 'My lungs are fit to burst!'

'Quiet!' Magnus snapped from several yards up. 'We are nearly at the top.' He turned back, leading them once more up the snowy mountain without, it seemed to them, so much as having broken into a sweat. The ever-silent Antonio remained by his side, apparently just as fit as Magnus.

By now, Sigbald and Njal were some hundred yards below, with Alof a hundred yards further back. The tiny figure of poor Ebel, flanked by Walter and Drogoradz, could barely be made out as he doubtless endured the teachers' abuse due to his slow pace.

Onwards they went, and soon the summit was in sight. It was marked by a pile of rocks stacked neatly on top of each other. Seeing this gave Leonardo new heart. He gritted his teeth and pushed himself upward, the sweat pouring from his back and soaking his shirt.

And then, they were there. Magnus and Antonio stopped, unphased, while Sebastien and Leonardo both collapsed to the ground with Gabriel just behind them. They had made it!

As they recovered, Antonio tossed a waterskin onto the ground between them and Gabriel lunged for it, gulping down the water greedily.

'Hey, leave some for us!' Sebastien complained, wrenching the skin from the dark-haired young man, taking a gulp himself before passing it to Leonardo. He drank gratefully, knowing he could have finished the whole lot himself, but decided it would be wise to save some for the others.

Once Leonardo had caught his breath, he stood to take in the view. He gasped. It was utterly breathtaking! He had been so absorbed in the climb that he had not taken stock of the dizzying height to which they had now ascended.

In the relative vicinity, the valley adjacent to their own formed an almost perfect bowl, filled by a small lake of dark blue water that rippled gently. To Leonardo's rear, was the valley through which he had climbed on the first day; long and thin with its steep sides, it was flanked by yet more mountains, and the countless peaks seemed to stretch away into the distance. Endless slopes of grey stone and scree were permeated with patches of snow that grew more frequent as the mountains grew taller.

To the north, some fifteen miles away, the peaks fell away to reveal the flat plains of the rich, agricultural land of southern Frankia that continued thus as far as the eye could see. To the south, Leonardo's view was obscured by yet more mountains, snowy peaks that seemed to rise just as high as, if not higher than, the one upon which he currently stood.

West was a similar story, with yet more of the epic terrain that made Leonardo feel as tiny as an insect.

He made his way over the rocky ground to stand with Magnus and Antonio as they gazed eastward. There, a colossal mountain rose from the earth, sloped gradually on one side and falling away steeply on the other with a bulbous, rocky summit. It was clearly the mightiest of them all.

Magnus heard Leonardo approach. He turned to see the young man's mouth open in wonder at the size of the behemoth.

'Ha! Yes, grand, isn't she? We call her the Dove. Look,' Magnus pointed. 'See the way it resembles a dove from the side? That's the chest there, and the head.'

Leonardo could see it, and marvelled at its scale, thinking it must be a whole day's march just to reach its base. To climb it would be a great undertaking.

Just then, Sigbald and Njal had arrived, copying Leonardo a minute before by collapsing onto the snow, looking spent. However, Magnus had other ideas than to allow them to rest.

'All of you, come here. It's important you learn what surrounds us.'

With a groan, they hauled themselves to their feet to stand wearily beside Leonardo as Magnus began to list off the names of the surrounding mountains, pointing at them in turn.

'That big one there's the Dove, then there's the Needle, then the Black Tooth, and the St Mary…'

Leonardo listened, trying to remember them all, but knowing it was hopeless. There were far too many to take in and he resorted instead to admiring what must have been the most beautiful sight his eyes had ever beheld. He promised himself that, no matter how long he was destined to live at the monastery, he would never take such a wonder for granted.

Presently, Alof had joined them and soon they were waiting only for the rear guard, delayed by the slight Ebel, who was lagging so far behind that Leonardo had begun to feel chilly. Now that he had stopped, the sweat that had soaked his clothing was making the wind all the colder.

A good length of time had passed when Ebel finally made an appearance on the summit, his usually dark skin several shades whiter and his eyes fluttering open and closed. Apparently, the only thing keeping the lad conscious was the intermittent shoves from Drogoradz, as he and Walter appeared just behind the young man.

'Unfit! Look at the runt we've been sent!' Walter called up to Magnus, who eyed Ebel with a frown. The boy collapsed onto the ground at his feet, his skinny arms quivering from what was likely to have been the greatest feat of physical exertion his thin body had ever achieved.

'Eye,' Magnus glowered. 'He seems to be lacking vigour…' Ebel gulped helplessly for air, apparently unaware of the conversation that was taking place above his head.

'No matter,' Drogoradz grinned ruefully as he looked around at the rest of them, speaking loudly so that his deep voice carried to all present over the wind. 'One of two things will happen; either the boy will adapt, or the mountain will claim him. Either way, we won't have to wait long to find out.'

There was an uncomfortable silence as Leonardo watched his colleagues Njal and Sigbald exchange a worried glance, as their imaginations conjured up visions of what that could mean.

'True. Very well, it's time we headed back. On your feet, boy!' Magnus barked, already striding away back down the route they had taken, as the wind whipped at his long, white hair and beard. Gabriel scrambled after him, as did Leonardo and Sebastien, but not before they had hauled their suffering colleague to his feet.

Soon, they were retracing their steps over the snow. Before they knew it, they were taking off their wicker snow shoes at the edge of the snow fields and scrambling down the rocky scree in Magnus's wake, kicking up clouds of dust into the July air.

By the time they arrived back at the cleft of the monastery, they were all glad to see the familiar, blocky stone buildings. The seven initiates shed their gear by the storehouse, copying the example of their instructors.

While Walter instructed Ebel and Alof to rearrange the kit, Magnus's piercing blue eyes had found Gabriel.

'You, boy. Cook lunch for us all.'

By God, it's only lunch time! Leonardo thought in dismay.

'You will find frozen meat in the ice cave behind the store, and grain in the great hall,' Magnus went on.

Gabriel's eyes widened at that. 'But, Teacher, I... I don't know how to cook!' he stammered in panic.

Magnus's eyes narrowed as he turned back to him. 'Well, you'd better bloody learn quickly, then. Because if you produce something that doesn't please the tongue, you'll be sleeping with the goats tonight! From now on, you'll all be taking it in turns!' He glared around at the rest of them before disappearing into the great hall, leaving Gabriel looking lost.

Leonardo and Sebastien decided they would help him and, together, they found the meat frozen amongst great blocks of ice in a small cave hewn into the mountainside, which shielded it from the rays of the sun. An hour later, using the herbs they found in the great hall, the three of them had managed to create something resembling a stew and bake several decent loaves of bread, albeit a little burnt around the edges.

Magnus had given the stew a sniff, then a taste, leaving Gabriel waiting in tense suspense before he finally gave a grunt that must have been approval. Then he, Antonio, Drogoradz and Walter took their fill and sat, allowing the rest of them to follow suit.

The seven of them ate in silence and, for once, their instructors didn't need to bark at them to stop talking, for their mouths were occupied with wolfing down the plain bowl of stew and hard bread.

After that, it was back out in the yard, where Magnus had them sit on the stone cross-legged as he took out the equipment they used on the mountain to explain its purpose.

'These you used today, they are called snowshoes.' He held up the wicker platforms. 'You saw how they strap to your feet and prevent you from sink... Hey!' He roared suddenly, making them all jump, as he glared as the wide-eyed Alof at the back.

'Falling asleep, boy? Want to climb the mountain again? Well?'

'N-no, Teacher!'

'Then concentrate! I won't repeat myself.' Next, he produced a coil of hemp rope and demonstrated several knots, letting the boys try each in turn as he explained their uses. 'This one comes in handy when you need to lash yourselves together. There is a glacier at the base of the Black Tooth with deep fissures in the ice that can swallow a man up. This knot is used in certain situations where it becomes necessary to bind yourselves together in threes – should one man fall, the weight of the other two will prevent him from plummeting to his death. Here, try it.' Magnus tossed the rope to Leonardo. 'We will head there in several weeks' time, so it's good that you learn now.'

The seven of them fumbled with various other knots for a while. Magnus then threw down a sack of barbed iron pegs with loops forged onto one end, designed to be hammered into the rockface to allow a rope to pass through. They took all the information in and learnt as best they could to keep Magnus happy and, though they all wondered what mountaineering had to do with becoming agents of Christendom's most elite holy order, they knew better than to ask.

Here, at least, Ebel fared better than he had in the morning, and his tongue stuck out in concentration as his nimble fingers dextrously practised the knots. Njal, the big Norwegian, had less luck, and was soon grunting impatiently as Magnus corrected him for the eighth time.

'By Christ, boy!' Magnus tutted over his shoulder. 'Loop that end underneath. No, give it here!'

An hour later, Walter had appeared and handed them each a worn, leather satchel that looped over one shoulder and rested comfortably on their backs.

'Form a line!' he shouted, once Magnus had taken his rope back. 'Put the bags down in front of you, quickly now! You, Englishman! Did I ask you to look inside? Leave them there and head to the store in single file. Go!'

The seven of them turned and hurried over to the store, with Walter snapping at their heels. It was becoming a common theme that every task, great or small, was to be done quickly with no small degree of urgency, Leonardo was discovering.

At the storehouse, they were all issued with a bundle of equipment that they collected and placed on the earth before their bags.

'Shawl!' Walter stood before the seven initiates with his own bag, demonstrating that he kept the same equipment the trainees were receiving. 'Use it to cover your face, or you'll end up as red as him!' He pointed at Njal, whose particularly fair skin was already burnt by the sun from their morning excursion. Njal, who had apparently not yet noticed, touched his face gingerly with a huge hand, frowning at its sensitivity.

'Water skin!' Walter held up the next item in his own bag. 'If I need to tell you what that's for, there's no hope for you. Blankets! Two are necessary in winter, but even then you'll feel the cold. Wait and see. Ice axe!'

He went on, explaining the use of the items that were apparently theirs to keep for the duration of the training.

'There will be times ahead during which the only things between you and death are the items in this bag,' he continued. 'Take care of

67

your equipment and it will take care of you! Now, put everything back in the bunkhouse and return here, quickly!'

They did as they were bid, storing the bags in the chests at the foot of their beds and hurrying back out into the yard. Walter then took them to the mountainside to point out the different types of snow and what each indicated the conditions of the weather to mean.

Then, he taught them about the common sicknesses of the mountain, not limited to sickness of altitude and frostnip, making them wince at his tales of the loss of limbs claimed by the cold and death due to exposure.

Finally, it was time for their evening meal, which was wolfed down as greedily as their lunch. Leonardo felt he could have consumed double that, had he been allowed.

Once they finished eating, Magnus addressed them at their table in the corner.

'Tidy up in here. Tomorrow, wake and be ready at dawn.' With that, he and the other three instructors disappeared to their quarters up the stairs, leaving their charges to their own devices.

They headed sluggishly back to the bunkhouse. As Sebastien started a fire, the rest of them collapsed wearily onto their beds and they were finally allowed to speak freely.

'Why on earth do we need to learn about different types of snow?' Gabriel asked the room incredulously. 'I came here to be a soldier of the Order, not a mountaineer! I thought we were going to learn how to fight!'

'I'm sure we will in time,' Sebastien said as he crouched by the hearth. 'I'm sure it's no mistake that the Order chose this place as their training ground.'

'Aye,' Alof said in his heavily accented Frankish as he unlaced his boots. 'It's all a damn test! I think I hate the mountains already.' He began massaging his feet. Yet, that was a sentiment Leonardo found he could not share, remembering the spectacular view from the summit of the climb earlier that day.

Little Ebel sat on his bed in silence, a worried expression on his face.

'What is it?' Leonardo asked him.

Ebel looked up into Leonardo's green eyes for a moment before answering. 'I'm not sure I'm cut out for this. You're all much fitter than me.' He looked ashamedly down at the wooden floorboards.

'Bah!' Sigbald exclaimed from the adjacent bunk, leaning over to give Ebel's shoulder a friendly punch that nearly knocked him off his bed. 'You'll be alright. Give it time, you'll see. It's incredible what the body can adapt to.'

'I hope that's true,' replied Ebel. 'It isn't like I have a choice, anyway. You heard what Drogoradz said, either I get fitter or...' He trailed off, leaving an uncomfortable silence.

'Do you really think other initiates die up here?' Njal asked, finally.

Gabriel, who was lying on his back and staring at the ceiling, sat up at that and laughed cruelly. 'Ha! I would not be surprised! Just wait until winter, this mountain will become our personal freezing hell.' He sighed and added, 'Maybe we shouldn't have come here. Maybe I would have been better off back in Porto...'

'Speak for yourself!' Sebastien scoffed. 'I've naught waiting for me from where I came from. At least we get a couple of hot meals a day, even if they are always goat stew,' he added with a grin.

'Ah, Sebastien!' Sigbald cooed with a smile. 'I'm looking forward to your turn to cook. I shall be your biggest critique!'

'Ha! Prepare to have the experience of a lifetime, my ugly Danish friend! For, my cooking exploits are known up and down the entire island of Britain!' Sebastien said proudly, his hands on his hips.

They laughed. 'Well, I will hold you to that!' Sigbald grinned. 'We can call you Sebastien, King of Lunch!'

Sebastien gave a mock bow before the fire as it crackled warmly behind him. 'And ye, my subjects, will be rewarded greatly for your loyal service!'

'Hurrah!' Njal's deep, booming laugh filled the bunkhouse. 'All you need now is a Queen! Fancy it, Ebel?' They all laughed again at Ebel's frown.

'Aye, now that's something we're missing! The Order could do with a few more women!' Alof piped up.

'It has women,' Leonardo added, and the rest of them listened in fascination as he recounted the instructors' conversation he had overheard on his first day. Once he was done, an incredulous silence followed.

Gabriel crossed himself and said, 'Unnatural! For women to be assassins?' He shuddered.

'Well, I'd certainly be a victim!' Sebastien said, as he hopped onto his bunk and clasped his hands behind his head. 'God knows, I would jump at the chance to lie with a woman again. If she so happened to want me dead, I'd never see it coming!'

Leonardo couldn't help but agree; he had lustful urges toward women as much as any man. When he lay in bed some nights, he often remembered the few sinful fumbles with peasant girls in whatever hideout he had called home back in Rome, and he felt his breathing shallow with desire.

'Supposedly, the second baptism allows agents to lie with women without being wed, if that's what their mission requires,' Alof said with a grin.

'Really?' Njal asked, eyebrows raised hopefully.

Gabriel tutted. 'The second baptism is probably not a vow we should take lightly,' he counselled pompously. 'And who knows what else it involves…?'

Sebastien snorted. 'Might as well find out then, eh?'

'Perhaps we should focus on getting through tomorrow for now,' Leonardo suggested. 'We could all use some rest.' The seven of them found that idea to their liking and lay down on their bunks, bidding each other good luck for the morrow, before wrapping themselves up in thick, woollen blankets.

As Leonardo stretched himself out on the lumpy straw mattress, he thought it was the most comfortable thing he had ever felt, and let out a sigh as his sore joints were allowed to rest. He wondered what the next day would bring as sleep took him a moment later.

Chapter 6

GASCONY

Leonardo woke with a start. He sat bolt upright in his bedroll, his chest heaving, covered in a sheen of cold sweat. He had been dreaming again. Of late, they had not been the good sort; they had been the kind that made his sleep fitful and fleeting, and so disruptive that he often dreaded lying down at night, for he knew the torment his mind was bound to subject him to.

He looked around the camp to see Sebastien moving to light the fire. It had been several days since they had rendezvoused and received their mission from Queen Eleanor and, ever since, the dreams had got worse. Seeing Sebastien again had brought back a flood of memories of everything that had happened at the monastery, all those years ago. Though Leonardo dimly remembered the pleasant times, it had to be said they were greatly overshadowed by all the suffering, and all the death.

Leonardo had always been a private man, reserved even, and quiet. Particularly for one who led a life such as his, it was nigh on impossible to have any kind of relationship with a woman, or even a close friend for that matter. Sebastien had been the closest he had ever come to replacing one of his real brothers, yet now he was as distant as he had ever been, and Leonardo felt as isolated as ever. He supposed he should be used to it by now; he had walked the same path for over a decade. At least he had God for comfort; at least he had his faith. Surely, that ought to be plenty?

Just then, Sebastien looked over to see that Leonardo was awake and watching him. Their eyes met, yet neither bid the other good morning and Sebastien had soon turned back to lighting the fire. Leonardo wiped the sweat from his brow and hauled himself out of bed. In the past, he and Sebastien had shared countless camps, yet none had been so quiet as this one, he remarked.

He packed up his bedroll before heading down to the nearby stream to fill up his waterskin and pat his horse. He and Sebastien had left Bordeaux to travel south, passing through Belin and then on to Mont-de-Marsan, where they had stopped at an inn for the night before picking up the trail and heading for the countryside north of Pau.

They were now well and truly in the heart of Gaston de Bearn's vicomte and had already noted that here, on Gascony's southern tip, the ambience was far more relaxed and shared none of the tense apprehension of Bordeaux. Clearly, the people believed they were safe from the fallout of the rebellion that was taking place, in large part, further to the north. But that did not mean that the Vicomte of Bearn played no role in it, for, if what Queen Eleanor said was true, Gaston had been rather proactive in his efforts to thwart the English king.

It seemed that Alfonso, King of Castile, had backed him, funding him with gold and equipment so that Gaston could be a thorn in King Henry's side in his stead and to do anything he could to weaken Henry's grip on Gascony. Moreover, Gaston's vicomte was well situated to receive anything that came over the Pyrenees; for, on the mountain range's western side, the peaks were not so tall or dense as they were in its centre and there were, therefore, many more viable routes over.

Yet, in both Leonardo and Sebastien's estimation, those routes would all culminate here, north of Pau, before the goods were carted off north toward Aiguillon and Casteljaloux, where Gaston's allies, and perhaps the man himself, currently resided – in the thick of the action.

They had already spent several days scouring the countryside for their prize; figuring that they were looking for something like a slow-moving, lumbering cart pulled by several oxen, complete with an armed escort. For the time being, however, they had found nothing. It was not improbable that they would be there for some time before anything interesting passed their way.

Presently, Leonardo returned to the camp to find Sebastien rebaking a loaf of bread ~~he had bought the~~ previous day. Leonardo sat himself down on his bedroll and stared into the flames. The hazy morning air was filled with birdsong as they chirped happily from nearby trees.

He took a gulp of water before tossing the skin onto the leafy forest floor beside Sebastien, saying, 'Here. Drink, if you like.'

Sebastien looked at the container for a moment, before muttering, 'Thanks.' He uncorked it and took a swig and then decided his bread was ready. He took it from the rock it sat upon and hesitated, before breaking it in two and passing the smaller half to Leonardo, who leant over and took it.

'Appreciated,' he said, nodding in thanks. That was about the extent of their conversations since leaving Bordeaux.

They ate in silence, listening to the fire crackle and the forest around them awaken. Here, it was teeming with life, and Leonardo thought that, if they were there another night, he would snare them a rabbit.

'We should find some higher ground soon,' said Sebastien, breaking the silence. 'That hill we saw yesterday evening, it should provide a good enough vantage point to watch the road from.' He indicated in the direction behind him through the trees.

Leonardo nodded. 'Very well, then let's make for it.'

A minute later their camp was broken, and the pair led their horses by the reins through the trees, in no particular rush to get there. It took them an hour to find a suitable position and no more was said between them as they settled down to wait on the ridgeline, each of them picking a tree to rest their backs against, a good fifteen yards from the other.

They had tied their mounts up loosely on the grassy bank at the far side of the hill so they could graze, and then it was just a question of waiting. Sebastien had produced a whetstone from his saddlebag and the air was filled with the *'Shing! Shing!'* sounds of him running the stone along the length of his short sword that he kept concealed at his waist under his cloak.

Meanwhile, Leonardo had unrolled some expensive paper from a leather tube and he spread it across his knees, deciding he would try to capture the scene of the plain before him. It was still summer, and peasants tilled the rich fields below. The road they observed was a busy one; farmers carted goods off toward Pau or the surrounding towns, the peasants meandered along in ones and twos, pushing barrows with their hoes tucked under their arms, as they chatted to one another from under the brims of their straw hats that shaded them from the hot sun.

Sebastien had forgone his robes; there was no sense in the disguise now, for it would serve little purpose. He had finished sharpening his blade and began to practise a few thrusts amongst the trees. Leonardo watched the movement from the corner of his eye, as he attempted to capture the curves of the hills on his paper with charcoal crayons. It seemed that his old comrade had not lost any of his martial prowess; indeed, his technique appeared even more crisp.

Sebastien had soon worked up a sweat and paused to mop his brow with his shirt, glancing back down at the road, only to find that there was nothing interesting happening. He sighed and settled himself back down to wait.

Leonardo had less luck with the trees. He had always found that they were more difficult to capture, for the lines and shapes were so random; there was no formal structure to them. His favourite thing to sketch were great works of architecture such as cathedrals, especially the more modern ones, for he found that their repeated geometric shapes, archways and spires were incredibly pleasing to the eye. Still, he would settle for whatever he had before him, as the times during which he was allowed to pursue what was becoming one of his favourite pastimes were few and far between.

Sebastien stood, grunting something about going to find some food and that Leonardo should be sure to keep a lookout. Leonardo nodded and Sebastien marched away into the woods.

A couple of hours passed when Leonardo felt his senses tingle and turned sharply to see Sebastien several paces away, gazing at his drawing from over his shoulder. Leonardo narrowed his eyes. Had Sebastien been trying to sneak up on him? Or was he just showing off that he could still move as silently as Leonardo?

Sebastien held up a small sack and said simply, 'Food.'

Leonardo gestured for him to approach and pulled out a section of his cloak on which he sat, so that Sebastien could pour out a selection of whatever lay in his sack. A collection of berries, nuts and mushrooms tumbled out onto the woollen fabric. Leonardo dipped his head in thanks and packed away his sketching materials to eat, but not before Sebastien had gotten a good look at the canvas.

'Hmm,' he uttered dismissively.

Leonardo narrowed his eyes. 'What?' he snapped.

Sebastien shrugged. 'Your trees. They look a little... squashed.' Then he turned away, taking up his previous seat on a rock twenty paces away. Leonardo looked back down at his sketch and felt a flash of annoyance as he saw that the trees were, indeed, a tad squashed, but otherwise not terrible. He bit his tongue to stop himself responding in anger and decided to occupy himself with the food.

It crossed his mind to check that the mushrooms were not the poisonous variety, but he dismissed the thought immediately. Sebastien was not the kind of man to try to poison him, even with everything that had happened.

They ate in silence and whiled away most of the afternoon in any way they could.

Soon, the peasants had begun to pack away their things and make their way back to their hovels, for the day's light was starting to fade, and they would pick up where they had left off on the morrow. That was when Leonardo saw it.

He jumped to his feet and pointed. 'There! What's that?' he asked. Following his gaze, Sebastien leapt up and marched to the tree line, squinting into the horizon.

Riders had appeared, six of them. They were followed by a huge cart, covered with a thick tarpaulin, hauled along at a snail's pace by a team of four oxen. Four more mounted men took the rear guard. Even at that distance, Leonardo and Sebastien could see the metallic gleam of helms strapped to the pommels of the riders' saddles and lances couched in their sheaths.

They were soldiers then, or even knights.

Sebastien stroked his chin as he peered at them. 'Hmm, ten mounted men and two more driving the cart. A dozen soldiers to escort one load of cargo. I'd say that could be exactly what we're looking for.'

'It's certainly the most promising thing we've seen yet,' replied Leonardo. 'I say we follow at a distance and wait until they've made camp for the night, to confirm. It shouldn't be long now, anyhow.' He glanced at the position of the sun.

'Aye, that'd be best,' said Sebastien. 'Let's be about it then.'

Several hours later, Leonardo and Sebastien were crouched side by side within the trees, watching through the darkness at the activity happening in the little camp the armed men had set up.

They had pulled their precious cargo off the road and lit a campfire, once the horses had been unsaddled and the oxen relieved of their yoke.

'Why do we 'ave to mount the guard?' one of the soldiers was complaining to their leader, a knight by the look and sound of him, Leonardo guessed. 'It isn't like the woods are crawling with enemies or anythin'. The roads down 'ere are safe, anyway.'

'Nonetheless, we will mount the guard,' the knight instructed him sternly. 'You know as well as I do that were anything from that cart to go missing, our Lord de Bearn would have our balls on a stick before you knew it.'

Leonardo and Sebastien exchanged a knowing look in the gloom; they had found what they were looking for, it seemed.

There was a little grumbling from the other men, but they accepted what the knight said to be true. A pair of them stationed themselves facing outward on opposite sides of the camp, whilst the rest laid out their bedrolls and chatted by the fire.

'Let's wait until they're asleep,' Leonardo whispered. 'Perhaps you could circle round to the other side, then we can attack on my mark.'

'No,' Sebastien replied. 'I'll circle round for the other guard, but we'll attack on *my* mark.'

Leonardo clenched his jaw in annoyance. 'Fine,' he hissed back, but Sebastien had already turned and begun to crawl noiselessly over the foliage and through the trees to carry out his task.

Leonardo sighed and resigned himself to wait, listening to the laughter of the men around the fire as they handed out meat and cheese and drank weak ale. Once, one had stood, passed the sentry, and left the safety of the camp to head directly toward Leonardo's position. Leonardo had stiffened tensely as the man had dropped his breeches no more than ten yards away to take a shit.

However, once he was done and fully clothed again, the man had headed back to the fire, none the wiser that there had been a killer lurking in the bushes a stone's throw from his improvised latrine.

Then, Leonardo had nothing to do but wait. An hour passed, and the men had since lain down to sleep in the warm, still night, with nothing at all to suggest there was any kind of threat waiting in the trees. Another hour went by and the guards changed, waking their fellows as they occupied the recently vacated bedrolls. And then another hour passed and it was midnight.

An owl hooted. A cricket chirped. The air was still.

Any moment now, Leonardo thought. It was as good a time as any. The light of a full moon shone through the canopy, down upon the little clearing of the camp, and the embers of the fire glowed a dull red. The guards yawned, leaning on their spears, while the horses, lashed to a nearby tree, slept.

Leonardo decided it was time to move forward and began to crawl, ever so slowly, through the bush that had been his hiding place, aiming for the guard who stood watch at the edge of the camp closest to him. He had drawn his twin daggers and gripped them tight as he went, ready to leap up at a moment's notice.

When he was as close as he dared, say fifteen paces, he focused his gaze at the far side of the encampment, where the second guard stood. Leonardo waited with bated breath for the first sign of movement that would be his cue to attack. His chin rested on the layer of dead leaves covering the forest floor and his breathing was shallow and fast, so that it barely disturbed the leaves below.

Any moment now…

The guard nearest to him adjusted his weight, cleared his throat and scratched his testicles. Leonardo decided to risk getting just a little closer. He was protected by a holly bush and the darkness. It was enough. Ten paces away. That was as close as he dared.

He glanced over to the other guard who stood silently at the far edge of the clearing. Where was Sebastien? Leonardo began to grow impatient. Had he somehow managed to get himself lost? Leonardo reassessed and wondered whether it was achievable on his own. He eventually decided that twelve was too many, even if he did have the element of surprise; that might only allow him to dispatch one or two before the others woke. No, he had to wait.

Then, without warning, something big and dark dropped from the treetops and cannoned into the furthest guard. The moonlight reflected briefly from a wicked blade before it disappeared down into the flesh, between shoulder and neck. They collapsed with a flurry of limbs and a loud clatter that shattered the silence of the still night.

Leonardo's guard turned with a surprised 'Oh!' and froze as he saw a dark stranger rising from the body of his fallen comrade. Yet, he had no time to react, for Leonardo was already behind him and was raking one of his razor-sharp daggers across the unarmoured flesh of the man's neck. He died with a gurgle and hit the ground, just as the commotion had alerted the others around the campfire.

'Argh!' one of the soldiers cried as he woke, only to find himself in his worst nightmare. 'Attack! We're under attack! Att—' He didn't finish, for Leonardo was thrusting his blade into the soldier's bare chest. Leonardo watched as the look of petrified horror on the man's face changed at the realisation of his demise, and then it went blank.

On the other side of the camp, Sebastien had produced his buckler, a small duelling shield, and had managed to dispatch another soldier.

The knight was shouting, 'To arms! To arms!' A second later, he and the rest of his men were reaching for their weapons and scrambling to their feet, their eyes searching for the enemy.

It soon presented itself, and they were set upon from both sides by two dark figures, slashing and thrusting their blades in the night, pushing the men back to the fire. Two more died before the soldiers came to their senses and managed a counterattack.

'Quick! Hand me that shield!' the knight ordered, as Leonardo wrenched his weapons from the guts of a man clad in nothing but a pair of stockings. The man gave out an inhuman wail as he bent double and fell onto all fours, blood spilling over his fingers and gushing from his mouth. His wail faltered as he choked on the thick, warm liquid.

Suddenly, Leonardo was attacked from two angles. He stepped back and parried the knight's longsword with a clash of steel upon steel. He had to sidestep a spear thrust and leapt forward so that he was within its arc and gripped the shaft of ash, watching the bearer panic before he slashed him square across the eyes, causing him to screech in pain and drop the weapon. In the same moment, Leonardo sidestepped another hasty chop from the knight, who hadn't had the time to pull on his armour before the action began.

The knight was flanked by an older man and a youth, who trembled as he extended forth his cooking knife, apparently not having been able to find his sword in the dark. However, the knight was not so green. Though he was clearly afraid, he had now recovered somewhat from the shock and snarled, advancing on the tall, cloaked figure with their glowing green eyes.

Leonardo waited and let him advance. The knight thrust, Leonardo parried; the knight stumbled, Leonardo thrust. The knight then tripped and fell onto the leaves in his attempt to dodge the attack. Leonardo used the moment of confusion to kick the longsword from the knight's fingers, and the knight had no choice but to crawl back in fear, back between the legs of his companions.

Meanwhile, the air was filled with clashes and thuds as Sebastien duelled three men at once, who had managed to encircle him, thinking to gain the upper hand. With a lesser man, the strategy would have worked, yet Sebastien was very nearly as fast with a blade as Leonardo, and that was plenty.

Sebastien lunged his feet wide, the buckler protecting the back of his head, as his blade buried itself between two ribs, and the scream of agony that followed caused nearby pigeons to fly from the trees. His short sword was yanked free and brought around, just in time to parry and thrust as he stepped back from an attack. Giving himself space to manoeuvre, he launched his own attack, causing the other two soldiers to take the backfoot.

Leonardo turned his attention back to his own adversaries. The older man licked his lips and stepped forward tentatively with a mean-looking falchion and accompanying shield. Leonardo sensed his experience and tested him with a thrust. The man blocked it with the shield and replied with a swing of the falchion. Leonardo stepped back neatly. The last thing he wanted to do was take the full swing of a falchion; those weapons had been known to lop off limbs with ease and he himself wore no maille, only a light gambeson that would have done little to protect him against the sword.

He switched the dagger in his right hand to an ice pick grip and darted forward, feigning a thrust with the left that predictably caused the soldier to raise the shield high in defence. Leonardo then punched the dagger in his right hand down hard, piercing deep into the wood of the shield so that it stuck. When the soldier tried to step back and pull the shield down to see where Leonardo had gone, Leonardo fought against him using the leverage of his dagger still buried deep in the wood.

Instead, he yanked his right arm backwards and, since the soldier's arm was looped to the shield through straps of thick leather, he was pulled with it. The soldier swung hastily in attack as he realised what was happening, but Leonardo was ready for it and redirected the blade with his left-hand dagger before plunging it deep into the soldier's neck.

'No!' the knight cried. He dived for his sword as Leonardo finished off the youth, who had hesitated for far too long. The knight crawled forward, his fingers finding the hilt. However, as he rolled over to push himself up, he felt a boot planted firmly on his chest and a dagger dripped blood onto his face, its point directed right between his eyes.

'Don't,' Leonardo's voice commanded. The knight was no fool; he knew he was beaten, and let his sword fall to the earth, raising his hands in surrender.

In the background, Sebastien straddled a man writhing around in agony, clutching at his face. Sebastien gripped a handful of the man's hair to tip his head back, so that his short sword would find the soft flesh of the man's neck easier, and the soldier was put from his misery.

'That one is unharmed?' he called, as he straightened in the moonlight and made for the next groaning soldier.

'Aye,' Leonardo replied.

'Then keep him that way. We will need someone to take word back to the Vicomte.'

'I was going to.'

The knight looked over in horror at Sebastien's butchery and cried, 'No, wait! Please, have mercy on them!'

'Be quiet,' Leonardo said softly, and the knight took one look at those glowing green eyes to know that it was a command he should heed.

Sebastien dealt with the last of the soldiers, dragging him back into the space by the fire. The man had managed to crawl two dozen yards into the trees, leaving a bloody trail behind him before he, too, had his throat cut.

Quietness descended upon the forest once more. As Sebastien occupied himself with checking the contents of the cart, Leonardo knelt to gaze at the wide-eyed knight by his feet.

'Tell me,' he said, 'where is your master now?' Leonardo's dagger was still inches from his nose and the knight went cross-eyed trying to keep its tip in focus. He gulped before replying.

'North, he will be north,' the man gasped. 'Most likely with Amaneus d'Albret and Bernard de Bouville. I know not where, exactly. I swear! Maybe Bazas! Probably Bazas.'

'Hmm.' Leonardo thought for a moment about why Emilio had sent him to Gascony in the first place. He glanced up to make sure Sebastien was out of earshot. 'Those are military supplies, yes?'

There was a nervous nod.

'Sent to your lord by the King of Castile?'

Another nod.

'What do you know about King Alfonso? What are his designs?'

A frown passed over the knight's face before he replied. 'He would have Gascony for himself. With my Lord de Bearn's help, he would take it from the English king now that it is easy pickings.'

'And was that Alfonso's idea? Or someone else's?' asked Leonardo. It was a long shot.

'Please, I don't know,' the knight replied. 'I swear upon all the saints!'

Leonardo grunted. He believed the man, for he would have no idea of the goings on within the courts of the Spanish kingdoms. It had been worth a go, however. Looking up, he saw that Sebastien had climbed onto the cart and was examining a military grade crossbow, one of the newer composite designs favouring a doublet pulley.

Sebastien didn't need to know about his other business, Leonardo decided. After all, for all Leonardo knew, it could be *his* master who was stirring the pot between the other Fingers. No, Sebastien didn't need to know.

'Very well.' He rolled the knight over unceremoniously and began to tie his hands together with a length of chord, and then his ankles, until the man was trussed up as good as a hog over a fire.

'Take a look at this,' Sebastien said as Leonardo approached the wagon. He tossed down the crossbow, which Leonardo caught. It was the latest in military technology and sure to add a significant advantage on the battlefield; unlike the traditional longbows that took archers years to master and at a great expense, a team of levied peasants could learn to shoot these crossbows in an afternoon.

'Interesting,' Leonardo said.

'Yes, there are a hundred more here and thousands of bolts to boot,' replied Sebastien. 'I'm sure we can assume that the rebels already have a good number of them. Ah, what do we have here...'

Sebastien stooped to rummage around in the back of the cart, pulling out a small, locked chest. He held it up and shook it. 'I can guess what's inside!' he exclaimed triumphantly as he clambered down with it clutched in his arms.

As the pair made their way back over to the constrained knight, Leonardo looked across at Sebastien. 'You took your time back there. I thought you might have fallen asleep. I almost went in to get the job done alone.'

Sebastien glanced at Leonardo's impassive face covered by shadows, unable to tell if there was the suggestion of a smirk on his lips. Eventually, he turned away and snorted.

'You're quick, I'll give you that. But a dozen men? Not a chance!'

'I suppose we'll never know for sure,' Leonardo replied as he stooped to fish around the knight's clothes to search for the key, his back conveniently turned to Sebastien, for he hadn't been able to contain his grin. He found it, the knight not daring to protest nor resist, and tossed it to Sebastien, who pushed it into the lock.

'Now then...' It turned with a click and the lid opened to reveal several columns of neatly stacked ingots of gold. Sebastien tutted down at the knight. 'Your master's a naughty boy! I think we shall have to confiscate these.'

Leonardo glanced back at the wagon. 'We should burn it,' he said.

'Agreed,' replied Sebastien. 'And I'll take the gold. My Lady the Queen can put it to good use, I'm sure.' He stuck out his chin defiantly as he met Leonardo's gaze, half expecting him to protest.

Leonardo shrugged. 'As you wish.'

They set about their work and, an hour later, the wagon was ablaze, the valuable cargo of crossbows and bolts becoming nothing more than charcoal.

Before they left, Leonardo and Sebastien stripped two of the soldiers' bodies naked and strung them up by their ankles to the thick branch of a nearby beech tree by the road, so that the grim spectacle could not be missed. Their message was clear: this is what happens to rebels.

The knight was left tied up by the fire. He would be discovered by the locals come the morning and would undoubtedly relay his news back to Gaston de Bearn, who would think twice before accepting military aid from the King of Castile, or at least be kept awake at night knowing that there were bloodthirsty loyalists running around in his territory.

Finally, they butchered the horses and oxen on the way out, so as to leave nothing of use for Gaston's men. After all, their masters wanted to keep Gascony in the hands of the English, at least for now, and that meant the two of them were at war with the rebels – and, in war, all was fair.

It was brutal work; Leonardo and Sebastien had just killed eleven men between them, enough bloodshed to make any sane man baulk at the sight. But such was their experience that they didn't even blink, for what difference did a dozen more make when their hands had already claimed the lives of countless others? The men of the Order of The Hand of God were rare indeed.

Before Leonardo mounted his horse, he knelt and crossed himself, whispering a quick prayer, knowing that his God would forgive him for acting for the greater good. Sebastien followed his example and, a moment later, the two of them were mounted and riding abreast along the road north, as the first light of the sun rose in the eastern sky.

Sebastien sighed contentedly and patted his horse's neck. 'It looks to be another fine day.'

'Indeed,' was all Leonardo said in reply, and they lapsed into something that almost resembled a companionable silence, broken only by the rhythmic thuds of their horses' hooves on the beaten earth of the track.

Chapter 7

TWELVE YEARS AGO

rogoradz's naked upper body was laced with thick knots of muscle, looking even more imposing now he had removed his shirt. He grinned at them all from under his enormous straw-blonde moustache, curved upward at its tips.

The seven initiates waited nervously before the big man in the yard.

'You!' Drogoradz said, pointing at Njal. 'Step forward!' Njal stepped forward hesitantly and, though he was a little taller than Drogoradz, he was not quite so bulky, and the look in Drogoradz's eye was the opposite of comforting.

Leonardo felt it was no accident that the biggest of them, Njal, had been selected for the demonstration of their first wrestling lesson. Leonardo had woken far earlier than his body would have liked, bleary eyed and lacking for sleep. He had, nonetheless, hauled himself out of bed and eaten a little bread he had saved from supper, before they found themselves in the cold morning air, carrying out the menial daily chores that kept the monastery alive. Before long, Drogoradz had begun ushering them out to one side of the yard that was free of rocks and made up of packed earth, instead.

Presently, the big man beckoned Njal forward. 'Come, come! Don't be shy!' he said with a nasty grin. It seemed that the day's lesson would be of an entirely practical nature, with little actual teaching and more showing.

Njal gulped and stepped forward, stretching out his arms in anticipation, as Drogoradz began to circle him like a cat would circle a mouse.

Njal spread his feet a little wider and was sure to keep his body facing the leering Drogoradz. The latter, clearly enjoying himself, pulled up his plain brown trousers over massive thighs to give himself more room to move, and then he changed direction, circling the other way.

Drogoradz chuckled as Njal backed away fearfully, his arms outstretched, waiting for the moment Drogoradz would strike.

Then, a second later, it came. Drogoradz dived in an athletic leap under Njal's guard, hooking his arms around both knees and using the weight of his momentum to tackle the Norwegian to the ground.

Njal barely had time to let out an 'Oof!' before Drogoradz was on top of him, twisting his arm painfully in a manner that made him cry out and tap his superior's shoulder in submission.

'Ha!' Drogoradz laughed as he leapt to his feet and beckoned Njal up. 'Stand! Again! Give me a challenge this time!'

Njal clambered reluctantly to his feet, knowing that the outcome would be the same.

Sure enough, a moment later, Drogoradz had leapt at him and Njal landed flat on his face, this time with a mouthful of dirt, only to find a thick, hairy forearm wrapped around his neck choking the life from him until he tapped.

Leonardo and the rest of the initiates shifted from foot to foot nervously, seeing the ease with which Drogoradz had neutralised the strongest amongst them.

After Njal was floored for a third time, he was allowed to rest as Drogoradz selected his next victim.

'You!'

Sigbald stepped forward. A brief flurry of limbs later, and Sigbald's fate was much the same as Njal's.

'Aargh!' was all he could manage as the big man's knee pressed into his gut. Twice more, Sigbald hit the earth before he, too, was dismissed.

Then, it was Leonardo's turn.

'Step forward,' Drogoradz commanded. Leonardo did so, licking his lips as he felt every inch the prey, as his adversary tucked away a strand of his long, straw hair that had come loose from the bun atop his head. The grin under the moustache twitched.

Leonardo rolled up the sleeves of his linen shirt, making sure the hem was tucked into his trousers as he began to circle his opponent. He had no idea what he was going to do when Drogoradz inevitably leapt at him, only that he was determined not to submit easily.

Leonardo spread his feet wide and sat down into his hips, trying to gain as much stability as he could. Drogoradz bared his yellow teeth, his great shovel-like hands spread open, ready to grasp at Leonardo's wrists.

Then, without warning, he lunged and Leonardo barely had time to leap back and then sidestep as a long, thick arm nearly managed to wrap itself around his waist.

Drogoradz let out a bark of laughter, his smile widening. 'Yes, that's it. Don't make it easy for me!'

He lunged again and Leonardo leapt to the side, but then his eyes widened in a moment of panic as he realised that Drogoradz had made a feint and the big man darted after him and was upon him. Before he knew it, Leonardo had crashed to the earth and felt a great weight fall onto his legs, before his ankle was being twisted excruciatingly.

He hissed in pain through clenched teeth and tapped his instructor's heavily muscled back. Drogoradz laughed and let him stand up.

'Again!'

Leonardo hopped up, giving his ankle a quick massage before he readied himself once more, narrowing his eyes at Drogoradz and thinking about how best to combat him. Yet, before he had a chance to formulate a plan, he was on the defensive and managed to dodge another attack. Leonardo tried to escape to the left, but was cut off. He went right, but Drogoradz had blocked him again.

The giant was advancing on him, bent low, his powerful legs ready to propel him forwards. Leonardo waited for the right moment until...

Now! Drogoradz darted forward and Leonardo leapt, vaulting clean over the bigger man's back so that his massive arms clutched only at the air in the space Leonardo had vacated. Then, Leonardo was behind him and, before Drogoradz had a chance to recover, jumped on him, his right arm twisting itself around his instructor's neck and he squeezed with all his might.

However, Drogoradz knew exactly what to do. He calmly wiggled his fingers into the crook of Leonardo's elbow, then pushed until his hand was through, then his arm and then he could breathe again before he twisted violently. Leonardo had the wind knocked out of him as he was thrown to the earth once more.

It was then Leonardo's turn to be choked out and he was soon struggling for air and tapping Drogoradz's thigh, and a knee was released from his neck a moment later.

Drogoradz roared with laughter and hauled Leonardo to his feet as easily as if he were made from straw. Leonardo felt a big hand slap his back, and he looked around at his watching comrades as they grinned at him and nodded in approval.

'That's the spirit!' shouted Drogoradz. 'Good effort, boy! My, you're a slippery one, too! Once more, then!'

The pair squared off for a final time, but it was much less eventful. After a minute of manoeuvring, Leonardo was caught yet again and forced to submit.

'Good!' was Drogoradz's verdict. So far, it was the only verdict, before he was summoning Alof onto the cleared patch of earth.

Alof had less fortune than Leonardo and was thrice submitted in quick succession, one after another. He left the training ground rubbing his shoulder, muttering something to himself, a sour look on his face.

Gabriel fared similarly, but each time he was beaten he gave great cries of frustration and pounded the earth in anger.

'Hey!' Drogoradz barked the third time. 'Letting your frustration get the better of you won't help you win!'

Next was Sebastien, and he circled their instructor with an intense look of concentration on his face. To no one's surprise, he was taken to the earth a moment later, but then he did do something that surprised them. When Drogoradz was manoeuvring Sebastien into one of his submissions from an apparently inexhaustible list, Sebastien countered and escaped, then launched an attack of his own, attempting to wrap Drogoradz's limbs into a compromising position.

But Drogoradz was too good for that. The counter was countered, and Sebastien soon cried out in pain as his arm was being bent at the elbow in entirely the wrong direction.

'Good!' Drogoradz commented with a grin once they were both back on their feet. 'Looks like someone has wrestled before, no?'

'Just a little,' Sebastien replied as he rubbed dirt from his face.

'Well then, show me!'

Sebastien leapt forward, crashing into Drogoradz's legs and, after a moment's struggle, they both fell to the earth, though in whose favour it was impossible for the watching audience to tell. They rolled around together for a moment or so, each jostling to gain the upper hand by straddling their opponent, a feat all the more impressive for Sebastien as he was clearly far lighter than the enormous Drogoradz.

Finally, the inevitable happened, and Drogoradz had Sebastien face down in the earth, his great weight on the younger man's back as he pulled his leg at a painful angle. Sebastien begrudgingly tapped the earth.

'Ah! Not terrible,' said Drogoradz. 'There might be a little potential there. Once more!'

This time, the combatants remained mostly on their feet as each sought a takedown by tugging on the other's limbs or shirt, trying to pull the other forward or push them over. At one point, Leonardo had to leap back out of the way as the two of them almost came barrelling into him before regaining the centre of the wrestling ground.

A brief struggle later and they were on the earth again. Drogoradz had, of course, prevailed, yet it was clear to them all that Sebastien had been the most successful amongst them. As Sebastien limped to Leonardo's side with a wince, the rest of the initiates didn't miss Drogoradz give a pleasantly surprised 'Hmm!' and a nod of satisfaction, before Ebel was being beckoned forth.

Poor Ebel. He must have been half the weight of his instructor and trembled slightly under the look of disdain Drogoradz gave him. Though Ebel was not short, he was skinny, and Leonardo had to wonder why his master had chosen him for the Order's most gruelling rite of passage.

Ebel must have known he could not win, not even close. Yet, Leonardo had to give the lad some credit, for, before Drogoradz had the chance, Ebel had charged him, throwing all his weight into the big man's waist in an attempt to knock him back.

It was almost pitiful. The impetus of his charge was not enough to so much as force Drogoradz to take a step back. Then, Ebel was being picked up and quite literally thrown to the earth before Drogoradz fell upon him and forced him to submit.

The two consecutive submissions were over just as fast. Yet, Ebel, at least, had had the courage to take the initiative each time, regardless of whether he had succeeded or not.

A moment later, Drogoradz was standing before them with his hands on his hips, grinning at the way all seven of them seemed to be massaging some minor wound or injury he had inflicted. Drogoradz had more than made his point.

'Right, now I have a feel for your abilities. But, more importantly, you all know how much you have yet to learn. Now, I'm going to teach you the basics. You!' He pointed at Sebastien. 'Step forward so I can demonstrate.'

They spent the rest of the morning performing the drills with Drogoradz until they were all completely sick of them, not to mention sore. When midday finally came around, they trudged into the great hall wearily in single file, and were happy to eat in silence as their instructors chatted amongst themselves at the table by the fire.

The afternoon brought their first lesson with Antonio, who, silent as ever, led them to the storeroom where they were handed wooden training swords. Antonio's teaching style seemed to be a little different to that of Drogoradz; instead of throwing them in at the deep end, he had them all stand in a line and then, with his back to them, he demonstrated a lunge with his own training sword, beckoning the seven of them to try.

He gave a motion with his hand for them to continue, then moved along the line, stroking his neat, dark beard as he reviewed their technique, pausing every now and again to demonstrate the thrust once more, or otherwise give an initiate's feet a tap or adjust the position of their arms.

Then, he showed them how to lunge with the thrust, then cut. An hour passed before he allowed the initiates to rest for several minutes as they all rubbed their shoulder muscles gingerly. As they soon discovered, holding the heavy, wooden training swords at arm's length for any period of time caused their muscles to burn painfully.

Gabriel was particularly vocal about his suffering. 'I'm hurting all over!' he complained. 'If it goes on like this much longer, we'll burn out for sure!'

'I have a feeling that's what they want to find out,' said Sebastien. 'It's their way of testing us to see if we give in, or if we can weather the storm.' He tossed a waterskin to Njal. 'Let's just stick at it for now.'

'Well, it isn't as if we have much of a choice,' Gabriel muttered.

Thwack! Antonio had appeared out of nowhere, the sound of his footfalls as absent as his voice. Gabriel was rubbing his ear from where Antonio had smacked it, looking up at his teacher to see his finger over his lips in a gesture for silence.

Then, Antonio was beckoning them all to several posts set in the ground at one end of the yard, where they spent much of the rest of the afternoon jabbing at them with their training swords under his guidance.

By the end of the second day, the seven initiates were even more sore than they had been at the end of the first, and collapsed onto their cots with a sigh of relief.

The third day, like the first two, was packed with activity, so much so that Leonardo found he had barely time to relieve himself, though he appreciated that the time went quick. They learnt languages with Magnus in the great hall, improving their Frankish, Italian, Latin, Arabic and a handful more.

Leonardo found he enjoyed that as much as anything else, and was surpassed in the group only by Ebel. At last, the dark-skinned Greek had found something he excelled at.

Alof and Njal, the latter in particular, were not so adept and soon found Magnus growling at them when he asked them to repeat a phrase he had just uttered.

Then there were more theory lessons, such as politics, where they had to memorise the names of major players that dominated the political landscapes in each of the great European kingdoms.

Geography, too – Magnus brought out various maps. Rare and interesting documents, created by a cartographer that had laboured for many weeks to produce them, the maps were usually reserved for the nobility and seldom fell into the hands of the common man. Magnus taught the initiates how to read them, explained what all the little symbols meant and how to orient oneself with the map's north.

The fourth day was more physical. The morning was swordplay with Antonio and then, in the afternoon, Drogoradz brought them to the far end of the cleft in the mountain, where a landslide had caused the level cliffside to fall away perilously.

There, Drogoradz had previously hewn boulders into enormous rough balls of stone of various sizes. He demonstrated what he wanted the seven of them to do by wrapping his gigantic arms around one of the largest and began waddling with it to the other side of the training ground.

None save Njal managed to get it all the way without dropping it, and Ebel hadn't even managed to get it off the ground. Leonardo had a newfound respect for Drogoradz's great strength, for he had made it look easy. Leonardo had also previously thought that his body couldn't feel any sorer, but yet again he found himself corrected.

At least, he consoled himself, they were allowed to eat well. During the day, while they were having lessons with one of their teachers, apparently two or more teachers went hunting, for it seemed that, at this time of year at least, there was plenty of game in the mountains, especially in the wooded valley floor. It was not an uncommon sight to see Walter and Antonio climbing back up the steep track to the monastery, with a deer or goat tied by the ankles to a pole that spanned the gap between their shoulders.

They made good use of the donkey in the stables, too, to haul hay from the villages back up to feed their goats. These were used to make milk and cheese, both of which tasted a little sour, but at least provided a good boost of energy.

The fifth day brought another excursion into the mountains, and this time Magnus led them further afield. Leonardo had the older man's back in his sights the whole way, with his white hair and beard whipping around the side of his head as he led the pack at a rapid pace.

As the day wore on, the gap between the groups widened. Those at the fore included Sebastien, Njal and Leonardo, whilst the middle trio were made up of Alof, Gabriel and Sigbald. Ebel, of course, fell far behind and was soon out of sight.

This time, they made a great loop, heading down the track, down into the beautiful, secluded valley below the steep cliffs of the monastery. They passed between pine trees and ferns, moss and boulders, where little patches of snow hid in the shade and small streams intersected the path here and there, where a gentle trickle of meltwater formed miniature waterfalls and small pools that were filled with water, that was the most clean and fresh that Leonardo had ever tasted.

He was so taken with the outstanding beauty of it all. One of his favourite things to do, in his exceedingly rare spare time, was to stand out by the cliff's edge near the barn and take in the breathtaking view that had not yet lost its novelty.

Yet, on the march, Leonardo had not the time to take in his surroundings, for Magnus's pace left no room for idling. It was early afternoon by the time the first trio made it safely back, and the second was not long behind them. Ebel, however, made his appearance an hour later and Walter never let him hear the end of it, making the lad scrape the shit from the barn whilst the others ate in peace.

The sixth day was a Sunday, and Magnus allowed them to rest – or, at least, their bodies, for in the morning he took them to the chapel for prayer and communion. Both initiate and instructor sat in silence beneath the enormous, gilded silver cross that glinted in the candlelight and, again, Leonardo noted how odd it looked in such a plain setting.

In the afternoon, they were advised to repair their kit and revise their previous lessons. Walter had smugly informed them that he would be testing them the following day on everything he had taught them to date, and anyone who did not meet his standards would be holding one of Drogoradz's boulders above their heads until their strength failed them.

Leonardo suspected that none of them would succeed in meeting Walter's standards. Sure enough, the following day, the seven of them found themselves lined up, grunting with the effort of holding a rock high above their heads, willing Walter to take pity on them – of which, they were learning, he had little.

Yet, he was fair if nothing else, and, considering Ebel had remembered the most, he was allowed to rest first. Leonardo and Sebastien followed together soon after, having scored similarly and were soon groaning and massaging life back into their shoulders and forearms.

Gabriel and Sigbald were next, leaving Alof and Njal gritting their teeth. Walter left them there until Alof inevitably dropped his rock, only to find that Walter had appeared above him shouting in his ear to pick it up. Njal soon followed, despite the Norwegian's strength, and received a similar treatment.

Alof was finally released from his punishment, but not Njal. Walter had made it abundantly clear that Njal's answers to the test had been so far below the acceptable threshold, that he wondered if Njal had been present at all for his lessons. The minutes went by and Njal dropped his rock several more times, eliciting a smack around the ear from Walter and more abuse as he did so.

Finally, he was allowed to rest and collapsed into a heap on the ground, panting and covered in sweat.

Leonardo was quickly learning that his instructors were punishing them for their incompetence and so he deigned to follow all instruction to the letter, to listen and absorb as much as he could of their teachings. That way, he discovered that he was more or less ignored, as his superiors picked on easier targets.

It was good, he learnt, to be generally adept at all things rather than to excel in one discipline and lack in another. Amongst the seven of the initiates, a hierarchy had begun to form, and Leonardo found that both he and Sebastien seemed to be leading the way as they were both rather good at everything.

In fact, Leonardo found that he was proving to be quite excellent at swordplay, and Antonio had little to correct on his form, instead giving him a nod of approval at his nimble thrusts and cuts, before moving on to critique the next initiate. During their sparring, none was faster, and the others had quickly come to fear the tip of Leonardo's wooden sword, knowing the sharp pain as it jabbed into their exposed rips or thwacked their shoulders.

Yet, Sebastien, though not quite on Leonardo's level, always gave him fierce competition, and the two friends found themselves grinning at each other as they traded flurries of blows, panting and sweating all the while.

However, if Leonardo was the best with a blade in his grasp, Sebastien always had the upper hand during the wrestling. There, he had his revenge, and when Drogoradz allowed them to pick their sparring partners, he always chose Leonardo, beckoning him forward with a mean cackle, though the amusement in his eyes gave him away. Leonardo would flash him a rueful grin, knowing he was likely to beat the Englishman perhaps once in ten attempts, and even then he was not entirely convinced that Sebastien hadn't let him win.

And so the training wore on. July became August, and August turned to September. By then, they had all fallen into a rhythm, and found that their bodies had indeed adapted to the rigorous routine of physical activity. Their marches in the mountains were now far more pleasant, instead of a desperate bid not to fall behind. Drogoradz's boulders didn't seem quite so heavy, and their training swords, too, were lighter in the hand. They repeated every knot until it was ingrained into their minds, and they knew by heart all the potential dangers of the mountains.

Politics, languages and geography were all concepts less foreign and Leonardo actually found most of it quite interesting.

The seven initiates had fallen into an easy camaraderie, with Sebastien and Sigbald lifting their morale by doing the most larking around in the bunkhouse at night as the rest of them laughed along.

Sebastien was witty and quick with a remark in a positive manner, and it was difficult to dislike him.

Leonardo was his usual reserved self, quiet and encouraging, always there to help when one of the others struggled with something. His capabilities were not lost on the others. He and Sebastien had a natural bond, and no one was quite sure who would be their leader, if they had to have one, but knew it would have been one of the two.

That was not to say the initiates were entirely without conflict. Once, Leonardo had lost his temper with Gabriel, who was often chafing at the spirits of the others with his constant winging about this and that. He had been taken aback at first when Leonardo had rebuked him, but the surprise had quickly turned to anger and the pair had tousled in the bunkhouse, with Leonardo gaining the upper hand, before their fellows pulled them apart.

Sigbald and Njal, too, had come to blows once, when Njal had helped himself to Sigbald's precious cache of smoked ham that he was saving for a later day. The fight took place in the yard one morning and, unfortunately, they had been observed by Magnus, who soon had them crawling up and down the rocky track on all fours until their elbows and knees were bloody as punishment.

Such things were easily forgotten, however, and for the most part they were seven friends. Leonardo, for the first time in a long time, was happy. He enjoyed the banter and the camaraderie. They all spent every waking moment of every day together and were quickly becoming something akin to brothers.

When Leonardo thought of it that way, however, it made him sad, for it harkened back to his old life in the streets of Rome when he had had two real brothers. Being older than Leonardo, they had taken care of him; and a sister, too! But they were now dead or gone, hunted through the streets and butchered by other beggars and thieves, and for what? A dispute about who held sway over the streets.

The memories were still fresh enough in Leonardo's mind; it had only been a handful of years prior, and he still remembered the way his brothers had told him to run when they had both turned in the alleyway to face down a gang armed with knives and makeshift shivs, buying him just enough time to escape. They had been afraid, though; he had known them well enough to see it plainly on their faces.

That had terrified him. His big brothers afraid? But they had been fearless! They were the toughest around, and he knew it. In the end, they had only been boys, as old as he was now. And they were gone. Dead. As was his sister, though whether she still lived he knew not.

On occasion, when the nightmares were vivid enough, Leonardo sometimes woke with silent tears running down his face, tears that were caused as much by his shame as the loss of his family, for he had left them in their time of need. That was reason enough to live a life of penance, he decided.

At least he could take comfort from the fact that he'd had his revenge since. Emilio had helped him with that. The thugs that slew his brothers were now just as dead, and Leonardo had been blooded. Yet, instead of keeping the storm that Leonardo felt brewing within him at bay, that act had merely caused it to churn all the more violently.

Fortunately, Leonardo had learnt to control the white-hot rage over the last few years, for he knew that, should it consume him completely, there was no telling what he might do. At the monastery at least, life was as calm as it had ever been; and, though Leonardo struggled daily, it was the kind of challenge he relished, and his success in the training was as good a goal to focus on as any.

But he knew he could not become complacent, for winter would soon be upon them. The mountains would transform into an altogether different beast.

Chapter 8

TWELVE YEARS AGO

The end of October was almost upon them and, with it, winter. Already, Leonardo had felt the air around the monastery begin to bite at his skin, and the initiates had taken to wrapping themselves up in thick, woollen cloaks on their way to their lessons, or to walk from the bunkhouse to the great hall. The first snow had arrived several weeks prior, and had since melted, yet the temperature was consistently cool enough now that the snow had begun to stick, and their daily chores had been altered to include its removal from the yard.

They had also grown used to the nuances of life at the monastery. Should they need water to drink, they had to collect ice and snow from nearby snowdrifts and melt it by the fire, before pouring it carefully into a barrel in the corner of the bunkhouse.

Similarly, there was no other way to bathe than to strip naked in the snow, scoop up a handful of it and rub it all over their bodies, before they gingerly ran barefoot across the earth and back inside to the warmth.

The seven of them had made it a tradition on the Sunday afternoons that they had off to descend down the mountainside with wicker baskets strapped to their backs, filling them with firewood from the valley below, with the intention of stockpiling for the winter, for it was certain that everything was soon to be covered with several feet of snow. They knew that their instructors were hardly likely to make the suggestion themselves, and all of them could very well imagine Magnus saying, 'Cold, are you? I suppose you should have thought of that!'

The older men, too, were preparing for winter. Their hunting trips had become more frequent and the ice cave, where their food was stored, was full. The meat was harvested, salted, then packed between great blocks of ice, that Leonardo guessed would have been cut from a glacier each year before the spring arrived. At least they didn't have to worry about the flies getting to it, for, as high as they were, there were almost no insects at the monastery year round.

One day, the initiates had been handed several large chunks of rawhide, cat gut and a needle and Walter had shown them all how to make their own boots. They had passed a pleasant afternoon on one of the last truly warm days, stitching away in the sun in silence, their backs to the stone wall of the great hall, forming the boots to their feet and gluing the layers of thick leather, several deep, with sticky pine tar.

Magnus, Antonio, Drogoradz and Walter still kept their charges on their toes. They were forever prone to being snapped at for asking stupid questions, or punished with physical toil for not doing exactly as they were asked. Yet, these occasions were becoming less frequent – though, whether it was due to the fact that the seven of them were improving, or that their instructors were mellowing to them, Leonardo could not say.

The initiates continued to eat in silence at their table in the corner of the great hall, while their superiors talked and laughed together. This, they were well used to and had even learnt that, by listening to the snippets of the older men's conversation, they gleaned what little information they could about the Order in its wider existence and of the men who were teaching them.

Magnus, they learnt, was the oldest and most successful agent that currently lived, all the more impressive for a man of his age, because the life expectancy of agents was decidedly short. Walter had once killed an archduke by flinging him from a balcony, and Drogoradz had travelled to the ends of the earth in pursuit of one of

99

his targets, to a distant land of tropical forests and tribes they called India. Antonio, of course, did not speak; every so often, however, his comrades would nudge him at the dinner table to recount one of his exploits and say, 'Hey, Antonio, remember when you…' and he'd grin and nod. Each of them was still somewhat of a mystery, though less so than when Leonardo had first arrived.

They were no less thorough in their teaching, however, and the same routine of learning from dawn to dusk was maintained. Leonardo was pleased to find his body was adapting well, for now his sword arm no longer ached with fatigue, and he could whip the heavy training swords through the air with ease without tiring. He could even lift the heaviest of Drogoradz's boulders and carry it a short distance – though, not quite so far as Njal. New muscles rippled under his shirt and he had never felt so strong. His lungs, too, felt as though they had a deeper capacity, and keeping up with Magnus was now no great challenge.

The most impressive transformation, however, had to be awarded to Ebel. A couple of days prior, he had stripped to his waist in the bunkhouse and Sebastien had exclaimed, 'By Joseph, Ebel! Where did you get all those muscles?' The others had all turned to see Ebel grinning with pleasure, looking down at his body that could now no longer be called skinny, for his shoulders had filled out, and his chest had a little shape to it.

Indeed, though he was yet the weakest of them, he could now keep up and no longer suffered Walter's stream of insults during their mountain excursions.

Unfortunately, however, some of the others did not share similar drastic improvements in their own lessons as Ebel. Njal, though fit and capable in all physical trials, struggled with the theory and often drove Walter to fits of rage when he could not remember the contents of the last lesson.

Magnus, too, had noticed it, and had begun to single Njal out more and more, directing his questions at the big Norwegian, leaving him red-faced and stammering as he desperately racked his brain for the answers. Even when both Leonardo and Sebastien helped him on an evening before bed, with the three of them sitting cross-legged before the little hearth in the bunkhouse, revising together what they had learnt that day, Njal seemed incapable of retaining any of it. He would hiss in frustration and smack the side of his head over and over with a meaty palm, until Sigbald would roll over in his cot and shout at them to keep it down. There was only so much Leonardo could do to help him.

Worryingly for Njal, the content of their lessons had only grown more complex. With Antonio, they had begun to train with all manner of different weapons, including but not limited to axes, bows, spears and other polearms, maces – and Leonardo's favourite, daggers. Antonio had shown them what constituted a good weapon and what constituted a poor one.

Antonio had handed out several swords to the group for them to examine and weigh in their hands. Then, he had pointed at one initiate and wagged his finger with a shake of the head.

'It's no good, teacher?' Sebastien had asked. 'Why?'

Antonio had demonstrated, placing his finger under the middle of the blade where it balanced. Then, he took the sword he esteemed to be good and balanced it in turn. The point of balance was clearly much closer to the handle, allowing the bearer to flick it through the air with much greater control.

'Ah!' Alof realised. 'It moves better!' Antonio nodded in reply.

Then he showed them how to correctly sharpen a blade, which soon became one of his tests. The initiates had to bring a dull blade to shaving sharpness in the space of an hour, or they would be set to crawling up and down the track on all fours, this time with a layer of thin snow covering the hard ground.

As for Walter, he had begun to show the group more subtle ways of killing someone, through the use of poisons and other concoctions, for example ways that made the victim look as though they had drifted off to sleep, never to wake up. During these lessons, it was exceedingly important that they all listen carefully. Walter was sure to remind them all, with a pointed look in Njal's direction, that should they to fail to get the dosage right, they could fail their mission – or, worse, harm themselves.

As well as the lessons in language, politics and geography, Magnus had added disguise onto the list. The seven initiates had been given a demonstration when Magnus had walked with them down into the valley, stopped them by a cluster of pine trees and asked them what they saw. They all gave a different, but ultimately incorrect, answer.

'Trees?' Njal had guessed.

No.

'Um… mountains?' Alof tried.

Magnus sighed.

'A series of random shapes and colours, lacking any pattern or shared structure,' Ebel reasoned.

But that, too, was wrong, as were the rest of their answers. The initiates soon learnt what they had missed, however, as a particularly thick tree trunk gave a mighty roar and leapt at Gabriel, who jumped several feet in the air with a feminine shriek of shock.

Then, the tree trunk boomed with laughter, and they realised it was, in fact, Drogoradz, wearing the most elaborate suit of camouflage Leonardo had ever seen, allowing him to blend in with the bark through the use of face paint and special, textured garb. They all had a good chuckle at that, and Magnus's point was well made.

A fortnight later, the temperature began to fall faster, never jumping much higher than the point at which water turned to ice, and sometimes falling far below that. It was mid-November and the snow was beginning to pile up. Training regularly in the yard had became an impossibility; wrestling and swordplay lessons now took place in the great hall, which was plenty large enough, if a little gloomy.

Familiar paths were dug afresh each morning leading from the great hall to the bunkhouse, then on to the store and chapel, then the barn. The goats and donkey were now unwilling to leave their enclosure, preferring to huddle together at the back of the barn in the hay until their next meal of a half-frozen bale was tossed in their direction.

The female goats were milked regularly, something Leonardo had been ordered to do on occasion. He didn't mind it, for it meant at least they would have milk and cheese.

Though the bunkhouse had a fireplace, it was becoming insufficient as a source of heat. Gabriel, particularly loathsome of the cold, grumbled until he had nailed the shutters closed, for violent gusts of wind would often cause them to fly open. He had also collected rags to pile up around the cracks between shutter and sill. Even so, they all shivered when they hopped into bed at night, pulling thick blankets around their bodies to form a protective cocoon.

Then, one day in late November, they had their first real storm. The wind howled like a banshee and blew so hard it ripped Gabriel's nails from the shutters. The boys had to work together to stack the empty cots against the shutters before the bunkhouse filled with the snow that was falling at such an alarming rate, they could not see further than two yards from the window.

In the morning, it took two of them to shoulder the thick door open, for the snow had built up to the height of their necks and it took a half hour of digging after dawn before they even laid eyes upon one of their instructors, carving a trench of their own from the great hall.

Magnus decided that it was the perfect time to show them how to dig emergency shelters from the snow, should they ever find themselves caught out in it. So, that was what they spent the day doing. They split into two teams, one man stomping around on the top of the snowdrift to pack it tight and dense, while the others dug a little channel upwards with short-handled shovels, creating a dome that was just large enough to allow three men to lie abreast, if they really squeezed.

'That's it, dig upwards so the warm air stays in,' Magnus said. 'Make them strong enough. You wouldn't want them to collapse on you tonight, would you?'

'Tonight, Teacher?' Sebastien asked, confused.

'Well, I'm not making you build them for nothing,' replied Magnus. 'Tonight, you'll all test them!'

At that, there were a few forlorn faces. Gabriel even let out a long groan, his shoulders sagging. Magnus growled, waded through the deep snow and smacked him.

'I've had enough insolent noises from you, boy!' He glared at Gabriel, who rubbed the back of his head with his hand, and returned Magnus's glare, though did not dare to say anything in reply.

The two of them remained like that for a moment, with Gabriel displaying combative body language. The rest of the group looked on fearfully at what Magnus might do.

'Careful, boy,' he growled in a menacingly deep tone. 'Don't forget who you are dealing with.'

After a moment's pause, Gabriel conceded and looked down. 'Yes, Teacher,' he muttered through gritted teeth.

Magnus turned away to leave them to it, the catastrophe having been averted.

'What was that all about?' Ebel asked Gabriel once Magnus had gone. 'Are you mad?'

Gabriel was clenching and unclenching his fists. 'I'm just so sick of this damned cold and this damned stupid mountain!' he roared, his fury quickly carried away by the wind that had picked up again. No one said anything. Instead, they let Gabriel cool off.

The shelters were surprisingly warm inside, especially since they were crammed with bodies. Ebel, Njal, Sebastien and Leonardo all shared one, and found themselves groaning with laughter when Njal passed wind in the enclosed space.

'By God, what have you eaten?' Sebastien moaned, covering his mouth and nose with his cloak.

By now, they were all so familiar with one another that Leonardo felt he knew them as well as he had known his own brothers. They had all shared their stories at one point or another, and had come to realise that they had much in common. Perhaps they were the same traits that had set them all upon this converging course to begin with.

They did everything together; they ate together, trained together, learnt together and suffered together. They shared, they laughed, joked and talked; occasionally, they argued, too. But that was what brothers did. There was in Leonardo's mind, a strong sense of kinship that translated into a team. Each helped the others when it was required, as each knew the shortcomings of the rest and when a supporting hand would be necessary.

However, Leonardo could not fail to notice that, as winter wore on, the bond between them was tested. Gabriel was the most vocal of his hatred for the omnipresent cold that they felt then on the first day of December, and often the others had not the energy to tell him to shut up. They were all glum and shivering, constantly trying to rub life back into the tips of their fingers.

The fires in the hearth at night were smaller now. Ebel had made a quick calculation and realised that they would need to ration their stockpile of firewood in order to survive the winter.

'What in God's name am I doing here?' Gabriel muttered to Leonardo, as the pair of them shovelled snow to form a path, an almost daily activity now. Their hands were wrapped up in as many linen bandages as they could get their hands on. Yet, after a few minutes outside, their fingertips still felt numb. Nor did it help that the wind blew snow right back into the channel they had just created.

It took them an hour to get to the great hall. When it was done, the massive wooden door banged open and Walter's face appeared.

'Hey, you two!' he called over the howling wind. 'Why haven't you dug to the chapel yet? The dawn broke an hour ago.'

Leonardo felt Gabriel seethe with anger next to him and feared he would snap at Walter – which would, of course, have been the worst thing he could have done.

'Apologies, Teacher,' Leonardo said quickly. 'We'll see it done right away!'

Walter narrowed his eyes at the pair of them. 'You'd better.' He closed the door on them with a bang and Gabriel spluttered indignantly.

'That bastard! We've been here all morning, freezing our arses off doing this! Does he think we enjoy it? Why do they never do it themselves!'

'Careful, you don't want him to hear you say that!' Leonardo reminded him as they turned away from the great hall.

'Pah! Fat chance of that over this fucking wind! It never stops!'

'Come on, let's just get on with it,' said Leonardo. 'The sooner we're done, the sooner we can get inside the great hall for lessons.'

They dug in silence for a few minutes, Gabriel still seething with anger, muttering occasionally about this and that. Then, he stopped and tapped Leonardo on the arm.

'Hey, you've seen the big pile of lumber at the back of the great hall. I say we break in tonight and take some.'

Leonardo saw a mad gleam in Gabriel's eye and knew he wasn't joking.

'Don't be a fool!' he shouted so Gabriel could hear him. 'If they catch us doing that, they'll probably skin us alive!'

Gabriel 'tsked' and gave a shrug that turned into a shiver. 'Fine. I just want the cold to stop.'

Later that day, the great hall was full of activity. Countless candles were now permanently lit in sconces that were covered in melted wax, or were piled into corners or on the tables at the edges of the room – anywhere that might provide a little more light during the short, winter days.

Tucked away in the corner, Antonio was re-fletching his hunting arrows as he sat opposite Magnus, who appeared to be drafting a letter to some unknown recipient. A pot of ink was placed alongside his parchment, and a quill darted back and forth between his wizened, leathery fingers.

Walter was crouched by the fire, experimenting with several brightly coloured powders in small, clay jars. He turned the flames a wonderful shade of green as he poured the contents onto the embers.

The tables had been cleared as usual, giving Drogoradz room to instruct the more technical aspects of his particular specialty.

'If you want to take a life with naught but your bare hands, you have to be strong. So, manoeuvre yourself into a position of strength, like this.' He demonstrated with Sigbald, moving to his back and looping his arms around him.

They drilled the movements and were grateful for it; for, even in the great hall with the fire blazing in the hearth, the chill that seemed to have permeated deep into their bones was near impossible to shake.

The great hall was soon filled with the sound of thuds as bodies hit the wooden floorboards, eliciting an 'Oof!' each time one of the initiates was toppled, as the pairs squared off to practise the techniques.

'Mmm, good,' said Drogoradz as he moved between them. 'Yes, that's it. Try to get your arm around further, don't give him the chance to escape.'

Then he made his way over to where Gabriel and Alof were training, and frowned. 'Hey!' he said to Gabriel. 'If you're going to do it, at least put some effort into it! That grip of yours looks to be about as rigid as a damp rag!'

Gabriel, however, instead of replying with the customary 'Yes, Teacher', as was expected, shrugged with disdain and said, 'Who cares? I'm probably never going to use this, anyway.'

It was as though a switch had been flicked. The atmosphere in the great hall changed in an instant. The other pairs stopped their wrestling, shocked at the tone with which Gabriel had spoken. The other instructors, too, had overheard. Walter had turned at the hearth, his beady eyes locked onto Gabriel. Magnus's quill quivered in his hand, inches from the paper, as he looked up from his work. Antonio watched impassively, one eyebrow raised.

As for Drogoradz, his face displayed a brief look of disbelief at the manner in which his student had just addressed him, before his nostrils flared in anger.

'What did you just say to me, boy?' He took a menacing step toward Gabriel, who gulped, though held his ground.

It seemed Gabriel's temper had finally gotten the better of him, because he appeared determined to pass the point of no return.

'I also want to know why the Order uses a training facility thousands of feet up the mountainside!' Gabriel found his courage and began to splutter indignantly while the occupants of the great hall looked on. 'I mean, it's stupid… each time it snows, we have to spend half the day shovelling the stuff, and the drinking water has all frozen by morning, meaning it needs to get heated by the fire while we go thirsty and… and I'm sick of this damned cold, too! What's the point?'

There it is, Leonardo thought. *The point of no return*. Gabriel had most definitely crossed a line. Leonardo could not remember any of them speaking to one of the instructors before with such a tone. None of them had dared to.

The silence in the hall was broken only by the howling wind outside. A look of rage flashed across Drogoradz's face. He took another step forward and the floorboards creaked under his weight until he stood only feet from the younger, smaller man.

'Congratulations, boy,' he growled. 'You've just earned yourself a trip down the track on all fours, and I don't care what it's like outside.'

Gabriel puffed out his chest to make himself seem bigger in an attempt to match Drogoradz's breadth. It was futile.

Just as Leonardo thought the atmosphere in the great hall couldn't get any more tense, Gabriel replied.

'And if I refuse?' His eyes flashed, and Leonardo remarked that at least he was no coward, for a lesser man would never have dared to contradict Drogoradz in such a manner.

Drogoradz's chest heaved and his nostrils flared dangerously again. He checked himself and shot a questioning look in Magnus's direction. After a brief pause, during which those piercing blue eyes flitted from Gabriel to Drogoradz and back, Magnus gave Drogoradz a small nod.

What happened next happened fast. Drogoradz exploded into action with a single, devastating punch that arced horizontally from his side in a wide loop, his entire weight behind it. Gabriel watched it coming with open-mouthed surprise, but was too slow to be able to do anything about it. Before he knew what had happened, a gigantic fist had collided with his jaw at great speed and his world went dark.

The rest of them, however, looked on appalled as Gabriel's head was jerked back violently from the force of the impact and he went as limp as a ragdoll, falling as if in slow motion with the momentum of the strike. Evidently, he was already unconscious, for his arms were hanging uselessly at his side and did nothing to brace himself before the impact with the floorboards that rushed up to meet him.

There was a sickening 'thud' as his limp head bounced off the hard wood floor, before his body went still. Blood began to trickle from his mouth as two teeth, rear molars from the look of them, clattered across the floor and came to rest at Leonardo's feet.

Njal had gasped and Alof, who had been standing the closest, recoiled in shock. Leonardo could see the same look of wide-eyed surprise displayed on the faces of all his fellows. It had been a brutal punch and none of them even dared to move, lest they be next.

After a pause, Drogoradz knelt by Gabriel, putting an ear to his nose, just as Magnus stood from his bench. 'He's still breathing,' he grunted over his shoulder to Magnus.

'Hmm! Perhaps you ought to have struck the wretch harder,' Magnus replied. 'Get him to bed. Hopefully, he will remember this latest lesson when he comes to.'

At that, Alof and Sigbald were shaken from their stunned silence when Drogoradz barked at them to see it done. Once they had scooped their unconscious comrade from the floor, they returned with their arms empty, and the lesson tentatively resumed.

The next day, Gabriel was cowed. He spoke to no one and, when Leonardo asked him how his jaw felt, he waved him away with a flick of the wrist, yet wouldn't meet his eye. As the morning wore on, Leonardo would catch glimpses of him tonguing the spaces in his mouth where his two back teeth had been.

During the lessons, Gabriel was silent, even when Magnus announced to them that, in the coming days, they were to prepare for their most arduous outing into the mountains yet. Gabriel said nothing and did not so much as acknowledge it. His brooding continued up until the morning of the excursion, when they woke before dawn to crunch out onto the snowy ground outside, their leather bags loaded with the kit they would need, and their bodies wrapped in triple layers as their breaths steamed in the cold.

The scenery outside was now completely whitewashed; snow covered everything, and it was there to stay. Leonardo's feet sank deep into the powder in his new leather boots, which were wearing thin sooner than he had hoped. Sebastien appeared by his side, shivering beneath his cloak. He pulled it about him as his breath created great clouds of steam that dissipated as it rose.

'At least the wind has subsided some,' he remarked.

'Don't speak too soon. It's never far away,' Leonardo replied as he watched the rest of their comrades file from the bunkhouse. Gabriel was last, his shoulders hanging lower than usual, his gaze focused on the snow between his feet. For once, he did not complain about the cold; in fact, Leonardo could not remember him saying anything at all since the lesson in the great hall.

Ebel clapped his wrapped hands together and jumped up and down on the spot in an attempt to get his blood moving.

Sigbald was diving into his leather bag, pulling out a set of iron eye bolts and a mallet, asking Alof, 'Do you reckon we'll need these?'

Njal took a piss against the side of the bunkhouse, making yellow patterns in the snow, before the door to the great hall banged open and their instructors marched forth.

'Right!' Magnus barked. 'Today, we aim for the Biskill.' The Biskill was one of the peaks that lay on the path to the Dove. Though a lesser peak and closer to the monastery, it was much less daunting than its gigantic sister, yet still further and higher than they had been to date. 'Let's be off.'

And, without further ado, Magnus began to cut a path down the track, leading the little procession of men over the virgin snow and into the valley below, where they headed eastwards.

It was hard going, and all of them had their snowshoes on, some making use of makeshift walking sticks from straight branches. Their line soon stretched over a hundred yards, which was the way Magnus had taught them. In winter, now that there was snow upon the peaks, there was the risk of avalanche, even as cold as it was. The more they spread out, the less chance there was of all of them being caught by one.

Leonardo was content enough to climb up and down in Magnus's wake, his footsteps following in the tracks left by the lead instructor, and he soon worked up a sweat, even shedding a layer and was the warmest he had been in weeks. The good weather held, and the progress was steady enough.

Once, they had all stopped to eat, with the older men sitting to one side while the initiates formed their own group some yards away. Gabriel didn't join them, however. He sat alone, brooding and eating nothing.

They took the march up soon after, and it wasn't long before they were in the shadow of the Biskill, with the Dove looming ominously in the distance. Magnus had them gather so that he could address them.

'Now, the Biskill is a glacial mountain, which means in places it's covered with a permanent river of ice that can be up to forty or fifty feet deep in places. There are fissures in the ice; if you fall down them, it could be fatal. From here on, we'll rope up in threes. Understood?'

The initiates nodded and produced coiled lengths of rope, tying them at their waists with well-practised knots. Leonardo found himself with Sebastien and Antonio, and glanced round to see that Gabriel had landed himself with Ebel and Magnus, with the remainder forming another three and a two.

When Ebel tossed Gabriel his end of the rope, it hit his chest and fell into the snow, for Gabriel had made no attempt to catch it. For a moment, Leonardo thought he was going to refuse to tie it to himself, but then he let out a loud, defeated sigh and stooped to pick it up reluctantly.

Once they were all ready, Magnus addressed them again. 'One more thing. The fissures may be hidden by the snow, so be sure to follow exactly where I lead.' Leonardo didn't need telling twice. He had no intention of tumbling to his death between two walls of ice that day.

They began the climb, the peak of the Biskill sitting far above their heads. Progress was even slower now, for the mountain was steep, and Magnus took them on a zig-zagging route that avoided all the dangers the steep glacier presented.

Leonardo soon learnt what Magnus had been referring to. They passed places on the climb where the ground fell away to one side into great cracks in the land, the sides of which seemed to give an ominous blue glow. Leonardo craned his neck, but could not see the bottom.

The fissures marred the earth, deep marks on the Biskill's face that were lethal wrinkles. Leonardo needed his wits about him. He kept the length of rope between himself and Antonio slack, as Sebastien took up the rear, and upwards they went in silence.

But then, their luck began to change.

'Magnus!' Drogoradz shouted from the rear and Leonardo turned to see him pointing to the north. Great billowing clouds had formed from nowhere, vast and dense. As soon as Leonardo laid eyes upon them, the wind that had been unusually absent that morning began to pluck at his robes.

Magnus stopped and turned, grimacing at the sight of the wall of grey and white that was rapidly approaching them. Leonardo watched as the cogs in the instructor's mind whirled, and Magnus gazed from the clouds to the summit of the Biskill and back.

Eventually, he seemed to come to a decision. 'We must turn back!'

'What was that?' Walter shouted, for the wind had now begun to howl and carry their voices away with it.

'Back! We must turn back now!' Magnus roared. Walter, cupping a hand to his ear, nodded when the diluted tones of Magnus's voice reached him.

'Aye, I'll retrace our steps!' he yelled back.

And so the procession of cloth-swaddled men turned on their heels, each of them glad that their leader had made the decision. The morning's good weather seemed to have been a cruel trick, for the storm that approached them looked to be a particularly vicious one.

'Slowly!' Magnus called from up the slope, now at their rear. 'Do not rush lest we fall into the fissures!'

Walter knew and, though there was some urgency to get out of the path of the storm, he instructed Alof and Sigbald, who shared his rope, to take care where they placed their feet.

The route back down the glacial slope was not much faster than their ascent, and Leonardo could see that they were well engaged upon it, having travelled at least several hundred yards across its surface.

Glancing north, he could see the clouds approaching at an alarming speed, and felt a knot of apprehension form in his gut. The last thing they wanted to do was to get stuck on the exposed face of the glacier once the storm hit them.

The wind was now so strong that it threatened to bowl them over, and they had to shield their eyes from it with wrapped hands, wincing and squinting as it made their eyes water. The deep rumbling of thunder rolled ominously toward them and the procession seemed to come to some unspoken agreement to increase the speed of its descent.

Yet, for one of their number, that was simply not fast enough. Over the wind, Leonardo heard shouting behind him, as did both Antonio and Sebastien. The three turned to see Gabriel yelling at Magnus, his arms making wide, angry and desperate gestures as he stumbled in the snow from the gusting wind.

Leonardo strained his ears, but could only hear some of what Gabriel said before the wind whipped his words away. He caught, 'Fuck this mountain!' and 'If we don't get off here now, we'll all die!'

A moment later, Magnus had begun to roar back at the young man until he was red in the face, the tip of his long, white beard pulled horizontal, ice already forming between the hairs. A moment later, Drogoradz and Njal had stopped as they also heard the shouting, and then Walter, Sigbald and Alof.

Nobody could really make out what was being said, but they didn't need to, for Gabriel and Magnus were quite clearly hurling insults at one another.

'Don't you speak to me like that, you little brat!' Leonardo managed to hear.

The wind howled and the sky darkened as the clouds began to pass overhead.

'Magnus! We need to move!' Walter was calling from the fore. Magnus, of course, could not hear him, as he was too absorbed in his shouting match with Gabriel, rage contorting his face into an angry grimace as he jabbed a finger at Gabriel's chest.

Leonardo squinted uphill, shielding his eyes as best he could, when he heard Gabriel shout, 'Fuck this and fuck you. I quit! I quit this damned place! I'm done!' Then, he began to fumble with the knot at his waist, untying it and freeing himself from Magnus and Ebel.

'Don't be a damned fool!' Magnus roared after him. 'Get that rope back around your waist, now!'

But Gabriel was hearing none of it. In his snowshoes, he clumsily began to jog directly down the slope, taking the fastest route to the valley floor.

'No!' Magnus shouted.

Sebastien, too, had cupped his hands to his face and began to yell into the storm. 'Gabriel!' he shouted.

Leonardo took up the call, realising the peril his friend was running toward. 'Wait! Gabriel, stop!'

But it was no use. Gabriel could either not hear them, or simply ignored them. He picked up speed, cannoning down the slope at a dangerous pace, as if he meant to sprint the several miles to safety. They all watched as Gabriel ran awkwardly in his snowshoes, shielding his eyes from the wind as he went. However, the near verticality of the mountainside soon caused him to lose all semblance of control as Gabriel hurtled onwards.

And then, to Leonardo's horror, he vanished. Gabriel's feet had suddenly found nothing but thin air beneath them, and he fell, his arms scrabbling momentarily at the sides of the fissure before it swallowed him up, and he had plummeted to his doom.

Chapter 9

GASCONY

rogo de Barentin frowned as he scratched his chin under his beard. He was armoured and mounted, with his helm strapped to the pommel of his saddle, which was how he usually left it for travel. The horse on which he sat snorted as it grazed on the grass of the hillock, swaying gently to and fro.

Drogo let it, for he was too preoccupied with the two men facing him on their own mounts. He peered at them from under a bald head, his dark, calculating eyes flitting from one to the other. Both he recognised; the one with the fair, shaven hair and bright green eyes he had met in the cathedral square at Bordeaux several days ago, and the other, freckled with short, chestnut hair and a square jaw, frequented the parliament building, an advisor of sorts to his Queen, Eleanor of Provence.

They had introduced themselves as Father Leonardo and Father Sebastien, respectively, claiming to be of the Church and carrying instructions from the Queen herself. It was strange, for they did not seem like monks or priests.

Drogo had been a military man almost all his life. He had seen plenty of churchmen and plenty of soldiers. The men before him were not the bookish type. Indeed, they seemed dangerous; there was something about them that reminded him of his hardened household knights who had known many battles and skirmishes. It was the way they carried themselves, he decided. Their confidence, their air of competence.

But then he glanced over their shoulders at the fortified town of Langon, the rooftops of its buildings visible several miles away over the canopy of trees, and his frown deepened. Behind him, the small force he had managed to scrape together from the remaining loyalists and his own men awaited instruction on the road, the men-at-arms kicking their boots into the dusty earth, wondering what the hold-up was at the vanguard.

'Hmm.' Drogo tugged at his beard thoughtfully with a gloved hand. What the two men were suggesting was sure to save him plenty of trouble were it to succeed, but he was not entirely sure how they intended to execute their proposed plan.

Two days prior, Drogo had sat in conference with the Queen as they discussed the preparations that needed to be made before the arrival of King Henry, now said to be imminent – a matter of perhaps several days.

Queen Eleanor had suggested that they retake Langon from the rebels, serving to both provide a base of operations for the inevitable sieges of La Reole and Bazas and to show that they had not been idle in their governance of the region.

Though Drogo answered to the King and the King alone, he had agreed with Queen Eleanor. Drogo had always thought of her as an impressive woman. He had also formed the opinion that, had she been King in lieu of her husband, then England would be a far mightier nation – though, that, of course, he had never voiced aloud.

Eleanor had also insisted that her two 'best men' accompany Drogo's force, uttering vaguely that he might find them useful. And there they now sat.

'So, what you're saying is that you can get me into that town without having to lose a single man?' he asked incredulously. One of his thick eyebrows rose so high it threatened to run away over the top of his polished dome.

'We can certainly try,' Father Sebastien said nonchalantly, in a manner so calm it was as if he were discussing the chances of them successfully baking an apple pie instead of infiltrating a city full of hostile rebels. He certainly seemed to believe it was a possibility, though perhaps he was simple, or just plain mad.

Drogo glanced at the other and was met by hard, piercing green eyes that had not an inch of give behind them.

'But how?' He shook his head in bemusement. If any other churchmen had offered to recapture an entire town from rebel forces, he would have laughed in their faces. Yet, there was something about these two...

'You leave that to us,' Father Leonardo said. 'Just make sure your knights are ready to ride for the gates at dawn.'

'And what if you should fail?' Drogo asked.

'Then you won't have to put up with us any longer, and all you'll have lost is a day,' Father Sebastien offered helpfully and followed it up with a rueful grin.

Drogo looked the pair up and down, his frown deepening. The two 'churchmen' were lightly armoured, with brigandines and gambesons worn over plain shirts and trousers, not at all the garments expected of a priest. Moreover, each wore a belt from which a sword and dagger – or, in the green-eyed one's case, 'daggers' – hung. The weapons appeared to be plain, but of good quality and well-worn, and Drogo had to draw the conclusion that they must, in fact, be some special sort of soldier, perhaps mercenaries hired by the Church.

That was distasteful, as far as he was concerned. Yet, the order had come from the Queen herself, who vouched for the men. He would otherwise have turned them away.

Eventually, Drogo shrugged. What did it matter to him if he waited a day? He would take Langon on the morrow and if, by some miracle, these men could have the gates open by dawn, then more the better; he would lose less of his own. He shook his head incredulously.

'Very well,' he said. 'I shall make camp a mile away in the woods, and will come with all of my best knights to wait for a signal at dawn. If it is as you say, and you manage to open the gates for me, then we can do the rest. Without the advantage of the walls, those farmers inside will stand no chance against my men.' Drogo shot them a satisfied smile and gestured to the horsemen at his rear.

The soldiers' faces were hidden by the steel plate of their great helms, their shoulders bulked out by thick links of maille. Each wore a triple protection of brigandine and gambeson over their vital organs, while sporting a long lance canted on their shoulders in the resting position. There was not an inch of them that was not armoured, and though they were few in number, Drogo's King had equipped them with the latest and finest gear. Drogo, who trained with them regularly, knew that they were lethal instruments of war.

However, the two priests before him simply cast a lazy glance in their direction and dismissed them with a curt nod, that caused Drogo to narrow his eyes a little.

'We will see it done, Sir Barentin. Until the morning, then,' Father Leonardo stated, turning his mount to follow his associate, and they trotted away through the trees, leaving Drogo to scratch his head and turn to one of his knights with a perplexed look. The knight shrugged, just as bemused. Drogo shook his head once more, waving his men to follow him as he trotted downhill through the woods to make camp.

He assumed that whatever the two churchmen would do, they would do under the cover of darkness so as to try to catch the enemy unawares. As Drogo selected a decent spot for their camp and began to post sentries, he was struck with the thought that the rebels holding the town must certainly have heard by now that the King's men had been en route to wrestle them from their position, and would almost certainly be ready and waiting. How did those priests expect to storm a fortified town, without the element of surprise whilst being greatly outnumbered?

Drogo decided he would like to find out. Once the camp had been made and the sergeants had managed the men-at-arms to guard it, Drogo took his knights toward Langon. As they approached the town, they picked their way stealthily through the trees, knowing that the clank of their armour would give them away if they got too close.

Drogo was an experienced soldier and wisely thought to leave a good quarter mile between them and the walls, picking a decent vantage point from which to sit and watch as he tied his horse to the trees, letting the horse rummage around in the blanket of dead leaves beneath its feet.

'What are we waiting for then, sir?' a knight asked.

'I'm not entirely sure,' Drogo said, squinting at the stout wooden gates of Langon, constructed from thick slabs of oak. Sentries patrolled the wooden palisade here and there, with bows slung over their shoulders.

Even from such a distance, he could tell their armour was poor and they were but peasant farmers, with few warriors amongst them. But, even then, they were many. Drogo thought that even with his small collection of elite knights, little more than a dozen, he might struggle. But two? It was daft.

Drogo sighed and muttered to his men that he was going to take a nap, and that they were to wake him should anything happen. He lay on the soft sheet of leaves and twigs that made up the forest floor and settled in to wait. He was good at waiting, all soldiers were. And it was a pleasant enough day, to boot.

Drogo interlocked his fingers over his chest, put one ankle over the other and closed his eyes, drifting off into an easy sleep. When he woke, it was dark and he sat up in the cool night air, glancing around to see that his men were either sleeping or standing watch, gazing through the point where the trees began to thin out at the palisades of Langon.

Drogo joined them and waited some more. He whiled away a few hours like that and the night remained silent, save for the usual sounds of the forest behind him, the hooting of an owl, a feral squeal, some gentle rummaging in the branches overhead. It was peaceful.

Then Drogo began to pace back and forth, becoming absorbed in his thoughts. He wondered what strategies the King would employ when he finally arrived and how long it would take him to crush the rebels. Would he take a similar tact to de Montfort, or would he be a little more diplomatic? Sometimes, it was hard to tell with Henry; he wanted to be the image of a pious king, like his cousin, King Louis of France. Generous, humble, wise. Henry was generous, Drogo granted him that, but he was far too impatient and tempestuous to be humble or wise. Drogo did his best to give sound advice on the rare occasion that Henry would listen, which was not so often.

Eventually, his thoughts turned to home. He was an older man now and enjoyed the comfort of his estate in South Oxfordshire. He had a pretty wife and several children to raise and had enjoyed playing the farmer in times of peace when his services were not required, as constable of Windsor castle. Just as Drogo thought, with a pang of guilt, that he was going soft, one of his men whispered to him.

'Sir! Something's happening!'

Drogo looked up sharply and went to stand by his knight. Lit torches were bobbing up and down behind the wooden palisade. Then he heard a shout, then another. Soon, there was much shouting, and the sounds that followed a second later, though faint, were unmistakeable to his ears; he heard the clang of steel upon steel and knew there was fighting within the walls.

'Boys!' Drogo hissed, clapping his hands to wake the sleeping men around him. 'Saddle up! Make ready to ride!' The forest around him woke into a hive of activity and, in moments, his knights were horsed and prepared to move on his command. He led them to the edge of the trees, making sure they had a clear path to ride over the pastures to meet the road and then on to the gates.

Now he waited – though, again, he was not entirely sure what for. The sound of a fight continued to break the peace of the night. Drogo had no idea what was going on; all he could see was the bobbing yellow light of distant torches. Drogo ground his teeth, tapping his fingers on the pommel of his saddle impatiently. He hated not knowing what was happening in there.

Clearly, the two 'priests' had found a way in and were fighting, but who knew how that was going? Drogo cursed. He was a fool to have even entertained the idea they might have succeeded. Of course, they were about to get skewered by a bunch of pitchforks!

Even as he thought it, he watched as a flaming torch was hurled from the gatehouse and over the ramparts. It tumbled slowly, end over end through the night sky, before it clattered onto the road before the gates.

That had to be his cue.

Drogo kicked his mount into a canter, urging it forward as his men followed suit, gripping the reins with their left hands and the shafts of their lances with their right. Great helms were stuffed hastily onto heads and mailed gorgets were prodded to check they were still in place.

Incredibly, when Drogo and his men reached the easy ground of the road, the gates of Langon began to swing slowly inward, and the sound of the fight within reached them loud and unobscured.

'Hya!' Drogo shouted, kicking his steed again and breaking into a gallop, lowering his lance as he went.

The gap between the gates widened, and he could now see the source of the noise. One man was holding back a dozen with a single spear. They almost surrounded him in a half dome and carried blazing torches and makeshift weapons of pikes, billhooks, scythes and other farmyard implements, with the occasional sword or falchion that gleamed in the firelight. The lone figure moved with an astonishing grace, seeming to be able to turn and thrust with his spear at several different targets within the same instant. It struck the other weapons, parrying blows and delivering attacks of its own to cries of pain as it struck its targets.

The gates were now plenty wide enough for Drogo and his men to ride through three abreast. As he closed the distance, a second man leapt out into view to join the first, holding off the horde of rebels between the pair of them.

Yet, Drogo had no time to admire their martial skills, for he was fast approaching. 'Get out of the way!' he roared. The two men had heard his approach and dived for cover just in time.

Drogo thundered through the open double gates, his heart pounding in a wonderful mixture of fear and excitement, as he charged the rebel line, his men shouting war cries from his side.

He selected a target with his lance, and was barely able to register the look of terror on the man's face before Drogo ran him through with such force, he was taken off his feet. The charge of heavily armoured knights and horses struck the peasants like a wave washing away a twig and they were spun in all directions, as Drogo and his men drew their swords and dismounted, hacking away at those who thought to resist.

He was vaguely aware of the two churchmen rejoining the fray, catching sight of their unfamiliar movements and fighting style from the corner of the slit in his helm, as they fought beside his men against the host of peasants. Amongst their enemy, there were several armoured men, perhaps lowly hedge knights or something of the sort, and they tried valiantly to rally the defenders. They succeeded for a short time to bunch themselves into a tightly packed defensive blob that blocked their attackers' advance any further into the town. However, Drogo and his new allies had regrouped and hacked into the defenders' line with such savage ferocity that, in the bloody minute that followed, all hope of resistance was squeezed from the rebels, and they were soon throwing down their arms in surrender.

Drogo's men gave a cheer, just as his sergeants led his men-at-arms through the gates behind them, who looked on the scene in dismay as they realised they'd missed out on all the action. Drogo made a quick assessment of his knights; finding that they were all unharmed, he set them to securing their prisoners and the town.

He looked around to see the earth around the gates and main street was littered with bodies from the short, bloody combat. There were yet more lying further afield, some dangling from the palisade forty yards away, and he knew none of his men had gone so far. He turned to find the Queen's priests approaching him, breathing heavily and spattered with blood and grime, their swords hanging loosely at their sides.

'Sir Barentin.' The freckled one acknowledged him with a nod. 'You have good timing.'

'Thank you,' Drogo replied, taking off his helm. He didn't know what else to say.

'Might we leave you the town and be on our way?' the freckled one asked, looking up questioningly.

'Just like that?' Drogo gave them a perplexed look.

'Just like that.'

He shrugged. 'As you wish. I'll see to its garrisoning. And what should I say when I report to the King of Langon's capture?'

He watched as the two men exchanged a glance. The green-eyed one then spoke. 'We would prefer it if you didn't mention us at all.'

Drogo raised his eyebrows. 'So, you're saying I can take all the credit?'

'That's exactly right.'

Drogo barked with laughter. 'That suits me just fine!'

The freckled one shot him a wry smile. 'I hoped you would say that. Until next time, then.'

The two men gave him a last nod and Drogo held up a hand in farewell, as the pair turned away and headed for the open gates, disappearing into the dawn a minute later.

Strange, Drogo thought, shaking his head in bewilderment yet again. Still, he felt as though he had come away much better with that deal. He had taken a fortified town without losing a single man and had something to show for his efforts to the King when he arrived. He nodded pleasantly to himself as he rode forward and began barking orders to his men.

It was turning out to be a very good day.

Chapter 10

TWELVE YEARS AGO

Magnus let out a string of curses. 'Boy! Can you hear me?' he shouted hopefully. Nothing.

Then, the wind picked up to an entirely new level and the blizzard was truly upon them. Now, there was nothing to hear but its howl, and suddenly the visibility dropped to several yards in front of Leonardo's face.

The few areas of his skin that remained exposed were pelted with snow and ice. It became so painful that Leonardo hissed with pain through gritted teeth and did his best to shield himself with his arms.

He hesitated, looking to Magnus for direction, but found that he could not see him. His world had become a swirling, freezing white hell.

Leonardo sought Antonio next and traced his gaze up the rope that linked them, only to find that the other end of the hemp lifeline had been swallowed by the storm. Its bearer could not have been more than five yards ahead and, had it not been for the fact that the rope suddenly pulled taught and tugged Leonardo, he could not have known for certain that they were even there.

He allowed Antonio to pull him downhill, or where he thought downhill was, for that too was impossible to see. Behind him, he felt the rope go tight as he, in turn, pulled Sebastien, and the three of them came to the silent agreement that they had to get to shelter.

Leonardo had no time to think about the fact that his comrade had just plummeted down a crevasse of ice. For all he knew, Gabriel could be lying dead or broken. Knowing that, should he not wish a similar fate, he understood they had to get off the mountain.

With the appalling visibility, it took them a quarter of an hour of toil to move several hundred yards. Then, finally, they had reached the end of it. Leonardo suddenly bumped into Antonio's back, and a huddle of dark, robed figures came into view.

Then, Magnus and Ebel were there, too. He heard Walter shouting, 'There's a cleft in the mountain here. We should take shelter and wait out the storm!'

'Aye!' Magnus shouted back through the blizzard. 'But stay close!'

The cold bit deep, despite the ten of them being well wrapped up. They shuffled forward through the snow, each clutching the cloak of the man in front, as Walter led the strange procession along. They came to where the rock bulged from the mountainside and offered a little protection from the wind, and there they sat on the snowdrift, taking all their remaining blankets from their leather bags and draping them over themselves in their three groups, packed together like fish in a barrel.

They waited there, hugging one another and sharing their bodies' warmth, initiate and instructor alike, hoping that the storm would soon subside. Leonardo wondered how it was possible to be so cold. Even with Antonio and Sebastien pressed up against him, and a thick square of wool pulled over their heads and tucked under their feet, acting like a tent to mitigate the relentless sting of the wind, he still felt his teeth rattle in his jaw.

Leonardo turned to look at Sebastien. His lips were blue and his eyebrows and eyelashes were caked in snow and ice. Leonardo had never seen him looking so miserable. There was no sense talking, for the wind was howling so loud he would never be heard.

Tucking his hands under his armpits and pulling his knees up to his chest, he wondered what had happened to Gabriel. Could he have survived? Was he now alive at the bottom of that crevasse waiting out the storm, too?

Leonardo certainly hoped so. Despite their differences, Gabriel had nonetheless become something akin to a brother these past few months. For the moment, however, there was nothing they could do but wait.

It took an hour for the worst of the storm to pass over them. One moment, they had been huddled together, wondering whether they would succumb to the cold, and the next, the wind had subsided. Several minutes after that, it was gone completely.

Antonio was the first to move. He wriggled his way from the blanket and hauled it from over their heads to reveal a bright, blue sky. The storm had gone as quickly as it had arrived, already moving off into the distance to terrorise the rest of the Pyrenees.

Leonardo followed suit and had to fight the snow off, for they had been almost completely submerged by it. He was grateful to be able to move, for he had lost all sensation in the tips of his fingers. He remembered one of Walter's lessons about some of the dangers of the mountain; specifically, when the body was subjected to temperatures well below freezing for extended periods of time and became so cold, it sacrificed the fingers and toes to keep the blood near the heart pumping for as long as possible.

Anxiously, he rubbed the life back into his fingers, hoping they were not lost. Around him, hooded heads were popping up from the snow as his teachers and his comrades freed themselves from their own shelters.

Magnus's white-haired head and beard were soon visible and, before any of them had managed to collect themselves, he was already barking orders.

'Up! Up! We must go back for the boy!' No one argued and they were all soon ready to retrace their steps once more. There was a sense of urgency about them, for they knew that if there was any chance that Gabriel still lived, they had to find him soon.

Leading the procession, Magnus tore up the mountainside, and it was not long before they had reached the place they suspected Gabriel to have fallen. As Magnus, or any of the other instructors for that matter, had never shown even the slightest hint of warmth toward their charges, Leonardo was slightly surprised to see the man so agitated, and wondered whether there was some humanity behind those cold blue eyes after all. Or perhaps he simply didn't want all the lessons to have been in vain.

'Careful!' someone shouted. 'The fresh snow is hiding the fissures, be on your guard!'

A minute later, they were all shouting into the glacier's many folds and chasms.

'Gabriel! Gabriel! Can you hear us?'

There was no reply.

'Gabriel! Where are you?'

But their cries went unanswered, and Leonardo began to fear the worst.

When it was clear that Gabriel, in whatever state he lay, was unable to respond, Magnus split everyone into two teams of five, each selecting their lightest members to be lowered down into the glacier's crevasses, one at a time, in a methodical manner. They would search every one if they had to, Magnus had stated.

Ebel and Alof were lowered down in their makeshift harnesses and hauled back up when it became clear that the fissures were empty. The going was slow at first, but the teams soon got into a rhythm, four lowering the fifth, waiting for them to shout 'All clear!' and then hauling them back to the top to search the next.

Hours passed and they began to fear that they would never find Gabriel. Suddenly, there was a shout.

'Here!' Alof's voice echoed off the walls of ice. 'I've found him!'

The other team rushed over to lend a hand, peering below into the crack that was barely wide enough to fit a man, where Alof and the rope disappeared from view.

'Does he live?' Magnus barked down.

There was a pause.

'No. He is dead,' Alof's desolate voice came back from the blue well. He had spoken with such bleak certainty that none on the surface doubted the truth of the statement.

Leonardo put his head in his hands and sank to his knees. Sebastien cursed. Ebel ran a hand through his hair and tugged at it despairingly. Magnus sighed and closed his eyes.

The afternoon sun had returned and shone above, mockingly. When they hauled Gabriel's body to safety, it was stiff and cold. His eyes were screwed tightly shut and his face, white as a sheet, displayed a twisted grimace, the muscles frozen there to forever display the final suffering of his death throes.

They would later discover that the fall had broken his back and he had lain at the bottom of the fissure paralysed, unable to warm himself as the biting, piercing, terrible cold had slowly killed him. *Poor Gabriel,* Leonardo thought. *Poor Gabriel. He had died alone and in pain.*

It was night by the time they made it back to the safety of the monastery. The solemn procession had been led by the brooding Magnus as pairs had taken it in turns to carry the body, now wrapped in layers of wool.

The mountain paths were awkward, and they were all tired and had long since eaten all their food. They dropped the body into the snow on several occasions, a sight that might have been comical had it not been the corpse of their friend.

Leonardo could hear Ebel snivel as he took the lifeless legs of his friend onto his shoulders, and felt the lump in his own throat grow.

Then, they were home, and the body was placed upon the stone-flagged floor in the chapel. It was unwrapped, cleaned, washed and prepared for burial. Gabriel's comrades paid their respects and Leonardo was not ashamed to find silent tears rolling down his cheeks as he wept for the young man.

'Be with God, friend,' he whispered as he took the cold, lifeless hand in his own. Then, the face was covered, and the body wrapped again, but this time in layers of white linen.

In the great hall, Magnus told them that, come the morning, they would bring the body further down the mountain. For, as high as they were, those patches of ground that were not covered by feet of snow were far too rocky to allow them to dig a grave.

Someone prepared a hot broth and the ten men who lived in the monastery upon the mountain ate in silence, realising how hungry they were and ate greedily, despite the circumstances. Then, with nothing more that they could do, they sat quietly, huddled around the fire as they stared into the flames, the absence of one of their number all too evident.

The mood in the bunkhouse on those long, winter evenings was often bleak. Not solely because they still mourned the loss of their friend Gabriel, but because life at the monastery had become quite the struggle.

Leonardo had never felt so cold. It never truly left him, from the moment he rolled out of his cot in the morning, to the moment he climbed back in at night. The climate around the mountains was so incredibly hostile, that he tried to imagine why God might had made it so. Perhaps mankind was trespassing there? Perhaps it really was where God and all the angels lived? Either way, Leonardo knew that man had not been created for it.

Their tutors, quickly becoming their tormentors, often forced them outside, whether that be for some lesson, to clear snow from the yard, collect ice to melt, or feed the goats. Since Gabriel's death, they seemed to have tightened the screws and the discipline they demanded had doubled.

Sometimes, without warning, Walter might burst into the bunkhouse in the early hours banging two pots together, waking the initiates into action, their eyes bleary in the freezing night. They would be rallied, handed the heavy wooden training swords and shoved toward the training posts and told to attack one or other of the teachers, with Walter banging his pots and shouting at them all the while. When it was done, they were all left panting and told they could return to bed, at which point none of them had the urge to sleep. After that, they had learnt to become light sleepers.

Antonio was taking great pains to ensure they all took the utmost care with their equipment. He would appear silently from thin air, as he often did, and single one of them out, gazing at them intently with his hand out, demanding to inspect their weapons or gear. He had explained to them with his creative hand signals and gestures that their lives might depend on their equipment, and had made them always carry upon their persons some form of weapon.

When one of them handed their weapon over, Antonio would inspect the blade carefully for any spots of rust, then roll up the sleeve of his robes and check if it could shave the hairs from his arm. If one of their blades did not meet his standards, he would punish them all by making them haul around Drogoradz's boulders. Leonardo had used what little free time he had to keep everything he had been given neat, orderly and well maintained.

Magnus, too, had made it his mission to ensure that his every command was obeyed without hesitation. Any deviation from his high expectations resulted in a clout around the ear, or he would force them to clutch blocks of ice until their hands were painfully cold. Once, he asked Alof to recite which herbal remedies should be used for which aliments for the fifteenth time, and Alof had made the error of sagging his shoulders in fatigue.

For that, Magnus had forced him to strip naked and literally kicked him out into the freezing air and left him there until his lips were blue and his skin was as white as the snow. That lesson had taught them all that, when a command was given, the only appropriate response was, 'Yes, Teacher.' The obedience was beginning to become ingrained within them.

Now that the nights were long and the light of the sun graced their valley for a depressingly short time before it disappeared behind the peaks, the practical things they could do during the day were limited and a new kind of lesson had been introduced to their routine.

Either Magnus or Walter would take them all into the chapel and give them what was part lesson and part sermon.

'Understand this,' Magnus would say, 'though we may play different roles, we are nonetheless men of God. All that we do is for His glory. We are sworn servants, humble servants. Remember that.' And then they would pray.

The six initiates would kneel before the stone altar of the chapel, beneath the great, gilded silver cross, and clasp their hands together. Sometimes, such as on Sundays, Magnus, Walter, Drogoradz and Antonio would kneel amongst them, and the chapel would be full of whispered prayers and promises to their Lord. Leonardo had come to learn that his new masters were, in fact, more devout than much of the rest of the ecclesiarch.

But then, how could it be any other way? he reasoned. The tasks the men of the Order were set, required them to have a strong relationship with God. It was during those lessons – or, perhaps, more accurately, sermons – that Leonardo was first introduced to the idea of balance. Magnus would teach them why the Order existed, and why they needed balance and to maintain the natural order of things. He taught them that their task of fighting for the greater good was of the utmost importance and that, without them and men like them, the world would soon descend into chaos.

Leonardo had never questioned this. In fact, he had liked the idea and had taken to it like a duck to water. He could serve God in the most meaningful of ways and, at the same time, channel that brimming pool of energy inside, whatever that was. For he did not yet understand it, but somehow knew it was not positive.

However, for some of the initiates, it had taken a little more to convince them. Once, Leonardo had seen his friend Sebastien staring into space thoughtfully after one of these sermons.

'What is it?' Leonardo had asked him.

'Nothing,' replied Sebastien. 'It's just… I had always thought that the Order existed to protect the Christian faith, like a… like a shield between it and evil.'

Leonardo had frowned at that, perplexed. 'Yes, that's exactly what it does.'

Sebastien's eyebrows had knitted together in concentration. 'But the way Magnus describes it, describes *us*, it's as though we are more a spear than a shield.'

Leonardo had shrugged. 'Yes, perhaps, but what difference does that make? Surely, all that matters is that we serve God and preserve His message, no?'

'Yes, yes. You're right, of course. Forget it.' Sebastien had shaken the thought from his head and the comment had been forgotten.

Leonardo had found that life at the monastery was opening his mind; that he was forever hungry for answers. It served as a little comfort to the harshness of life. He had come to realise that, had he not believed in what they were doing there, he would not have survived that winter. Perhaps that was why Gabriel had perished? He had not given himself wholly and completely to the cause.

Little did Leonardo know that Gabriel's death would not be the only tragedy to befall the men of the monastery that winter.

Chapter 11

---◆•◆---

TWELVE YEARS AGO

It was mid-January and the conditions had never been more arduous. Christmas had been and gone with little ceremony and the six initiates had begun a new year, as fresh as the powder that crunched underfoot. The moaning wind seemed to torment them at all hours of the day, and the cold was cemented deep within the very marrow of their bones. It had been at least a week since they had last ventured beyond the confines of the monastery's boundary, and knew they were due another outing into the snowy peaks beyond.

Of late, at least two of their instructors had been suspiciously absent from the monastery at any one time with no explanation given, and the initiates were beginning to whisper amongst themselves that it must have something to do with them. Sure enough, Magnus soon summoned them to the great hall to brief the six of them on their next mission.

'Now,' he barked in his usual severe tone, 'it is time you all learnt to think for yourselves. Tomorrow, you will be given a task that you must undertake alone.' He paused for effect and glared around at them all as they sat on the simple wooden benches before him. The initiates exchanged worried glances with one another, but said nothing.

Magnus continued. 'These past few months, we have been teaching you of the surrounding area, its dangers, how to survive, how to navigate – and, of course, the mountains and their names. Tomorrow morning, you will each be given the name of a lesser peak, some provisions, and two days.' He paused again, his mouth working under his stark white beard as he ensured that he had their full and undivided attention. He did.

'You will have noticed that some of us have been absent this past week. That is because, on each of these peaks, we have deposited a coloured flag that you will have to collect and present to us within the given period of time. That way, we will know that you have been successful in your mission. Is that understood?'

Sebastien raised a hand tentatively.

'Speak,' Magnus barked.

'Um, which peaks will we be given, Teacher?' he asked.

'Ah!' Magnus wagged his finger. 'Not so fast. That is part of the test. You will be given the name at the moment of your departure, and you will be expected to know in which direction your mountain lies. If you have been paying any attention whatsoever, then that will be the easiest part of the test.'

Njal shifted uncomfortably next to Leonardo.

Now Alof raised his hand slowly.

'Yes?'

'What if we don't make it back in time? What if we fail, Teacher?' he asked hesitantly.

Magnus's eyes narrowed. 'Fail? Have I provided failure as an option? Well?' Alof shook his head hurriedly. 'Fail and we will perhaps reconsider whether you are worthy of this opportunity.' Magnus spread his arms wide and indicated the bare stone walls of the gloomy great hall that had become their home.

'If you become agents, you will often find yourselves working alone,' he continued. 'So the sooner you get used to thinking for yourselves, the better.'

After that, they were dismissed and they sidled off to the bunkhouse to prepare. Once inside, Njal began to moan about the task ahead.

'I bet he gives me the most obscure one!' he complained. 'He'll probably send me up the Dove, knowing my luck…'

Sigbald snorted. 'Don't be daft. You can't climb that thing in winter, it's impossible. I'm more worried about remembering all the smaller ones. There must be close to thirty mountains around here that Magnus has given us the names of!'

'Exactly,' Alof agreed, his shoulders sloping dishearteningly. 'How in God's name are we to remember them all? We'll all look fools if they send us off and we have no clue in which direction to head. Imagine stumbling around for two days, freezing our bollocks off for nothing!'

Ebel was rubbing the fluff on his chin thoughtfully. 'Do you really think they would send us away if we fail?' he asked, addressing no one in particular.

'Let's not find out,' Sebastien replied. 'Ebel, your mind is the sharpest among us. Do you think you can help us remember the names of all the mountains?'

Ebel thought for a moment and shrugged. 'Perhaps not all, but most. I think.' His expression turned into a worried frown.

'Listen, then,' Sebastien went on, getting the attention of the other five. 'There's still some daylight left. I say we go up the monastery's mountain and make sure we know what's what.'

'That's a good idea,' Leonardo agreed. 'We can pool our knowledge. Surely one of us will know the names, and fill the gaps of the rest for everyone else.'

'What are we waiting for, then?' Sigbald said, striding to the door and pulling it open without waiting for the rest of them. They followed and rushed up the side of their mountain to get a better view of their surroundings. The six of them spent the last of the light pointing into the setting sun, naming the summits one by one, repeating them several dozen times each and memorising their shapes and characteristics.

'Look!' Ebel said, pointing into the distance. 'There's the Hawfoot, the Pale Ridge, the Magdalene and the Buck.'

Leonardo felt an anxious knot in his gut, thinking about what Sigbald had said. He was worried that, come the morning, Magnus would provide him with the name of his peak and all he'd have in response was a blank look. He also knew that if he felt anxious, Njal must have felt doubly so, for he had always been the slowest to learn in the group.

At least Leonardo had a decent grasp of the area now and felt confident that he could navigate his way around it. He was not so sure that Njal, on the other hand, could. But there was little he could do for him now, save help him to remember as much as he could.

'What's that one there?' Leonardo tested Njal, pointing to a rocky summit. The big Norwegian screwed up his face in concentration, whilst Sebastien, Sigbald, Alof and Ebel had trudged through the snow several yards away to their rear to debate the names of two adjacent mountains in the far valley.

After a moment, Njal sighed in exasperation, letting his thick arms drop to his sides as he exclaimed in frustration, 'I don't know!'

'That's the Hog's Hoof,' Leonardo said quietly. It was the third time he had told the Norwegian. Njal looked glumly down at his boots, half buried in the snow.

'I'm never going to remember, am I?' he said miserably. And, though he was tall, strong and had grown a thick beard since they had arrived last year, Leonardo saw the boy in him then, and Njal suddenly seemed much smaller. He seemed afraid.

'You'll be alright,' Leonardo said, trying to reassure him. 'In a couple of days, this will be just a memory. We'll all be laughing about it in the bunkhouse around the fire.'

Njal shot Leonardo a forlorn look, his big, fearful blue eyes watery in the last of the evening light. 'If it's not this I fail at, it'll be the next one. I'm not as smart as the rest of you,' he grumbled, gesturing toward the others. 'I'm just a big idiot…' He kicked his leg out of the snow angrily, sending a plume of perfect white powder into the cold air, where it drifted down prettily.

'Come on, Njal. You've come this far, don't lose heart now!' Leonardo urged him. 'It'll be spring before you know it, and it'll be so hot we will be able to train shirtless in the yard, like we did last year.' He squeezed his friend's shoulder reassuringly.

Leonardo liked Njal. He was always quick to laugh, and the sound of his deep chuckle booming around the stone walls of the bunkhouse was as familiar and comforting to him now as the crackle of the fire. Njal found it particularly funny when Sebastien gave them his impersonation of the sour-faced Walter, and he would strut around the bunkhouse, elbows flared, looking down his nose at them all in an uncannily accurate representation. To Leonardo, it was just as funny to watch Njal lose it as he rocked back with laughter than the impression itself.

Moreover, he had come to learn that Njal was not a malicious man; though he may have looked the most fearsome, he might have been the gentlest among them. Leonardo had previously doubted whether Njal would have been able to take a life, had he been asked to. Yet, that did nothing to detract from his likeability; perhaps it even enhanced it. Njal was a good companion to have around, and was no pushover; that much could not be denied. But his mind did hold him back, and Leonardo feared it would be the undoing of him.

They stood there, pointing at all the familiar peaks, reciting their names until the last of the light had faded and they could no longer tell the silhouettes apart. They were then forced to descend back down to the bunkhouse, where the only thing left to do was to sleep, which was fitful enough.

In the morning, Leonardo rose stiffly, uncurling himself from the foetal ball that kept him warm, and throwing off the several blankets that were the only thing stopping him from shivering himself to sleep. He dressed, throwing a thick cloak over his shoulders as the others stirred around him, and was just reaching for the door, thinking to go outside to relieve himself, when it burst open and Magnus stormed in, followed closely by Walter.

'Up!' he roared without ceremony. 'Up you get, all of you!' He kicked Alof's cot and the younger man gave a yelp of surprise from under the covers.

Walter clapped his hands loudly as he, too, strode into the room. 'No time to waste!' he shouted. 'By God, it stinks in here. What have you foul pigs been doing...' he added, turning his nose up at the stale odour.

The others were soon dressed, hauling on their cloaks and shouldering their leather satchels as Magnus and Walter continued to berate them, cajoling them toward the exit and the mountains that waited beyond.

A minute later, the six initiates were lined up in the yard outside, with Drogoradz and Antonio looking on from the far side as the last of them hurried into place.

'I sincerely hope you all prepared your equipment the night before,' Magnus said as he walked around to face them. 'Tough luck if not. Now it's too late.'

Leonardo glanced back to see the glowering figure of Walter, who stood barring the doorway to the bunkhouse.

Magnus gestured at Antonio, who Leonardo noticed carried a scrap of parchment in one hand, just visible in the dim morning light.

'One by one, you'll each go to Drogoradz and Antonio to receive the name of your summit,' said Magnus. 'Then, you will have two days to retrieve your flags. Alone. Do not try to form pairs or groups, as there will not be time for you to travel to more than one of the targets in the given time. Questions? No? Good. It's a simple enough task, so if by the grace of God you have been listening to me these past months, then we'll soon discover which among you possess a brain.' He glared around at them all, lingering a little longer on Njal's tall form.

'Very well!' Magnus snapped his fingers and pointed at Ebel. 'You! Go forward.'

Hesitantly, Ebel made his way across the snowy yard to Drogoradz and Antonio, adjusting the weight of his sack in preparation for the march. As he reached them, Leonardo strained his ears, but could not make out what Drogoradz said to him.

He watched as Ebel cocked his head to one side as if in thought, then strode confidently away down the track. Of course, he knew where to go.

Next, Sebastien was called forward after a delay of several minutes. Leonardo muttered, 'Good luck,' breaking the silence under which they had waited.

'Quiet!' Walter growled behind him as Sebastien turned to reply, who then thought better of it.

He made his own way to the end of the yard, received his destination, and set off. Next was Alof, then Sigbald, with a delay between each. Alof seemed to hesitate for a good moment before trudging slowly down the track, and Leonardo could imagine him racking his brain to remember where his mountain lay.

'You! Njal. Forward.' Magnus regarded the Norwegian with scrutiny as Njal gulped and crunched over the snow toward Drogoradz and Antonio. Antonio held up his parchment for Drogoradz to read from and the summit was given. Leonardo watched, with some concern, as Njal seemed to have frozen. Did he know which it was? Why wasn't he moving?

He seemed to stay that way, swaying a little in front of Drogoradz, until the big man barked at him to get a move on. Njal then jumped into action, walking off down the track. Leonardo hoped that meant he knew where he was going.

Then, Leonardo was alone, and Magnus was soon waving him on. 'Go on then, boy. Off you go.'

Leonardo made his way over to his other teachers, following in the trail of footsteps his brothers had left behind. *Please,* he thought, *please let it be one I know.* He stopped in front of Drogoradz, who consulted Antonio's parchment paper once more before looking down at Leonardo disinterestedly.

'The Snout, that's your mountain. Your flag's colour is red. Now bugger off.'

Leonardo walked past them and, for one panicked moment, couldn't think for the life of him where the Snout was. *Oh no!* he thought, his heart sinking with despair. *I can't remember. I'm going to fail and be told to leave the monastery. Maybe I'll even have to go back to my old life of begging in the streets!*

But then it came to him in a flash. They had been near there, not so long ago, but before the snow had truly set in. He'd never gone up the mountain, but Leonardo remembered the two large ponds of meltwater that sat at the mountain's base, from which its name was derived. East. He had to head east. It had taken them half a day in summer, meaning that the current climate would likely delay him several hours.

139

No matter, it was dawn and he had time. He breathed a sigh of relief, sure of his bearings now, and set off into the valley below.

Leonardo shielded his eyes against the sun and gazed up at the Snout. He had just passed over one of the meltwater pools, knowing it was there even though it was covered in the same thick blanket of pure, virgin snow as the rest of the surrounding area, for it was completely flat.

He had made good time through the several valleys that had lain between the monastery's mountain and the Snout. Leonardo had remarked that it had been the first time he had truly been alone for months. Though he enjoyed the company of his newfound brothers and their banter, the peace was refreshing, and the only sound was that of his own breath and the crunch of his snowshoes underfoot.

Now his route would begin to climb steeply for several hundred feet and Leonardo took a deep breath to begin it. He walked with a long, straight stick that had a ring of iron nailed to the bottom as a third point of contact to aid him on the march. After several minutes, Leonardo planted his stick in the snow to pause and remove a layer, for, though it was cold, the climb was warming his blood.

It took a little over an hour to reach the summit, at which point Leonardo found himself to be short of breath despite his new and improved level of fitness. As he rested for a moment, his hands on his knees, he scanned the area for any signs of a red flag.

There was nothing. Frowning, Leonardo took several paces onward, making absolutely certain that he was at the true summit as the wind whipped at his cloak. He peered around, but his eyes found nothing, only snow and rock.

Shit, Leonardo thought, beginning to panic. *What if I've climbed the wrong mountain?* He turned to look back down at the path of his ascent. There were the two pools Magnus had pointed out to them in the fall. They were the mountain's namesake, he had said. They were why it was called the Snout.

Yes, surely, he had to be in the right place, so where was his red flag? Leonardo searched the area once more, his heart fluttering anxiously. What if the flag had been blown into oblivion by the wind? It was strong, after all. What if he had to go back to the monastery and explain that to Magnus? He would scoff in disbelief, Leonardo was certain.

'Please God, let it be here,' Leonardo muttered under his breath. Just as he'd said it, his eyes caught sight of an oddity in the field of pure white.

What was that? It was as white as everything around it. Leonardo marched over as fast as his snowshoes would allow him. Then, as he approached, it took shape. There was a pile of rocks, almost completely submerged by a snowbank that the wind had battered so that the snow had built up on the side facing Leonardo. A branch had been lashed to one of the rocks with rope and, to it, a piece of material hung, frozen stiff at a diagonal.

Confused, Leonardo could see that it was white and not red. He reached out and touched it, feeling the thing crunch under his wrapped fingers.

'Ha!' he laughed, as the ice and snow fell away. A patch of red showed beneath the spot he had broken, and Leonardo wrenched the branch from its base and shook it. More snow broke away and he smiled in triumph at his prize. Leonardo knelt and crossed himself, muttering a prayer.

The moment of victory was short lived, for the wind had picked up, and Leonardo wasted no time in stashing the flag in his satchel and beginning the descent. The sun would soon set, and he would be out of light. The only thing to do now was to find a decent place to build a shelter to wait out the night.

Leonardo was not looking forward to it; no matter how good he built his shelter, he knew he would still be shivering himself to sleep that night. Resigned to it, he scanned the area during the descent for a suitable location when, all of a sudden, he heard a howl in the distance.

Leonardo froze, his ears pricking up. Then there was another one. Long, low and drawn out, it sounded eerie in the silence, carried along by the wind.

Wolves.

Leonardo had heard them before from the monastery, though never so close, and he had never actually seen the elusive creatures. He decided he would like to keep it that way, for the howls had made the hairs on the back of his neck stand on end. They reminded him that men were not the only predators patrolling the Pyrenees.

Sebastien had told him once that wolves almost never attack men, yet that information did little to reassure Leonardo. The grateful feeling that he'd had earlier in the day at the marvel of his solitude had evaporated, and he recognised just how vulnerable he was.

Leonardo continued on, picking up the pace and thinking to make some kind of shelter as soon as he could. There was another howl, though he thought it might have sounded a little further away this time.

Several minutes went by and no more howls pierced the air. Leonardo felt himself begin to relax again as some of the tension left him. The wolves must have been heading in the opposite direction, he decided, relieved.

By the time he had reached the bottom of the mountain again, more pressing matters dominated his thoughts. Looking up, he knew he had no more than two hours of light and would need all that time to build an igloo if he was to survive the night.

He found a suitable spot and began to compress the snow beneath his boots as he'd been taught, packing it high on a deep snowdrift. He did that for an hour, stopping once to uncork his waterskin and take a gulp, before he commenced the hollowing out of a simple little tunnel, only deep enough for him to lie in without his feet sticking out the end, and only tall enough for him to sit cross-legged, provided he dipped his head.

Once complete, Leonardo pushed his meagre affairs inside and blocked the entrance with a little snow, leaving only a slit at the top to protect him from most of the wind, before proceeding to make a little nest from the woollen blankets he had in his pack. He lay there, propped up on an elbow, helping himself to some smoked ham wrapped in linen as he wondered how the others were getting on.

Had they found their flags? He hoped so. Then he wondered what the spring would bring, should they make it that far. Leonardo lay down and covered himself as best he could. And what about after the training? What would life be like then? Would he travel the world and discover all of its wonders? He smiled to himself and closed his eyes, imagining what incredible things he would see and do, and what characters he would meet, as he drifted off to sleep.

Chapter 12

GASCONY

Trumpets blared as the King's ships arrived in the port of Bordeaux. The streets were lined with, what seemed to Leonardo, all the remaining loyalists in Gascony. They cheered the long-overdue arrival of Henry III and the army that was going to bring peace back to the land.

Handkerchiefs waved as the city folk leant over the railings at the dock, just as the first of the ships bumped against the jetties and the sailors hopped out to secure them. Whooping men and women stamped their feet and clapped in approval as a crowned figure appeared at the prow of the flagship, dressed in a fine cloak of red velvet.

He was a short man, and plump, with curly brown hair that fell to his chin and was parted neatly on either side of his head. He had a well-kept beard and carried himself in the regal manner in which only the upper echelons of society were taught. Leonardo concluded that he must be King Henry. Leonardo pursed his lips and turned away, leaving his vantage point to be filled by the eager townsfolk that surrounded him. He was certain he'd see plenty of the King in the coming weeks and didn't feel the necessity to witness the pomp of his disembarkation.

Leonardo slunk back through the streets and made for the inn that he had been using for his lodgings, near the parliamentary building.

Though basic, it was by his standards a luxury. Striding through the door, he nodded to the innkeeper and jogged up the stairs. He then locked himself away in his first-storey room to write to Emilio.

He kept his master well informed. While Emilio rarely replied, Leonardo knew he liked to be kept in the loop whenever possible. He kept the contents of the letter brief, recounting their capture of Langon and the situation in Gascony as he understood it, noting which factions had sided with which and the names of some of the more influential nobles that were loyalists or rebels. He finished the letter with an estimation of what he suspected might happen; that the rebels would surely have little chance against the English king and his entire army. That was, if Henry could afford to keep them employed. The threat of the Castilian invasion was another matter entirely, however, and the outcome was, for the moment, unclear.

Leonardo paused before sealing the letter. There was much he could have included that he had not. For instance, he had thought that the rift between him and his old friend Sebastien was beginning to heal while they had worked together to capture Langon. Yet, he had been mistaken; as soon as they had arrived in Bordeaux, Leonardo was pushed to one side and Sebastien took to meeting with Queen Eleanor and her ladies in private.

Leonardo was rarely invited and, when he was, it was always in the presence of Roger de Ros or some other such administrator. The discussions always revolved around the mundane topic of the state of the King's finances, leaving Leonardo with the strong suspicion that such meetings were designed merely to appease him, while he was sure that the matters of substance concerning the Queen were resolved without him.

Leonardo was there as a courtesy, a request from the English Finger to help secure Gascony for the English king, using all the methods that politicians and soldiers could not. So far, it seemed to Leonardo, Sebastien was doing his best to keep Leonardo at arm's length, though whether that was because of the animosity he still harboured after everything that had happened at the monastery, or some other reason, Leonardo could not say.

145

It had been twelve years since they had last met, and they were both different men. Sebastien had become almost impossible to read. Leonardo sighed. At least Sebastien could not keep him from the parliament that was scheduled for the morrow. Leonardo tilted a candle over the letter, dripping hot wax onto its surface, before pressing his signet ring with the symbol of the Order into its surface. He finished by tying the letter with a string and set it aside, to be given to a messenger service later that day.

Leonardo stood from the writing desk and walked to the window, where the shutters were opened to the late summer air and he had a good view of the townsfolk making their way through the streets, being about their business. Leonardo leant on the windowsill for a while, watching with the slightest feeling of curiosity – and, perhaps, even envy – as a proud-looking young man strutted along with a giggling maiden on his arm.

He sometimes wondered what it would be like to have a significant other in his life, to take a woman and settle down to start a family. But it was too late for him; he had been alone for far too long. He wasn't sure he was even capable of such feelings anymore. Over the years, his emotions had been dulled to distant pangs and he did not feel much of anything.

Once, when Leonardo had been younger, the world had been so full of possibilities, full of hope for what might be. But, as the years had slid by and his brutal work had consumed him, he had come to understand that his fate was one of service to a higher order.

As time wore on, those doors of possibility had been closed to him, and he had climbed the ranks of the Order, the only organisation suited to a man like him. It was fulfilling in some ways, to be sure, but so very lonely. For the agents of the Order, marriage was forbidden – and, even if it were not, Leonardo would not be so irresponsible as to do so. How could he, in his position, have anything like that?

No, his was a life of servitude and penance; it was the only logical option. Leonardo closed the shutters and lit some more candles, before removing his clothing and folding them in a neat pile on the stool. He stripped naked and took up his whip, gripping the familiar worn handle as he knelt in the middle of the room and prepared himself.

Leonardo grunted as he swung the thing over his shoulder and the thick straps of leather smacked his back at great speed. He swung it again and again until he had drawn blood, and added another scar to the countless that already covered the pale skin stretched over his spine. The crack of his whip was the only thing he really felt these days. Of late, it served not only to punish Leonardo for his ungodly thoughts, but to remind him that he was yet amongst the living.

'Quiet! Quiet! The King approaches. All kneel!' the nobleman, Peter Bonefans, shouted to the people gathered in the parliamentary hall in Bordeaux. Peter had been appointed joint Seneschal of Gascony, along with Drogo de Barentin, in the King's absence. He stood at the centre of the grand hall, where many rows of benches were lined along the walls, facing him and the raised dais that stood opposite the great arched double doors of the entrance.

A hush fell over the waiting crowd of knights, nobles and other important men as the King himself strode in with Queen Eleanor on his arm, followed by an entourage that included his master of household knights, Drogo de Barentin, and master of the wardrobe, Roger de Ros.

Leonardo had luckily managed to find himself a spot at the back of the hall, which was packed with people, all the spaces on the long, ornate benches having long since been occupied. Leonardo was content to lean with his back against a wall surrounded by countless others, and he noted how the parliament seemed to have been opened to anyone with half a reason to be there.

The waiting men knelt as Henry made his way with Eleanor to the dais. Henry sat upon the throne, directing his wife to sit beside him.

'Please stand, friends!' he called out.

Leonardo straightened to find the King of the English wearing a sweet smile and beaming around at them all. Now that he was closer,

147

Leonardo had the impression that the King was quite an inactive man. His stomach was a little larger than it ought to be, and his pale face looked unaccustomed to the sun. Henry steepled his fingers regally before him as a shuffling filled the hall and his nobles regained their seats, or stood where there were none.

Leonardo watched the pair and followed Eleanor's gaze as it lingered on a figure on one of the principal benches at the far side of the hall. It was Sebastien. He was never far from his mistress, it seemed. The moments Leonardo had spent in his company since they had returned from Langon had all been in the presence of Eleanor and, though they were fleeting, he could not help but notice that the pair of them were quite familiar with one another.

Presently, the King cleared his throat and addressed the waiting men. 'Good to see you all, gentlemen! To those of you I have not yet seen, good morning!'

There was a mumbling of 'Good morning' from the crowd before Henry went on. 'Now, I've been updated as to the situation here and was… surprised to find that things had deteriorated a little more than I had initially come to understand.' He shifted uncomfortably in his throne for a moment and Eleanor looked at the floor.

Leonardo found it hard to believe that Henry could have failed to grasp the gravity of the situation when it had been reported to him that the great nobles of the region had risen up against him, and he suspected that was Henry's way of saying, 'I should really have got here sooner.'

'Nevertheless,' Henry continued, 'I'm here now, and have already had a correspondence sent to La Reole informing the de Pins family that I intend to stay until peace is brought once more to the land, and that I am open to some form of dialogue. I have made it abundantly clear to William de Pins that I plan to rule in a way that is far more sympathetic to their wishes, very much unlike Simon de Montfort. With any luck, we'll hear something back from him this morning.'

'You can't reason with these treacherous dogs, Your Highness. I say we lay the siege tomorrow!' a boisterous young noble shouted from one of the front benches, to a grumbling of assent. That was Roger Bigod, who would command a good portion of the King's forces in the coming campaign. Sitting next to him was John de Gray, another well-known household knight who commanded his own host of men. He nodded in assent at Roger's words.

Henry rolled his eyes. 'Yes, thank you, Roger. However, perhaps the Christian thing to do would be to offer a parley before we level half the cities in Frankia. Now, since many of us have only just arrived, I suggest we defer to Peter Bonefans and Sir Drogo de Barentin, who will have much more detailed knowledge of Gascony's circumstances, I'm sure.' Henry looked pointedly at his two seneschals, who had taken a seat with the rest of his entourage on another bench facing the dais. 'Might either of you be able to tell me where Gaston de Bearn is at present?' The King asked.

'Erm, we believe he is somewhere in central Gascony, united with Amaneus d'Albret, Your Highness,' Peter Bonefans offered.

'Hmm.' Henry steepled his fingers thoughtfully. 'And, you say it is he who has been responsible for inciting many of the rebel lords to action?'

'It would appear that way, yes, Your Highness,' came Drogo's gruff voice.

The King leant back in his throne with an annoyed frown on his face. He tugged at a lock of hair nonchalantly, deep in thought and quite unperturbed by the hundred or so men who watched and whispered amongst each other. Leonardo suspected kings were used to such things.

Eventually, Henry spoke. 'That's unfortunate, as I'm rather fond of Gaston.' Now it was Eleanor's turn to roll her eyes, though she said nothing. 'Perhaps now that I'm here, Gaston will see reason and lay down his arms. Was his quarrel not with de Montfort's rule, after all?'

Peter Savoy, of the great Savoyard family, stood. 'I'm not so sure, Your Highness. There's been rumour that he's in league with Alphonso of Castile and accepts bribes to continue his disruption of Gascony. There is even talk that the King of Castile wants Gaston to conquer Gascony as his Frankish general, and rule it in his place.'

A serious murmur of disapproval rippled through the hall at those words and a shadow passed across the King's face. 'Yes, I have heard such rumours. But I know Gaston, I do not think he would go so far!' For a moment, Henry had sounded like a hurt little boy whose friends had refused to play with him. No one present seemed to share Henry's convictions, however.

'And I would have thought that Bernard de Bouville would know better than to join Gaston!' he continued. 'To think of everything I've done for him and his family!'

'We should burn their cities to the ground, Your Highness!' Roger Bigod interjected again.

'Alright, alright, Roger, we all know what you think!' Henry held up his hands in exasperation. 'Let's try to exhaust our other options first. For heaven's sake, what is it they want? Can we appease them?'

'Might I offer a suggestion, Your Highness?' Peter of Savoy asked politely.

'Very well, let's hear it.'

'I've been in direct communication with the vicomtes of Fronsac and Castillon,' said Peter of Savoy. 'They have suggested to me that they would be willing to lay down their arms, if you would agree to pay them an annual fee of two hundred pounds each for the next five years.'

Henry waved his hand in disgust. 'Certainly not! I can't spare a single pound! Don't they know I've a crusade to fund?'

There was some muttering at that. Not everyone shared the King's crusading fervour, and many were of the opinion that the King ought to focus his attention and resources on matters closer to home. However, it was said that his heart was well and truly set on the crusade to the Holy Land, and he would hear no word against it.

'Do they not have any demands that are reasonable?' he asked the room.

'Men like Gaillard de Solers, who have been personally wronged by de Montfort's rule, might appreciate the man being put on trial,' suggested John de Gray, and all de Montfort's enemies present stamped their feet in assent at the words. Yet, there were just as many who growled angrily at the suggestion.

The King sighed. 'We tried that, remember? De Montfort may have had a heavy hand, to say the least, but the Solers family want his blood, and that I cannot give to them. Simon is married to my sister, after all.'

Earlier that year, Simon de Montfort had been put on trial before the English parliament at Westminster, after the mysterious death of Rostand de Solers in de Montfort's custody had led to riots, eventually snowballing to rebellion.

The disgruntled Gascon nobles had stood before the English king in Westminster with no end of accusations to throw at de Montfort, though none of the accusations had stuck for one reason or another, and Simon had been acquitted. Then, to everyone's shock, de Montfort had sailed to Gascony, hired several thousand mercenaries and sacked La Reole. King Henry, of course, had to depose him as Seneschal of Gascony before the situation was further exacerbated, paying de Montfort a total of seven thousand marks when he refused to quit the position. The latter eventually retired to his Earldom in Leicester once the sum had been paid. From there, it had all unravelled fairly quickly for Henry.

'We could ask Alphonse of Poitiers for help, Your Highness,' Peter Bonefans interjected.

Henry gave a very unkingly snort. 'Don't be ridiculous, that fool wouldn't lift a finger to help me! Nothing would make Alphonse happier than to see me lose control of Gascony. He'd jump at the chance to snap some of it up for himself, I'm sure.'

Just then, running footsteps echoed off the stone-flagged floor of the corridor and a panting messenger burst in through the open door. He skidded to a halt in alarm as he saw the hundreds of faces that made up the English court turn to frown at him for the interruption.

'F-forgive me, my lords, Your Highness,' the messenger puffed, bowing deeply.

'What is it?' the King asked testily.

'News from La Reole, Your Highness. William de Pins has your answer.'

'Ah!' Henry exclaimed with a smile, leaning forward in his throne with the look of a man who expected good news. 'Tell us!'

The messenger gulped. 'I-I think it's best if, perhaps, you were to read it in private, Your Highness.'

Henry frowned. 'Why? Does it not concern the fate of La Reole?'

'It does, Your Highness, but—'

'Then read it aloud, for heaven's sake! I haven't the time!'

With shaking hands, the messenger unfolded his note and read the words of William de Pins. 'We extend our welcome to King Henry, but regret that he will soon have to board his ships earlier than expected. We will no longer recognise the reign of the English crown over our lands and will fight to keep them independent of his rule. La Reole is ours.' The messenger finished the brief note to look nervously up at the King.

Henry sat back with a look of outrage and hurt spread across his face, just as the hall broke out in a murmur of frantic whispering.

'The sheer insolence!' Henry cried. 'Very well, if William de Pins, Amaneus, Gaston and all the other fools want a fight, we'll give them one!'

The hall erupted in a cheer now that a decision had been made. Roger Bigod jumped to his feet with a broad smile on his face and shouted, 'You see, Your Highness, I told you there was no point—'

'Oh, shut up, Roger!' Henry interrupted him. 'And lay siege to that damned city, will you!'

Several minutes later, Leonardo was pushing himself off the wall and used the distraction of the excited nobles to make his exit, along with a plethora of other men who left in the wake of the King's generals to make the preparations for war. It seemed that the King's attempt at diplomacy was over before it had begun.

Leonardo made his way out of the hall as people streamed past him and turned when he felt a tap on his shoulder. He turned to see Sebastien and raised his eyebrows questioningly.

'What is it?' he asked coolly.

'The Queen would see us presently.' Sebastien's reply was curt and his brown eyes hard.

'She asked for me specifically, did she?' Leonardo guessed.

'She did,' Sebastien conceded. 'She needs all the help she can get.' Leonardo nodded and followed Sebastien back down the hall to the office where he had first met the Queen, and glanced at the familiar guard stationed there before he and Sebastien slipped inside to wait for her.

They sat before the big desk in comfortable chairs, in an uncomfortable silence, before the Queen entered. She was followed by Sir Derek, Roger de Ros and, to Leonardo's surprise, Peter of Savoy. He and Sebastien stood, and the necessary introductions were made, with the Queen brushing off Peter of Savoy's questions toward the two churchmen as the Queen insisted they were simply trusted advisors.

Though the shrewd Peter of Savoy frowned at that, he did not press the matter, and waited for the Queen to speak, just as Sir Derek took up his usual position by the door.

'You'll both be aware of Peter by name, I'm sure?' Queen Eleanor asked, remaining standing behind her chair at the desk. Both Sebastien and Leonardo nodded, for who hadn't? The Savoyard dynasty had ruled over a large region of south-eastern France for centuries, turning what was initially a poor country into one of Frankia's most wealthy provinces through diplomacy, trade and the control of certain Alpine passes to make them a well-respected power on the continent.

'Peter's family and mine share a long history, and both of us have a vested interest in quashing this rebellion as fast as possible,' the Queen went on.

Peter nodded as he pulled up a chair and placed himself down, crossing one leg over the other elegantly. 'Yes, rebellion in Gascony is very bad for business,' he said through pursed lips.

'Quite,' the Queen agreed. 'Now, the longer this insurrection goes on, the more damage it does to England. Not only does it damage my husband's and my reputation and rule, but it is costing us money we simply do not have. Henry will let no one touch the funds he has set aside for his crusade and, as a result, the royal treasury is about to run dry.' Leonardo detected a hint of exasperation in Eleanor's voice as she gripped the back of her chair from behind the great desk.

'Sir Ros, please inform these gentlemen of the sum that was required just to transport the King and his army to Gascony.'

'Of course, Your Highness.' The short Roger de Ros sifted through a pamphlet of documents that seemed to be a permanent fixture about his person, before pulling one out and quickly scanning its contents. 'Four hundred and nine pounds, Your Highness.'

There was a sharp intake of breath from the listening men, and Leonardo grimaced at the enormous sum.

'Those were my thoughts exactly!' Queen Eleanor said as she watched their expressions. 'Rebellions are not cheap affairs and, at the current rate my husband seems to be throwing his money around, our pockets will be empty before Christmas if we're lucky.'

Eleanor was quiet for a moment, allowing the information to sink in. She looked around at them pointedly to ensure that they all understood the gravity of King Henry's position. If the rebellion was not crushed soon, Henry's army would mutiny from lack of pay.

'What can we do to help, Your Highness?' Leonardo asked, looking up at the clever young Queen.

'That's where Peter comes in,' she replied, indicating the Savoyard Duke. 'He knows the politics of Gascony far better than I and has an idea of how we might raise a little more cash.'

Peter of Savoy cleared his throat. 'Well, they were just ideas and perhaps a little unrealistic. However, I see no harm in voicing them here.' He turned to Leonardo and Sebastien, who waited with interest. 'King Henry will soon march on the Vicomte of Benauges. I take it you will have heard the name Bernard de Bouville in relation to the rebels? It is his vicomte – though, with it being so close to Bordeaux, he will know it is a primary target for Henry and, moreover, it does not have the defences to stall him in a lengthy siege. Bernard knows this, too, and will have fled the city – somewhere further east, I would imagine, perhaps Ste-foy-La-Grande, on the southern side of the Dordogne.

'Now, the thing about rebellious noblemen is that, if they surrender under terms of a defeat, you can only squeeze so much money out of them, as their voluntary surrender would likely have won them favourable terms and mitigate any financial losses they would otherwise suffer. By that point, it will be too late for our purposes, anyway. However, if you capture them during a campaign, not only can you demand their immediate compliance, but you can also ransom their release for a hefty sum.

'If, by some miracle, the King were able to capture a Gascon noble or two with the status of Bernard de Bouville, he could raise enough cash from the proceeds of the ransom to extend his campaign by a month. But, as I say, it's just an idea.' Peter of Savoy finished with a dismissive wave of the hand, as if the proposal was entirely impracticable.

'If the timeline is as constrained as you say, Your Highness, buying ourselves a month would help a great deal,' Sebastien mused aloud.

'I'm sure there is a way to get to Bernard de Bouville,' said Leonardo. 'Is Ste-foy-La-Grande well defended?' He turned to Peter of Savoy questioningly.

Peter of Savoy looked confused for a moment. 'You can't mean to go and capture him yourselves, can you? You're men of God!' He looked between Leonardo and Sebastien with surprise.

'We can be very... persuasive, Lord Savoy,' Leonardo replied simply and heard the Queen chuckle knowingly.

Peter of Savoy raised his eyebrows, held his hands up and said, 'I will ask no more! And yes, wherever Bernard is, he will be guarded.'

'It's worth a try, I'd say,' the Queen decided. 'Father Sebastien, Father Leonardo, would you do your best to bring me Bernard de Bouville?'

'We won't let you down, Your Highness,' Sebastien said with a smile, which the Queen returned. He then stood, as if to make for the road immediately. Leonardo stood with him and, as they headed for the door, the Queen called out after them.

'Oh, and gentlemen, please do be careful.'

Leonardo turned and saw that she was staring rather intently at Sebastien, and had the impression that the warning had been meant for him alone.

'Always, Your Highness.' Sebastien dipped his head and they left. Leonardo's brow creased and he was left wondering, not for the first time, what the nature of Sebastien's service to Queen Eleanor truly was.

Chapter 13

TWELVE YEARS AGO

Leonardo was running. He was always running, just like he had always been running. Running barefoot in raggedy trousers, his grubby feet slapping the flagstones. At first, there was a great big grin spread across his boyish face, making his green eyes twinkle. He giggled helplessly as he ran, his older brothers laughing and trying to catch him, chasing him this way and that playfully.

Left, then right, up some stairs, through a doorway, out the other side, left, then down the street. He squealed delightfully as he felt their fingers tickle his sides and sped up, darting, hopping and leaping.

But then the air changed, just like it was always destined to. Clouds of fog, cold and grey descended upon them and Leonardo's smile faltered. Something sinister approached and his brothers knew it, too.

They shouted at him to run and Leonardo looked back at the pair of them to see fear and panic in their eyes. Their expressions never left him. It was an image seared into the core of his mind. It scared him more than anything ever had, that look of fear. For his big brothers were fearless! Weren't they?

Leonardo's step faltered and he almost fell. His brothers caught him and pushed him onward, shouting at him in desperation to get out of there, to run! Go, they had said. Run. And so he had. He had left them, but not before he had glanced over his shoulder and witnessed, to his horror, that cold, ruthless fog had swallowed them up.

Leonardo woke. Something was happening. He heard noises, and tore himself from the dream world, trying to discern what was corporeal and what was a construct of his imagination. Blinking in the darkness, he remembered where he was – tucked in blankets in his little snow tunnel.

What was that noise? There was a scraping at the entrance. Something was scooping away at the snow. Something was trying to get in; to get at him!

Leonardo squinted in the darkness through the little slit he had left at the top for air when, silhouetted in the dim light of the moon outside, a shape appeared. Straight, grey fur, pointed ears, a long snout and a glistening wet nose. Then, a cold, yellow eye gazed in and the creature snarled, baring sharp, canine teeth.

Leonardo's eyes widened in horror as he realised what had woken him up. The wolves, they had found him! The scraping recommenced and Leonardo's heart hammered in his chest. There was not much snow between him and them; it was only supposed to act as a heat shield, not a defence against hungry predators.

He scrabbled around for his satchel, fumbling in it and feeling for his dagger. His hands found it in the dark and he wrenched it from its sheath, pushing himself as far back into the tunnel as he could.

Some of the snow at the entrance fell away to reveal a great, shaggy grey head. It growled, as a string of saliva dripped from the beast's mouth.

Leonardo felt the fear knot his guts and shouted at the thing as it bared down on him, slinking its way up the snow tunnel toward him, its breath steaming in the freezing night air.

'Hey!' Leonardo yelled desperately. 'Hey! Get away from here! Leave me alone! Get away, damn you!'

The wolf snarled in response and came close enough for Leonardo to smell its rancid breath. His back was now firmly pressed up against the wall of snow and ice behind him and he braced himself against it, preparing to deliver a kick to the wolf's snout or slash at it with his dagger.

Leonardo was vaguely aware of other shapes moving behind the wolf, and another snout appeared between the first's legs, sniffing hungrily, licking its chops at the thought of a fresh kill. It growled, too, seeming to urge the first on.

The wolf facing Leonardo tested him with a snap of its jaws, trying to bite at his ankle. Leonardo drew his foot back and kicked, scoring a glancing blow that caused the wolf to snarl and bite again, and again.

'Get off me!' Leonardo shouted in desperation, kicking wildly as the wolf tried to clamp its jaws around his foot. There was a flurry of limbs and teeth in the darkness, and snarling and panting as Leonardo fought a desperate battle with the animal, until it successfully caught his foot as he tried to kick it. He cried out in pain as he felt the beast's jaws grip his ankle with frightening force, its sharp front teeth biting clean through the leather of his boot and sinking deep into his flesh.

The wolf began to drag him backward, out toward the open so that the rest of the pack might tear him apart from either side. Leonardo wailed in pain and fear as it yanked him on and he slipped and slid over the surface of the snow. The other wolves caught scent of the fresh blood and howled hungrily, snapping at one another for the first bite of fresh prey.

Leonardo slashed wildly with his dagger, catching the wolf on its snout and it yelped, releasing him and reeling, allowing Leonardo to push himself back inside the tunnel. The gap the first wolf left allowed another to fill it, and Leonardo was soon met with another pair of merciless yellow eyes. It tried to bite him, and he kicked it and thrust with the dagger, tearing at the thing's ear.

The wolf was more wary after that, yet it snapped and bit with just as much force as the first, its paw managing to pin Leonardo's leg once as it bit again. However, Leonardo rebuked it with a another cut from his blade, thanking God that Antonio had been so insistent that they honed them until they were shaving sharp.

The beast backed away and another in the pack vied for position, snarling at the others to take its turn at the terrified young man curled up in the hole in the ground.

Leonardo's chest heaved with adrenaline as he braced himself at the rear of the snow tunnel once more, before it started all over again. Biting, snapping, snarling, growling, the stench of hot breath, wet saliva flicking onto the snow, inch-long teeth and a mass of matted fur.

Leonardo fought desperately. He was a cornered rat fighting for survival, knowing full well that, were he to drop his guard, the wolves would drag him out into the open to feast on his living flesh. He didn't know when, but he realised that he had begun to growl himself at some point. His terror was beginning to become diluted with a cold, black rage that boiled within him.

'Come on, then!' he cried in agitated defiance. 'Which one of you is next? Come on! Fight me, you beasts!' The wolves faltered before another member of the pack tried its luck. With a snarl of his own, Leonardo took the offensive before the wolf could make an attack and thrust his knife into its face, skewering it clean through the eye. The beast howled in pain, leaping back with a spurt of blood.

The wolf whinnied and cried pitifully, moving from Leonardo's narrow field of view. The other wolves hesitated, glaring at him and baring their teeth.

'What are you waiting for?' Leonardo roared. 'Come and get me! I'll make a meal of you yet!' He felt his courage growing as he heard the strength in his voice, and let it warm him. None of the wolves made to attack him and Leonardo even dared to shuffle a little closer to the exit of his shelter to goad them some more.

'Are you afraid?' he shouted in the night. 'Fight me!' One of the wolves howled, another barked and snapped, but none attacked. It seemed they were learning to be wary of this indomitable man and his long, steel claw.

The alpha gave a final, angry snarl and barked at the others, turned, and trotted away through the snow in search of easier prey.

The rest took one last, longing look at Leonardo before they turned and followed their alpha, and soon they had gone, fading into the night just as quickly as they had appeared.

Leonardo was sweating, despite the cold, and his chest heaved deep breaths for minutes after the wolves had gone. Then, he laughed.

He laughed at his success. He laughed in relief and then at the sheer misfortune of it. He glanced down at his bloody dagger and vowed to keep one at his side forevermore. Then, once the fear had abated, the adrenaline had washed away and the cold began to creep once more into his blood, Leonardo thought to rebuild the little barricade of snow separating him from the outside world.

Leonardo winced in pain and felt around his ankle, running his fingers over wide puncture marks where the first wolf had bit deep. He cursed and wrapped the ankle up as best he could. Then, he crouched in the tunnel, his dagger clutched in one hand, the other hand wrapped around his knees, his eyes fixed on the slit of the starry night sky, which was all he could see of the world outside.

He stayed like that, his eyes open and his body wide awake, until the morning came and the slit turned from black to a dark blue. As soon as there was enough light to see properly, Leonardo punched his way through and gathered his things, stepping out into the morning to check that the coast was clear.

Squinting around, he could not see or hear the wolves that had attacked him during the night, but there was plenty of evidence of their movement. Paw prints and tracks criss-crossed in the snow, concentrated around the entrance of his shelter where the fighting had occurred. Leonardo could see several individual trails of blood that were not his own and knew he had scarred at least one of the beasts. Perhaps that would make them think twice before they tried to make a meal of men.

Leonardo took a deep breath, knowing that the journey back to the monastery would leave him vulnerable out in the open, but also that he could not stay there forever. He took a swig from his waterskin, shouldered his satchel, and set off.

It was early afternoon by the time Leonardo reached the track up to the monastery. He hobbled up, his injured ankle sending jolts of pain up his leg with every step. He had leant heavily on his stick during the return journey, and his slow progress meant that the cold had buried deeper into his skin. By the time he laid eyes upon the familiar cluster of stone buildings, his jaw was chattering, and he was tired, cold, hungry and thirsty. But he was still alive, and victorious!

Leonardo smiled to himself, wondering who had got there first. He clambered up to the door of the great hall and pushed it open, sighing in relief as he felt a wash of warm air engulf him and he let his eyes adjust to the gloom.

Several faces looked up at him from the closest table. Sebastien was there, of course. Ebel too, and Sigbald. They had all made it back safely and, Leonardo guessed, successfully, for they were sitting slurping at bowls of stew or tending to their equipment.

'Ah ha!' Sebastien cried in delight at the sight of his friend. 'Little late in the day, isn't it? Did you find an inn to stop at for lunch?'

Leonardo grinned. 'Nonsense, I was giving you lot a head start!' He shook his friends' hands as they stood to greet him, and Sigbald plucked Leonardo's red flag from his satchel and waved it in the air triumphantly.

He tutted mockingly at Leonardo. 'Coming fourth isn't like you, my friend!'

Leonardo shrugged. 'I had a little... setback.'

'Oh?'

However, before Leonardo could reply, he heard footsteps on the wooden stairs at the far end of the hall and turned to see Magnus appear in his billowing black robes that contrasted with his white hair and beard. He caught sight of Leonardo and beckoned for silence.

'You. Leonardo. Bring it to me.' He held out his hand for the flag and Leonardo snatched it back from Sigbald, noting that it was the first time Magnus had ever addressed him by his actual name instead of the familiar 'boy' that he had grown accustomed to.

Leonardo limped over and presented his prize to Magnus with a triumphant smile.

'Hmm,' he grunted as he took the flag and weighed it in his hand. 'I expected you here sooner. Nevertheless, here you are.' To hear something other than a reprimand from Magnus made it sound almost like a compliment.

Magnus glanced down at Leonardo's bandaged leg. 'What happened?' he grunted.

'Wolves,' was Leonardo's simple reply. 'They attacked me in the night, Teacher.'

Magnus raised his eyebrows in surprise. Leonardo could hear his comrades whisper in astonishment behind him, as they had been listening with interest.

'Wolves, eh? Well, it's probably for the best you didn't let 'em get you. You wouldn't have made much of a meal, anyway.' Leonardo imagined he could see the hint of a smile playing on Magnus's lips under the wild white beard, and couldn't help but grin.

'Yes, Teacher.'

'Good. I'll have Walter see to that wound. There's stew in the pot, boy, help yourself.'

Leonardo was allowed to catch up with the others and they wasted no time in clamouring at him for details of his near-death experience. They chatted, each regaling the others of their first solo adventure in the mountains as they waited for the rest of their party to show.

The sun had set when the door to the hall banged open once more and the huddled silhouette of Alof let himself in, shivering and miserable looking. He, too, had been successful, and presented his own flag to Magnus before falling upon the hearth and sticking his blue fingers over the fire.

As the evening wore on, however, it became more likely that Njal would not show. At one point or another, the rest of their instructors had made an appearance. Walter had cleaned Leonardo's wound and rebandaged it before dinner, whilst Magnus had paced the great hall as Antonio and Drogoradz ate behind him.

The five initiates present were soon dismissed and told to retreat to the bunkhouse, where they were to rest in preparation for lessons as usual upon the morrow.

The next morning, there was still no sign of Njal, and when morning turned into afternoon Leonardo and the others began to fear the worst.

'What if he fell, or something…?' Sebastien trailed off as he, Sigbald and Leonardo cleaned the barn, the goats bleating around them.

'Hmm,' Sigbald grunted, chewing his tongue in thought as he forked at a bale of frozen hay. 'Maybe he's just lost somewhere?' he speculated. 'These mountains can be disorienting. I was almost lost myself, and I only managed to find my way back because I spotted Ebel's tracks.'

'If that's the case, he won't last long out there,' Leonardo concluded grimly.

When the evening came, there was still no sign of the tall Norwegian. Ebel muttered in low tones at the dinner table that he had heard Walter and Drogoradz talking; they had said that those who did not return on the fourth day were usually presumed dead. There would be a search party sent out, of course, but that was hardly likely to yield fruit; it would be like searching for a needle in a haystack.

It wasn't until the day after that, that Njal finally made an appearance. The other initiates were out in the yard, wrapped up in cloaks, furs and mittens, as they swung at the training posts with wooden swords under Antonio's supervision.

Sebastien had been the first to lay eyes upon the tall, hooded figure stumbling up the track. He cried out, dropping his training sword and running over, Antonio hot on his heels.

Leonardo followed and saw that it was, indeed, Njal. He caught a glimpse of his comrade's gaunt face, the skin white as a sheet and stretched thin over his bones. Njal looked like death incarnate, when his eyes rolled up into the back of his head and he collapsed into the snow.

They all helped carry him into the great hall and Magnus was summoned, followed closely by Drogoradz and Walter, as they descended to see what had become of their sixth initiate.

Njal was placed before the fire and he seemed to babble deliriously, only half conscious.

'What's he saying? Is he trying to tell us something?' Alof asked. They all leant a little closer, crowding over Njal as his cracked lips moved.

'I'm sorry, I'm sorry!' he kept muttering. 'I just wanted to lie down in the snow to rest my eyes for a minute. It was only supposed to be a minute, I swear!'

His friends leant over him with anxious faces. 'Make way!' Walter snapped, shoving them aside to tend to the young man.

Walter crouched over Njal, with all the other inhabitants of the monastery watching closely. He snapped his fingers over Njal's eyes. 'Can you hear me, boy? Can you see me?'

Leonardo looked around. Njal had not arrived with his bag, let alone the coloured flag that he ought to have collected. He must have run out of food and water some time ago; he would have had to slake his thirst from the snow itself. It was a grave error to eat the snow, Magnus had taught them, for the body lost much energy melting it once it passed down the gullet.

'My hands,' Njal muttered. 'I... I can't feel my hands. Or my feet. I'm sorry.' Walter looked down at Njal's thinly bandaged extremities and began to peel them away gently. What was revealed beneath made the initiates gasp in horror and take an involuntary step back.

Njal's fingers and thumbs were black as tar. They looked grotesque, like charred sticks at the bottom of a fire; malformed, twisted and terrible. The discoloration stopped abruptly just before the last knuckle where the fingers met the palm; where Njal's body had sacrificed the digits to save heat for the valuable organs in his torso.

Magnus had taught them about this; it was an extreme reaction caused by severe exposure to temperatures well below freezing. One thing was abundantly clear to all who were present: Njal would never grip a sword again.

It was as if he had a moment of consciousness, for Njal seemed to come to, and brought his head up a little from where he lay upon the floorboards. He held up his hands and, in the light of the fire, he wailed in horror at the sight of his shrivelled, blackened fingers.

'Nooo!' he cried, tears rolling down his cheeks at their loss. He seemed as aware as the rest of them that, though alive, he would now live out the rest of his days as a cripple. 'Nooo!' He lay his head back on the floorboards and screwed his eyes shut, letting his mangled hands fall to his sides as he wept.

The onlookers exchanged grim looks. Walter removed Njal's boots to find that his toes had fared no better; they, too, would have to be removed. This seemed to be decided when Walter glanced up questioningly at Magnus, who gave him a grim, curt nod. Walter stood, heading upstairs.

'Lay him on the table,' Magnus commanded. The others, knowing what was coming, gritted their teeth and hoisted Njal's weeping form onto the nearest of the pine tables, wincing as he cried out in pain between his mutterings.

Walter returned, carrying a leather pouch that he unfolded upon the adjacent table to reveal an array of wicked-looking surgical implements. Leonardo sighed and closed his eyes. He had no desire to be present for what was to come next, but knew that it was a necessity. If the fingers were not cut away, they would surely go bad, and sickness would spread to the rest of the body.

He gripped one of Njal's ankles as Walter made to start on the right hand. Sebastien was grimacing as he held Njal's wrist, and Ebel looked ready to vomit.

'Hold him steady,' Walter ordered them, as he inspected the blade of a fine-toothed saw and tested it with his thumb. When the gruesome work began, the great hall filled with jarring screams of agony as Njal's weakened form bucked and writhed under his brothers' grips. He wailed pitifully as the saw sliced through the dead flesh and bone.

Thankfully, after several minutes of the macabre procedure, he fell into a state of unconsciousness. Walter was allowed to finish the operation by stitching up all Njal's stumps carefully, his hands and feet now sporting uneven nubs instead of fingers and toes.

The atmosphere in the hall was solemn as Walter wiped the blood from his hands.

Sebastien turned to Magnus once it was done and asked, 'What will become of him, Teacher?'

Magnus sighed sadly. 'If you can't hold a weapon, you can't be an agent. We'll send him down to Arreau to recover for a while, and then he will take the journey back to his master. The Order will find a purpose for him.' Magnus nodded, tugging thoughtfully at his beard.

They took Njal to his bed, throwing big logs into the fire and, for once, disregarding Ebel's careful system of rationing so that their brother might be warm. They wrapped him with blankets and checked his bandages, administering him with water and meat, opening his mouth gently and encouraging him to eat during his more lucid moments.

'I'm sorry,' he would mutter occasionally. 'I was lost. I swear, I only stopped to rest my eyes for a moment. It was just going to be a moment, I promise!'

'Shh, shh now,' Sebastien soothed as he sat beside Njal, stroking his forehead like a mother might to a sick child. 'It's alright, Njal, you're alright. Just rest now. Go on, close your eyes. That's it. Sleep.'

'I'm sorry...' Njal whispered before his eyelids fluttered shut and he drifted off into oblivion.

The next morning, Leonardo woke and, with the help of Alof and Ebel, prepared Njal a sack for the journey down the mountain. He would best recover in Arreau, where the winter was not so harsh.

Meanwhile, Sebastien and Sigbald helped Njal out of bed, but had to stop as Njal tested his weight on his feet. They clearly caused him great pain and Leonardo wondered if he would ever be able to walk properly, even once he had recovered.

Fortunately, the day outside was clear and, an hour later, the donkey was braying next to Drogoradz, who had volunteered to shepherd the wounded initiate down the mountain. Before he went, Njal turned to his brothers and clasped each of them in a teary goodbye. He was despondent, they could tell, and they promised to pray for him.

Sebastien had fashioned a crutch for Njal in the night and handed it to him, taking his other arm and helping him over to Drogoradz. Then, the pair of them hauled Njal up gingerly onto the donkey's back and he was ready to go.

They stood back, shoulder to shoulder, Leonardo, Sebastien, Sigbald, Ebel and Alof, and watched as Drogoradz led the donkey down the track by the reins, the slouched and defeated figure of Njal sitting upon it.

He turned back to them, his face upturned into a mask of sorrow, and he raised a maimed, bandaged hand in a gesture of farewell, that all five initiates returned with lumps in their throats as they clasped each other for comfort. Njal turned away to leave the monastery, his time there done. It was the last time any of them would ever see him again, and his fate would be lost to the world.

He would leave alive, but not in one piece. The mountains had broken him. The Order had broken him. Leonardo sighed, fighting back the tears, and looked around at his comrades.

Now, they were but five.

Chapter 14

GASCONY

Leonardo sat in the corner of a tavern, sipping a tankard of weak ale, his hood pulled up over his head despite the warm weather. They had arrived in Ste-foy-La-Grande earlier in the day and Leonardo had had to quickly cover his features upon their entry to the large town for, in the courtyard, he had passed none other than Gaillard Solers, the noble youth he had struck on his first day in Gascony. The last thing he needed was to bump into a hot-headed rebel who already had it in for him. He had, therefore, secreted himself in a dingy tavern that he suspected a man like Gaillard would not frequent.

They had been waved into the city by a guard, who didn't look twice at the two travel-worn priests leading their mounts under the arch of the gates. Leonardo had watched the roads on the journey, during which he and Sebastien had hardly spoken. Country folk of the different provincial communes had brought grain, wine, wool and other produce by the wagonload from the unguarded villages to the safety of walled cities, now that word had spread that the King's army was marching forth from Bordeaux, and Ste-foy-La-Grande was no exception. At least in the towns it could be guarded, for anything of value in the villages was sure to be confiscated by greedy soldiers.

Along with Leonardo and Sebastien, many villagers and country folk were entering the town in search of refuge, far from the fighting, and the atmosphere was layered with a hint of urgency. Leonardo had remarked, too, that Ste-foy-La-Grande was well guarded. It seemed to be a safe haven for nobles and peasants alike; for, when he and Sebastien had led their horses down the main street, he had turned to come almost face to face with Gaillard Solers, who had been deep in conversation with one of his knights and had looked up just in time to see a priest pull a dark hood over his face.

For a moment, Leonardo had feared that there might have been a hint of recognition pass over his face, though it seemed, a moment later, that Gaillard had dismissed the notion. From then, Leonardo and Sebastien had decided that it would be prudent for him to stay off the streets lest he have another chance encounter with the youth, and that Sebastien would scout out the location of the Vicomte of Benauges in the meantime.

Leonardo was content to wait and, though he didn't dare to risk heading outside, if he leant forward in his seat to look out of the window he could see, through the gap between two buildings, the lazy water of the Dordogne flowing west toward Bordeaux and the Bay of Biscay. Outside, the air had begun to change a little. It was slightly cooler now that it was mid-September, and winter would see it fall to what would universally be considered cold, though it had nothing on the harsh winters he had known high in the Pyrenees.

Leonardo had been revisiting his memories, reliving the events that had unfolded at the monastery there, brought back to the forefront of his mind by Sebastien's presence. Although twelve years had passed, it was as if it had been only yesterday since they had parted ways in anger. Leonardo sighed and doubted things would ever be as they once were.

He wiled away the time by watching the folk in the tavern around him, the talk of the English king's arrival the principal subject on their lips.

'I heard King Henry's sent three thousand o' them archers to Benauges. Three thousand!' a toothy old man informed his apprentice incredulously, after taking a great swig of ale and mopping his beard with a grubby shirt. 'S'only a matter of time before Benauges falls,' he added, giving his apprentice a knowing look.

'But what about La Reole and Bazas?' the young apprentice asked. 'They're both big cities with thick stone walls, turrets n'all! Folks say they can't be taken!'

'Aye lad, that's right,' said the old man. 'That King Henry'll struggle with 'em, no doubt. But 'es got an army behind 'im, that aint nothin'.'

'I suppose.'

'Least there'll be plenty of work for carpenters like us once this is over, if it's anythin' like Taillbourg.' The old man stuck his chin out proudly, as if being old enough to remember the aftermath of the famous battle was an achievement.

The apprentice seemed impressed enough, however. 'Were you there? What happened?'

'I wasn't there myself,' replied the old man, 'but that King Henry burnt much afterward when Louis gave him a right spankin'! Did it out of spite, I reckon. Either way, everything's been going downhill for him ever since. But, anyway, such things ain't for you and I to worry about, lad.'

Just then, Leonardo spotted Sebastien enter through the door and watched him scan the room out of habit. Once Sebastien was satisfied, he made his way over to Leonardo's table in the corner and sat himself down.

'Bad news,' he grumbled.

'What? Is Bernard not in the city?' asked Leonardo.

'Oh, he's here alright,' replied Sebastien. 'But he's surrounded by twenty knights.

'Shit. Where?'

'He's gathering his forces to him in an encampment outside the walls, to best decide how he'll combat Henry. At present, Bernard is with the Bishop, but he'll be joined by some lesser nobles who'll bring their own men. And then, of course, there's your friend Gaillard, who has a small force of his own. In two days, this place will be teeming with rebels.'

'I see. So it's now or never,' Leonardo concluded grimly.

'That's about the gist of it,' Sebastien agreed. 'In essence, we have two days to kidnap a vicomte from an armed encampment of God knows how many men, and successfully escape with him through fifty miles of hostile territory.' There was a pause as the two of them contemplated the difficulty of the task before them.

'Shit,' Leonardo said again into the silence.

'Indeed.' Sebastien scratched the stubble on his chin. 'I may have a solution, however.'

Leonardo leant forward in his chair. 'Let's hear it then.'

'We are ordained priests, are we not?'

'We are,' Leonardo confirmed with a nod. It was true; all agents of the Order were confirmed as practising priests once their training was complete, for they were, after all, men of God.

'And what is it priests do?' Sebastien pressed, the hint of a smile on his lips.

'Preach?' Leonardo tried.

'That's right. I say, we give the vicomte a sermon,' Sebastien said with a grin.

Bernard de Bouville's encampment was situated a short way upriver from Ste-foy-La-Grande. Evidently, the soldiers had not wanted to bathe in the filth that tended to float downstream from riverside settlements, opting instead to camp upon several fields by the woodlands at the edge of the villagers' settlements, the steeple of Ste-foy-La-Grande's church visible in the background.

Leonardo remarked again at what a beautiful part of the world it was, as they approached with their horses. Golden meadows of wheat shimmered in the afternoon breeze as the soldiers lounged around under the sun by their tents, fiddled with their equipment or prepared supplies. There was no great sense of urgency amongst their ranks, however, for they knew that any hostile forces were at least two days' march from their position, and they could yet enjoy the peace of the day.

Opposite, a neat orchard of apple trees was planted and a group of peasants were milling amongst their trunks with barrows and sacks, shaking the branches so that the greenish-red fruit fell to the earth with soft 'thumps' before being collected for the annual cider brew. Behind the camp, where there was not crop or harvest, rich woodland covered the ground and birch, oak, beech and pine swayed gently, the faintest hint of yellow beginning to appear on their golden-green leaves.

The military camp was picketed with lookouts, and already the comings and goings from knights, men-at-arms, horses, oxen and carts had beaten away the grass, creating a track leading to its heart. Two soldiers stood guard, with bored expressions on their faces as they leant on their spears.

The first straightened, eyeing the two approaching churchmen suspiciously as they rode up.

'No further, fathers!' he declared, looking the newcomers up and down. 'Official business only within the camp.'

Sebastien and Leonardo dismounted, enabling the guards a better look at them. Both were dressed in their most pristine priests' robes, cowls and all. Leonardo had an expensive strip of wide purple cloth tied around his waist in a sash, mimicking the colours worn by the priests in the Papal States.

Sebastien gave the guard who had spoken a withering look. 'Oh, don't be tiresome!' he said, with all the confidence of a man speaking to one below his social station. 'Let us through so we might be about our business!'

The guard bristled indignantly. 'I don't know what your business is, father, but I have my orders. I—'

Sebastien cut him off. 'Excuse me! But do you know who this is?' He gestured to Leonardo, with a pointed look toward the guard, his voice hitting the perfect tone of righteous indignation. The guard paused as he shot a baffled look from one priest to the other.

'No. Should I?'

Sebastien gave an exasperated sigh. 'This is an emissary sent by the Pope himself, straight from the Vatican no less. He has a message to convey to your Lord Bernard. I trust the Vicomte Bernard is here, is he not?' Sebastien made a show of looking over the guard's shoulder into the centre of the camp.

The poor guard looked awfully confused. 'But..' he stammered. 'From the Pope, you say?'

'Yes, the Pope!' Sebastien's voice took on a condescending tone one might use to lecture an unruly child. 'Do you know who that is? Would you like me to inform your Lord of how his men gave the Pope's messenger such a rude welcome? Well?'

Leonardo took his cue and blessed the soldier in Italian, making the sign of the cross before him for good measure.

The flabbergasted guard seemed not to be able to speak for a moment, but he managed to collect himself somewhat and blustered, 'Alright, alright! No need for that. The Lord Bernard ought to be in his command tent back there. It's the big red one.'

'Well now, that wasn't so hard, was it!' Sebastien, the pompous priest, chided the man as he grumbled and stepped aside, allowing the two of them to pass.

As soon as they had led their horses out of earshot, Leonardo muttered, 'You were quite good at that.'

'I know,' Sebastien said with a smile. 'Here, let's stable the horses first. Then we can get to the hard part.'

The first phase of their plan had gone off without a hitch. However, as Leonardo and Sebastien secured their horses in a paddock that served as a temporary stable, they both knew the difficult part was yet to come and was as much a gamble as the first.

They made their way back through the camp, trying to look as though they belonged there, but elicited a few curious glances from the soldiers, nonetheless. The camp was not gargantuan and housed perhaps a hundred or so men, who milled about carrying out their various duties, and it was not hard for them to spot the command tent.

'Remember, for this next part, just follow my lead and I'll react to the situation as it comes,' Sebastien said in a low voice.

'So, you're improvising?' Leonardo asked.

Sebastien paused and cocked his head to one side. 'Yes, I suppose I am.'

A moment later, they had reached the large red tent, where the banner of the house of Bouville hung loose from atop a lance planted into the earth. A long-haired knight stood, half armoured, at the entrance eating an apple. He looked the pair of them up and down as they approached.

'Who the bloody hell are you two?' he asked, taking another bite of his apple as his gaze fixed on Leonardo's purple sash.

Sebastien cleared his throat. 'We have a message from the Pope himself addressed for the Vicomte!' he declared importantly.

The knight shrugged and nodded toward the entrance flap, which was propped open with a wooden pole to allow the light to enter. Inside, several men could be seen poring over a campaign table, deep in discussion.

'You'll find my Lord there, fathers.'

'Thank you,' Sebastien said, sharing a look of apprehension with Leonardo before they ducked inside.

The command tent was typical of campaigning armies. The interior was spacious and filled with various items of furniture: a writing desk, chairs and a campaign table upon which a map of Gascony lay spread. There were also a number of chests lining the walls that would have been filled with parchment and paper listing the names of the men under the vicomte's employ, equipment that he had at his disposal, correspondences from the other rebel lords – and, of course, gold to fund the campaign. Candles provided extra light here and there, and soft furs lay over the chairs for comfort. Briefly, Leonardo wondered how many such tents dominated the numerous other rebel encampments set up around Gascony.

Three men looked up from the table. Two were clearly more household knights; weathered-looking soldiers that had seen their fair share of war. The third was undoubtedly Bernard de Bouville, for he was dressed in a wonderful cloak of blue lined with an expensive-looking wolf pelt that hugged his shoulders. Beneath, he wore an armoured brigandine, the unblemished metal scales of which shone in the light.

Bernard was an average-sized man of around forty. His dark brows furrowed at the intrusion, as the conversation he had been having with his knights ceased at the disruption.

'Yes?' he asked in confusion, looking up at the two newcomers.

Leonardo spread his arms wide and declared a greeting in Italian to the vicomte, laying on a thick accent for authenticity, which he followed up with a deep bow. He breathed a sigh of relief that there were no other churchmen in the tent besides themselves, for, if there were, Leonardo doubted their guise would have held up to a great deal of scrutiny.

Sebastien cleared his throat. 'This is Father Benedict, Lord Vicomte. He has been sent to you to deliver a message from the Pope himself. I have been tasked by the Bishop Odo to bring him to you and to translate his words, should it please you.'

There was a stunned silence in the command tent as the three men processed the information. Bernard de Bouville's dark brows threatened to disappear into his thick head of curly black hair.

'From the Pope?' he asked incredulously. Though Bernard was a high-born noble, being sent a message from the Pope himself was not only a rarity, but an honour of the highest degree. Usually, the Pope would only deign to address Kings, Queens, Emperors and Dukes. Even men as important as Bernard were well off his radar.

'Indeed, Lord Vicomte,' Sebastien continued seriously. 'Father Benedict here has ridden directly to you from Rome to be before you today.'

The look of surprise had not faded from Bernard's face. 'Well, what does the Pope want with me, Father Benedict?' he asked Leonardo.

Leonardo played his part dutifully and shot a questioning look in Sebastien's direction.

'Ah, Lord Vicomte,' Sebastien said with an amused smile. 'Father Benedict doesn't speak a word of Frankish, I'm afraid, so I'll be translating for him. And, err, I dare say he's rather thirsty after such a long journey...' Sebastien trailed off and looked pointedly at Lord Bernard.

'Ah, yes, forgive me. Where are my manners?' said Bernard. 'Let's get this man some wine!' He snapped his fingers and one of his knights turned and strode over to the writing desk, where a jug of wine stood with several cups. He hastily poured a cup and stroke back to Leonardo, who maintained the disguise with his best pious smile, graciously accepting the cup that was offered to him, before the knight poured one for Sebastien, too.

The two knights and Lord Bernard waited impatiently, each staring intently at Leonardo as he took a sip of the rich wine. He prolonged the silence a little, nodding his head in appreciation of the wine, before he began to ramble away in Italian, using elaborate hand gestures to emphasise a point to the listening men before him, who clearly did not understand a word.

He finished a minute later, and the three watching heads turned in unison to face Sebastien, waiting for the translation. Though Leonardo's heart hammered from the stress of their deception, he had to stifle a grin as Sebastien puffed out his chest and began to translate the fiction.

'The Pope has heard of your rebellion in Gascony, Lord Vicomte, and sends his deepest sympathies to your cause.'

'He does?' Bernard asked in disbelief. 'I thought the Pope would take Henry's side?'

Sebastien shook his head. 'On the contrary! Our Father in Rome is all too aware of the mistreatment the men of Gascony have suffered at the hands of the English crown. He shares your indignation, Vicomte!'

Bernard rubbed the short beard on his chin. 'How interesting, I had no idea,' he mused. 'But why does the Pope address me?'

'Ah, well, my Lord Vicomte, the excellent lineage of your family is known to the Pope, and he therefore directs his message to the man he believes ought to be the leader of this war against the English king.' Sebastien continued without missing a beat, laying the flattery on thick.

It worked, too, for Lord Bernard had puffed out his chest pompously. 'I suppose it should come as no surprise that the Pope would favour me over the other vicomtes,' he said, though Leonardo could see his surprise was poorly disguised. 'There is no leader of the rebellion per se, for Gaston is merely a mouthpiece. However, if there were, I see no reason why it should not be me...' Bernard trailed off, his mouth twisting into a smile at the thought, and his two knights nodded vigorously in approval.

'Yes, of course, Lord Vicomte,' said Sebastien. 'In fact, that brings us to the purpose of Father Benedict's visit. He wishes to discuss with you, on the Pope's behalf, the possibility of sending Papal funding to support yourself and the rebellion in order to punish the mischievous King Henry for the neglect of his loyal subjects.' He delivered the line expertly, putting the slightest emphasis on 'Papal funding'.

It was not lost on Lord Bernard, for he breathed, 'Papal funding?' His eyes glazed over in a look of wistful greed.

Just then, Leonardo touched Sebastien's arm and interjected with another babbling stream of Italian.

'What's he saying?' Lord Bernard asked, looking up sharply at Leonardo, then back to Sebastien, having no clue as to the words he was speaking.

'Ah, yes, apologies Father Benedict,' said Sebastien, turning back to the vicomte. 'It is no secret, Lord Vicomte, that the Pope is extraordinarily fond of the late saint Hugh of Cluny.'

'Really? I had no idea!' Bernard replied and, again, Leonardo struggled to hide his amusement. Their guise had clearly fooled the vicomte and he hung on Sebastien's every word.

Sebastien nodded knowingly. 'Yes, he is, and he has it on good authority that Hugh took his monastic vows in a village two miles south of here before relocating to Cluny. The Pope laments that he could not visit such a place of holy significance himself, as his duties keep him well occupied in Rome. Instead, he has instructed Father Benedict here to come in his stead and relay to him a description of the place. I thought we might discuss the matter of financial support along the way? Time is, after all, one thing none of us have an unlimited supply of.'

'Certainly!' Bernard said at once, ignoring the uneasy looks his household knights gave one another at the thought of allowing their master to travel the roads at such a time as this. One of them leant in to whisper something into his ear, but Bernard waved his hand in dismissal. 'Bah! Nonsense! Henry's forces are far from here yet, I'm sure there's no danger. Come then, Fathers! Let's be on our way!' Lord Bernard declared with an accommodating smile and gestured for Sebastien and Leonardo to follow him to their horses.

Outside, one of the knights whistled to several of their waiting fellows, and Leonardo's heart sank as three more armoured men stood from around a campfire and joined the small party as they made their way to the horses. *No matter*, he thought, *between the two of us we can deal with the extra men.*

A minute later, the small party was saddled, mounted and riding from the encampment at a lazy walk as Bernard sat himself between Sebastien and Leonardo, asking the would-be translator all sorts of questions to direct toward Father Benedict. Two of the knights took the vanguard, while the remaining three guarded their Lord's rear and scanned the road ahead as well as the trees that flanked them, searching for any danger to their master, for they were at war after all. Little did they know that the real threat was already amongst them.

'Ask him, if you would, Father, how it is that the Pope came to learn of my family's fine lineage?'

Sebastien dutifully directed the question to Leonardo over their mounts, who gave a reply after pretending to think for a second.

'The Pope learnt of your history from the Duke of Flanders during his visit to Rome some five years ago. The duke holds your family in hight regard, too, Lord Vicomte.'

Bernard's eyes lit up. 'The Duke of Flanders!'

Leonardo grinned, thinking it had been all too easy to fool the vicomte, and he began to enjoy the ruse. They continued that way for a half hour or so, meandering down gentle country lanes under the canopy of trees, heading further from Ste-foy-La-Grande and its surrounding villages. The road was quiet now, and almost void of traffic.

'Here is as good a place as any,' Leonardo said to Sebastien in Italian and Sebastien nodded.

'What did he say?' Bernard asked impatiently.

'Father Benedict thinks that's a wonderful idea,' replied Sebastien. 'He added that the Pope would most certainly approve of the construction of a ship named after his favourite dog.' He turned to Leonardo and replied back in his own rudimentary Italian. 'I'll take the two at the front, if you take the three at the back?'

178

Leonardo nodded. 'That'll work.' He touched the hilt of his daggers hidden up his sleeves for the seventh time, making sure they were where he could reach them, and shot a glance over his shoulder to better gauge how he might dispatch Bernard's men. His heart pounded with the anticipation, and he saw, out of the corner of his eye, Sebastien stiffen in preparation for action as the vicomte chatted away.

But then, all of a sudden, the sound of galloping hooves met their ears and a dozen mounted knights erupted from the trees, surrounding the small party with canted lances, their faces covered by great helms and their limbs clad in maille. Horses whinnied and bucked, and both Leonardo and Sebastien tugged at their own horses' reins in confusion, as the vicomte lost all control of his own mount for a moment.

The knights circled them and one cried, 'Halt!'

The party was stopped in its tracks. The vicomte's knights had drawn their swords, but quickly realised they were surrounded and outnumbered, and that any attempt to fight would be futile. They looked to their lord for direction and, as the vicomte finally managed to calm his mount, he looked around with ruddy-faced anger at the armoured knights.

'Who are you?' he roared. 'Do you know who you're interfering with?'

The nearest rider kicked his mount forward to face them, and came to a halt a yard away before removing his helm.

Sebastien cursed as the familiar, triumphant face of Gaillard Solers revealed itself and locked eyes with Leonardo. Leonardo's heart sank and he cursed himself for having antagonised the young man back in Bordeaux. The smug look of victory displayed on Gaillard's face made Leonardo seethe with anger.

'Solers!' Lord Bernard exclaimed. 'Is this some kind of joke?'

'Forgive me, Lord Vicomte, but these men you are travelling with are not who they seem,' Gaillard said with a silky drawl, his eyes never leaving Leonardo's.

'What the devil do you mean? This man has been sent from the Pope himself!' Bernard indicated Leonardo.

'Lies, Vicomte,' replied Gaillard. 'They're all lies!'

'But… but… the message was meant for me. From the Pope!' The utterly confused Lord Bernard and his knights were looking from Gaillard to Sebastien and Leonardo and back, all of them suddenly unsure of what Bernard's trusted ally was telling him.

Gaillard Solers snapped his fingers. 'Search them!'

Several horsemen kicked their mounts forward to apprehend the two churchmen. Leonardo saw Sebastien's hand move to his side, where his short sword was concealed. Leonardo shook his head warningly, for even they could not hope to win against so many well-armed men.

Rough hands patted them down and their weapons were soon discovered and confiscated. Lord Bernard watched in a horrified silence as Gaillard's men revealed their deception, and Leonardo and Sebastien resigned themselves to their capture, neither seeing any chance of escape.

It slowly began to dawn on the vicomte that they had made a fool of him, and his face reddened in a mixture of both rage and embarrassment.

'You treacherous bastards!' he spat.

'Oh, come now, Lord Bernard, we were getting on so well,' Sebastien chided, the mischievous grin returning to his face. Leonardo knew him well enough to understand that cracking a joke was his way of making light of a particularly bad situation.

But the vicomte did not see the funny side. He was apoplectic with rage.

'Would Henry stoop so low as to employ such skulduggerous tactics!' he roared at them. 'What a bloody waste of my time! Solers, make sure these swine suffer, will you?'

'With pleasure,' Gaillard cooed. 'You're not really churchmen at all, are you, friends?' He smiled nastily at them.

'Actually—' Sebastien began, but Leonardo gave him a sharp kick him from his horse, and he fell silent as the knights manhandled them, winding lengths of rope around their wrists and pulling them taught.

'Unbelievable!' the vicomte seethed. 'Come!' he called to his knights, not wanting to prolong his embarrassment any longer. He shot a last look of pure venom at his deceivers, before turning his mount and galloping away with his knights, leaving Leonardo and Sebastien in the custody of Gaillard Solers.

'Well, well, how fate has an interesting way of shaping our destinies,' said Gaillard. 'I thought I'd recognised you at the gates of Ste-foy-La-Grande. Two for the price of one!' he cackled, as he turned his mount and allowed his men to lead the now bound Leonardo and Sebastien away into the trees.

Leonardo exchanged a gloomy look with Sebastien, who grimaced. Fate had not gone their way at all, it would seem. Their mission's objective was galloping away up the road and they had allowed themselves to be captured by a malicious young noble, who not only harboured a deep animosity for them, but knew they were enemy spies to boot.

It would be a miracle if they lived to see the morning.

Chapter 15

TWELVE YEARS AGO

'Do you want to know why we are here? Do you want to know why the Order chose to build its training facility here two hundred years ago?' Magnus paced before the altar in the chapel, the sound of his boots hitting the stone floor echoing from the walls.

Leonardo, Sebastien, Ebel, Sigbald and Alof sat upon the benches in the first row, listening carefully. It had been over a week since Njal had left and each of them felt a vacuum created in their group from his absence. This had been the first time since that Magnus had taken them for one of his 'sermons' in the chapel – if you could call them that. Usually, the sermons all followed a similar theme; he would teach them of the balance that was the Order's goal to maintain, and why it was so important for Christendom that they serve the greater good.

That day was different, however. None of their instructors had ever told them why it was that the monastery was located so high in the mountains, in an almost impossible to reach location, completely isolated from the rest of the world. Leonardo had wondered, more than once, why the Order's agents were not trained in a secluded farmstead in the plains of northern Italy, or somewhere else with a far more temperate climate. He waited for Magnus to continue.

Magnus glared around at them all in his usual manner, one of his bushy white eyebrows raised as he checked that they were all listening closely.

'The Order chose this place because it is hell.' His usual harsh, gruff voice lowered to barely a whisper and the initiates had to lean in to hear.

'This place,' Magnus spread his arms wide, 'represents suffering. These mountains want to kill you. They're dangerous, make no mistake. That cold that you can feel gripping your bones, it can kill you just as effectively as any blade or arrow, as you have seen. You see, to be an agent in the Order of The Hand of God requires more than just brute strength.'

He continued to pace before them, his voice rising a little. 'That's what the other holy orders exist for; hot heads capable of naught but fighting. The Order of The Hand of God, however, demands that you be... *more.*'

Magnus put emphasis on the last word and began to tap a finger to the side of his head. 'The Order requires you to use this. You have to think. That's what the mountains do, they require you to think to survive. Just like you will have to do, should you graduate and return to your masters. You will surely have to use your minds whilst being hungry, tired and cold.'

He turned away from them, his hands on his hips, to face the great gilded silver cross hanging on the wall. 'That's what we are trying to teach you to do here. If you can survive this place, you can survive most.'

Magnus turned back to them. 'Your suffering does not go unnoticed. God sees all. He knows that you sacrifice in his name, that you suffer for his glory. But you should not do so blindly or without purpose. You should do it because it will make you strong, because it forces you to use your minds.'

Magnus sighed as his charges looked up at him silently. 'You have all had the opportunity to flee this place, though none of you have done so, despite the fact that it can be hostile and miserable. Have you ever asked yourselves why?'

The initiates exchanged questioning looks with one another. The conversation in the bunkhouse had, on occasion, turned to their individual motivation. Interestingly, however, despite the loss of Gabriel and Njal, the thought of abandoning their mission here had never crossed their minds. Perhaps Gabriel was part of the reason, Leonardo theorised. Perhaps God had punished him for losing faith and opened up the earth to eat him. Or perhaps he had merely slipped.

Leonardo knew he had his own motivation for staying; as far as he was concerned, he had a debt to repay to God and sins to atone for. He would never leave. Besides, where else would he go? He knew that Sebastien had similar reasons, and the others, too. Something had pulled them all here, something had weaved their fates together. And Magnus seemed to know it.

'I think, the reason you are all still here,' he continued, 'is because, deep in your hearts, you have the desire to serve a higher purpose. You know that, if you left, you could return to your old lives as… what, beggars? Thieves? You would be nobody and nothing. But you must have realised by now that this suffering is an opportunity for you to do more, to be more.'

Magnus looked at each of them in turn. 'But to do that, you have to use this.' He tapped the side of his head again, hammering the point home. 'Have you understood?' he asked.

'Yes, Teacher,' the initiates echoed in unison, as they realised it was not a rhetorical question.

Magnus raised a bushy white eyebrow once more and grunted a 'Hmph!' before adding, 'Well, we'll soon see about that, won't we?'

Leonardo felt the air changing and smiled. Spring would soon be upon them in earnest and, with it, warmer temperatures. He longed for the sweltering summer days he had always taken for granted, to train in weather so hot he would have to take his shirt off lest he soak it with sweat. The idea alone was almost enough to warm him.

He sighed. That wouldn't happen just yet, however. It was March and, though not so harsh as January had been, it was still brutally cold at night. A more intense sun had brought other dangers, too; Magnus had been warning them of the heightened possibility of avalanches and what to look out for.

He had been drilling it into them during their latest theory lessons until they were almost bored of hearing, 'Cornices, look out for those,' or 'and sudden changes in temperature, and rocky patches on the mountain above,' or 'avoid traversing steep inclines in the afternoon when the sun's been out for a while.'

Yet, they would all happily embrace the risk if it meant being a little warmer. Ebel's log pile had almost run out, and they had halved the nightly ration so that they woke in the bunkhouse each morning shivering, despite the layers wrapped around them.

Sometimes, however, they had found that the days of late could actually be pleasant, especially when the sky was void of cloud, and nothing stopped the sun from gracing their skin.

They trained in the yard on such a day, stripping back to just two layers as Walter instructed them on the use of a bow. They had been incorporating all sorts of weaponry into their training of late, archery included, and also the use of several very modern and expensive-looking crossbows, with intricate mechanical winching systems that Leonardo found fascinating.

Walter clearly preferred a regular longbow, the dreaded weapon of the English skirmish troops that he was able to shoot at an impressive rate. The first time Leonardo had tugged on its string he had grunted in frustration, finding that it was far more difficult than Walter had made it look, and it had taken some weeks for his muscles to grow accustomed to.

'Come on, Ebel!' Sigbald chuckled as he watched his comrade struggle with the weapon. 'Just pull it back!' He flashed a grin and shot an arrow into a straw target twenty paces away.

Ebel flashed him a look of annoyance as he released his own arrow, though at nowhere near the speed of Sigbald. 'These damn things are heavy. It probably takes years to master them,' he mused, turning the weapon over in his hands.

Walter sidled over to inspect their technique. 'Years? It can come quicker than that if you put your mind to it, boy. Again!'

Walter gave an exasperated sigh as Ebel missed the target completely with his next arrow, and spent a minute or two correcting his technique.

'Hey, Leo!' Sebastien nudged Leonardo and nodded to his painted straw target. 'I'll bet you my chunk of bread tonight that I can get a bullseye with this one.'

'Yeah, right!' Leonardo scoffed. 'Let's see it then!'

Sebastien turned to his target and licked his lips with concentration, fitting an arrow onto his bowstring and holding his fingers either side of the shaft. Then, taking a deep breath, he drew back slowly, his eyes never leaving the red-painted dot at the centre of the target. With a grunt, he let the arrow fly and it thudded into the target a handspan from the centre. Sebastien frowned.

'Ha! Not bad, though,' Leonardo allowed. 'Let's see if I can do any better...' He took aim and loosed. Leonardo's arrow thudded into the straw an inch closer to the centre than Sebastien's and he turned to his friend with a triumphant grin.

'Alright, alright, you win.' Sebastien rolled his eyes as Walter appeared behind them and spotted their work.

'Acceptable,' he grunted. Leonardo and Sebastien exchanged a pleasantly surprised look; coming from Walter, it was the equivalent of the highest praise. They didn't have time to enjoy it, however, for Walter was standing before them and gestured for them to lower their bows.

'That's enough for now,' he said. 'Unstring your bows, but do not pack them away. I want you to hold on to them. Our food stores are depleting, and Magnus has asked that I send you all out to score us some game. Alone, mind. I don't want to see you leaving together; you're supposed to be thinking for yourselves, after all. Now, clear off! I expect a feast on the table by tomorrow evening!' And with that, he left them, slinking away back to the great hall.

Once dismissed, the initiates excitedly rushed back to the bunkhouse to discuss their latest mission. Lately, it was not unusual for them to be given tasks to complete out on the mountainside on their own, whether that be to simply reach a certain point and return, or fetch some commodity that daily life at the monastery required. It was all a test of a sort, they knew. But they had never been asked to hunt yet.

'Ah, it's been too long since I hunted!' Sebastien said enthusiastically. 'I never got to use a bow like this, though…' He ran a hand down the bow's shaft, as Alof sat down heavily onto his bed.

'What a pain!' Alof complained. 'Anything we catch we'll have to haul back up. Maybe it's better to pretend we didn't catch anything?'

Ebel scoffed. 'You know full well that if we return empty handed, Walter will have us strip naked and lie in the snow until our balls turn to ice!'

Alof sighed. 'I suppose you're right. Where's the best place to go, anyhow?'

Sigbald piped up, his back to them all as he rummaged around the wooden chest at the foot of his bed. 'Down in the valleys, for sure. I've seen mountain goats come this high, though it's rare. We could be waiting all day for them.'

'Aye,' Sebastien confirmed. 'Where there's trees, there's game. We'll find something.'

'Hey, can anyone feel it getting warmer?' Ebel asked the room. 'By God, what I wouldn't give for it to be warm enough to sleep at night with the covers off…'

Sigbald whistled through his teeth. 'Now there's a dream. Say, Ebel, if you had to choose right now between a hot summer's day or having a plump young maiden naked in your bed, what would you choose?' he asked with a wicked grin.

Sebastien barked with laughter as he wrapped up a sheaf of arrows. Ebel shot him a disapproving look.

'That's not a particularly pertinent question,' he replied.

Sigbald rolled his eyes. 'Suit yourself. What about you, Alof? What would you choose?'

Alof gave the question a considerable amount of thought, stroking his chin seriously as if he were contemplating a deep, philosophical concept.

'I'd take the plump maiden,' he said eventually and grinned.

Sigbald laughed and clapped. 'That's the spirit!'

Sebastien raised his hand and asked, 'Can I have both?'

'Both?' Leonardo asked with a grin. 'That sounds too good to be true!'

'Exactly, too good to be true for a bunch of misfits like us,' Alof said, flopping back onto his cot and pulling a cover around him. 'I'm not sure I can even remember what a woman looks like!'

'Hey, Alof, don't you need to prepare your gear?' Sebastien asked, glancing over at Alof's bow that lay across the floorboards where he'd left it. It had been a lesson that, for most of them, had been learnt the hard way – prepare and maintain your equipment when you have the chance, or it could cost you.

'I'll do it in the morning,' Alof yawned. Sebastien shrugged and turned back to his own pack. Alof was not stupid, and he was physically capable, too, but he had never been particularly industrious or energetic in the tasks that he was left to do on his own. He wasn't quite lazy, but would only do the bare minimum that was required, unless one of their teachers instructed him otherwise.

'Hey, what say we all walk down together tomorrow?' Sigbald asked the bunkhouse.

'You heard Walter,' said Ebel. 'He said we're to go alone.'

'Yes, but once we've passed down the track and are out of sight of the monastery, he'll be none the wiser!' replied Sigbald. 'Just once we get to the bottom of the valley.'

Ebel thought about that for a moment and could see no reason why it would be an issue. He shrugged. 'Alright, I'm in.'

'Absolutely!' Sebastien said enthusiastically. 'That'll be the first time we'll all have been out on the mountain together without the other lot.' He tipped his head in the direction of the great hall where their instructors resided.

And so it was decided. The next morning, they rose and prepared to leave. Pulling their cloaks about them, they collected their bows and trudged out into the snow where, under the watchful, beady-eyed gaze of Walter, they walked down the track, one by one at long intervals, until the monastery had faded from view.

Where the track meandered down around a hillock, they each waited until their group of five was reunited once again. The unusual absence of their superiors' solemn company, combined with the good weather and their unchecked, boyish camaraderie, meant that the five of them became almost giddy with the joy of their freedom.

Sigbald wasted no time tackling Ebel into a nearby snowdrift, making them all laugh. Ebel got him back by launching a snowball that exploded on Sigbald's forehead with a cloud of white powder. A minute later, snowballs were being fired in every direction amidst fits of breathless laughter as they chased one another, pelting each other with the makeshift projectiles.

Sebastien had made a little pyramid of snowballs and was hurling them at all of his fellows, while Alof wrestled with Sigbald as each tried to topple the other into the fresh powder, made all the more difficult through their fits of laughter. Leonardo and Ebel were standing at opposite sides of the track, trying to launch two snowballs simultaneously so that they might collide in mid-air. They succeeded, and the snowballs smashed together and vanished in a plume of crystallised flakes, and they threw their arms in the air and cheered, their mission quite forgotten.

It was a wonderful morning; the first time any of them had been allowed to offload some of the stresses they had endured that winter, and Leonardo had not realised how much he'd needed it. It was good to play.

Eventually, however, once they were all tired and out of breath, it was decided that they'd better get going down the track and focus on catching some game, lest they suffer Walter's wrath. They descended the mountain in good spirits, laughing and joking all the way. After an hour or so, they had reached the zig-zagging valleys, where the shelter of the cliffs allowed the trees to grow.

'Right, I suppose we'll have to split up now?' Ebel asked the group.

'Yes,' Sebastien confirmed. 'We won't catch anything if we're babbling together like this. We can meet back here in a few hours, though, and climb back up together?' They all agreed to that and parted ways.

Leonardo remembered a secluded valley to the south that had a good covering of trees and plenty of places for small game to hide. He strung his bow and made his way there, keeping his eyes open for any signs of movement. He saw plenty of birds circling above him, but they were too small a target for him to hit. Occasionally, he spotted a hare that would have been perfect, but he was too slow, or otherwise alerted them to his presence at the last minute by snapping a twig underfoot.

He was surprised to see just how much life there was now that they had travelled a considerable way down the mountain. It seemed that no one and nothing was as foolish as they to live so high as the monastery.

Leonardo was content to loop his way between the trees, making his way deeper amongst them, when he spotted his chance – a little marmot was sitting on a rock thirty paces away, licking its paws contentedly. It had not seen him.

Carefully, he brought his bow up and took careful aim at the small mammal. It was a long shot, but not an impossible one. He released. The arrow flew true and struck the marmot in the side, the impact causing it to fly from its perch and into the snow, killing it instantly. Leonardo smiled to himself. That would do the job.

He extracted the arrow and gutted the creature where it lay, ripping out the organs and intestines and flinging them onto the blanket of pine needles under a nearby tree, where some other scavenger would undoubtedly have them, before washing his hands in the snow.

Once done, he tied the marmot to his pack and began to make the journey back to their designated meeting place. He hummed cheerily on his way, happy enough to be out in such fine weather, for it was afternoon and the sun was warm enough for him to unclasp his thick cloak and pack it away.

Half an hour into the climb, a voice called out.

'Hey!'

Leonardo turned to see Sebastien stepping out from behind a boulder with a triumphant grin on his face. He jogged down the slope to Leonardo's side and turned, showing him the large hare he had slung on his back.

'Mine's bigger than yours!' he grinned teasingly as he fell into step beside his friend.

Leonardo shot the hare an unimpressed glance. 'What did you do? Bore it to death with that joke you always tell about the midget and the pig?'

Sebastien pretended to look offended. 'Actually, I told it that joke and it died of laughter.'

Leonardo chuckled and shot back, 'The hare didn't deserve to live, with a sense of humour like that!' Sebastien laughed and clapped him on the back, and the pair made their way amicably up the slope.

Leonardo decided that it felt good to have someone he could joke with, for he hadn't done that with anyone since his brothers had been killed, and that had been years ago now. Sebastien was a good friend, probably the best friend he'd ever had. He knew his time at the monastery would have passed with much more difficulty had Sebastien not been present.

They crossed another ridge and gazed up at the next part of the mountains they had to climb. There, a rocky gully wound its way up the mountain with sheer cliffs on the left. To the right, there was a much shallower route, but it would take them a good half hour longer, for the gully was a much more direct way to the top.

'We should go right,' Leonardo said immediately. 'It'll take longer, but that gully doesn't look safe. See that cornice to the left? Looks dangerous, especially in this temperature.'

'Aye,' Sebastien said, nodding in agreement. 'I was about to say the same thing. The long way up it is.'

On the way, Sebastien passed the time by turning the conversation to wrestling, and the pair discussed at length the best way to beat Drogoradz in their sparring sessions.

'You're not going to win out of brute force,' Leonardo reasoned. 'That's for sure. But he's not as flexible as you. Maybe you could get to his back and use one of those obscure ankle bars.'

'Hmm. Maybe,' said Sebastien. 'The problem's getting to his back in the first place, he's too good!'

Leonardo opened his mouth to reply, when a tiny voice called out from below. 'Hey! You two! Down here! Hey!'

The pair of them turned, squinting to see a small figure far below waving up at them.

'Ah, it's Alof!' Sebastien exclaimed as he waved back.

Alof shouted something up at them and hauled a shape from his shoulders into the snow. Sebastien cupped his hands to his mouth and yelled, 'What was that?'

'I said, look at this!' the tiny Alof shouted back up to them, pointing at the shape in the snow. 'I got a whole ram!'

'A whole ram!' Sebastien shouted back. 'Well done, brother! Now all you have to do is get it up here!' he chuckled under his breath.

'Wait for me there, then!' Alof shouted back and proceeded to haul the ram onto his shoulders once more. He stood at the point Leonardo and Sebastien had been minutes before.

Leonardo could see him scan the hillside for a route up. His eyes found the gully and Leonardo watched as he made for it, trudging up to the steep dip in the mountainside.

'Wait, Alof!' he called. 'Don't go left, go right instead. There's a cornice there that could go at any minute!'

'What?' Alof shouted back, his voice echoing slightly.

'I said, there's a cornice that could go at any minute!' Leonardo shouted. 'It could be dangerous!'

'Bugger that!' the tiny voice cried back from below. 'Going right will take ages! I'll take my chances!' Alof then set upon the gully once more, making his way deeper into its fold as Leonardo and Sebastien exchanged an uneasy glance.

Sebastien called down to their friend once more. 'Seriously, Alof, stay clear of the gully. Magnus warned us about this, remember!'

'Well, Magnus isn't here, is he!' Alof called back. 'And who are you, anyway? My mother? It'll be fine!' He was a good hundred yards into the gully now and, as Leonardo watched him climb, he felt a growing sense of trepidation knot his guts.

'Alof!' he called desperately, fearing what could happen. 'Go back! Please!' But Alof was ignoring him, his powerful legs pushing him further up into the trench of the valley.

Just then, movement caught Leonardo's eye. Some of the snow up at the cornice had moved, cascading several layers of it down the mountainside and into the dip of the gulley above Alof.

'Alof! Look!' he called out. However, Alof had already seen it and had frozen, watching the snow slide to a halt fifty yards above him. Leonardo and Sebastien watched in shock, waiting with bated breath for something else to happen. But the mountain was as still as they were, and it seemed as though that was all it had to offer.

Alof stood, craning his neck upward, looking to see if there was any more to come. When nothing else happened, he called back up to them. 'Alright, I'll take the right-hand path.'

The minor cascade had been enough to convince him, and Leonardo breathed a sigh of relief as he saw his friend turn around and make his way back down the route he had come.

For a moment, everything was fine; but then, from the top of the peak, there was a noise. Low and rumbling, it was not dissimilar to the sound of rolling thunder. Both Leonardo and Sebastien turned to look up the slope where, at the very top of the gully, an enormous mound of snow seemed to be shifting in slow motion. It began its journey down into the 'U' of the gully, dragging the surrounding snow with it until it became a slow-moving wave.

'Alof, run!'

Alof didn't need telling twice. He tossed the ram onto the ground and began to sprint down the slope, hoping to reach safety before the avalanche reached him. All Leonardo and Sebastien could do was watch in horror as the wave of snow, ice and rock grew in size and speed.

They had seen an avalanche once or twice, but always from afar; they'd never been close enough to truly understand their terrible power. The noise grew and the world was filled with it; a continuous rolling boom that drowned everything else out. Birds took to the sky in the valley below as Alof ran desperately toward the trees.

'Run!' Sebastien shouted at the top of his lungs, as if that would make a difference. The wave of snow was now travelling at a speed that far outmatched the sprint of any man, and was getting faster by the second. It cascaded down the gulley, bouncing off the sides and throwing great clouds of powder into the air as it pulled everything that was loose down with it, shrub and rock alike.

The power of the avalanche was God-like, and Leonardo could believe that such things were the product of divine intervention. He watched, unable to breathe, as the wave of snow and ice descended upon the tiny form of his helpless friend.

It charged, a colossal writhing beast of white, dwarfing Alof, who appeared like a fly next to a whale. And, in one horrible moment, Leonardo knew that there was no chance for Alof to outstrip it now.

The last he saw of Alof was of the German glancing over his shoulder in panic as he hurled himself down the slope, before he was engulfed by a gargantuan, angry titan of pure white that shot right over him, devouring him greedily. Then, Alof disappeared forever.

Leonardo and Sebastien watched, in open-mouthed horror, as their brother was swallowed by the massive wave of snow. They stood frozen to the spot as the avalanche ran its course, throwing debris deep into the valley beyond, flattening trees and sending boulders flying. The sheer destructive power was terrifying; thousands upon thousands of tons of snow, ice and rock had hurtled down the mountainside at the speed of an arrow in flight, and it took a minute before the avalanche had finally run its course.

Then, the valley fell as still and silent as it had been moments before, as if nothing had even happened and everything was back to normal.

'Alof!' Leonardo shouted, breaking the pair of them from inaction. In the same moment, they threw down their gear and ran back down the path they had climbed, fixing their eyes on the point they had seen Alof disappear.

Several minutes later and they had reached the spot, pouncing on the freshly moved snow and digging desperately with their hands.

'Alof!' Sebastien cried in the hopes that his call would be answered. 'Alof!' There was no reply.

Though the pair knew it was futile, they kept digging, for what else could they do? They kept going until their fingers hurt through their mittens and their clothes were soaked through. They tried different spots, would dig several feet deep in one for any signs of Alof's black robes, then move further down the slope when they saw none.

Leonardo and Sebastien must have dug fifty holes each – no, a hundred – before the sun began to set and the reality had sunk in that Alof, wherever he lay buried, was long since dead. The sheer mass of snow that had been shifted in the space of mere seconds was terrifying. After hours of hopeless digging, Leonardo stood and walked to where Sebastien knelt, clawing at the snow. He placed a hand on his friend's shoulder, who ceased at the touch.

'Come on,' Leonardo said hoarsely. 'We need to tell the others.'

Sebastien sniffed and wiped his face and Leonardo realised he had been crying. He helped his friend up and, together, they made their way back to the monastery in silence, the jovial mood of the day shattered as the mountain had claimed another one of their own.

It was dark by the time they pushed open the door to the great hall, causing the inhabitants within to look up in surprise. Ebel and Sigbald sat at a table at the back of the hall and were tucking into a goat's leg, biting the meat from the bones and grinning to one another happily. They turned to see their comrades enter and their smiles faded when they caught sight of their grim demeanours.

Walter, Magnus, Antonio and Drogoradz were all sitting at another table by the fire, discussing something amicably. When Leonardo banged the door open, Walter stood angrily and looked at them.

'Where in God's name have you two been? You ought to have been back hours ago!'

Neither Leonardo nor Sebastien spoke for a moment. They simply stood at the entrance, a look of utter sorrow displayed on their faces.

Magnus regarded them shrewdly for a moment. 'What is it, boys? Speak up!' he growled. 'Where is the other?'

Sebastien cleared his throat and swallowed before he muttered his reply. 'Avalanche. Alof was… he…'

'You saw it?' Magnus asked, eyeing them carefully. The room was silent as all eyes turned to Sebastien.

Sebastien nodded. 'We both did.'

'There was so much of it,' Leonardo said, blinking back tears in the dim light. 'Snow, I mean. We tried to dig him out. We tried for hours!'

Magnus stood and approached the pair of them as Leonardo's voice reached a desperate pitch.

'I'm sorry, Teacher. We tried to dig him out, we tried to—'

'Stop,' Magnus said softly, placing a hand on Leonardo's shoulder. 'Stop.'

Leonardo clamped his mouth shut, his jaw trembling.

Magnus looked at them each in turn. 'If it is as you say, then you could have dug for weeks and never found the body. He is gone.'

'We tried to tell him, Teacher,' Sebastien said, his voice cracking. 'We called out to him to take a different route, but he wouldn't listen!'

Magnus sighed and closed his eyes.

'Forgive us, we should have done more!' cried Sebastien.

Magnus opened his wrinkled eyes and looked at the pair of them with something akin to pity. 'There is nothing to forgive, it is not your fault. He would have been alone at some point and would have made the same decision. At least the pair of you were there to witness his fate. At least we know what became of him.'

The men of the monastery held a service for Alof in the chapel the next day. It was a solemn affair; yet, this time, there was no body to bury, just a memory. Magnus gave the burial rite regardless and they each knelt and whispered prayers for Alof, initiate and instructor alike.

Leonardo thought bitterly that he ought to have gotten used to saying goodbye to friends lately. Yet, that didn't stop his eyes from welling up once more and he felt the pain of Alof's loss in his chest, like something vital had been ripped from it. It didn't seem fair; Alof had been a good man, capable and strong. He had dedicated himself to a higher cause, but had fallen along the way.

For that, Leonardo hoped he would be awarded a place in heaven. If he was lucky, perhaps they would meet again in another life, where they might laugh and joke together once more. But, for now, Leonardo remained amongst the living and would have to honour his Lord in this life before that eventuality might come to pass.

No one in the bunkhouse spoke that night as they all climbed into their cots. No one had anything to say that the others did not already know. However, each of them kept stealing glances at the empty bed near the door. Alof should have been lying there; he should have been tucked away under his usual pile of blankets, snoring soundly. But he wasn't, and the blankets remained folded at the foot of the bed.

Leonardo didn't sleep for some time. What a journey this had been so far. What a misery! Who else would die before it was over? Himself? Emilio had never told him it might be this difficult. Had Emilio known what awaited him within the snowy peaks of the Pyrenees?

Leonardo shook his head. Of course he had; Emilio knew everything. Leonardo sighed.

The mountains had claimed another of their number and now only four remained.

Chapter 16

GASCONY

Leonardo shielded himself as best he could as Gaillard Soler's boot thumped into his side. Gaillard was out of breath and had been at it for some time already, though Leonardo had not yet given him the satisfaction of crying out in pain. Gaillard squatted down next to him in the dirt and Leonardo caught a glimpse of the red birthmark that worked its way up his neck and finished at his square jaw.

Gaillard pushed his medium-length chestnut hair from his face, so he could better see his captive. His handsome features were smug as he gazed down at Leonardo, who looked back with a pair of hard, green eyes that glowed in the darkness. Night had fallen and the light came from the flickering flames of the campfire that Gaillard's men had made in a secluded spot in the forest, where no one was likely to disturb them.

'I told you I'd get you back for touching me,' Gaillard smirked. 'How do you feel now, spy? I'll bet you feel like a fool. You certainly look like one!'

'Master Solers, if you are going to kill us, would you please do us the courtesy of getting on with it?' Leonardo replied dryly.

Gaillard stood and kicked him again. He carried on that way for a minute or so, kicking Leonardo as hard as he could, with Leonardo powerless to prevent it, since both his wrists and ankles were bound.

Again, he made no sound as the blows landed and had to bite his tongue to keep from crying out.

Sebastien lay several yards away, similarly bound, as Gaillard's men watched and laughed from around the fire. Sebastien's face was, by now, as bloody as Leonardo's, as they had both been beaten by Gaillard and his men. They had been stripped of their priests' robes and lay where they had been unceremoniously thrown into the dirt, naked from the waist up.

The young nobleman seemed to take great pleasure in Leonardo's suffering, for he had not yet tired of thumping him. By the campfire, the knights were busying themselves with two, long lengths of rope that they were tying neatly into nooses, testing them with a few tugs to ensure the knots held. Another of them was squinting up into the darkness at a thick branch, twelve feet from the forest floor and some yards from where the horses were tied, marking it out as a potential target to throw the nooses over.

Leonardo knew he and Sebastien didn't have long. As soon as Gaillard tired of beating him, they would be hung. He despaired inwardly. This was where he was going to die, then, ignominiously in a patch of forest in the middle of nowhere. Gaillard probably wouldn't even bother to bury them; he'd just let their corpses swing and the crows peck at them until their decaying flesh had fallen from their bones.

It was a harrowing thought, though Leonardo had long since hardened himself to the idea of his own death; for, in his line of work, it was unlikely he'd see forty. Gaillard kicked him again and Leonardo spat out a mouthful of blood and leaves, wiping away the dirt on the back of the hemp rope that bound his wrists together.

'There, how righteous do you feel now?' said Gaillard. Leonardo was momentarily dazed as Gaillard's boot connected with the side of his head again.

Then, from behind Gaillard, came a low chuckle. Gaillard turned and frowned, and when his men realised it was their second captive that had made the noise, they fell silent to listen, too. Sebastien continued to chuckle from the edge of the clearing where he lay, as if his circumstances were reversed, and he were the captor and not the captive.

'What's so funny?' Gaillard scowled, standing with his hands on his hips, looking down at Sebastien.

Sebastien smiled a bloody smile up at him. 'What a brave young man you are! Beating your restrained prisoners. How very courageous of you!' No one present could fail to miss the sarcasm dripping from his words.

'Be quiet, you wretch!' Gaillard sneered. 'What do you know about me? Silence, or I'll have you gagged.'

Sebastien chuckled again. 'You're such a big, grown-up boy. I bet you do Mummy proud! Look at you, gallivanting around with your merry band of pansies!' The men sitting by the fire stiffened in outrage at that. Gaillard strode over to Sebastien and delivered a brutal kick to his gut that only made Sebastien laugh harder.

What is he doing? Leonardo wondered. He was only going to prolong their deaths. Did Sebastien have a plan?

'Yes, that's it! Kick me, you cowardly brat! We all know you've never won a fair fight!' Sebastien managed to finish the sentence, just as his head rocked back from another blow.

Gaillard was seething in rage at the insult, struggling to maintain his cool at this slight on his honour. His knights around the fire watched the events unfold with interest, looking on to see how their leader would deal with their insolent prisoner.

'You don't know me, damn you! I'm no coward!'

'Really? Why don't you prove it then, you wet sissy!' Sebastien shouted defiantly up at him from the dirt. Leonardo began to laugh, finally understanding what Sebastien's intentions were. The two of them began to chortle together, despite their circumstances, making a mockery of Gaillard before his men, who watched in silence as their two, half-naked captives creased upon the forest floor.

Gaillard trembled with rage and kicked Sebastien again, but this only made him laugh all the harder, and soon both he and Leonardo were in hysterics.

'Shut your fucking mouths!' the youth hissed through clenched teeth, turning to stomp on Leonardo's head as his body racked with laughter.

'Here, Solers!' Sebastien called. 'I bet you wouldn't even have the balls to wrestle me before all these men!'

'Do you think I'm a fool?' Gaillard sneered. 'Untie you and give you a chance to escape? Ha!'

'You don't even have to untie me! I'd wrestle you with my arms and legs bound,' Sebastien challenged. For a moment, Gaillard Solers paused, and it seemed as though he were contemplating the bout. His men watched him closely and Leonardo could tell that they were keen on the idea; watching their young master wrestle a captive would surely add to the evening's entertainment.

But then, Gaillard had dismissed the idea. He snapped his fingers, gesturing to the knights.

'I thought not,' Sebastien taunted as the eleven knights stood from around the campfire and tossed the two nooses over the thick branch, where they hung, swaying ominously in the firelight. 'Not with those little rat-sized bollocks between your legs.'

By now, Solers was ignoring the taunts, but Leonardo could tell the words were getting under his skin.

Leonardo decided he would try a different tac. 'Why not accept the bout, Master Solers?' he called out for everyone to hear. Gaillard turned back to him, but said nothing, his eyes narrowed. 'I assume you've yet to fight in a battle with these men,' Leonardo continued, nodding toward the listening knights. 'Why not prove you're a worthy leader?'

There was a tense silence and Leonardo realised he'd hit the mark.

'What can it hurt, Master? They're bound, anyway...' muttered one of the watching knights, and Gaillard held up a hand to silence him, his mouth twitching in anger.

'I need to prove nothing,' he hissed, though Leonardo was unconvinced. He licked his lips, glancing up at the swaying nooses, and tried one last time.

'It is said your father Rostand died in de Montfort's custody.'

At that, Gaillard took a menacing step forward, as if he intended to kick Leonardo again. 'Don't you dare speak my father's name, you dog!' he shouted.

Leonardo held up his bound hands defensively and said hastily, 'Folk say he was a good man! An honourable man.'

Gaillard paused, and some of his men even nodded in acknowledgement.

'It is said he was poisoned as de Montfort's prisoner,' continued Leonardo, 'that he died poorly, and he was ill treated for a man of his station. Would you treat us the same and, in doing so, become as crooked as your worst enemy?'

Now, Leonardo knew he had *really* got to Gaillard. He watched as the young man wrestled with a wave of emotions, trying unsuccessfully to keep them from his face.

'But *you* are not honourable, like he was,' Gaillard snarled. 'You are not from great families or noble houses. Why should I show *you* any respect?'

'Aye, we may be scoundrels,' Sebastien interjected. 'But there's no reason for you to become as bad as de Montfort was. Prove that you're an honourable man! Fight me!'

The knights stirred behind the conflicted Gaillard, and another of them spoke up. 'Why not, Master? We can always hang the devils afterwards.' Leonardo heard the hopefulness in his voice and could tell that they were all dying for Gaillard to fight Sebastien.

Gaillard clenched his fists in frustration, clearly torn between wanting to kill Leonardo as soon as possible, and prove to his men that he was no coward. Eventually, he caved to their will and shouted, 'Fine!' His men cheered in response.

The men formed a half-circle to watch the excitement unfold, their faces full of glee. Gaillard unbuckled his sword and dagger, tossing the belt with them onto the earth by the fire. He unfastened his brigandine and lifted it over his head, along with his shirt of maille and padded gambeson, until he wore only trousers and an arming doublet.

Leonardo pushed himself up to his knees with a grunt to watch, as Sebastien hauled himself to his feet.

'Why not make this fair and untie me?' Sebastien gestured to the rope securing his arms and legs.

Gaillard hesitated, then gestured to one of his men. 'Free his legs, but keep his hands tied. He said he'd fight me bound, did he not?' He grinned as the knights laughed nastily, and one of their number stepped forward to cut the ropes from Sebastien's ankles.

Sebastien stretched his cramped legs, testing his weight on them and finding his balance. Leonardo watched him closely, keeping an eye on the sword belt that lay on the ground near the fire. He pursed his lips; it was closer to Gaillard's knights than it was to him.

'Best of three?' Sebastien asked with a cocksure grin on his face. Gaillard nodded and rolled up his sleeves to reveal powerful forearms.

The watching men cheered as the two began to circle one another, and Leonardo felt a pang of fear for Sebastien as it struck him that Gaillard might actually be rather good. The young nobleman looked comfortable enough as he sidestepped around the clearing, his hands stretched out before him, mirroring Sebastien's movements.

Sebastien licked his lips, his eyes wide with concentration. Though his hands were tied at the wrist, he held them out before him defensively, anticipating the attack that was sure to come. A hush descended on the watching men as Gaillard tensed, then leapt forward, closing the gap between himself and Sebastien, attempting to grab hold of the other man's wrists.

Sebastien shook him off and sidestepped back. There was an 'Ooooh!' of excitement from the watching knights as Gaillard grinned, deftly circling back around. Leonardo watched as Sebastien faltered and Gaillard attacked again. This time, he caught a hold of Sebastien and the two of them toppled onto the leaves with a thud, rolling around to the whooping cheers of Gaillard's men as they vied for position.

For a time, it was unclear who had the advantage, until Sebastien found himself on top of Gaillard and, with a grunt of effort, tried to clamp his hands around Gaillard's throat to suffocate him. Leonardo thought Gaillard was done for, but then the younger man bucked, rolled and pulled Sebastien from him and the advantage was lost. Gaillard's men cheered as he then mounted Sebastien, trapping his bound hands under his body as he manoeuvred around, eventually finding a binding lock on Sebastien's arm and twisting it painfully until Sebastien cried, 'Yield!'

Gaillard's men roared and stamped their boots as their leader rolled to his feet and spread his arms wide in victory, a triumphant smile stretching from one ear to the other. Leonardo frowned. What was Sebastien playing at? He was one of the best wrestlers Leonardo had ever seen; even bound, he would not struggle with most men. Was Gaillard really that good?

But then, as Sebastien made a show of panting and pushing himself wearily to his feet, he locked eyes with Leonardo for the briefest of moments and shot him a wink and Leonardo knew it was all a ruse.

'There, spy! Do you think I'm a coward now?' Gaillard gloated, his handsome features leering in the firelight.

Sebastien spat a mouthful of dirt. 'Careful, boy. You haven't won yet,' he replied and beckoned Gaillard on for a second time.

The nobleman narrowed his eyes at being referred to as such. One of his men shouted, 'Get the bastard, Master Solers!' as the others howled in delight at the spectacle unfolding before them. Leonardo saw a skin of wine being passed amongst them and wondered if any of them were already drunk.

Then, without warning, Sebastien had darted forward, surprising Gaillard. He caught him by the wrist, pulling the young man down before him so that Gaillard fell to one knee. Sebastien wasted no time in pressing his advantage and hopped around Gaillard, looping his bound hands over his head and falling back, so that they fell to the earth again. Gaillard had to fight to keep Sebastien from choking him, as the latter's legs locked around Gaillard's waist.

As they rolled around, Leonardo had to dive out of the way, for they almost collided with him, and used the opportunity to move a yard closer to the discarded sword belt. No one seemed to have noticed it, for the watching knights were far too engrossed with the bout to pay him any mind, and he risked edging a little closer.

Meanwhile, Gaillard was still struggling to pry Sebastien's hands from his neck and Sebastien seemed content to let him try for a while. The watching knights had subconsciously stepped forward, narrowing the circle so as to get a better look of what was happening. Eventually, Sebastien tightened his hold and Gaillard had no hope of escaping from the iron grip and tapped Sebastien's wrist in submission.

Sebastien released him and Gaillard let out a disgusted curse as the watching knights moaned in disappointment. Sebastien couldn't resist his own mockery and, with a gleeful grin on his face, he said, 'You can't even beat me with my hands tied! What do they teach you high-born whelps these days? Or did they have you sewing with your mother and sisters?'

Gaillard growled in anger. 'Again!' he shouted, readjusting his shirt where it had been torn in the fight.

'Come on, Master Solers! Kick his arse on this last one!' someone shouted.

'Aye, beat him quick, so we can hang the mouthy bastard!'

Leonardo moved a little closer still, his heart pounding with trepidation as he feared that, at any moment, one of the knights would glance over and discover his ploy. He looked around, searching their faces for any sign that they might have seen what he was up to, but again they were too enthralled with the fight. Leonardo was almost close enough to be able to lean over and grab the sword hilt where it lay. If he could only move just a little farther…

Gaillard was angry now and he leapt at Sebastien furiously, swatting away his attempt to catch his limbs and cannoned bodily into him, knocking Sebastien from his feet and falling on top of him. But Sebastien didn't allow the younger man to stay there for long; a second later, they were rolling around again and Gaillard's men cheered as the two fought for the advantage once more. Then, they had split apart and both were scrambling back onto their feet, panting and wary of their opponent. Leonardo was almost able to reach the sword now and his heart hammered in his chest with anticipation as he waited for the perfect moment to strike.

He exchanged a quick glance with Sebastien and gave him a brief nod he hoped the other had registered, for no sooner had Sebastien looked away than Gaillard had roared with anger and charged him again. This time, they remained standing and tousled violently, each trying to spin the other to the ground. The watching men shouted their encouragement to their leader, just as Leonardo reached for the sword belt.

Sebastien must have seen it, for a second later he had grabbed Gaillard by the shirt, spun him and caught him by the neck once more, the rope of his bindings biting deep into the soft flesh and making Gaillard splutter.

In the same moment, Leonardo had snatched the belt, leapt up to his feet and drawn the sword. There was a cry of alarm from the watching knights as they all dived for their weapons, the clearing exploding into a hive of activity mixed with shock, anger and confusion.

However, two of the men were already too slow and Leonardo had slashed at them, severing an artery of the first and blinding the second, using the distraction to hack at the rope between his legs. Gaillard was shouting in rage as he saw what was happening and struggled to free himself from Sebastien's grip, but Sebastien was too strong and he was no longer playing.

One of the knights had recovered and had drawn his own sword and advanced upon Leonardo, just as he had managed to shed the bindings from his ankles. Leonardo parried the oncoming blow, gripping the hilt of Gaillard's sword with both hands and praising God that the youth had good taste in blades, for it was both sharp and well balanced – and, in Leonardo's hands, utterly lethal.

The knight screamed in pain as Leonardo replied with his own lunge and the man reeled, clutching at his breast and howling as the blood began to soak his unarmoured shirt. Leonardo kicked the sword belt toward Sebastien, for the dagger was still sheathed upon it. Sebastien wasted no time in tripping Gaillard, falling on top of the young man with an 'Oof!'

Gaillard and Sebastien scrabbled for the dagger at the same time. Sebastien had to release his grip on the nobleman for a second, climbing his way up Gaillard's body and pushing his face into the dirt as he snatched the dagger from the other man's fingers, causing Gaillard to bellow in a muffled cry of outrage. Sebastien took the dagger, cutting away at his remaining bindings, as Gaillard struggled to dislodge him from his back.

On the other side of the clearing, the rest of the knights had rallied, and their weapons were drawn. Leonardo observed that not all had removed their armour and frowned at the added complication. Fortunately, none of the men had had time to replace their helmets or mailed gloves that protected their hands, though the steel shirts of maille were sure to make things more difficult. Leonardo would have to be careful, for he was still bare chested himself.

There was a series of clangs and metal clatters as he parried a blow and then another, and another. The remaining knights had begun to circle him, stepping over the bodies of their fellows who were either dead or crying out in pain at the wounds Leonardo had already inflicted. Leonardo was forced backward, attacking with his own strikes that either glanced uselessly from maille or caused minor wounds. At least they caused the knights to pause, for though they were many, they had already learnt to be wary of Leonardo's blade.

The knights closed in around him, spreading out and brandishing their weapons menacingly. These were no peasants; they were knights, heavily armoured and trained for war, and they would not baulk at one swordsman standing before them. With grim determination, they came forward and Leonardo readied himself for the attacks that would follow, realising that even he did not have much chance against them now that the element of surprise had been expended. It was only a matter of time until he would be overwhelmed.

'Stop!' a voice roared from behind him. Leonardo risked a glace over his shoulder and could see that Sebastien had a dagger pressed up against the red birthmark on Gaillard Soler's neck, its very tip already drawing blood, for it was buried under the skin of the youth's throat. Gaillard's eyes were wide with fear, and he cried out in pain as Sebastien twitched the dagger, causing another bead of blood to drip down the red skin of the birthmark.

Leonardo turned back to the knights to see them pause and falter in their advance. They exchanged questioning glances at one another at this development and none seemed to know what to do.

'Back!' Sebastien shouted. 'Stay back or I'll gut this fucking weasel, with God as my witness I swear I will!' The tone of his voice left no room for any doubt that Sebastien would do it, and the knights, seeing how Leonardo had already dispatched several of their number, had frozen with indecision.

'Back, damn you!' Sebastien shouted again and twisted his blade once more, causing Gaillard to cry out again and whimper with pain. That seemed to settle it, and the knights took a step back, giving Leonardo space to run toward the tree the horses were tied to and hack away at their ropes.

'Hey!' one of the knights shouted, taking a step toward Leonardo, whose blade levelled at the man the moment he had moved.

'Are they really worth dying for?' Leonardo asked him, nodding toward the horses. The knight stopped in his tracks, eyes fixed on the tip of Gaillard's sword that Leonardo held steady, the blood of his comrades dripping portentously from it.

Leonardo could practically smell the tension in the men before him. He could sense the adrenaline coursing through their veins. They were ready for a fight, and it wouldn't be long until one of them decided to forsake their leader and attack him.

'All of you, see sense!' he shouted to them. 'No more men have to die tonight. Make one wrong move, and my colleague here will take great pleasure in slitting the throat of your master. Then there will be two of us to fight.' Leonardo let his words sink in, watching the hesitation in the knights' faces as they stood with their weapons outstretched toward him. After seeing the way Leonardo had handled their fellows so easily, the thought of facing two such demons must have given them some doubt.

'Besides,' Leonardo added, 'if young Master Solers here dies, who will pay you?' He beckoned to Sebastien with his sword to come to him, and the latter shuffled awkwardly over with Gaillard still hissing in pain under the tip of his own dagger. Sebastien eyed the watching knights warily, scouting for any signs of movement, the grip on his blade solid and unflinching.

'I'll… get you for this!' Gaillard grunted through gritted teeth.

'Quiet!' Sebastien snapped as he reached Leonardo, who had presently untangled the horses and slapped the rump of most of the beasts, keeping two for themselves and causing the rest of the mounts to flee into the darkness.

'I swear I'll kill the pair of you!' Gaillard went on. 'When I'm finished with you, you won't—' However, he never got to finish his sentence, for Sebastien had struck him in the temple with the pommel of the dagger, making a sickening '*crack*' and the young man went limp.

At that, one of the knights made a start, but Leonardo roared at him. 'Back! Lest you want us to kill him for good!'

Sebastien hauled the unconscious young man onto the horse Leonardo held for him, hopping up nimbly and returning the tip of his dagger to the nobleman's throat, glaring menacingly at the group of knights.

'Toss me our weapons,' Leonardo commanded and, once he had been obeyed, hopped up onto his own mount. There was a pause as he surveyed the scene a last time, his eyes flitting over the glowering group of knights and those that were lying on the forest floor, clutching their wounds and crying out in pain. The nooses still dangled from the large branch, though it seemed that the knights would have to wait to prove their knots were up to the job, for their condemned men were free and had captured their leader.

'Come,' he muttered out of the corner of his mouth to Sebastien. 'Let's be gone.'

'Aye.' Sebastien hawked and spat before the armed men. 'The company here was getting tiresome, anyway.'

They pulled on their reins and galloped off into the trees, casting furtive glances over their shoulders as the knights stood around the campfire and faded from view.

A minute later, they found the road and Sebastien breathed a shaky breath, the adrenaline slowly leaving his blood. 'That was a close one,' he said, shaking his head incredulously.

'Too close,' Leonardo agreed after a short pause. 'It was a good idea. To goad the boy, I mean.'

Sebastien shot him a grin. 'Pompous little fool rose to it too easily!' he said, as he patted Gaillard's unconscious back.

Just then, Leonardo had a thought and broke into a smile, letting out a low chuckle of amusement.

'What?' Sebastien asked, glancing at his comrade from the corner of his eye.

Leonardo turned to him. 'Well now, your mistress said she wanted a nobleman to ransom, did she not? I wonder if the Solers' firstborn will do!'

Sebastien tipped back his head and roared with laughter into the night. 'Yes, perhaps not the one she wanted, but I think he'll do just fine!'

The two men grinned at one another and chuckled amicably as their horses took them westward under the silvery light of the moon.

Chapter 17

TWELVE YEARS AGO

Leonardo panted as he ran through the trees, snaking his way between the trunks and up the slope, his bare shoulders catching on the dry bark every now and again, causing bits of debris to stick to his tanned, sweat-covered skin. He gritted his teeth as his chest heaved, hearing Ebel and Sebastien hot on his heels behind him.

He darted out of the trees and onto the familiar, rough, rocky track that led up to the monastery. Stones crunched under his boots and the ground was almost entirely void of snow. It was a hot day, and they were all training bare chested, as they had been able to do the last few weeks; the skin on Leonardo's back had already turned a rich, golden bronze.

Spring had passed and summer had begun and, as the snow and ice had gradually retreated up the mountain, life was following in its wake. Just that day, they had spotted a herd of deer plucking at the flowers on the mountain slope, and a bear clawing at a tree trunk, too.

Leonardo ran up the track ahead of his brothers, trying to gain a lead on them. But Sebastien wouldn't be beaten that easily.

'Not... so... fast!' he panted between breaths. 'You're not... getting there... before me!'

Leonardo didn't respond, but increased his pace and shot back a smile, causing Sebastien to growl in irritation. The pair of them pulled away from Ebel and Sigbald, who took up the rear, and ten minutes later the buildings of the monastery were in sight.

'Ha!' Leonardo shouted triumphantly, but no sooner had he uttered it, than he felt a hand grab the waistband of his trousers and pull him back. He stumbled, to see Sebastien laugh as he took the lead.

'You little cheat!'

'Still ahead though, aren't I?' Sebastien cackled.

Leonardo redoubled his efforts and the pair came skidding to a halt, side by side, before Drogoradz and Antonio, who had been observing their ascent. The pair collapsed to the earth, panting and sweaty before their instructors.

'Hmm, not bad. Faster than before,' Drogoradz said, inspecting the candle marked with lines at set increments in the wax that gauged the time elapsed as it burnt. 'Up you get! Time for some sparring!'

'What? Now?' Sebastien asked incredulously. 'Can't we have a rest first, Teacher?'

'Ha!' Drogoradz barked as Ebel arrived, followed shortly after by Sigbald. 'That would defeat the point now, wouldn't it, young Sebastien! I want to see what you can do when you're spent!'

He tossed Sebastien and Leonardo a training sword each, which they caught. They then entered the sparring zone marked out in the yard by branches laid on the ground, and began to circle one another.

Since winter had ended, Leonardo had observed that their superiors were not quite so cold toward them. Drogoradz, for example, had actually bothered to learn their names. And, in the great hall during mealtimes, they were not reprimanded for talking amongst themselves as they had been at the beginning, though none of them could say exactly when this change had happened.

'Let's see if you're quick enough to beat me today, then!' Sebastien teased presently, causing Leonardo to smile, as he knew full well that Leonardo almost always won.

Leonardo dipped into a stance of readiness and faced off with Sebastien, who bared his teeth with mock ferocity. Sebastien took a tentative step forward and tested Leonardo with a thrust. It was deflected easily, and Leonardo reposted with his own toward Sebastien's thigh that the latter barely managed to leap back from.

Sebastien followed up with a flurry of neat thrusts in quick succession, displaying a fine martial prowess that any swordsman could be proud of. But Leonardo was simply too fast. With each attack, he stepped back, parried and dodged, goading Sebastien forward until his rear foot was inches from the sticks forming the boundary of the training area.

Thinking he had Leonardo cornered, Sebastien leapt forward with what ought to have been the finishing blow in the form of a crisp lunge to Leonardo's chest, but Leonardo was ready for it. He twisted to one side, surprising Sebastien and, in one fluid motion, deflected the thrust, chopping down sharply on Sebastien's exposed wrist.

Sebastien cried out in pain and dropped the wooden sword, shooting Leonardo a look of annoyance and massaged his wrist, knowing full well that, had the edge been steel, he might very well have been missing an extremity. Leonardo winked at him and bent to pick up the training sword, flipped it in his hand, and handed it, pommel first, to Sebastien.

'Fast enough for you?' he asked.

Sebastien shook his head with a rueful grin, snatching his sword back and making ready once more. 'Again!' was all he said.

They fought on, with Ebel and Sigbald sparring in the adjacent ring. Their instructors were giving advice from the edge, Antonio in the form of elaborate hand gestures that they had all grown accustomed to, while Drogoradz barked commands and criticisms through cupped hands.

The four of them moved with a new confidence, the blades feeling now like an extension of their arms as they whipped them through the air, the sweat dripping down their young, athletic bodies that had packed on a good deal of sinewy muscle since they had arrived. It could not be argued now that they were youths, for the rigorous physical activity had transformed them. Even Ebel was unrecognisable from the skinny young thing that had climbed the mountain almost a year prior.

'Good, Ebel, good!' Drogoradz called as Ebel managed to score a slash onto Sigbald's shoulder, causing the Dane to stumble in surprise. 'Remember to whip that arm back once you've made your attack, Sigbald. Linger too long and he'll punish you like that!'

Meanwhile, Antonio had tapped Sebastien on the shoulder and had made a rapid succession of hand gestures, pointing to Leonardo, then back to Sebastien and tapping his head.

'You want me to… anticipate his movements?' Sebastien asked. Antonio nodded rigorously and gave the thumbs up, gesturing for them to try once more.

Sebastien licked his lips and squared off to Leonardo once more. This time, he did a much better job of imagining what Leonardo's next move would be, delaying his defeat by several seconds more, yet the result was ultimately the same. Leonardo was too quick and too canny.

'Damn it!' Sebastien cried out in frustration. 'Again!'

Leonardo had come to learn that his friend was the type of man who hated losing. He knew that, if he let him, Sebastien would spar until he had scored a point, or until one of them dropped from exhaustion.

Leonardo sank down into a fighting stance once more, his sword held high in readiness. But, just as they were about to begin, Antonio placed a hand on Sebastien's chest and shook his head.

'What is it, Teacher?' Sebastien asked confused. Antonio held his hand out silently for his sword.

'Ah, I understand,' Sebastien said with a grin, knowing that Antonio wanted to try. Sebastien loved it when Leonardo and Antonio sparred, for their silent instructor was the only person that could beat Leonardo, and Sebastien took great pleasure in seeing his friend struggle against the master.

Leonardo grinned begrudgingly, for he had never beaten Antonio, not even once. However, he recognised that the man was a phenomenal swordsman and knew that, if he wanted to improve, Antonio was his best chance. Drogoradz had barked at the other two to take a break and, a moment later, he, Ebel, Sigbald and Sebastien had all stopped to watch the two Italians face one another.

Antonio rolled up his sleeves and shot Leonardo a pointed, questioning look, that Leonardo had come to learn meant, *Are you ready?*

Leonardo took a deep breath, blowing the air back out through his cheeks to calm himself, before he nodded. Antonio began to circle him, not yet bothering to adopt a fighting stance, his sword hanging loose by his sides as his dark eyes fixed on Leonardo's. He moved with the easy confidence of a predator, as agile as a cat.

Leonardo took the centre and decided to wait until Antonio made his move. He didn't have to wait long for, without warning, Antonio had sprung into action a second later, closing an impossible gap of several yards in one great bound, the tip of his sword aimed straight for Leonardo's face.

Leonardo barely managed to duck and recover as Antonio paced around him once more, the hint of a smile playing on his lips that gave the impression he could have ended Leonardo then and there had he wanted to. He smoothed his straight, black hair back over his head.

Leonardo gritted his teeth and waited. Another attack came. Antonio moved incredibly fluidly, using such flawless technique that Leonardo would have found quite beautiful to behold were he not on the receiving end of it. He parried and stepped back, barely managing to keep up with the master.

Once, during a lightning-fast chain of strikes, he thought to counterattack, but played into his opponent's hand and was jabbed in the ribs by the tip of a wooden sword. 'Oof!' Leonardo managed, clutching his side as Antonio straightened with a smile and made a circular motion with his finger.

Again.

The onlookers grinned and exchanged amused glances at the master's skill. Drogoradz let out a low chuckle, shaking his head knowingly.

Leonardo narrowed his eyes and nodded to Antonio, signalling that he was ready. This time, he would take the initiative, he decided. He flew at Antonio with a series of blows that would have brought any of the others to their knees, or at least disarmed them; yet,

Antonio managed to deflect them all, returning with his own attacks and Leonardo was soon on the defensive.

He dodged and ducked, circling back to the centre and buying himself a moment of respite. Panting, me made ready once more as Antonio nodded and gave him an impressed smile that said, *Well done, most would not have survived that.*

However, the next time Antonio attacked, Leonardo was unable to hold him off for more than a few seconds, before he felt the edge of the wooden sword smack into his arm and then his leg, causing him to stumble back.

There was laughter and a smattering of applause from the watching crowd as Leonardo righted himself, and he turned to see that they were beaming at him. Leonardo panted and grinned back. Though he had lost, he was satisfied to see a bead of sweat trickle from Antonio's forehead and knew that at least he was giving the master a challenge, albeit a little one.

'Well done, Leonardo!' Drogoradz called from the edge of the training ground. 'Even I can't make that bastard work so hard!'

Antonio nodded again in appreciation and made the circular motion with his finger, accompanied by a raising of his eyebrows.

Again?

Leonardo nodded. Antonio began to circle him with all the certainty of a man of his spectacular skill. Leonardo clenched his jaw in concentration, breathing deeply through his nostrils. He could do better than to just make Antonio sweat. He drank everything in, from Antonio's leather boots and how they twisted in the beaten earth, to the way he sat on his hips, his knees slightly bent and ready to propel himself forward, to the grip on his sword and the way his arm moved it before him.

Leonardo was fast enough; he was sure of it. Now, he just needed to understand what Antoni was thinking, what his next move would be, and where the tip of his blade would appear before it got there.

Leonardo attacked. There was a rapid flurry of limbs, and the sound of the wooden training swords clacking together filled the summer air as the spectators watched, in open-mouthed wonder, as the two men fought, thrusting, slashing and parrying at unbelievable speeds.

Back and forth they went, with one taking the offensive and pushing the other back, just as the tide seemed to suddenly change and then it was the other's turn to advance. Their technique was so clean, so perfect, that it looked almost choreographed. Leonardo watched in grim satisfaction as his master's brow furrowed in concentration.

Clack, clack, clack! The swords moved incessantly, directed in elegant stokes by their bearers, clashing together several times within the space of a single second.

The two men moved tirelessly, circling, attacking, leaping back, sidestepping, dodging and ducking. A minute went by, then two, then three.

By now, the onlookers gazed upon the beautiful spectacle in amazement as both Antonio and Leonardo dripped with sweat, kicking up dust here and there as their nimble movements and swift directional changes disturbed the ground.

On and on they went, quite losing track of time as neither seemed to be able to gain the upper hand. Eventually, sometime during the fifth minute, they finally began to tire visibly, yet were still so fast that no one watching could really say for sure what was happening.

It wasn't until halfway through the sixth minute that the bout stopped abruptly when Antonio overstretched and straightened, to find the tip of Leonardo's wooden blade prodding at his neck, his student standing behind him, grinning triumphantly as his chest heaved.

Silence fell over the training ground as the pair stood frozen, a look of surprise dawning on the master's face as he realised he had just been beaten. None of the onlookers could believe it, either. Drogoradz looked even more surprised than the others, if that were possible.

Then, Sebastien began to slowly clap, his face transforming delightfully until he wore a smile that seemed to stretch from ear to ear. The others began clapping, too, then cheered, Drogoradz amongst them, for what a spectacle that had been! Leonardo had beaten the master!

Antonio took a step back and bowed deeply to Leonardo, who felt compelled to return the gesture. When he straightened, he saw that Antonio wore a broad, rare smile, showing two rows of perfect white teeth. Antonio made a couple of complex gestures, then pointed at Leonardo and to himself.

You are lucky to have such a good teacher, he mimed.

'Ha, yes!' Leonardo laughed. 'I would have to agree, I am lucky.'

Leonardo's friends rushed over to clap him on the back. Not giving him a chance to regain his breath as they cheered him, they pulled his arms in the air in triumph and Leonardo laughed as they hoisted him onto their shoulders.

'Bloody well done, boy,' Drogoradz clapped appreciatively. 'Bloody well done!' He allowed the initiates to have their moment of victory, before he was barking at them to put their swords away and make ready for a lesson from Walter, about poisons made from berries. They did so willingly, discussing amongst each other how incredibly fast Leonardo was and how there couldn't have been a swordsman in a thousand miles to match the pair, as Leonardo listened with a contented smile on his face.

They were all improving, in every aspect of their training. A fortnight after Leonardo had bested Antonio with the sword, Sebastien, apparently seeing that as a challenge, managed to subdue the mighty Drogoradz at wrestling.

Leonardo had watched as Sebastien dextrously flipped their enormous instructor, once the pair of them had toppled to the ground. Sebastien had locked his arm up in such a favourable position that even Drogoradz's mighty strength hadn't been sufficient to break the hold. Sebastien had bent the elbow in a direction the joint was not built to accommodate and Drogoradz had tapped in submission with a deep cry of surprise.

A breathless Sebastien had leapt to his feet, sporting a gleeful grin as he looked down at the wrestling master. However, his smile had quickly faded when he saw Drogoradz's expression; he was sitting, frozen, looking up at Sebastien with a face that was quite unreadable.

For one horrifying moment, Leonardo had thought that the giant was about to climb to his feet and pummel his subordinate; but then he had roared with laughter and pushed himself up, clapping Sebastien so hard on the shoulder he sagged a little at the knees.

As a result of their joint success, the initiates seemed to have won themselves a newfound respect amongst their instructors. They could now ask questions without being told to keep silent and their superiors were more forthcoming with information. Drogoradz had told them, for example, that those initiates who survived the first winter were much more likely to survive the second, giving them all a feeling of hope that they might come out of this ordeal in one piece.

Though they all undoubtedly preferred the summer over winter, life at the monastery was still hard and their superiors pushed them to their limits relentlessly.

Drogoradz demanded that they lift heavier and heavier boulders, or that they complete the timed run to the tree he had marked halfway down the first valley quicker. Walter had them memorise the recipes for a dizzying number of lethal concoctions, and demanded that they were capable of naming each part of their anatomy and how best to track a man down, be that in a natural environment or an urban one.

Magnus, too, had been introducing new lessons in the form of detailed family trees of the high nobility of European kingdoms, or describing at great length the customs and cultures of distant lands that would help them to blend in should they ever need to travel there. They even studied Arabic, the language of the heathen, for Magnus had decreed it was important to understand their enemy, too.

The four remaining initiates reacted well to the pressure. They absorbed the knowledge, their minds becoming as fast and capable as their bodies, and they learnt to think for themselves. Their competence was not lost on Magnus, and that summer sparked a new level of difficulty in the tasks they were set individually.

Once, he had given Leonardo four days to reach a town at the southern frontier of the Pyrenees, telling him to find the old man that tended the vineyards upon the northern slopes. Leonardo was to observe the old man without being seen and return to provide Magnus with a detailed description of him and a summary of his daily activities, so that Magnus would know he had been successful. Leonardo relished the challenge, and realised that it was the first time he had seen another human being outside the monastery since the previous year.

The town at the far edge of the kingdom of Navarre was quaint and small. It was not difficult for Leonardo to find the old man, who plucked at the grapes of the vineyard with two sons. Leonardo smiled to himself as he had watched from afar, remaining unseen by using all the techniques of camouflage and stealth he had learnt.

The other initiates had been given similar tasks and they had all completed them without issue, finding that navigating the mountains in summer was simple child's play to what they had endured in winter. The winter had hardened them, and Leonardo understood now why such a hostile environment had been selected, for he found that nothing was quite so difficult once the biting cold and howling wind were removed from the equation.

Then, midway through the summer in late June, Magnus had them all travel to the city of Pamplona, where they stayed at an estate belonging to the Catholic Church. Their lodgings were simple and rugged, and the estate was inhabited by local monks who welcomed them, though stayed clear, keeping their interactions to a minimum with the men of the Order, for they seemed to understand that they were a different kind of churchman.

Leonardo remembered that time vividly and quite fondly, too. They spent it 'playing games', as Drogoradz called it, where the initiates would have to hunt their instructors through the streets, picking them out from a crowd, and sneak up on them to either deliver a mock killing blow or otherwise steal something from their personage.

The city was a myriad of bright colours; sounds, smells and visions of civilisation that all four initiates had forgotten. It was all so foreign, new and exciting. Leonardo found that almost everything he had learnt was put to the test; his physical aptitude, his grasp of foreign language and custom – and, perhaps most importantly of all, his ability to think independently and to analyse various situations.

He loved it all, the disapproving look of the city guard as he pushed his way through the crowds, the shouting of haggling merchants and buyers at the markets, the sway of the hips of the young, dark-haired Spanish maidens. It was so refreshing to be back in a city once again. Albeit Pamplona was not nearly as vast as Rome, a city was a city and Leonardo was, after all, a simple street urchin. He was in territory he knew how to navigate.

Once, Walter took lodgings in an inn at the heart of the city, and Leonardo and Sebastien paired up to try to catch their teacher off guard in his room. They had made an attack in the night, thinking to climb through the window and managed it without being detected; but, as soon as they had dropped in over the sill, they were met with the sight of Walter sitting on a stool with his back to the far wall, a crossbow aimed at their chests and an eyebrow raised in their direction.

It was fantastic fun, however, and they found that they were learning plenty about how to infiltrate an enemy position. There was a villa several miles from Pamplona that was apparently owned by the Order, for it was unoccupied and a little run down, but Magnus had the keys to the front door, and they used it to stage mock attacks or defences.

One time, Leonardo and Ebel were awakened in the middle of the night as the door splintered open with a crash and Sigbald and Sebastien charged in with a roar, their training swords held high in gleeful victory as they descended upon their unprepared brothers.

During the day, they learnt how to scale walls with hook and rope, or breach doors equipped with the newest types of locks. Much of it, too, was observation, and Magnus would discuss at great length the importance of information gathering so that they might make an informed decision before jumping into action. He was careful to make it very clear that they were not training to become merely elite soldiers of the Church, but that they were to be extensions of their masters and would have to act on their behalf, carrying out their will in their absence and whatever that might entail.

One day, they had all been sitting on a low wall before their lodgings on a hot afternoon, as Magnus had just concluded one such lesson. Behind him, monks sweated as they tilled fields of golden wheat under a hot sun, sweating under their shirts. Beyond, the gentle rolling hills faded into the summer haze, as a cooling breeze pulled gently at the trees displaying leaves of vivid green.

'Teacher, may I ask a question?' Sigbald had said.

Magnus had turned to him with a wave of his hand. 'Very well, boy. What is it?'

Sigbald swallowed. 'When we become agents – sorry, *if* we become agents – what kind of things will be asked of us?'

Magnus sighed. 'By God, boy, what do you think? We haven't been teaching you how to use a sword, only to stick you in some backwater priory somewhere to sing hymns!'

Sigbald reddened. 'Forgive me, Teacher. It's just, you have never told us exactly…'

'That's because there is no exact answer, boy,' said Magnus. 'You will have to do whatever it is your masters ask of you. That might be anything from subterfuge to spying, from tracking to impersonating.' He looked at them all pointedly. 'Sometimes, killing too. But know that, so long as you serve the Order and fight to preserve the balance, your sins will be forgiven – even killing. You will all have to adapt to the situation. Allow yourselves to be malleable, for I have no doubt that whatever the Fingers ask of you, it will certainly be dangerous. You might find yourselves in a foreign land at the edge of the world, and be completely alone with a complex task to carry out. *Then* you will understand why brute force alone is insufficient.'

He tapped the side of his head again. 'Use this, and maybe you'll live to serve God another day. That's all any of us in this organisation can ask for. Honour your masters and give glory to God. At least then your lives will have had meaning, eh? That's a rare enough thing to find these days. Understood?' They all nodded solemnly.

The thought of travelling to a foreign land at the edge of the world filled Leonardo with more than a little trepidation, but his excitement far outweighed his anxiety. What was it that lay there?

he asked himself. What oddities and interesting things did the world have yet to reveal to him? What horrors?

He almost asked Magnus this, but bit his tongue at the last second, sure that whatever came out of his mouth was bound to sound stupid.

'What kinds of things did you do for the Order, Teacher?' Sebastien asked boldly, shaking Leonardo from his reverie.

The others watched with bated breath as Magnus turned slowly to Sebastien. None of them had had the courage to ask such a brazen question to their superiors before, least of all Magnus. His piercing blue eyes were unreadable as he considered the young Englishman for a long time.

Sebastien squirmed uncomfortably, unable to hold the older man's gaze, and worried that he was about to be punished for his boldness. However, to their collective surprise, Magnus replied.

'I have done plenty in service of the Order, boy. If you're wondering if I've killed men for the Order, then yes. Too many to count.'

They watched as Magnus's gaze drifted to a stone in the grass by his feet. He seemed to focus on it intently before continuing. 'There are things I have done – that you will all have to do – that I am not proud of. But I did them because they served the greater good. I could see what good became of them and I know that, by doing them, I left the world a better place as a result.' He looked back up at the group of younger men with an unshakeable conviction in his eyes.

'Commit an unsavoury act for the right reason, restore the balance, and God will forgive you,' he added. 'That is why our Order exists. I believe it is a force for good.'

Now, it was Ebel's turn to surprise them all. Encouraged by Magnus's openness, the shrewd olive-skinned young man put forth his own question. 'And the people that we will be sent to… eliminate, Teacher. Who decides whether they interfere with God's balance or not?'

At that, Leonardo saw Magnus's nostrils flare and his eyes flash with annoyance, before he calmed himself and pursed his lips under the thick white beard that covered most of his face. 'That, boy, is a matter we leave to the Fingers to decide. They are the most devout amongst us. They are voted into the inner circle and chosen for their competence and devotion to our cause. You'd do well to be careful with such questions. Do not think to imply that corruption infects our upper ranks!'

'No, Teacher, forgive me. I meant no offence,' Ebel said quickly, bowing his head in subservience as Magnus narrowed his eyes at the youth.

'The Fingers,' said Magnus curtly, 'who are also your masters, know best. And let that be the end of it. No more questions. Go, see what Walter has to show you.' He turned his back to them and the initiates scrambled to their feet, not wanting to push their luck with the older man, who had already been unusually forthcoming.

Leonardo couldn't speak for the other Fingers, for he knew only Emilio, the Papal Finger. That was the way it was supposed to be. They were strictly forbidden to talk about their masters to the others, having taken oaths to protect their identities. For, should they babble, it could compromise the secrecy of the men of the Order.

Leonardo thought to himself that he was glad he had Emilio for a master. Emilio would know what was best for the Order, surely. Emilio would always act in its best interests. Of course he would – he was the cleverest man Leonardo had ever met. The alternative was too uncomfortable to even consider; so much so, that Leonardo point blank refused to do so. Emilio was a man of God, and that was that.

Their time in Pamplona regrettably came to an end, as all thing must. During the sixth and final week, Magnus had the initiates participate in their longest exercise yet. Over the course of four days, they split into pairs, with Leonardo and Sigbald pitted against Sebastien and Ebel. Magnus gave one pair a scrap of parchment with a note written upon it, and it was the job of the other pair to steal it from them, using all their guile and resourcefulness.

Startled locals leapt out of the way in shock as the four young men barrelled around the streetcorners, sprinting after one another within the confines of the bustling city centre. When they were inevitably caught, a scuffle would break out and, once the parchment had been wrenched from grubby fingers, the whole thing would start again after they had relayed the contents of the parchment to Magnus.

By the end, the four of them were quite exhausted, as none had had more than a couple of hours sleep as a result of being hunted mercilessly by their comrades. The final scores had been nine to eight in favour of Leonardo and Sigbald, though Sebastien had insisted that had only been because the city guard had stopped to reprimand him for crouching by a noble lady's skirts for cover, allowing the others to catch up to him.

Needless to say, they all left the Navarran city in good humour and high spirits, and as close as they had ever been. During their two-day trek back up the mountain toward the monastery, they would march side by side with their instructors. And even they, with perhaps the exception of the ever-sullen Walter, didn't bother to rebuke the initiates for their constant chatter and jokes.

Indeed, during the breaks they took to eat and drink, they all sat together, instructor and initiate alike, and passed around waterskins and smoked meats. Drogoradz would regale them with a tale set in the Far East, of bears that could be made to dance, while Walter told them of the vast ocean of sand that lay south of Egypt and stretched farther than the distance of Normandy to the Black Sea.

When they finally reached the monastery at the end of the second day of their journey, a particularly good one as far as Leonardo was concerned, they were all glad to see the familiar collection of plain stone buildings, high upon the mountain, that had become their home. That fondness came even after the monastery had been a place of great suffering for them, as neither Leonardo nor, he suspected, any of the other three would forget the countless times they had shivered to sleep, or the times their instructors had made them crawl through snow while screaming at them to do better, or when they had fallen, failed and despaired.

Leonardo reflected that he had grown a great deal in the time he had been there; the youth that had climbed the mountain well over a year ago was not the same as the man that climbed it then. True, there had been loss along the way, awful loss. Gabriel and Alof had been killed, and Njal crippled, by the very same terrain that seemed so innocent and beautiful in the summer. Yet, Leonardo had become a harder man for it.

They fell back into the daily routine of life at the monastery in August with renewed vigour since their training in Pamplona. By now, the four of them were well used to it, and the time seemed to slip by quicker.

September was unremarkable, until one day when Leonardo spotted two men making their way up the track during a clear afternoon, when the four initiates were in the yard at the training posts. One of the men was very tall and slim, and his long, matted dark hair hung loose around his shoulders; his face seemed to display a permanent scowl, as well as a collection of scars. The second was of average height and build, and around the same age – somewhere in his late thirties. He had medium-length, light brown hair and symmetrical, well-sculpted features that made him look handsome.

They stopped before the great hall, where Magnus and the others greeted them cordially and bade them inside to rest their feet. The visitors stayed at the monastery for several days and, during hushed discussions and a few furtive glances during mealtimes, Leonardo, Sebastien and the others came to the conclusion that they were active-duty agents, perhaps come to visit their old tutors.

Once, the two visitors had joined the initiates during their sparring in the yard, taking their turn to face off with the younger men between the makeshift ring of branches. Leonardo had bested the short, handsome one with relative ease, though his technique had been excellent.

The taller one, however, was quite another story. His great height gave him an advantage of reach; and, coupled with the fact that he was almost as skilled as Antonio, this meant that, frustratingly, Leonardo won only four bouts of seven. The fearsome-looking man had bared pointed teeth in acknowledgement each time Leonardo had slipped his blade past the long limbs, and shook his hand out of respect once the fight was done.

It was not until the two men had taken their leave that the initiates learnt who they were. The taller one, Gustav, was supposedly the best tracker the Order had. It was said that no man could run from him forever; that he had a knack for sniffing someone out, no matter which corner of the world they tried to hide behind. Gustav found them all. Then, he would end them.

The other, named Geoffrey, had supposedly mastered the art of disguise. Apparently, he could play a role like no other and could fool anyone into believing he was a noble lord, or a beggar, a merchant or a soldier. Later, Drogoradz had told them a tale of how Geoffrey had killed a corrupt sheriff by disguising himself as a pretty young maiden and seducing the man, taking him to bed, at which point Geoffrey had slipped a knife from under his frock, much to the sheriff's surprise.

It was the first time Leonardo had properly met other agents. He was sure he had seen some in passing at Emilio's estate, yet those moments had been fleeting and he hadn't known who he was looking at. Regardless, it was a fascinating window into the world of the Order, an organisation that Leonardo had yet to fully comprehend.

The intrigue regarding their visitors ended when the pair made their way back down the track that would take them north, to Frankia, and it was back to business as usual. September wore on, and it wasn't until the third week that the initiates were subjected to a particularly cold bout of weather that made them shiver one morning and rush back into the bunkhouse to pull on another layer.

Leonardo remembered feeling a pang of anxiety twist in his gut as he realised that winter was just around the corner, and with it would come the long nights, freezing relentless wind and misery.

The others felt it, too.

'Winter is almost upon us,' Sigbald said glumly that same night, as he watched Sebastien light a fire in the hearth. So far, they had already prepared a vast stock of firewood that dwarfed their collection from last year.

'Yes,' Ebel replied, trying to sound positive. 'But you heard what Drogoradz told us. If we survived last year, our chances for this year can only be greater. We have so much more experience now!'

'Ebel's right, boys,' Sebastien said as flames licked around the bundle of kindling he had made, and he stood to face them. 'We can do this! We're almost there. All we have to do is stick together. Agreed?'

They muttered their assent, coming together in the centre of the bunkhouse to form a loose ring.

'Aye!' Sigbald affirmed, nodding vigorously, his spirits beginning to lift. 'So long as we help each other out, we'll be agents in a handful of months. We're brothers, after all, eh?' He grinned around at the rest of them, and they grinned back. 'That's what brothers do. They look out for each other.'

'Yes, that's right!' Ebel replied with a smile. 'We are brothers now, aren't we?'

'Of course we are!' Sebastien cuffed him on the shoulder playfully. 'We'll be brothers for life!'

'Until the end,' Leonardo agreed with a nod. He felt a sense of kinship that warmed him. He was so terribly fond of the three men; the bond between them was so strong that he knew for a certainty that they would, indeed, be brothers until the end, whatever that end might look like.

Huddling close, they linked their arms over one another's shoulders and pressed their heads together.

'Well then, brothers,' Sebastien said through a smile, 'let's see what these damned mountains can throw at us next!'

Chapter 18

GASCONY

L a Reole sat high upon a rocky outcrop that overlooked the river Garonne. Its squat shape and thick, round towers might not have been described as pretty, but the word formidable certainly came to mind. It was a well-designed and well-placed fortress, now sealed to the outside world, and the men of King Henry's army milling around its base looked like tiny ants in comparison.

Many of the townsfolk had stayed, despite the advance of the King's army. They peered nervously from gaps in their shutters – wide, fearful eyes flitting this way and that, watching the bustle of activity through their streets as foreign soldiers shouted and stamped.

Fortunately for them, Henry had had the foresight to instruct his men not to mistreat the townsfolk, who had for the most part been ignored. Though Henry was conscious not to allow his occupation to devolve into something resembling that of de Montfort, there had been tales of other cases elsewhere in the countryside of Gascony of crops and vineyards put to the torch.

At least La Reole was spared from this, save for a handful of houses that were demolished to make way for a massive trebuchet. Its enormous timbers had been unloaded from a number of gigantic carts pulled by several oxen each, and the ground was soon churned to mud as the engineering team attempted to assemble the contraption.

It was raining when Leonardo and Sebastien rode into the town, pulling their cloaks about them and attracting bemused looks from the passing soldiers as their horses' hooves splashed through the mud. Leonardo could not blame them, for the sight of the struggling captive lain unflatteringly over Sebastien's horse garnered intrigued expressions. Gaillard Solers groaned indignantly into his gag, struggling at the rope around his wrists.

'Shh!' Sebastien said, twisting the young man's ear painfully. Solers fell into a furious silence as they approached the main hubbub of activity on one of the main roads through the town.

A little further down the road, Leonardo could see a large, ornate carriage painted green and trimmed with yellow that stood out amongst the drab houses around it. It was guarded by several mounted knights, and he guessed it must have transported the Queen.

They had learnt that Queen Eleanor had travelled to La Reole with her husband to oversee the installation of the siege, and had altered their course to find the King's army already well underway with the task. Clearly, Henry was keen to pacify Gascony as soon as possible.

The light drizzle continued to patter onto their heads and shoulders as they stopped by the carriage, and Sebastien wrapped his knuckles against its side. A shutter slid open and the pretty, auburn-haired lady-in-waiting looked up at him and positively beamed, clearly recognising the freckle-faced and lightly bearded Sebastien under his hood. Sebastien smiled warmly back.

'Might we have a word with your mistress, my dear?' he said softly.

'Yes, of course.' The girl blushed and Leonardo rolled his eyes. A moment later, the Queen's face appeared at the window and smiled at the two of them.

'Good morning, Your Highness,' Sebastien declared with a grin. 'We have come with a gift!'

'Ah!' Queen Eleanor's face lit up. However, as she peered over at the slumped form of Gaillard Solers, she frowned and said, 'Has Bernard de Bouville shed twenty years and changed the colour of his hair?'

'He has not, Your Highness, for this is not he,' Sebastien replied.

'Then, who?'

'This,' Sebastien began, flashing a grin at Leonardo, 'is Gaillard Solers, head of the Solers family of Bordeaux.'

'Ah, so *this* is the Solers boy!' Queen Eleanor stuck her head further out of the window and called to Sir Derek, who waited nearby. 'Would you fetch me Drogo de Barentin, Sir Derek?' Sir Derek nodded, and pulled on his horse's reins with a click and cantered away.

'He is not the man you asked for, though we thought he might do,' Leonardo explained. 'The Solers family is wealthy enough, as I understand, and ought to pay a fair price for young Master Solers' release.'

'Well, perhaps not quite so much as a vicomte, but he is far better than nothing! I must say, I'm impressed.' The Queen gave them an amused smirk as Gaillard protested on the horse. 'The money his ransom raises ought to fetch a good deal. Hand him over to Drogo, would you? He'll know what to do.'

A minute later, there was a clattering of armour and Leonardo turned to see the bald and thickly bearded Drogo de Barentin marching up the street, flanked by a group of men-at-arms. His mouth twisted slowly into a sly grin when he laid eyes on young Gaillard. Leonardo saw the latter's brow crease in return, and he gave a groan of worry from behind his gag.

Drogo stood with his hands on his hips, a satisfied grin on his face as he exclaimed, 'Master Solers! How nice of you to join us!' He snapped his fingers and two of his men-at-arms grabbed Gaillard by the belt and hauled him off the horse, where he fell into the wet mud and shit in the road with a splash.

Drogo laughed and stood over him. 'My, my, I must have done something to please God for him to drop a gift like you into my lap. You and I will have some fun together, Gaillard. Perhaps, by the end, you will even have learnt some manners.'

Drogo snapped his fingers again and the men-at-arms looped their arms under Gaillard's protesting shoulders and hauled him away, his boots dragging in the mud behind them. Then, Drogo turned to look up at Leonardo and Sebastien and gave them a nod of appreciation.

'That's the second time the two of you have done me a service. You have my thanks.'

'The pleasure is ours,' Sebastien returned the nod.

Drogo gave them a thoughtful look. 'You know, I could use the pair of you. Tomorrow, I'll be riding to Bazas to oversee the siege there. Roger Bigod will take over here whilst the King, Peter Bonefans and John de Gray will spread to the countryside. I wouldn't say no to a couple of staunch fighters, especially ones as resourceful as yourselves. What say you?'

Leonardo shrugged. 'I'd be happy to help you, Sir Barentin. That is, if the Queen has nothing more for me to do?' He looked questioningly at Queen Eleanor, who shook her head.

'That is all for now,' she said. 'I have matters to attend to at Bordeaux that do not require your skills, though I will send for you if necessary. Go with Drogo, do what you can to bring a swift close for Bazas. The sooner this rebellion is over, the better.' A dark shadow passed over her face and Leonardo guessed she was thinking of the state of the royal treasury.

Sebastien bid his mistress farewell, and the window to the carriage was closed. The driver whipped the horses into action and the carriage trundled away, back to Bordeaux, leaving Sebastien and Leonardo with the venerable Drogo de Barentin.

They left the town of La Reole the next day, passing a furious Roger Bigod, who was shouting at the engineering team with the trebuchet, who had somehow managed to misplace a vital beam of the siege engine, delaying its use by several days. The grey weather continued, with overcast skies and intermittent showers, reminding them that winter was just around the corner – though, at least in Gascony, it was often comparatively mild.

Sebastien and Leonardo rode to Bazas with Drogo de Barentin and six hundred knights, men-at-arms and other camp followers, all marching along the now quiet roads in an orderly fashion, quite undisturbed by enemy soldiers.

John de Gray had taken a contingent of mounted skirmish troops and had fanned out with his men the day before the King's army had marched from Bordeaux, chasing away the rebels further south and east, where they were suspected to be gathering under the command of Gaston de Bearn.

Leonardo enjoyed a pleasant journey, during which he, Sebastien and Drogo chatted at the vanguard of Drogo's force about the rebellion, the King of Castile, England and Christendom, and a plethora of other things and, by the time they got to Bazas, Leonardo found that he rather liked the older knight. He was wise and amicable, and a lifetime of military campaigning had given him a realistic and practical outlook on life that he used to advise the King when his opinion was asked for.

Their chat ended abruptly, however, when they came into sight of the town of Bazas. From nearby trees lining the road, arrows began to whiz through the air, one whipping right by Leonardo's ear and another striking his mount in the rump, causing it to rear.

Fighting broke out a moment later, as Drogo's knights charged the ambushing enemy archers and chased them down through the woods, where they were put to the sword, but not before they had taken a handful of Drogo's men with them. After that, Drogo remained sullen for the rest of the day, barking his orders to his men as the great doors of the castle of Bazas were closed and the last of the defenders scampered inside.

And so the siege began in late September and the castle of Bazas, less formidable than the one at La Reole, but nonetheless a considerable obstacle, was soon surrounded with loyalists and cut off from the rebels. A military camp was established, and a watch set in place to observe the sally points of the keep. The attackers soon learnt not to get too close to the walls, after one or two men had been picked off by crossbow bolts when the weapons were poked through arrow slits in the thick walls.

Leonardo and Sebastien were issued a tent and allowed to set it up next to Drogo's. They were welcomed by Drogo and his knights, often sharing meals with them around the campfire, and the conversation between them was easy. Drogo even involved the two men with his plans and listened when they offered their thoughts.

Drogo de Barentin was keen for a swift end to the siege and, to that end, on the second day, had one of his knights lead an attack on the southern wall. Leonardo had watched with fascination as hundreds of men ran to the walls in a great cry of defiance, carrying ladders and holding thick, wooden shields fashioned from scavenged scraps of timber above their heads. The defenders hurled down rocks, javelins, arrows, bolts and vats of boiling oil, and screams pierced the air as the attackers writhed in agony on the grass at the base of the thick walls.

Some attacking teams managed to climb several rungs of the ladders, before enormous boulders thudded onto their helmets and toppled them from their perches. The attack was abandoned a minute later when they realised their attempts were futile, and the defenders cheered, leering down at Drogo's men below as they dragged away the dead and wounded, shouting down curses and defiant insults.

The mood in the loyalist encampment after that was grim and Drogo could be seen frowning and rubbing his beard. They settled in, estimating that the defenders of Bazas likely had enough provisions to last them several months, and Drogo and his knights spent the days debating how they might get their men within the walls. Drogo had his own siege equipment and, on the third day, a trebuchet had been assembled in a field before the walls.

The defenders had peppered it with projectiles, but they had all fallen short. The engineers had done a good job of distancing the trebuchet and then, when the order was given and the pin hammered in that allowed the counterweight to swing free, it was the attackers' turn to cheer as the massive lever arm hurled a block of stone high into the air, where it fell somewhere within the walls.

Sebastien and Leonardo stood watching for a time as the engineers made minute adjustments to their kit, tossing out a few of the ballast stones from the counterweight. As the second projectile hurtled toward the keep, they argued about how long it would take to create a beach in the flat portion of wall that was the intended target.

A boulder weighing half as much as a man struck the wall in a direct hit, and the engineering team cheered and shook hands around the base of the enormous war machine as great chunks of stone exploded from the wall with the impact. Drogo ordered a constant bombardment of the castle and Leonardo and Sebastien soon retired for food, imagining how the incessant thuds striking the castle must grate upon the nerves of the men within.

The event of their near execution at the hands of Gaillard Solers had served to alleviate some of the coolness between them, and Leonardo remarked over the first days of the siege how he and Sebastien were able to joke together and even enjoy each other's company almost as they once had, though neither dared to bring up the events of the past. Leonardo was content enough to have Sebastien back on his side, and the two of them, along with Drogo and his knights, shared a wineskin one night as the men of the guard patrolled around them.

'The walls aren't as stout as we'd first thought,' Drogo had said. 'The engineering team tell me we'll have a breach within a week.'

'That trebuchet is quite something,' Leonardo mused as he stared into the flames of the campfire.

'Aye,' Drogo nodded. 'Imagine what ten could do. We'd have the castle in a day.'

'How many men are within?' Sebastien asked.

'A couple of hundred, no more,' Drogo shrugged. 'Once there is a breach, taking it will no doubt be hard. I'll lose men, for sure.' His face darkened.

'On this occasion, I'm not sure we'll be of much use to you, Sir Barentin,' Leonardo said apologetically as he passed the wineskin.

'Perhaps not,' Drogo agreed as he took a swig. 'Storming that breach will be about brute force alone.'

As predicted, Drogo had his breach within the week. Leonardo woke one morning to survey the devastation where a great pile of rubble had cascaded from the wall, forming a kind of ramp up which an attacking force might climb. Already, the defenders were attempting to repair it with makeshift barricades. However, Drogo had ordered his archers to pepper them with volleys and, even as Leonardo watched, several tumbled from the walls clutching fatal wounds.

'To arms, men!' sergeants were calling through the camp as the trebuchet continued to batter the breach, widening it as the morning wore on.

By midday, the men of Drogo's small army were armed and ready, checking and rechecking their equipment as their units were assigned positions several hundred yards from the breach.

Drogo's men-at-arms would lead the charge with large pavises that would protect the entire bodies of the men of the front rank. Drogo would follow with his heavily armoured knights to secure a foothold upon the breach, and both Leonardo and Sebastien had agreed to fight beside him. They had commandeered helmets, coats of maille and shields, their weight feeling unfamiliar on Leonardo's body, for he had not fought armoured for many years.

The men within the castle of Bazas had only to peek over the battlements to see that the enemy attack was imminent, and a tense silence fell upon the loyalists as they knew they would be charging a prepared enemy. The sound of the deep crack of the trebuchet's boulders smashing the walls to fragments of rock pierced the air.

Drogo de Barentin's voice rang out before the ranks of armed men, albeit slightly muffled, for he spoke out from behind a great helm, his dark eyes barely visible through the thin slits.

'Is everyone ready?' he called, addressing his commanders. They stood arrayed on the field before the breach, the commanders of each division of the army nodding their heads.

They brandished swords, spears, axes and falchions, the brutal-looking weapons designed to render another man's flesh, freshly sharpened by Drogo's armourers the day before. Then, the rain began to fall, and the dull rumble of thunder reached their ears as water pinged off steel helmets and trickled through the iron rings of maille, soaking the gambesons beneath.

The red surcoats displaying the King's livery were soon damp and the men waited anxiously for their commander to give the order. Leonardo and Sebastien stood side by side with Drogo's favoured knights, their sword and shield at the ready. Then, as the rain intensified and another rumble of thunder cracked the sky, Drogo shouted for the engineers manning the trebuchet to cease, the only sound now being the rain.

Drogo gave no inspirational speech to his men, for they all knew what was required of them. Instead, he pointed his sword toward the breach and shouted at the top of his lungs, 'For England! Chaaarge!'

The battlefield erupted into action as the attackers roared with fear and fury, the front rank of men-at-arms breaking into a run toward the breach. Leonardo followed a second later, shouting his own battle cry as he ran with the knights, side by side with Sebastien.

A moment later, they were within range of the defenders' archers and dozens of them popped up from behind the battlements, firing bolts and arrows down into the running men. There were screams and shouts of pain as many found their mark, and men tumbled to the ground as the lethal barbs punctured their flesh.

Then, the men-at-arms with the pavises had reached the breach and began to scramble awkwardly over the rubble, holding up the cumbersome pavises as they went and doing their best to deflect the rocks that were hurled in their direction. Inevitably, some of them died from the onslaught, falling face down amongst the broken stone, where their bodies were trampled on by their comrades as they tried to get to the enemy.

Rebels had formed a strong group in the crux of the breach, and a bristling wall of shields and spear tips defended its narrowest part, the men bracing as best they could on the uneven ground as archers continued to fire into the attackers from upon the walls on either side.

Even the endless hail of projectiles was not enough to ward off Drogo's men for long, however. With a savage cry of fury, the first wave of men-at-arms collided with the defenders and the air was filled with shouts, clangs of steel and the general clamour of battle.

Leonardo was still some way down the slope of rubble, unable to get any closer, for there was a great dense mass of writhing and pushing bodies all around him; and, even if he had wanted to retreat, he could not. He gritted his teeth and held up his shield as arrows and rocks thudded into the wood. A man to his left screamed as an arrow thwacked into his eye socket and he fell, clutching at the shaft.

Beside him, Sebastien fell with a grunt as a rock smashed into the side of his helm. Leonardo pulled him to his feet, holding his shield over his dazed friend to protect him against more blows as he regained his bearings. Behind them, the men below shoved them unceremoniously further into the breach. There, where the fighting was thickest, the defenders held staunchly; several ranks deep and bellowing defiantly, they maintained the advantage of the higher ground and pushed back.

Leonardo felt himself being crushed between two great forces and he cried out in pain as he found himself being carried along by the wave of men. He had no choice but to back down the slope, gripping Sebastien under the arm as they went, for he was still disoriented.

From his position, Leonardo could not see how the fighting was playing out in the front ranks, only the rise and fall of swords and falchions in mailled fists as their bearers rained down blow after blow. A spurt of blood erupted into the air several yards in front, followed by an inhuman screech of pain, though Leonardo could not say which side the victim belonged to.

The noise was a different story, however. His senses were assaulted by the cacophony of the battle, his world filled with shouts, yells, grunts, clangs and thuds. The air smelled of blood and damp cloth, and the rain continued to fall heavily until the ground below the breach was churned into a mud pit, and the attackers below began to lose their purchase upon it, slipping and sliding to and fro, the archers on the walls using the opportunity to pick them off.

The great, heaving force to Leonardo's rear lessened, and the loyalists began to fall back down the slope and, for one horrible moment, it seemed as though they might break and flee. But then, voices shouted from amongst their ranks as the sergeants, captains, knights and other commanders bellowed at the men not to give another inch of ground.

Leonardo caught sight of Drogo de Barentin hacking away with his sword, his great helm and surcoat spattered with blood and dust.

'Come on!' he shouted to Sebastien, pulling him onward. 'They need help at the front!' Leonardo sought a momentary break in the mass of men and squeezed himself into it, his sword arm held out before him. Sebastien followed and the two of them stumbled up the breach to the thick of the action, forcing their way through Drogo's ranks of men.

The noise intensified as Leonardo made it to the second rank and he could finally see what was going on. The fighting upon the breach was brutal, and so many lay dead that both sides hacked at each other from upon a carpet of corpses, two lines of bared teeth and snarling grimaces as they fought desperately.

The men-at-arms that had carried the pavises were nowhere to be seen, and the attackers were now led by Drogo and his heavily armoured elite. Opposite, similarly armoured rebel knights held the breach and, it seemed, were equally as determined to hold it. The man beside Drogo fell backward with a scream, clutching at a foot that had been stabbed at with a spear, creating a gap that Leonardo lunged into.

He stood side by side with Drogo. However, there was no time to greet the commander, for a sword thrust itself in his face, and he barely had enough time to hold up his shield to block it before another clattered from its rim. It was not at all the kind of fighting Leonardo was used to; here, he had no space to manoeuvre and much of his speed and skill with blades counted for naught. In the press of battle, spears and swords could come from any angle, and the best a man could do was grit his teeth and pray his fellows had his back.

Leonardo had no choice but to do just that and forced himself to remain calm as he thrust and hacked away. His sword claimed a life every now and again as it found opportune gaps in the enemy's armour, and Leonardo watched in grim satisfaction as they fell backwards and died.

He controlled his breathing, letting out great hisses of breath as he parried and lunged. An axe came from nowhere and struck him heavily upon the shoulder and, though the steel links of his maille shirt stopped his arm being hacked off, the brute force of the blow connected well, and he cried out as he felt something 'crunch' beneath the armour.

Then, the axeman was cut down as a blade was thrust through the man's throat. Leonardo glanced to his left to see that Sebastien had recovered and fought at his side. The breach was perhaps wide enough for only nine men to stand abreast. Leonardo held its centre with Drogo on his right and Sebastien on his left, and the three seasoned warriors fought with an unflinching calmness, each of their blows purposeful and well aimed.

before them and the defenders jabbed at them warily from behind their shields, edging ever backward as they shot furtive glances to the left and right, where their comrades struggled with yet more attackers.

The battle raged on for another few minutes before the rebels' resolve broke and they either fled into the squat stone tower of the keep, or threw down their weapons in panicked surrender. Drogo's men howled with carnal pleasure, and yet more screams filled the air as there was a great butchery of the defenders before Drogo was able to gain control of his men. Those that had not been cut down were taken prisoner, and one of Drogo's knights called up through an embrasure of the keep to negotiate the terms of surrender for the remaining rebels.

A panting Drogo de Barentin held up his sword and howled in victory and hundreds of men took up the call, waving swords and spears into the air. Leonardo found himself caught up in the ecstasy of their triumph and thrust his own blade into the wet sky, crying out in excitement, fear and relief as he felt the adrenaline still rushing through him. Sebastien howled next to him, and the pair embraced, each glad to find the other still standing.

They broke apart and returned the gesture to Drogo, clasping the knight in a clatter of metal as they laughed in relief.

'By God, that was a fight!' Drogo laughed as he pulled his great helm from a sweaty bald head, tilting it back and opening his mouth to let the heavens hydrate him. 'Thanks for your help back there!' He flashed a grin at Leonardo and Sebastien.

'What help?' Sebastien said, smiling back. 'From where I stood, you were doing all the work yourself!'

'Ha! Perhaps I'm not as old as I thought!' Drogo beamed, the excitement of the fight and joy of the attack's success filling him with energy. 'Come, we have a castle to garrison.'

There was no time to rest on their laurels, for Drogo's army was a professional one, and he was a level-headed and practical soldier. There were the prisoners to secure, the castle to clear of hostiles, repairs to be made now that it was theirs, wounded to tend to, dead to bury and whole host of other tasks that Drogo's men were put to, working incessantly under the equally incessant rain until nightfall, when they were finally allowed to rest and fill their bellies.

Whilst the battle on the breach of Bazas had been raging, word had arrived that Benauges, too, had fallen, and the thousands of archers sent to besiege it were now free to pepper other enemies of the crown with their lethal projectiles.

Leonardo had peeled off his armour that night, wincing at his bruised collarbone as he washed the blood from it and the rest of his kit, uncertain as to whom it had spilled from. He collapsed into his bedroll and fell into a deep sleep the moment his eyes were closed.

When he woke the next morning, he left the tent to find the smell of sizzling pork wafting into his nostrils from the campfire, where Sebastien sat with Drogo and his men, laughing and talking of the previous day's battle. Leonardo joined them and took some fried pork with bread and cheese, wolfing it down, before catching up on other news of King Henry's successes.

The household knight, Geoffrey Gascelin, had taken the castle at Lamothe-Landerron, and Peter of Savoy claimed Meilhan. Other lesser settlements had been taken, too, such as Duras and Labrit, and countless villages pledged once more to serve the English crown as King Henry's men swept south and east in a great wave of war.

There had been a clash with Amaneus d'Albret involving John de Gray and King Henry himself in the countryside, though it had been more of a skirmish than a battle, and neither force had come away with something they could call a clear victory.

Needless to say, the overall position of the English king looked favourable for him, and, as September turned into October, his priority was to securely garrison as many of the newly captured castles and towns as he could before the campaigning season came to an end.

Leonardo and Sebastien finally left Drogo de Barentin's camp in early October, clasping hands amicably as they wished each other farewell.

'Where do you go to next, Drogo?' Leonardo asked as he prepared a horse to leave.

The wizened knight scratched under his bushy beard and shrugged. 'Wherever the King demands. Perhaps Mont-de-Marsan in the south, or wherever the rebels still hold. I just follow the orders.'

'So do I. It was good to fight with you, Sir Barentin!' Leonardo replied with a smile and waved to Drogo as both he and Sebastien mounted and rode north.

'And with you both!' the knight called after them.

The strategic town of Bazas had fallen to King Henry and it seemed that the rebels would soon have no option but to capitulate. Yet, Leonardo knew that things seldom went according to plan, and that the next complication was sure to appear soon.

Chapter 19

TWELVE YEARS AGO

The wind blew in powerful gusts and Leonardo had to brace himself against the rock face, testing his rope again with his free arm to ensure it was tied securely to a pillar of sharp rock below. If he fell at this height, he would be dead without the safety of the rope. By now, however, he had grown used to such high stakes, but that didn't stop his heart from fluttering when he glanced below and saw the sheer drop that would spell his doom were he to make one wrong move.

He squinted up through the tiniest slit in the linen bandages that wrapped his head and kept the wind from pelting his skin with snow and ice. *Just another few feet*, he thought as he gritted his teeth and searched for the next handhold.

All around him, jagged spires of rock jutted up from the cliff face like a thousand broken teeth. Leonardo had crawled amongst those distinguishing features of the mountain they called the Black Needle, gripping onto them and using their dark, twisted shapes to haul himself upwards toward the summit.

It was the first time he had climbed the Black Needle and did so alone, being the last of his brothers to attempt it. The others had warned him the night before of the difficulty of the climb and the lethal drops found on every face.

'Take the eastern face,' Sebastien had said. 'It's the fastest way through, but you'll need to use your rope on the last section.'

That was where Leonardo was now, mere feet from the top. It had taken him a gruelling half hour of carefully seeking out a path, testing holds, circling back, then committing and repeating the process every fifteen yards. Even with this painstakingly long and deliberate procedure, he had still slipped backwards in a moment of panic several minutes before and fallen from his perch as a freakishly strong gust of wind had unbalanced him.

Leonardo fell and smashed into the rockface below as the rope around his waist went suddenly taught and halted his fall. He hit his head quite badly and was dazed for a few seconds, but managed to recover and resume the climb after the setback which, luckily, resulted in nothing more than a large lump on his temple.

Now Leonardo was within reach of the summit and, a moment later, was hauling his way over the last craggy rock formation, where the mountain came to a needle's point formed from the black bedrock, earning its namesake.

Up here, the wind howled around him, blowing from all directions and threatened to pluck him from the mountain. The visibility was poor. It was mid-February, and the worst of the winter was yet to pass. The weather was erratic and unpredictable and the resulting storms deadly. Despite that, Leonardo was smiling.

He had adapted to the harsh conditions of the high Pyrenees in winter, feeling as at home on their slopes as any of the mountain goats he saw picking their way over their rugged features. He had survived everything the mountains had thrown his way. They all had.

Perhaps it was a miracle, or maybe divine intervention; perhaps God had seen their devotion to a noble cause and spared them a similar fate to that of Gabriel or Alof. Either way, they were alive. And, as Sigbald had pointed out the day before, they had almost finished with their training in the mountains. Soon, they would all be granted the honour of the second baptism.

Leonardo could not see further than the next peak. On a clear day, he knew that the view from any of the nearby summits was spectacular. He would have been able to see the Pyrenees stretch out before him. They were less of a mystery to him now. He remembered when he had first climbed amongst them and thought that, if God had ever lived anywhere on earth, it would have been here.

Though Leonardo had now scaled the tops of many a mountain and had never seen any sign of God, or even any of the angels or singing cherubs that folk said must live so high, the mountains lost none of their magnificence as a result. Dangerous and beautiful, unmoving titans of stone, they were indifferent to him, but when Leonardo stood upon their points he felt like a king. He might as well have been, for who was there to contest him?

Up here there were no rules, no laws. Reality and reason had been left thousands of feet below, and up in the clouds the only thing that lived was the wind. Leonardo knew he couldn't stay long, however. He was far too exposed. Unlike the angels, his mortal body suffered from the cold and he had to keep moving. He sighed and squinted down at the knot of rope at his waist, giving it a testing tug. It held. He knew that if he was caught on the rocky cliff face of the Black Needle overnight, he would surely perish, for there was no shelter for him to dig. It was time to head back.

Two days later, on a Sunday morning, the initiates were preparing to head out into the freezing cold as yet another harsh winter day broke upon the monastery.

'Brrr!' Sebastien shivered as he stood up out of bed and began to clothe himself in more layers of wool and fur. 'It's so damn cold!'

Leonardo had heard that phrase several times a day since December and had come to feel it was inadequate in explaining the way the chill penetrated so deep. They had collected enough wood in the autumn to have the fire blazing away for most of the day and night, but even that did little to keep the cold at bay.

Once or twice, Leonardo had considered stepping directly onto the coals for his teeth chattered incessantly, but thought better of it. He took his mind off the freezing temperatures and asked the others, 'So, what will Magnus tell us today?'

Sunday was often a good day. The initiates usually had the afternoon and evening free to do with as they pleased. However, they found that any free time that they were awarded was best spent revising the theory they had been taught throughout the week, so as not to displease their teachers when asked to recite parts of the lesson. But, at least they could do that in the relative warmth and solitude of the bunkhouse.

Presently, Sebastien shrugged in reply. 'Who knows, these days? Did you hear what he said last week? I had no idea the Order owned a whole fortress in Tours! I thought that the Order left that kind of thing to the Templars.'

'They do, usually,' Ebel piped up. He rubbed his hands together and picked up a shovel leaning against one wall in preparation for the removal of the nightly deposit of snow outside. 'The Order of The Hand of God handed over most of its defensive strongholds to the other holy orders over a hundred years ago. It would hardly be discreet for a secret branch of the Catholic Church to own countless priceless castles all over Christendom now, would it? I dare say we wouldn't remain secret for very long. I think the only ones that remain are in Tours, Rhodes and one somewhere in the Alps...'

'And how on earth is it that you know that, Ebel?' Sigbald asked.

'Weren't you listening last week?' replied Ebel. 'Magnus was telling us some of the history. You really should listen every now and again, Sigbald. You might actually learn something.' He smirked playfully, though there was the slightest chiding tone in his voice that Sigbald did not fail to pick up on.

'Well, I can't be expected to know everything, can I?' Sigbald rolled his eyes as he arranged his bed.

'Ebel's right,' Leonardo spoke up to defend Ebel's words. 'We shouldn't lose sight of why we're all here – to protect the Christian faith and its followers.'

'Ah, Leonardo! So chivalrous!' Sebastien clapped his hands to his heart dramatically, though Leonardo knew he was being sarcastic.

Half annoyed, half amused, he replied, 'I'm serious! What Magnus tells us is important. The history is a key part of it.'

Of late, the lectures Magnus gave them in the cold chapel each Sunday morning revealed another of the Order's closely guarded secrets. Last week, he had told them of the history of its inception after the battle of Tours in 732. The Church had deemed it necessary to employ other, more subtle, tactics apart from military might alone to defend Europe from threats both foreign and domestic. That made the Order of The Hand of God just over five hundred years old.

Magnus had done his best to impress upon them that the Order served the greater good, that it acted as a shield against the evil in the world. None who heard his sermons could deny that the elderly man truly believed it, for such was the passion in his voice that they found themselves enraptured at his words, and he'd have both initiate and the other instructors alike nodding along at what he was saying.

As a result, Leonardo awaited Sunday mornings with anticipation, as the message Magnus gave filled him with hope.

Presently, Sebastien held his hands up in defeat. 'Yes, yes, you're right! I'll tell you what, I wish we'd had a speaker as interesting as Magnus at church when I was a boy...'

Sigbald nodded at that. 'Yes, he is quite good, isn't he? Anyway, speaking of church, it'll be time soon. Let's get a move on!'

They set about their work of shovelling a path from the great hall to the chapel across the blanketed yard, in the freezing air. Then, they filed into the chapel and began to light the many candles before sitting down on the benches to wait.

Before long, their superiors filed in, one by one. Walter, Drogoradz, Antonio and, finally, Magnus. The wind howled momentarily before Magnus shut the door behind him and turned the latch so it wouldn't blow open.

He made his way to the altar, stood before the great gilded silver cross and turned to glare around at them all, his lined skin creased into a frown that was a common feature on his bearded face. When he spoke, however, Leonardo knew that the contents of this sermon would not follow the same line as the others.

'Winter is almost over,' Magnus barked in his usual brisque manner. 'You have come a long way since you arrived here.' He addressed the initiates directly, shooting them each a piercing glance with his icy blue eyes.

'You have suffered in these mountains. You have understood the dangers they present and, in time, I hope you will understand why it had to be here that you were broken down and reformed. Your time here will soon be at an end, and there is but one more task we would demand from you.' Magnus paused. If he did not have their full attention before, he certainly had it now. Leonardo's breath caught in his throat and he saw the others around him visibly lean forward in anticipation.

A final task! Just one more and it would all be over! Could it be true?

'Thus far,' Magnus continued, 'we have encouraged you all to be independent. For you to be successful agents, you must have the capacity to think on your feet and act alone. All this is true, though there will be times that you are required to work together. This last task will test you in that regard.'

The initiates exchanged anxious glances as Magnus let the idea sink in for a moment.

'Individually, you have conquered all of the great summits of the Pyrenees, which is no small feat. Yet, the greatest of them is still a mystery to you – the Dove.'

There was a sharp intake of breath from the listening initiates. The Dove! Was climbing such a beast even possible? It soared high above the rest, its base at least a full day's march from the monastery. None of them had ever been asked to climb it until now, for they had assumed it to be an impossibility.

'So, the four of you will climb it, but you will not do so empty handed,' Magnus went on cryptically. Leonardo was confused and, glancing to his left and right, saw his confusion reflected in the faces of his brothers.

Then, Magnus stepped to one side and half turned, so that he could look upon the enormous silver cross hanging from two thick rods of iron on the back wall. Seven feet of thick, gilded oak, silver panels and inlaid rubies, the cross must have weighed more than even the mighty Drogoradz. The initiates followed his gaze and their eyes widened.

'This is a test that all must undergo,' said Magnus. 'Take the cross to the summit of the Dove and plant it there. Succeed, and we will see the light of God reflected from the mountain when the sun next shines. Fail, as many do, and all your training here will have been for naught!'

It was an unforgiving sentiment. All the many hours they had worked! They had bled for this, wept for it, and it could yet slip between their fingers. So many months of toil could be lost. It was a galling thought. And now, the obstacle that stood between them and success was the Dove, no less. Not only that, but they had to do it all with the enormous silver crucifix.

Magnus continued. 'Three days you will have, three more days of work. Climb the Dove, plant the cross and return within three days, and the second baptism will be yours. Do this, and it will all be over.'

The atmosphere in the bunkhouse was cowed. It had been that way for several days, ever since Magnus had given his final sermon. Once the magnitude of their task had sunk in, it had given them all pause.

'We can do this!' Sebastien had said to them all. However, he didn't sound as convincing as he'd hoped, and they all knew of the dangers that went along with such a mission. 'What was it Magnus said? This is a task all initiates must face. If they can do it, so can we!'

'Hmm!' Sigbald grunted. 'But what Magnus didn't tell us is how many of those initiates died on the Dove.' There was silence.

'Nevertheless,' Leonardo said as he leant by the fire. 'We have to try. We've worked so hard to get here, I'll not let this stand in my way. What say the rest of you? Would you fall at the last hurdle? Or see it through, until the very end?' His green eyes locked onto each of them in turn and they had nodded, knowing there was no other choice.

'Aye!' Sebastien said. 'Then, if we're going to do this, let's bloody well do it!'

It was the night before their departure, and they had made as many preparations as they could. The enormous silver cross stood leaning by the door ominously. It had taken all four of them to lower it safely from the wall and they had grunted with exertion at such a task.

'By God, it's heavy!' Sigbald had exclaimed. 'It must weigh as much as any of us.'

'More than that!' Ebel puffed as he lifted one end.

Up close, the cross was quite beautiful. The burnished silver was aged, though still reflected the light prettily. Thick plates of it were riveted to the oak beneath, and its surface was marred by a thousand tiny scratches. Here and there, it was studded with jewels, and Leonardo could see that certain recesses were empty and partly crumpled, perhaps where the rubies had been knocked free and lost. On the back, one of the silver panels had been bent away slightly where a nail had sheared to reveal the dark oak beneath.

It was a monstrous thing, and there had been more than a little debate as to how they were to transport it the many miles to the summit of the Dove. Eventually, after having experimented with several methods during the days after their mission was announced, the four of them had constructed a crude sled that they would take turns to haul along the flatter parts of the journey. Then, when the terrain grew too steep for that, they would haul it via a rope up each slope. None of them, however, had managed to come up with a viable solution on how they might haul the thing up the head of the Dove, where every side of the mountain became almost sheer for a hundred yards before levelling out at the summit.

Whatever happened, it was sure to be an inhuman effort.

'So we just leave it up there?' Sigbald mused to the room.

'Well, I suppose so. We plant it there and come back,' Sebastien offered by way of reply. 'Magnus didn't say anything about bringing it back down again.'

'Hmm,' Leonardo frowned. 'Then how is it here before us? He said it's "a test that all must undergo." If the last group of initiates had to do it, too, they must have brought it back down with them, no?'

The others exchanged a glance and they lapsed into silence as they thought on it for a moment, wondering if there was something the instructors were not telling them. But then Ebel let out an 'Oh!' of understanding and snapped his fingers.

'I get it!' he said to the others. 'One group of initiates must have had to take it up, and the next lot bring it down! That's how it's here now. The last lot must have been sent to get it.'

'Huh,' Sebastien muttered. 'That does make sense...'

The others seemed willing to believe this theory, though Leonardo was unsure. He sensed that they were missing something.

However, he didn't have time to dwell on the apprehensive nagging at the back of his mind, for the conversation in the room was already changing to the matter of provisions they were to take with them. That, too, had sparked some debate amongst them.

'Perhaps we should bring more than we need?' Leonardo had suggested. 'Would it not be good to be ready for anything?'

Ebel had shaken his head. 'I don't see the point. We have three days, any more than that and we'll have failed anyway. Three days should be all we need.'

'I agree,' Sebastien nodded. 'Besides, it isn't like any of us need anything else to carry with that damned cross.' He gestured at the seven-foot yoke standing by the door. 'I think we should try to travel as light as possible so that we might get there faster.'

That had decided things for their provisions. Then, there was the route. Ebel had scouted for them the day before, concluding that the most direct route would be to travel east and loop around the base of Mount Andosia – though, even then, it would take them up and down three separate glacial plains and valleys.

The distance, as the crow flies, would have been easy had the terrain been flat. That was not the case, however, and Ebel had estimated that it would take them the whole day to reach the base of the Dove. That meant they had the second day to heave the cross to the top and descend, and the third to return to the monastery. Given that they could make the climb, they were starting to see that it was theoretically possible, though none of them had ever attempted anything so difficult.

Over the past few days, they had tried to glean as much information from their instructors as their newfound informality with them would allow. However, when Sebastien had asked Drogoradz, usually the most talkative of the four instructors with the initiates, his answer had been evasive.

'It is not for me to say, but for you lads to find out for yourselves. What I will say is this – prepare yourselves, for the challenge ahead is greater than you can know.'

Later, in the confines of the bunkhouse, the initiates had discussed what that might have meant, but had ultimately drawn a blank. If anything, it only served to increase the knot of anxiety they all felt twisting their guts.

There was silence for a moment as they were all wrapped up in their own thoughts and fears, imagining what might happen on the morrow. Just then, the door to the bunkhouse was pushed open from the outside and Magnus let himself in.

They all stiffened; Magnus only came into the bunkhouse to scold them for its untidy state, though tonight it seemed he had no such intentions. He shut the door behind him with a dull thud and they waited for him to speak.

'Are you all ready?' he said after a pause. The four initiates nodded in unison. 'Good. Then I will speak to you now, as I will not see you in the morning. You should be planning to set out before daybreak from whence the time limit will have begun.' They nodded again.

There was a moment's pause, during which Magnus fixed his intense gaze onto the floorboards. The four initiates could see his mouth working as the thick, white bristles of his beard moved to and fro. 'Then I will bid you good luck,' he muttered. 'You have been fine students.'

There was silence as Leonardo and the others shifted uncomfortably. They had not expected such high praise from their teacher, for that was what it was, especially from the lips of Magnus no less, and Leonardo could think of no appropriate response to give. Fortunately, Sebastien spoke up.

'Thank you, Teacher,' he said. 'We will do our best not to disappoint you.'

'I'm sure you will not, my boy.' Magnus's eyes looked up and met Sebastien's, then he looked around at the others, his omnipresent glare softening for just a moment. 'Very well, then perhaps I will see you all on the other side of this.' He gave a curt nod, turned to open the door and left.

Perhaps. He had said perhaps. They all exchanged a look once Magnus had closed the door behind him.

'By Mary and Joseph!' Sigbald exclaimed. 'He spoke to us as if we're about to walk to the executioner's block!' He crossed himself, for Magnus's praise was more worrying than anything they had yet heard.

'Or, maybe he cares more than he lets on…' Sebastien mused. 'Anyway, are we sure we're all ready?' he asked, looking around at them all.

He received a nod of confirmation from the other three. They had all double and triple checked the contents of their leather satchels, ensuring they had everything they needed, as well as plenty of rope to haul the sled with. They were as ready as they would ever be.

'We should get some sleep,' Ebel counselled sagely, though they all knew that sleep that night was sure to evade them. Nevertheless, they climbed into their lumpy cots a moment later, huddled in furs and blankets as the fire crackled.

Leonardo stared into its flickering yellow flames until they had died to ash and ember, which glowed a dull red. His future hung in the balance, and it was unclear what would become of him. In several days' time, his life would change forever, one way or another.

When he woke, Leonardo could not remember falling asleep, but felt that he had barely slept. He swung himself from the cot as his brothers stirred around him. Silently, they prepared, checking again that their equipment was where it ought to be and that they had everything they needed. Ebel had volunteered to have the first go with the cross, and he and Sigbald hauled it onto the sled, lashing the cross to it with rope.

Once ready, they gave each other a nod and opened the door to the mountains that waited beyond, and began their final journey together.

The wind blew so hard it threatened to strip their cloaks from their shoulders. They had begun the day with clear skies that had now morphed into thick grey clouds overhead, and snow had begun to fall.

The going was slow; the huge, gilded crucifix was a mighty yoke and more than once they had cursed the undulating terrain. Had it been flat, it would have been almost easy, but they had no such good fortune. As it was, the slopes of the mountain tended to pull the sled left or right, threatening to yank the bearer downhill with it.

That had almost been Ebel's fate, when only an hour in, just as the sun had made its first appearance, he had staggered as the sled had begun to slip off the course of their path, down into a ravine. Leonardo had to run and dive to save both Ebel and their precious cargo.

Since then, the bearer had taken the lead and the sled had been flanked, when possible, by two of the others, while a third rested. It was hard going; they had to change the driver of the yoke every half hour, and had thought to have a second man help to pull, but soon realised that that would be impossible due to the narrow paths and steep sides of the mountains.

The snow was thick and deep everywhere and, even with their snowshoes, the initiates struggled, often leaning on their walking sticks to catch their breaths during the climbs. They went up and down, soon escaping the shadow of the monastery's mountain and descending into the next valley.

Climbing the other side was arduous; their route was lined with young pines, and wide enough for only one man to walk alone. It was Sebastien who had the bad luck of hauling the sled at that point. For a half hour, he cursed at the trees as the sled caught on their trunks, or otherwise on rocks that caused him to stumble and the rope to tug at his waist, halting him in his tracks and forcing him to turn to negotiate the release of the sled with violent tugs of his own.

Even with Leonardo and Sigbald pushing from below, Sebastien was soon crying out in frustration, the sound echoing from the sides of the lifeless valley before being lost to the wind. At least the activity kept them warm, Leonardo thought to himself. Though, that was little comfort, for their warmth meant that they were using a great deal of energy, and he had come to learn that managing his energy reserves in the mountains was crucial to survival there.

An individual expended much of it to climb a mountain and Leonardo had never had more of a ravenous appetite than when he'd returned to the monastery after conquering a summit. Once they had climbed to the other side of the valley, Mount Andosia was in sight, and there they stopped for some food and drink.

They each carried three days of provisions in their packs, consisting of several corked waterskins, for they had no good way of melting the snow during the trek, and a great block of cheese and leg of goat each that they tore into, biting great chunks off before washing it down with gulps of the icy cold water.

They didn't rest for long, however. They knew that the march ahead had to be completed before nightfall, as well as make some kind of shelter that was to protect them from the elements. As soon as they had slaked their thirst and filled their bellies, they were away.

The four of them spoke little during the journey. There was no joke-filled banter as there might otherwise have been; instead, they talked only when they discussed where the next leg of the journey would take them, or how to navigate a particularly difficult portion of the route with the sled.

The great cross lay mockingly, tall and outstretched, upon the sled; it was an anchor that they had all quickly come to resent. It had entered their minds briefly to cheat and they had debated whether they might find some other, lighter object that reflected the sunlight that they could plant at the summit of the Dove. However, they quickly dismissed the thought, when they concluded that, by the time they had found something like that, their three days would be up. They were, after all, in the middle of the Pyrenees in winter; it was a wilderness.

Onwards they went, into the shadow of Mount Andosia, which they had all climbed at some point or other, sticking to the ridges on the higher ground as much as possible to ease their passing. Even so, the ground was seldom flat, and they had all lost count of the ridges and trenches, hills and troughs they had traversed.

It was all a blur of brilliant white, the landscape covered with pristine snow that seemed to melt all of its features together. Their breath steamed in the air as they ploughed on beneath the freezing grey and white mass of sky, the clouds so dense overhead that it was hard to tell where the land ended and the sky began.

Beyond, the titanic craggy mass of the Dove loomed, with its great, rounded head of rock that made up the summit. It towered above them, growing larger and more intimidating with every hour that passed. It dared them to try to climb it; massive and indifferent, it would be utterly unforgiving.

'The weather's changing!' Sigbald called from the rear. 'There'll be a blizzard tonight, I can feel it! We need to get to the Dove fast!'

'Aye!' Sebastien called back from the front, squinting up at the sky as Ebel directed him over the virgin snow. 'Let's get a move on!'

They redoubled their efforts, knowing that their survival might depend on constructing an adequate shelter. It was almost impossible to determine what time of day it was; the sun was nowhere to be seen, and the light from above had dimmed to an opaque glow that the clouds had almost managed to blot out entirely.

The snow began to fall. Sigbald and Sebastien, who now sported thick beards, soon found them to be covered in crystalised ice where the freezing air had turned their breath solid.

The initiates soon descended into the last valley, awkwardly traversing the boulderous stream that cut through its middle, before beginning the climb up the other side, for which they were almost grateful, as it sheltered them from the worst of the gale that buffeted them constantly.

At least here there were no trees to impede them, just the steepness of the slope. They had to untie Sigbald and the other three had to laboriously haul the sled up between them. Once, about halfway up, Sigbald slipped back and fell heavily into the snow, letting go of the rope.

Suddenly, Leonardo felt the weight of the sled increase as he took up Sigbald's slack and was yanked backward, the motion causing him to shoulder Sebastien aside so that he, too, fell. In a flash, the rope was slipping through Leonardo's fingers at a rate of knots as the sled plummeted back down the hill.

Leonardo cried out as he desperately gripped the hemp rope, which flew between his hands so fast it burnt through the layers of cloth he wore on his fingers.

'Arrgh!' he cried, and Ebel looked on aghast from above as the sled hurtled downhill. Leonardo knew he would have to let go at any moment and the sled would crash into the valley floor. They would have to restart their climb from the bottom, losing an hour of valuable time.

But then, Sebastien appeared at his side and his hands gripped the rope too, and the sled slowed. Sigbald was there, clamping down with all his considerable strength to stop the sled's descent entirely. The three of them stood, panting from the effort, as Leonardo gave the two of them a silent nod of thanks before they began to haul the cross back up to their position once more.

As the light began to dim, they could tell evening was approaching, and the need to get to safety was impressed upon them when the temperature began to drop, the way it always did when the sun had dropped below the mountains. The four comrades climbed from the valley in the gloom to find the Dove soaring up above them menacingly.

They would need to spend another hour of the next morning getting to the true base before they could begin the real ascent in earnest, but they were close enough to set up camp. Not that they had much choice, for the light was fading fast.

With practised motions, the different jobs of shelter building were distributed and they set about their work, anxious that the snow was now falling so heavily they could barely see more than fifty yards ahead.

'Quickly!' Ebel called over the wind. 'We won't last long in this!'

They dug with small shovels that were kept tucked in their packs, stamping the snow down here and there to condense it, so they might carve a recess into it that could fit the four of them inside.

'There's no time to do it properly,' Sigbald called. 'Just hollow something out and cover it with the blankets we have!' No one argued and, soon, in the snowdrift they had chosen, they had hollowed out a rough cave and covered the entrance with thick woollen blankets, over which they shovelled snow to insulate them.

They crawled inside, just as night fell and the blizzard passed above them, buffeting the side of their shelter with a vicious cyclone. It was so powerful it tugged one corner of the half-submerged blanket free, and Ebel had to sit with his arm stretched up to hold it in place until the gale had subsided some. They made the repairs, then lay down to sleep, each of them utterly exhausted from the gruelling day's work, as hard as they had ever known, and were disheartened by the fact they had two more days to survive.

The shelter was barely wide enough for them all to lie in and they were crammed together. However, they didn't mind, for it meant that their warmth was recycled, and it was the only way to stop their teeth from chattering with cold. Leonardo did not even have the energy to wonder what the next day might bring before he was asleep.

259

Chapter 20

GASCONY

Leonardo and Sebastien sat on a bench at the docks as they watched the men of the King's army board the ships, climbing awkwardly up the gangways, their grim faces resigned to the rough sea voyage that would follow. Every so often, a pair could be seen hauling a stretcher between them, its occupant covered by a blanket to protect them from the cold. The fabric was stained with blood where the man's weeping wounds had sullied it, a groan of pain escaping from his lips as he fidgeted half-consciously.

But they were the only reminder that a rebellion was happening outside of the city of Bordeaux, for it had remained loyal since the beginning and had enjoyed freedoms other cities in Gascony had not. Its ports had remained open for trade and ships constantly navigated the meandering waters of the Garonne that split Bordeaux in two.

Many such ships of late were English military vessels, and professional crews cast away from the jetties, their decks full of soldiers, wounded or otherwise, to take them back to England. Leonardo watched as the cog before them cast away and there was much shouting as the sailors called to one another, jumping around the ship to fiddle with the rigging, unfurl the masts or dip great oars into the water, whilst the soldiers on board watched, bemused, trying not to get in the way.

It was December and King Henry had run out of money. The campaign had stalled, falling just shy of the achievements the loyalists had hoped for before winter. More rebel towns had fallen into the hands of the loyalists and, not long after the siege of Bazas was won, Amaneus d'Albret and Bernard de Bouville, the greatest rebel lords of central and Northern Gascony, respectively, had sued for peace.

Henry had ultimately been lenient, for he wanted a speedy end to the whole debacle and pardoned his nobles in the hopes that the rest would follow their lead. It was not so. In the south, Gaston de Bearn was still at large, his rampant insurgence fuelled in large part by King Alfonso of Castile. Annoyingly, La Reole too had held out, the siege of the great fortress occupying much of King Henry's resources.

Now that the weather had turned, all campaigning activity had ground to a halt and many of the English noblemen, including the King himself, had returned to Bordeaux to pass the winter there. Though King Henry had been successful in stamping out most of the rebellion, what little Leonardo had seen of him he knew that the King was bitterly disappointed. His coffers were dry and he had been forced to send the great bulk of his men-at-arms home, after his sergeants had been caught pawning their armour so that they might pay for an extra meal.

The elite of his knights stayed on, however, and Henry had tried to maintain good relations with the Spanish kingdom of Navarre, going so far as to ask for military aid from the other side of the Pyrenees. But that was now too late, for the mountain passes were unusable for the time being and Henry would have to wait.

Leonardo and Sebastien, for their part, were doing plenty of waiting, too. However, at least for them, they could rest contentedly, knowing they had done all they could to ensure their primary mission was fulfilled – to keep Gascony in the hands of the English, so that the balance of power on the continent was maintained. It seemed that the question of the rebels' demise was only a matter of time.

In the meantime, there had been other distractions to occupy them. In early November, the pair of them had been invited to dine with Queen Eleanor. Although Leonardo had accepted, for it would have been considered extremely rude to do otherwise, he did so with a pang of apprehension, knowing that the meal was likely to be a very formal occasion and would undoubtedly include other powerful nobles.

Sure enough, when he and Sebastien had sidled into the banqueting hall of the King and Queen's lodgings in a royal house of Bordeaux, the room had been filled with people that towered over Leonardo on the social hierarchy. He greeted each of them in turn – the Queen's ladies-in-waiting, high-ranking knights and nobles, including Roger de Ros and Peter of Savoy, and there were not one, but two, bishops present.

Leonardo took his seat uncomfortably, flattening his pristine robes over his breast self-consciously. He had paid the washerwomen double to do an extra thorough job on them, but the garments felt inadequate amongst such company, nonetheless. Many candles lined the table and a fire burnt in the hearth, warming them from behind, as their cups of wine were never allowed to empty with the army of servants on hand that buzzed around like flies.

The table seemed to have been organised in respect to the occupants' rank. While the King and many of the nobles still campaigned in the countryside, the Queen was, of course, chief amongst them, and she flanked her seat at the head of the table with the two bishops and Peter of Savoy.

Leonardo and Sebastien had a place at the far end, for which Leonardo was grateful. Sebastien was soon chatting discreetly to the pretty, auburn-haired lady-in-waiting, making her laugh at something or other, a twinkle in her eye. Annoyingly, he seemed far more at ease than Leonardo, who had remarked that he would have much preferred a basic meal around a campfire in the company of Drogo de Barentin and his knights.

When the food arrived, however, he almost changed his mind. For the esteemed guests, no less than nine courses of food were served, the first of which were salted oysters, followed by pork pies and peas served with a rich, fatty sauce. By the fifth course, Leonardo had had enough, and finished his steak with a satisfied sigh, looking around to learn that it was apparently customary to only pick at each course and leave most on the plate. He wondered if one ever tired of eating in such a manner each day. The lavish food was a far cry from the basic gruel or stews he was used to; however, when the deserts were served, he couldn't resist trying a delicious lemon tart, and was pleasantly surprised to find that it tasted even better than it looked.

By the time the last plates were taken away, Leonardo was stuffed and content to endure the idle conversation of Roger de Ros. After having sat down for an hour or more, the guests stood and mingled amongst themselves. The wine was strong, and Leonardo felt it go straight to his head, despite the enormous quantity of food in his stomach, and signalled to one of the many servants requesting something weaker. He never liked to lose control of his faculties.

He seemed to be the only one, however – apart from the Queen herself, who appeared to be as sharp as usual. When Roger de Ros had finally gotten bored of Leonardo's curt, one-word responses to his chatter, he excused himself to search for someone more talkative. Leonardo stood back from the crowd, watching the Queen with a good degree of interest. She was laughing at something one of the bishops said, her smile reaching her pretty eyes, and she touched the man's arm, causing him to beam at her with delight, the slightly tipsy bishop looking incredibly pleased with himself for having brought her joy.

Leonardo was no fool and could see that, beneath the mask of innocent playfulness, everyone who met her loved her, for Queen Eleanor was a master politician. Leonardo edged a little closer to pick at the olives left on the table, despite his belly being fit to burst, so that he might hear some of the conversation.

'Yes, thank you, Bishop, so wonderful of you to say!' Eleanor's words met his ears over the hubbub.

'Oh, not at all, Your Highness. Anything I can do to help!' the Bishop declared with an enamoured smile.

Suddenly, Queen Eleanor's face turned serious and her eyes became big and round. 'Do you really mean that, Bishop? You would do anything to help?'

'Y-yes!' the Bishop stammered, suddenly worried he might have somehow offended the Queen. 'Anything at all, my dear. Just say the word!'

'Well, um, I suppose, now that you've broached the subject, there is something you can help me with, Bishop.' The Queen blinked her big, serious, hazel eyes for effect and the Bishop was hers.

'Name it! If it is within my power, I will see it done. You have my word, Your Highness!'

'Oh, you're such a wonderful man!' said Eleanor. 'The matter concerns my friend, William of London. He, too, is a great man of the Church, like yourself, and I wish him to become Bishop of Flamstead. Will you vouch for him before your brothers of the Church? Do you have such power as to get William elected? I think he would make such a good Bishop!'

The Bishop almost went down on one knee, bending humbly before the Queen. 'I do! And I shall, my Queen. I shall!'

Leonardo smiled to himself as he wandered over to the fire, tossing an olive pip into the flames, as a servant presented him with a cup of weaker wine that he took gratefully, taking a sip. The Queen had just used her charm to get one of her supporters elected to a significant political seat of power in England. She was clever and, Leonardo thought, an asset to her husband.

He stood there for a time, leaning on the carved stone pillars that flanked the enormous hearth, and stared into the flames, mulling around his thoughts and content to distance himself from the conversation of the upper echelons of the court.

A moment later, he was drawn from his reverie when a figure appeared at his side. When he looked up and saw who it was, he bowed deeply.

'Your Highness,' Leonardo said as he straightened. 'I am honoured by your invitation.'

Queen Eleanor smiled disarmingly at him and waved a hand dismissively. 'The pleasure is mine. You are, after all, Father Leonardo, a good friend and colleague to Father Sebastien, whom I hold in high regard.'

'A good friend,' Leonardo repeated stiffly, still a little uncomfortable in the presence of such people. 'Were those his words or yours, I wonder?'

Queen Eleanor gave him a shrewd look. 'They were his. Of a sort. In any case, he tells me you are as capable as he, if not more so. I can see that the two of you have a long history, though Sebastien has not told me how it is that you know each other.' Although the question was not asked, Leonardo could sense she was prying for answers, for she was not stupid, and must have seen that there was a rift between the two old friends.

'He does me a great service in saying so,' Leonardo deflected. 'I take it he has helped you previously with a similar manner of work to that which we have done for you, Your Highness?'

Queen Eleanor nodded. 'He has indeed. When I first learnt of his... talents, I knew he would be useful.'

'And how is it you came to learn of Sebastien and our organisation, if you don't mind me asking, Your Highness?' Now it was Leonardo's turn to pry.

'Not at all,' the Queen said. 'I know Sebastien's master. He is...' She trailed off, her eyes drifting to the flames licking over the logs in the fire, and Leonardo saw a look of what might have been discomfort flash across her pretty face, and the Queen shuddered visibly. Only one of the Fingers of The Order could make a Queen afraid.

'Ruthless?' Leonardo finished for her.

Eleanor collected herself and nodded. 'Yes,' she confirmed. 'And effective. Though, I know Sebastien to be a good man, with a good heart.' She smiled and the two of them glanced over to see Sebastien telling Roger de Ros a joke, at which the small man was laughing hysterically.

'I am rather fond of him,' the Queen said quietly, and Leonardo supressed a frown as she turned back to him. 'And you, Father Leonardo, do you enjoy the work you do?' Her hazel eyes fixed intently onto his green ones, and he felt he was under scrutiny.

'My work never usually takes me into the presence of such people,' Leonardo replied evasively. 'Though, strangely enough, Your Highness, you are the second Queen I have had the pleasure of speaking to in my life.'

'Oh, really?' Eleanor said, surprised. 'Pray tell, who beat me to it?'

'Actually, it was none other than your sister, the Queen of France.'

Eleanor's eyes lit up. 'Ah, Margaret! I do so love my older sister. We maintain frequent correspondences, you know. Tell me, Father, when was it that you met her?'

'In Cyprus, Your Highness. My work had taken me, along with the ill-fated crusade of King Louis, two years ago. I met your sister at the castle in Nicosia.' Leonardo remembered her well. Margaret had been stunningly beautiful and the envy of every man who laid eyes upon her.

'Ah, yes, she told me about the adventure,' replied Eleanor. 'What a shame it ended poorly. It is the reason, you know, that my husband pledged himself to crusade. He was inspired by Louis, even if the venture was not as successful as he would have liked.' The Queen was being polite, Leonardo knew. The seventh crusade had been a disaster and Louis' army had been all but wiped out, along with a whole host of elite Templar and Hospitaller knights, at the hands of the Egyptian Sultan's army.

'Yes. She was as enchanting as you are, Your Highness,' said Leonardo, and he allowed himself a smile that came too easily to his lips.

Retuning the smile, Queen Eleanor said, 'You are too kind, Father. Forgive me, I must check on my other guests.' The Queen excused herself to join the rest of the group, leaving Leonardo alone once more. After their conversation, he could not help but find that he liked the young Queen all the more, though felt that their talk had had a purpose. Leonardo had the feeling that Queen Eleanor had been attempting to gauge his character, perhaps deciding whether or not he was trustworthy.

Since Leonardo had been careful to give nothing of importance away that the Queen did not already know, he had no idea what conclusion she would have drawn about him. He watched as she made her way to Sebastien's side, placing a hand on his arm affectionately, smiling up at him as he looked down at her. By then, the other guests were either too drunk to notice, or had left already, for the hour was well past midnight. But Leonardo *did* notice, and it made him feel uneasy.

After the banquet, toward the end of November, many of the King's knights and the King himself returned to winter at Bordeaux, save for those who were garrisoned in captured towns. The city felt a little busier after that, and there were no more invitations to fancy dinners since there were a plethora of other, more noteworthy guests to appease.

Leonardo was content to pass the time training discreetly with Drogo and his knights. His face was known as a priest amongst the court, and he was careful not to be seen wielding a sword to those who had not already seen him use one.

Leonardo met regularly with Sebastien, too, and the pair of them had caught up over the much more basic meals served at the taverns of Bordeaux. Each regaled the other with the tales of their adventures since they had last met, filling in twelve years' worth of absence and, as the weather outside grew chillier, it seemed like the pair of them were as companionable as ever.

Or, they would have been, had the past itself not hung between them like a rotting cadaver. They let it fester, hoping that, by not mentioning the events that took place in the mountains, it would go away. And perhaps they were right; perhaps nothing needed to be said.

Leonardo was certainly happy to believe so. What mattered was that he had his oldest friend back, and he felt a wash of comfort to know that he was not completely alone in the world after all. For Sebastien understood him, shared all the same barriers that life had set for him, and could relate to all the many and great hardships that an agent of the Order had to endure.

The two of them had even gone hunting on occasion, galloping out of the city with bows slung on their backs, accompanied by Drogo and his knights, and Leonardo was reminded of the excellent team he and Sebastien made.

Leonardo would stalk the fields for deer, jumping out and making a racket when he spotted one, causing it to bolt right into Sebastien's path, and the creature would take an arrow straight to the heart.

They ate well, butchering the meat as they'd been taught and sharing it by the fire, laughing and talking of whatever sprung to mind.

Leonardo felt happier than he had for many years knowing that their friendship was all but repaired. There was just one thing gnawing at him that dampened his mood. Leonardo feared for his friend, and there was a question that needed to be asked that he wasn't sure he wanted an answer to.

Presently, they sat at the docks of Bordeaux, watching the activity as the soldiers sailed away downriver and toward the Bay of Biscay.

'I wonder how much ships like those cost?' Sebastien pondered absent-mindedly, as Leonardo thought how best to ask what had been troubling him.

'No idea,' he replied. 'Why? Are you thinking of becoming a ship's captain?'

Sebastien scoffed. 'Not bloody likely. Not with my wheat stalks for sea legs. Anyway, it isn't like I have the money to afford one.'

'Where would you go?'

Sebastien shrugged. 'Somewhere warm.' There was a pause as the two of them watched the goings on before them in silence for a time. Three men struggled with a fearful nag that had been spooked by the lurching ships, perhaps thinking that they were great lumbering timber sea monsters, and the creature bucked and brayed in wide-eyed fear as a fourth sailor ran over to help.

'Can I ask you something, brother?' Leonardo said finally, turning to Sebastien with a serious face.

Sebastien frowned for a moment and shrugged. 'Aye, go on then.'

Leonardo hesitated, wondering about the best way to go about asking it, eventually deciding it was best to just come out with it. He cleared his throat. 'You and Queen Eleanor seem very... close.'

Leonardo let it hang in the air as Sebastien narrowed his eyes.

'I've worked with her for years now. What of it?' he said suspiciously.

Leonardo sighed. 'You should be careful, Sebastien. I don't know what it is you do for her, *with* her exactly. But know that, to her, men such as us are pawns in a game. We are to be used and discarded.'

Sebastien bristled at that. 'Queen Eleanor is as honourable a lady as I have ever known. It has been a pleasure to serve her in any way she has demanded.'

Leonardo's heart sank as he felt a wall come up between them. 'Yes, I understand that,' he replied, 'but you must know that you are expendable. Besides, we both need to keep in mind that, should we fail to prioritise the Order and the vows we both made over any allegiance to what could be a fickle Queen, for all I know, then a far worse fate awaits us.'

At that, Sebastien's nostrils flared. 'Do you think I do not know that? I know my vows and I know the Queen better than you! I will not hear of any insult toward her. We will speak of it no more.' Sebastien had stood from the bench and stalked away, leaving Leonardo wondering if something had been left out.

Over the coming days when the pair next met, the conversation had been forgotten and Sebastien was back to his usual laughing self. Leonardo was glad and did not risk bringing the subject up again. However, he decided that there was indeed something that Sebastien was not telling him and feared that Sebastien was in well over his head.

Leonardo decided he would try to get to the bottom of it, for Sebastien's sake.

Twelve years ago

Leonardo was being shaken awake and opened his eyes to find Sebastien kneeling over him.

'Come on, Leo! No time to waste. It's light already!'

He rolled to his side and rubbed the sleep from his eyes and shivered. It had been a cold night; however, for once, he had not been woken by his own shivering, for he had been so very tired. He still was, he realised, but sighed, knowing that there would not be another chance to sleep for some time yet.

His legs cramped painfully as he tried to move them, and his belly ached for food and he remembered they had not had the time to eat the night before. Leonardo freed himself from the tangle of blankets and crawled from the makeshift shelter, straightening to see his brothers arranging their belongings, the only sound being the crunch of their boots on the fresh powder in the still, morning air.

The skies were clear and the sun was just peeking from the 'V' to one side of the Dove in the east, shining on them with a blissful warmth. It looked to be a good day.

But then Leonardo frowned. He looked around, confused at first, before beginning to scrabble around in the snow desperately.

'What the hell are you doing?' Sigbald asked.

'The sled! Where is the damned sled!' Leonardo cried out, searching around the virgin powder for any sign of it.

The others stopped in their tracks and exchanged a glance of panic as they realised that the sled was, indeed, missing.

'Shit! The snow must have buried it! Where was it last night?' Sebastien joined Leonardo, hunting around with his boots in the snow for a hint of gleaming silver.

'Over here, I think!' Ebel called back as he sank to his knees in the snow several yards from Leonardo and began to jab his walking stick down beneath its surface. As the four of them searched, the feeling of apprehension rose in their chests. They were well aware of the amount of snow one blizzard could deposit in just a single night. What if they never found the cross? What if they searched all day and all of the next and found nothing? What would Magnus say if they returned as empty-handed failures?

They all knew full well that he would scorn the idea of a second chance and he'd say something like, 'It was your damned fault you didn't mark its position! It's not as if you didn't know there was a blizzard outside!'

'Bollocks!' Sigbald cursed in fury as he hauled up another plume of dry, glittering powder that drifted through the air like pale confetti. 'We might never find it. I'm sick of this fucking mountain!'

'Alright, alright!' Sebastien shouted back at him, equally as frustrated. 'Complaining about the mountain isn't about to help us find the cross, is it? Shut up and get digging!'

Leonardo watched as Sigbald glowered and opened his mouth to reply, just as Ebel's stick hit something with a dull *thunk!*

'Here!' he cried. 'It's here! Quick, help me dig!'

The rest of them scrambled over to Ebel's position and, in their excitement, shifted several feet of snow in as many minutes until they locked eyes upon a ruby that glittered up at them out of the snow like an amused, twinkling red eye.

They laughed in relief and clawed away the rest of the snow, freeing the sled and tugging it onto the surface. They clapped each other on the back and, once Sigbald and Sebastien had muttered an embarrassed apology to one another, they wasted no time in setting off. Another long day awaited them, and they would need every hour of daylight they could get.

Leonardo began with the sled this time, but when he attached the rope to his waist and began to pull in the direction of the Dove, the sled seemed not to want to move, as if it had doubled in weight overnight. With a great effort, he hauled it into motion and decided that, in his fatigued state, he was simply weaker.

The climb began without them noticing, gradual at first, then the slope grew much steeper as they made their way under the rocky crag above, stealing glances every now and again at the enormity of the challenge that awaited them above. Soon, it was so steep they had to untie themselves from the sled and pull from higher up the slope, as they had the day before, anchoring it this time at intervals so that it couldn't fall into the ravine below.

They called up and down the slope to one another, coordinating the relay as they passed the rope to their fellows, then climbed above them to take it the next leg of the way. However, they could only do this for so long and, after a couple of hours, were forced to stop, for they had reached the Dove's iconic head of sheer rock, and the use of the sled became an impossibility.

The air there was thin, even thinner than they were used to. Looking around, they could see that they had been ascending steadily over the course of the previous day and that morning, reaching dizzying heights that already trumped most of the lesser peaks they had climbed that winter. But the hardest part was yet to come.

Though the sun shone bright, for which they were all grateful and prayed it stayed that way, the wind blew and the air was cold. The four initiates pulled extra layers onto their shoulders as they sat upon the wide ridge at the edge of the sheer face of bedrock.

They perched themselves on exposed stone, or the cross itself, and greedily tucked into their stores of meat, bread and cheese, pausing every so often to take long swigs from their waterskins that they had been careful to keep tucked between their bodies during the night. If the waterskins froze, they would become undrinkable and therefore useless.

They feasted in silence, each of them filling their bellies to bursting with salted meat and rich cheeses, consuming their quota for the morning.

Sigbald was the first to finish and he was soon standing, craning his neck and gazing upward at the Dove, deep in thought. Leonardo joined him a moment later, standing by his side.

'What are you thinking?' he asked.

Sigbald rubbed the beard on his chin. 'We can hardly use the sled. I say we make a couple of straps from the rope we have and loop them around the horizontal arms of the cross. Wear the thing like a pack as we climb.'

'Hmm,' replied Leonardo. 'That wouldn't be a bad idea if it was half the size. But it's seven feet tall and heavier than all of us.'

Sigbald sighed. 'Well, I'm all ears if you have a better suggestion.'

Leonardo racked his brain and was about to answer that he had no better plan, when Ebel spoke from behind them.

'How about this. We split into pairs, each taking a different route up and staying parallel, then each pair will have a rope attached to the cross that will hang between us. That way, we half its weight. We could even wrap it in our blankets to protect it.'

Leonardo and Sigbald looked at one another with the hint of a smile.

'You always were the clever one, Ebel!' Sigbald chuckled. 'Sounds good to me. Let's get to it, then.'

'Hang on!' Sebastien said, through a mouthful of bread and cheese. 'I have to finish this first!' They laughed as he brandished the loaf of bread.

'Move your arse, then!' Leonardo replied as they set about preparing the cross for the next part of the journey. The sled was abandoned, and they used all of the rope they had left to secure two equal lengths of twenty feet to the horizontal arms of the cross, testing all their knowledge of the knots they had learnt the last year.

As they worked, Leonardo could not help but steal glances at the head of the Dove. He was suddenly hit with the magnitude of it. The face they had chosen to climb rose up before them, several hundred feet of seemingly vertical cliff face intersected by a thousand different neat layers of rock, like the rings of a tree. It was naked and hard, a mass of dark grey, brown and black granite amidst a world of white. He swallowed. The top seemed such a long way off.

'We should leave our packs with the sled,' Sebastien suggested once he had finished eating. 'Take perhaps a waterskin each?'

'Yes, they'd only get in the way,' Ebel agreed.

'What of the second man?' Sigbald asked. 'What does the other in the pair do while the first climbs?'

'He could act as an anchor, tied to the first and a little higher up,' replied Leonardo. 'That way, if either of us slip, we'd have a chance...' He trailed off, not wanting to entertain the possibility of falling from such dizzying heights.

The rest nodded and Sebastien and Sigbald hauled the cross, now swathed in thick blankets, onto their shoulders to begin the march of several hundred yards up to where the climb truly began. They walked in silence, grateful that the weather seemed calm that day and the wind was only half as powerful as usual.

The deep snow changed to solid rock underfoot where it began to protrude through the surface. They were now so high and exposed that even the snow could not settle without being scattered by the wind. The hardy ice that remained was so carved by the wind that beautiful, wavy patterns had formed, cut deep into its surface that was not unlike the way sand was shaped by streams at the beach.

Unlike the sand, however, the ice was hard and cold and so too was the air. Leonardo's heart sank when he realised they would have to unwrap their hands so as to have better purchase on the rocks. He could only hope they could move fast enough so that they reached the top before he lost his fingers.

Several minutes later and they were basked in the light of an unobstructed sun as it began its own ascent through the heavens, shining its light on the cliffs above.

'At least that's something!' Sebastien exclaimed as he and Sigbald set down the cross, for they could take it no further on foot.

'Aye,' Sigbald muttered in reply. 'We could use a bit of luck.'

'The air's thin up here,' Ebel said to no one in particular.

'Right, who shall go with who?' Sebastien asked. They looked around, each weighing up the others.

Eventually, Ebel sighed and said, 'Perhaps I should go with Sigbald, since I'm the slightest and he's the stockiest.'

Sigbald clapped his companion on the shoulder. 'And don't you forget it!' he said, causing Ebel to roll his eyes.

Sebastien nodded. 'Yes, that ought to balance things out. I guess I'm with you, Leo!' He turned to Leonardo with an infectious grin that Leonardo could not help but return.

As the others busied themselves with the harnesses, Leonardo turned to look upon the mountains spread below. Once again, he was struck by their sheer beauty and thought that there had never been a more glorious place to pledge himself to God. He sank to his knees, clasped his hands together and began to whisper in prayer, closing his eyes as the sun warmed the skin on his face.

He asked his Lord to keep the strength in his arms, and the elements fair. He asked that God protect his companions and to keep them safe. And he asked, most importantly of all, for guidance and for God to show him the path forward, for it was not always clear to him. Surely his prayers could be heard here of all places, at the very tip of the world, where heaven and earth met.

'Help me do the right thing, Lord,' Leonardo asked. When he opened his eyes, he looked around to see his brothers knelt beside him, muttering their own prayers, and smiled.

How could God fail to protect such devout servants as they? He stood, and his companions stood with him. They turned to one another and exchanged grim nods. They were ready.

Silently, they took up their positions around the enormous silver crucifix and tied themselves to it and each other.

'Ready?' Sebastien asked them all. 'There'll be no going back once we begin.'

Ebel, Sigbald and Leonardo nodded in reply, and it was decided. The four initiates began the ascent.

Leonardo took a deep breath and set out to the left of Ebel, pleased to see that, up close, the rock face had plenty of handholds. He gripped the cold surface and found it rough beneath his fingers. His breath steamed onto the stone before his face as he looked down to place his feet.

Sebastien climbed by his side, pulling ahead as he would act as the anchor should Leonardo slip. To the right, Ebel too took that role while Sigbald, roped to the cross like Leonardo, would bear its weight as they climbed.

After twenty feet, Leonardo felt the rope at his waist go taught, and glanced down to see that the crucifix was beginning to rise from the ground. He strained against the mountain, grunting as he felt the extra weight that was half as much as his own again.

Cursed thing, he thought. The climb would have been arduous enough on its own, but with the cross it was a nightmare. After twenty more feet, Leonardo's forearms were already burning and he was beginning to think that the word nightmare was not suitable for the hell of the climb. He glanced over at Sigbald to see that he, too, was sweating and panting from the effort, the cold beads running down his forehead and into his beard, becoming ice almost as soon as they had left his body.

'We'll need to rest soon!' Leonardo called up to Sebastien. 'Find us a place!'

'There's a ridge just above me!' Sebastien called back. 'Another fifteen feet!'

'And enough space for us, too?' Ebel called back, his voice echoing from the rock.

'Aye, should be.'

Leonardo gritted his teeth and forced his body upward, hauling the yoke of the cross with him. Annoyingly, he felt it tug at him often, threatening to pull him off the rockface as Sigbald's movements to his right caused it to wobble between them, knowing that his friend must have felt the same thing. It meant he had to be extra sure of where he placed his hands and feet, testing the holds and moving painstakingly slow.

Then, there was a sharper tug and Leonardo looked down to see that the cross had been caught on a shard of rock that jutted from the cliff unevenly.

'Hey!' he called to Sigbald. 'Look!'

'Shit,' Sigbald cursed as he looked down and saw the problem. 'Here, see if you can disturb it with the rope.'

Leonardo made absolutely certain he had a good purchase with his left hand before freeing his right and leaning over to wiggle the rope. As he did so, he caught a glimpse of the ground that was already far enough beneath them to cripple them should they fall. The thought made his heart skip with fear and he focused his attention on the cross.

'Wiggle it more!' Sigbald shouted.

'I'm trying!' Leonardo shouted back, giving a great heave that caused the cross to fly free and swing around, its blanket-covered surface hitting the cliff with a reverberating *thunggg* like a smothered gong.

'That's it,' Sigbald panted. 'Now let's keep going.'

A minute later and the snail-like procession of climbing men had almost reached the ledge Sebastien had pointed out. The latter wrapped his hands over its lip and hauled himself over, disappearing momentarily before giving a shriek of alarm.

The others stopped in their tracks, looking up at the place where Sebastien had just disappeared.

'Are you alright?' Leonardo shouted up to him.

'Fine!' a voice called back after a moment's pause and Leonardo breathed a sigh of relief. 'There's a body!'

Leonardo was sure he had heard wrong. He exchanged a confused glance with Sigbald, who had clearly been sharing his thoughts.

'A what?'

'A body! There's a body up here!'

'Are you sure?' Leonardo shouted back incredulously.

'Of course I'm bloody sure! It's right in front of my eyes!'

'Alright, I'll be up in a second.'

Leonardo closed the last few feet to the rocky ledge with a few deep breaths and, as Sebastien helped to haul him over, he found himself face to face with a dead man. Two wide, open eyes gazed lifelessly back at him, the mouth open in an 'o' of surprise, as if his passing had come at a shock. Sallow, pale skin hung from sunken cheeks and, though it was clear he had not died recently, it was impossible to tell when exactly, for he was quite clearly frozen as solid as the rock they climbed. He reminded Leonardo of the pieces of meat that hung amongst the blocks of ice in the cave where they stored food back at the monastery.

Leonardo tore his gaze away as he helped Sigbald haul the cross to the ledge, before turning back to the body as he shook out his tired arms.

'Who do you suppose he was?' called Ebel.

Leonardo inspected the body once more. It was tucked onto the ridge, wedged there with barely enough space to lie without toppling off. It was clad in icy black robes and furs, not unlike the ones they wore themselves and, though the flesh was thin and half rotten, both Sebastien and Leonardo could guess as to the dead man's identity.

'It's another initiate,' Sebastien called back, his voice shadowed with a dark, gloomy tone. 'He didn't make it.'

There was silence as the others had nothing to say in reply. They rested there a while, regaining some of their strength, swigging from their waterskins as they stole glances at their dead companion, his ominous presence a grim reminder of the dangers they faced.

'Come on,' Sigbald called eventually. 'Let's climb some more.'

They began again and Leonardo craned his neck upwards to see that they were but a third of the way, and his heart sank at the distance that remained between them and success. He forced himself to master his emotions and dragged himself up with steely determination, the cross forever attempting to pull him to his death below.

They went on like that for an hour or more, resting regularly wherever they could, for their arms were soon weak from the effort.

Sebastien was right, there could be no turning back now. Their options were success or death, plain and simple.

Fortunately, their many months of arduous training had paid off and the four men's resolve had been hardened. Their limbs were strong, and they were fit; they would not be so easily cowed by a mere climb, even if the fall were a lethal one.

Leonardo refused to be beaten, and the view below, coupled with the realisation of the precariousness of their position, clinging to the rockface like bizarre wildflowers, was enough to make most men tremble with fear. But they were not most men. Surely, the elite of the Order of The Hand of God could conquer the King of the Pyrenees.

Leonardo seethed in pain as he felt the excruciating burn of his muscles, working doubly hard to pull the extra weight of the cross.

A gruelling hour passed.

'A little further!' Sebastien called from above. 'Come on, boys! Just a few more yards and we're there!'

'I need a rest!' Sigbald called back.

'There is nowhere to rest!' Ebel's echoing reply yelled.

'Look up! Just a little more, Sigbald. You can do it!'

Sigbald cried out in frustration, feeling the same fire in his arms as Leonardo, and knowing that letting go would spell his death. They hadn't rested for thirty agonising feet, for there had been nowhere suitable and the only option had been to plough on.

The ground below was now nauseously far away and there could be no hope of surviving such a fall. Leonardo seethed as he chose what seemed to be the millionth handhold and pulled his body upwards yet again.

'I'm up!' Sebastien shouted from just above him and Leonardo watched as his friend pulled himself over the lip of the cliff, followed shortly by Ebel to their right.

Soon, the rope that linked them was being pulled as Leonardo felt the slack removed, taking some of his weight as he climbed the last few feet until he, too, was at the lip. Sebastien grabbed a handful of his robes and hauled him over until he lay panting, giving his arms a chance to rest.

Once Sigbald was over and the cross had been pulled up, the four of them had laughed in triumph, but a quick glance up the slope told them they were not out of the woods yet. Though it was far from vertical, the slope was still steep, and covered with a fine scree of rock, mingled with snow and ice here and there, that was sure to be as perilous as the cliff had been. It continued like that for another fifty yards or so, before levelling out to a safer gradient.

'How do we do this?' Ebel asked them as they panted on the cliff's edge. 'One wrong move and we could all slide back over the edge.'

'I say we spread out as much as we can,' Sebastien suggested. 'Look, the ground in places looks firmer, we should seek that out.' They nodded, and took up position, well aware of the death drop to their backs.

'Ready?' he called out? They all nodded, and began to crawl upwards, ensuring they dug their toes as deep as possible into the earth before pushing themselves up.

Once, Ebel began to slip slowly backward with a surprised 'Oh! Ooh!' However, Sigbald caught the rope between them with a grunt and stopped him.

Both Sigbald and Leonardo pushed the cross up between them, its great weight threatening constantly to slide down over the abyss below. Then, gradually, the earth began to level out and Leonardo could finally stand without fear of slipping, and walked the last few paces until he met flat ground, tugging the cross with Sigbald all the while.

Sebastien and Ebel, meanwhile, looked around to see that, incredibly, they had reached the highest point of the Dove and expressions of shock and joy slowly formed on their faces.

'We've done it. By God, we've done it!' Sebastien cried out and gave a great whoop of elation as he realised they had succeeded. Leonardo began to laugh as he untied himself from the cross, and the four of them clasped each other in joy, shaking hands with big smiles on their faces.

'Of course we've done it!' Sigbald laughed. 'We're the best!' And he punched the air, giving a mighty howl that echoed from the surrounding peaks, before the others joined in.

They stood, congratulating themselves, until a gust of freezing air reminded them that they yet needed to climb down before nightfall.

'Come on, let's get this damned cross upright and get off this bloody mountain!' Sigbald exclaimed, untying the blankets that protected their cargo. The four of them spent some time searching for the best place to plant the cross as the wind buffeted them, knowing that they had to position it in such a way that it would catch the light and could be seen from the monastery's mountain, proof that they had completed their mission.

'Ouch!' Ebel exclaimed, as his boot hit something hard protruding from the ground. Looking down, he saw an iron peg had been hammered into the bedrock.

'Here!' he called to them. 'Look, there are three more of these… there, there and there.' He pointed to the ground around him and, sure enough, Leonardo saw three other pegs that had surely been used as anchor points for rope in the past. There was even a little hollow that had been chiselled out for the base of the cross to sit inside. Squinting into the distance, they could see that this was a good a spot as any. The obvious anchor points and the man-made hollow caused Leonardo to wonder just how many times the great crucifix had been hauled up the Dove.

'They must have used this in the past,' Sebastien said, inspecting the pegs. 'We have enough rope. We can secure it to the pegs here. Come on!'

As they removed the protective blankets, Leonardo wondered how the other teams had passed this way. Had they succeeded? Or had they, like the poor dead soul on the cliff face, failed?

With newfound urgency, the four of them carried the seven-foot cross to the pegs and stood it upright, leaving Ebel to hold its proud, magnificent form up to reflect the sun dazzlingly as they tied it to the earth. The jewels set in the silver surface twinkled prettily and, for once, they smiled to see it, for it was no longer a burden but a symbol of their victory.

Once it had been tied, Ebel tested it, jerking it with all his weight. However, he couldn't move it, for the taught ropes pulled from several directions and even the strongest wind would not disturb it. Next,

Ebel gave it a quick polish with one of the blankets before the four of them stood back to admire it for a moment, smiling and clapping one another on the shoulder as the cross gleamed magnificently.

A minute passed as they stood smiling, enrapt at the sight, before Leonardo reminded them they had to be down the mountain for sunset, lest they wanted to freeze at the top. Gingerly, they made their way back down the slope of scree and, with pounding hearts, lowered themselves back over the cliff to begin the descent.

It went as smoothly as they could have hoped, far easier than the climb now that they had only their own weights to worry about. Even the wind graciously held off trying to blow them to the bottom, as if rewarding them for their accomplishment. A mere hour later, and Leonardo was stepping off the cliff to safety, scouting out the route that would take them down to where they might set up a camp.

There was still light left, and the four of them were in extraordinarily high spirits, deciding they would use the light remaining to get a head start on the next day. They collected their belongings from the sled and abandoned the thing, for what use was it to them now? The good weather held, and they marched along, laughing together and joking, or speculating as to what would happen in the following days, or what the second baptism would entail.

That night, there was plenty of time to build an ample shelter, and the night was even calm enough for them to light a fire using branches they had collected from the sparse pines at the bottom of the first valley. The flames were a great morale booster – not that they needed that now, for each of them knew that, in just a couple of days, they would be agents of the Order and their training at the monastery would finally be over.

Leonardo slept well, despite the cold, and woke the next morning with a warm feeling in his heart, one that he saw reflected in his brothers' faces in the dim light of dawn. They broke camp to finish the march, knowing they had plenty of time to reach the monastery before sunset. They turned every now and again, to see with satisfaction that a tiny twinkle winked playfully at them from the head of the Dove; the fruit of their labour, and the end of their last ordeal.

It should have been a perfect day, one of achievement and laughter that eclipsed even the state of fatigued hunger that they all felt. They had eaten through the last reserves of their food and, as they rounded a familiar hillock to begin the ascent on the track to the monastery, that shouldn't have mattered, for they were home, and their journey was complete. Nor should it have mattered that their waterskins had run dry, or that their clothes were damp, or that they had only a couple of blankets left between them, for the others had been lost in the blizzard.

And yet, it did.

For, as Sebastien glanced up, he saw that their path ahead was barred by four robed figures standing stock still in the middle of the track. The others saw them, too, and stopped, squinting up to see, even from a distance, that there could be no mistaking the unkempt mass of white hair surrounding a wizened head, or the enormous, familiar bulk that they had all wrestled with aplenty.

It was their teachers, Magnus, Antonio, Drogoradz and Walter. They had been waiting for them. As they drew closer, a hundred different thoughts raced through Leonardo's mind. Perhaps they were there to congratulate them? Perhaps this was part of the second baptism?

But, as they neared, doubt gnawed at him, and a feeling of dread made his heart sink as he saw the grim expressions of their superiors. They stopped again, four initiates facing four teachers, their respective breaths steaming silently in the still air of the afternoon.

'We, um, we've done it, Teacher,' Sebastien said, finally breaking the silence as he addressed Magnus, indicating with his arm the direction they had come. Leonardo could hear the hesitation in his voice and knew that his friend sensed the same thing he did; something was not right.

Their instructors gazed at them all, each wearing the same stern expression, their eyes hard and unforgiving.

'I have seen,' Magnus replied harshly. 'But your work is not yet done. The real task is about to begin.'

Leonardo's heart sank. It turned out that there *was* something the instructors had been keeping from them, after all.

'What do you mean?' Sigbald asked incredulously, forgetting the formality of the title *Teacher* in his dismayed confusion. 'We've done what you've asked. It's over.'

Magnus glared at him. 'It is over when we say it is, boy!' His rebuke cut through the air like a knife. 'I'm telling you that the real test awaits, the one none of you are prepared for.'

'What's that then?' Sebastien shot back, the hurt at the realisation they had been fooled showing through his voice.

There was a pause as they waited, with bated breath, for Magnus to speak. 'You will go back and retrieve the cross. You will have three more days to do so.'

Silence.

The four initiates were lost for words as Magnus's order sank in. Go back? Do it all again? The prospect was more chilling than the winter air.

'But... but...' Sigbald finally managed to bluster, his face red with indignation. 'The mission was to climb the Dove and plant the cross! We've done that; now surely we are finished!'

'No,' Magnus said with brutal simplicity. Leonardo searched the familiar faces of his instructors for any sign that it might have been a joke, any chink in their dark expressions that could hint at a smirk. Yet, he saw none and knew in his heart that this was, indeed, the true test.

'What about our food? Water?' Ebel squeaked, his voice cracking. 'We've nothing left!'

'You will not be resupplying,' said Walter, speaking for the first time. 'What you do not have you must source from the mountains. Find a way to survive, or perish!' He regarded them with his gleaming, dark eyes that showed not a hint of mercy.

'This is ridiculous!' Sebastien spat vehemently.

'This is the Order, boy!' Magnus roared in reply, making them all flinch. 'You chose this, remember! You volunteered! No one told you it would be easy. No one said it would be without danger. Hear me, all of you! Feel free to return to your miserable lives. Go with your tails between your legs if you wish, but you'll do so without God's grace. For, if you turn your backs now, you will have forsaken him as well as yourselves.'

Sebastien glared back at Magnus, his fists clenched by his sides. For a moment, Leonardo feared he would try to attack the older man – though that would have been suicide, of course.

'You have two options,' Magnus went on. 'The first, you surrender in defeat, having let the mountains get the better of you. And it will be a failure that stays with you your whole lives, when you wonder what might have been if your resolve was but a little harder to break. The second, you go back and bring me that cross. The glory will be yours and that, I swear, will be the last of it. Three more days, and it *will* be over. The choice is yours.'

Leonardo felt outraged. He felt as though he had been swindled, that his superiors had unfairly set them up. Why hadn't they told them they had to bring the cross back, too? At least they could have prepared better. Then he realised that that was the point.

A moment later, he realised how obvious it was. Of course they had to bring the cross back – that had been the test for every group of initiates. It always had been.

Leonardo, Sebastien and the others had all been so willing to believe that it was over, that they had completed their training. But no. *This* was the test. Just when they thought they had done it, they were sent back. Leonardo understood then that it was designed to break them.

The four of them were cold, tired and hungry, and Magnus was suggesting that they embark on another three-day journey to an icy hell and back. Leonardo sighed and closed his eyes. They had no choice; they would have to return to the Dove.

'You can't—' Sebastien began, but Leonardo grabbed his arm and shook his head.

'We must go back,' he muttered, resigned to his fate. 'We cannot give up now, or all of this will have been for nothing!' He turned to look into the hopeless eyes of the others. 'We've all worked so hard to get here, all we need to do is survive three more days. We can do that, can't we? Just three more! Then it will be done.'

Sigbald ground his teeth together, his eyes shut as his large chest heaved. Ebel looked as though he had aged a decade in the space of a minute, all joy extinguished from his thin, dark features.

Magnus nodded in confirmation. 'Three days, as you say. Remember, all the elite of the Order pass this way. Do not think you are unique in your suffering.'

Sebastien cursed loudly, turning away from them in disgust and sinking to his haunches a few paces away, his head in his hands. Leonardo joined him and placed a reassuring hand on his shoulder, his face a mask of bitterness.

'Come, Sebastien, let us use the daylight.'

For a moment, Sebastien did not react. As Leonardo could not see his face, he worried that his friend was about to concede. But then Sebastien nodded and stood. He took a deep breath and let it out in a long, slow hiss, a grim shadow passing over his face as he, too, resigned himself to the task ahead.

'Three more days,' he whispered.

Just then, they were joined by Ebel and Sigbald and they, too, were nodding in assent.

'Three more days,' they muttered, one after the other. And it was decided. They would go back.

Sebastien shot Magnus a last, venomous glare before he shouldered his pack and turned, retracing their tracks through the snow. Ebel and Sigbald followed, as Leonardo gave a final glance back at his superiors, who had now become something more akin to torturers.

They stared back silently, impassively, an impenetrable barrier, the final barrier, between him and the tantalising promise of a future. He narrowed his eyes. He would be damned if he gave that up so easily. Leonardo wrenched his gaze away and left them, turning back to his comrades and the long, hard journey that lay before them. A test it would surely be, he knew. The most onerous he had ever known.

Chapter 21

GASCONY

The parliamentary hall at Bordeaux was a hive of activity. Men argued amongst one another as the King strode back and forth, red with rage and worry. The Queen shifted anxiously in her throne and the King's trusted generals exchanged apprehensive looks. Amidst all the noise, a haughty Castilian dignitary stood defiantly, one hand on his hip and the other holding an unfolded letter he had just finished reading aloud to the English court.

It was early February and the King's men were preparing to resume the campaign, when Cristoval del Soria had arrived with perfect timing to deliver the fateful message from Alfonso, King of Castile. Cristoval was adorned fabulously in bright yellows and reds, his hose matching his chequered doublet that carried the Castilian coat of arms, and a flowing gown draped over his shoulders, edged with stark white fur, that made him look more regal than even Henry. He wore a superior expression, and a pair of dark eyes surveyed the parliament with an unimpressed look under a head of medium-length, straight black hair that was neatly combed back over his scalp.

Cristoval had just finished delivering nothing less than a threat of open war from his King. Alfonso, knowing that the rebellion was not progressing in a manner that suited him, had declared that if Henry did not leave Gascony within the month, he would send the full might of Castile's army on an invasion fleet and destroy all remaining English forces.

Leonardo watched in dismay as the parliament fought amongst each other about what the best course of action to take might be.

'Do you think it's a bluff?' Sebastien muttered from the corner of his mouth, as they sat on one of the benches pushed up against the far wall.

'Perhaps,' Leonardo replied. 'But, even if it is, it's not one Henry can afford to call.'

'Exactly,' said Sebastien. 'He's got half an army and can barely afford to pay them. A Castilian invasion would be a complete disaster.' He huffed, clearly as put out by this development as Leonardo was. Leonardo had to agree; there was no way that Henry could beat the entire might of Castile with the meagre force he had left to him. And, judging from the King's reaction, Henry knew it too.

Henry continued to pace upon the dais, as his men shouted up words of advice. Eventually, he threw up his arms and called for silence. Cristoval del Soria waited patiently.

'Adjourned!' Henry shouted. 'I need time to think!' He then strode rapidly from the hall, much to the confusion of his lords. The level of noise rose yet again as the men of the parliament began to discuss what this meant for them and for Gascony.

Cristoval del Soria wore a smug look on his face as the King stormed past him, followed by several trusted advisors. He followed suit soon after, striding from the hall with a couple of mean-looking soldiers in tow, who were almost as well dressed as he was. Leonardo narrowed his eyes as he watched the man go and thought that he might like to have a chat with him.

He stood and looked back at Sebastien. 'I'll catch you up later. I have to go.'

Sebastien gave him a bemused look. 'To do what?'

'Run an errand,' Leonardo replied simply and he took his leave, following the Spanish dignitary from the hall and down the corridors. The colourful man strode from the building, clearly intending to await Henry's response in his lodgings in the city. As he crossed the busy courtyard, Leonardo jogged after him and called out.

'Master del Soria!'

Cristoval stopped and turned, his armed guard turning with him and blocking Leonardo from approaching any further.

'Might I have a word with you, sir?'

Cristoval gave Leonardo's plain black robes a long look, up and down, and turned his nose up at him. 'What do you want, man? Make it quick!' he said, assuming a tone of snobbery that suited him all too well.

'I was hoping you could provide me with some information. Concerning King Alfonso.' Leonardo kept the annoyance from his voice at being spoken to so.

'Information!' Cristoval said with a mocking smile. 'What sort of information?'

Leonardo took a deep breath. 'I wish to know of the King's character, what motivates him to fixate so stoutly upon Gascony?'

Cristoval del Soria shrugged. 'My King is an ambitious man. Where he sees opportunity, he strikes.'

'But, is there no one who directs him, who might be persuading him to disrupt the lands of the English crown in particular?'

The dignitary gave Leonardo another long, piercing look. 'Who are you?' he asked finally.

'No one,' Leonardo replied simply.

'Very well, then I shall say no more on the subject,' said Cristoval. But then he lowered his voice a pitch. 'That is, unless you have something to offer me?' He raised an eyebrow as he waited for Leonardo to answer.

'How does gold sound?' Leonardo suggested and the dignitary gave a short, cruel laugh.

'By the looks of you, you don't have a fraction of what it would cost to even tempt me.'

'You'd be surprised,' Leonardo shot back.

'Is that so?' Cristoval sneered. 'I doubt it. In any case, it is not gold that interests me, but information. Knowledge for knowledge, but I don't suppose you'd know anything worth knowing!'

Not anything that I could tell you without having to kill you, Leonardo thought, but he said nothing.

Cristoval snorted in derision. 'Thought not. Good day, sir,' he said, spitting the last word out as though it were an insult. He turned away and strode off across the square, his guards in tow, leaving Leonardo cursing in his wake.

Leonardo thought back to the other thing Emilio had asked him to look into – whether the other Fingers acted against the rest of the Hand's will. He had thought that he might learn a thing or two about who, if anyone, drove the King of Castile's ambitions from someone who was deeply embedded in his court, but the dignitary had not been as forthcoming as Leonardo had hoped. Though, he was left with the impression that Cristoval del Soria knew something. Whether that would be the information Leonardo needed or not remained to be seen. However, one thing was for certain – he would have to have another chat with the man.

By nightfall, King Henry had sent word back to the King of Castile with a marriage proposal between his son and Alfonso's daughter. It was, like as not, insufficient on its own to have brought lasting peace, but it was worth a try and it bought the English crown time.

Everyone who turned within the circles of the court was discussing the potential threat of invasion and the King's advisors never left his side all day. The Queen was as busy as she had ever been, too. The doors to her offices in the parliamentary building were kept propped open, for the amount of traffic coming through them was making the things beat like a drum.

Sebastien was never far away and provided his council when it was asked for, as more information trickled in from informants in the Castilian court. As for Leonardo, he found that there was little he could help with, but did not stray far from the goings on, for it was paramount that he understood fully what was happening.

Finally, by almost midnight, the talk ceased, and the men of the court were forced to retire to bed. Leonardo stood outside in the square and watched them file out, one by one, each going their separate ways to their lodgings, offered light by way of flaming torches or candles held by their servants.

A minute later, the Queen emerged flanked by Sebastien and the ever-silent Sir Derek. They looked up and spotted Leonardo standing there, stopping before him. Leonardo bowed to the Queen.

'Good evening, Your Highness,' said Leonardo. 'I hope your day hasn't been too long.' But, even as he said it, he saw tired rings around her eyes and knew that it had. The fate of the remaining lands of the English crown on the continent hung in the balance and it would be the King and Queen's family who suffered the most should they fall.

'Greetings, Father Leonardo,' she said wearily. 'I'm afraid it has been. It's been tiring, though I don't think I'll get much sleep tonight regardless, and I imagine neither will my husband.'

'I wonder if there is anything I can do for you, Your Highness?' Leonardo asked.

'No, thank you.' She gave him a tired smile. 'But get some rest yourself, we may need you tomorrow.'

'As you wish. Goodnight, then.'

The Queen bid him goodnight and turned to leave with her bodyguard.

Sebastien looked at him. 'Night, Leo. I'll escort the Queen back to her houses, so I'll see you tomorrow.'

'Alright, until tomorrow then.' Leonardo held up his hand in goodbye.

'Yes, we'll talk then!' Sebastien called as he walked backward, then turned and pivoted, jogging to catch up with the English Queen, their forms illuminated by the bobbing torch held by Sir Derek. Leonardo watched them go as a sudden thought occurred to him. He had never seen the Queen so unburdened of her regular troop of guards, ladies-in-waiting and advisors, and guessed they had been sent to bed already, given the circumstances.

That was not to say she was unprotected, for Sebastien alone counted for several men, but Leonardo could not help but feel it was an opportunity. Over the winter, he had had perhaps a handful of opportunities to tail Sebastien, something for which he had felt a little guilty at first, as Eleanor was a good Queen and Sebastien was his friend. Yet, Leonardo had eventually reasoned that it was a necessary evil if he should want to protect his friend from the ruthlessness of politics. That didn't stop him from being afraid to find out what it was that Sebastien was hiding. Leonardo was almost relieved when he discovered, unsurprisingly, that Sebastien was a very hard man to follow.

Sebastien's instincts were good, and he had long since formed a habit of checking over his shoulder and scanning the faces of those that walked behind him. Leonardo had to be extra careful, for if Sebastien glanced back, he would easily recognise Leonardo's gait, and the game would be up. As it stood, of the one or two times that Sebastien had been all but alone with the Queen, Leonardo had not been able to see or hear anything.

He had wondered if he was being paranoid, and if there was in fact nothing untoward happening at all. But Leonardo's own instincts had dismissed that notion fairly quickly; he knew Sebastien, well enough to know he was, indeed, hiding something. As he watched the trio disappear around a corner and the light from the torch fade into the night, he decided he had to know.

Leonardo pulled up his hood and followed at a stride. He rounded the corner a second later and could see the three of them. The night was dark and overcast and he thanked God for it, for the light from the torch would blind Sebastien, whereas Leonardo would be well adjusted to the gloom. All he had to do was stay far enough back.

He darted from building to building, grateful that the streets were all but empty, and took cover where he could, keeping his focus trained on Sebastien and the Queen. They were making their way toward the royal houses, a short walk from the city centre that the Queen would usually have taken in a carriage. This time, however, it seemed her mind was too preoccupied to have arranged for one to pick her up. *All the better*, Leonardo thought.

Queen Eleanor picked her way along the muddy streets, holding up the hem of her dress so as not to sully it as she chatted to her two companions. The going was slow as a result, but Leonardo was yet too far to hear what was being said. He stuck to the shadows, not daring to get any closer for the time being. Fortunately, Sebastien too seemed preoccupied and was not being as diligent as he normally was.

The streets began to widen, and the earth became a little surer underfoot, where there was not so much of a bottleneck created by the foot traffic like there was in the densely packed streets of the centre now that they were nearing the city's edge. After another few minutes, some of the grand stone buildings gave way to small vineyards and gardens, and the walls of the royal household loomed ahead. Leonardo had to be careful now, for there was less cover to hide himself behind, and he had to resort to crouching behind low stone walls or darting behind hedges. Lit braziers illuminated several guards standing at the gate, and Leonardo's heart sank, knowing that, once they had passed it, there was no way he could follow.

However, a moment later, his heart leapt as he saw the Queen stop twenty paces from the gates and signal to Sir Derek to go on without her. Sir Derek hesitated for a second, not liking the idea of leaving the Queen alone, even with someone she trusted. No doubt considering that she was, after all, only yards away from the most well-defended household in the city, Sir Derek finally gave a brief nod and walked through the gates, leaving the Queen and Sebastien alone.

Leonardo knew he had to get closer, but the hedge he was using as cover from the road ran out. He searched the darkness for anything that he could use to get a little nearer, and spotted a drainage ditch that followed the road on its right bank. Leonardo lay on his belly and crawled towards it, grateful for the fact that the moon was covered by cloud. Had it been daylight, he would have been easily spotted at this exposed point; but, as it was, the only substantial light flickered from the fire in the braziers by the gate of the royal houses.

Leonardo slithered into the drainage ditch, wincing as his body made a squelch in the damp mud. He froze, but heard no shouts of alarm and pressed onward. He could hear the low voices of Sebastien and the Queen, though they were but murmurs of blurred sound for the moment, as Leonardo was still too far away. He pushed on, as fast as he dared, elbow after elbow as he crawled along the ditch like a lizard.

Then, the ditch forked away from the road, and he could go no further. Leonardo lay and cocked his head, guessing he must have been no more than thirty feet from them. If he strained, really strained, he found he could just about pick out the odd word here and there.

'…you think it is a bluff?' came the deeper voice of Sebastien.

'I don't think so,' the higher pitch of Queen Eleanor replied, and she muttered something else that Leonardo could not make out.

'Yes, hopefully it will all be over soon…' Sebastien said, and then the conversation became too muted for Leonardo to hear, and he cursed inwardly. A moment later, however, perhaps the two of them had wandered a little closer to his trench, for the voices became clearer again.

'You've been so good to me, you know.' It was Sebastien's voice, but it was low and full of affection, and Leonardo remarked how he had never heard his friend speak like that. His heart began to pound. What was he about to hear?

More murmuring, until the Queen's voice became slightly more distinguishable. 'It's the least I could do. You're a good man and you deserve better.'

There was a low chuckle as Sebastien murmured something else that Leonardo couldn't hear. Then, the tone of Sebastien's voice grew serious and what he said next shocked Leonardo to the core.

'And the baby? How will we hide it?'

'It is winter, fortunately,' replied Eleanor, 'and I have several larger dresses that we will use to cover the bump. No one will be any the wiser.'

The baby. The baby! Leonardo could not believe it. Had Sebastien been having an affair with the Queen? And now she was pregnant? It was too much; it couldn't be true. Leonardo stared into the dark grass as his mind raced, piecing together all the clues he had gathered over the last few months. He thought of the close nature of their relationship, the touches of affection, the secret meetings. He wanted to cry out in frustration. Was Sebastien a fool? He would be a dead man walking for this. For, when someone found out – and if the

Queen was pregnant, that would surely be a matter of time – Sebastien would be tortured to death. Perhaps Queen Eleanor, too.

As far as he knew, the Queen had not given birth by Henry for some years, and there was speculation amongst the gossips as to why that was. If they could be believed, she was either infertile or the King impotent. Though, now it seemed that the Queen was fertile enough.

'…we will have the wedding ceremony once all this is over, then…' The Queen's voice became muffled, and Leonardo could not make out the rest of the sentence. He had heard enough, however. *A wedding ceremony?* Now they were getting married? But that was illegal, for Eleanor was already married, and no priest in their right mind would ever agree to perform the marriage rights for an already married woman, least of all her.

'…perhaps you can have your friend Leonardo administer the rights?' Queen Eleanor asked. There was a pause, as Sebastien seemed to seriously consider this. Leonardo lay in the ditch and had to clamp a hand over his mouth to stop himself from crying out in outrage. How could they think he would ever want to have a part in this? Had they completely lost their minds?

'I don't think so,' Sebastien replied finally. 'Leonardo means well, but he is the Order's man through and through. I'm not sure he would understand.'

Not sure I would understand? Leonardo scoffed inwardly. *How could I?* Sebastien had betrayed everything he ought to have held dear – his master, his King, the Order and the Queen, too. For he had as much condemned her with this idiocy as himself. Leonardo wouldn't have believed it had he not heard it with his own two ears. The Queen seemed like such an intelligent woman; how could she have been so stupid?

'The Order will come after you for this…' There was a good deal of worry in the Queen's voice as it trailed off. She obviously did not want to voice aloud what the Order would do if they caught up with Sebastien.

'There are places we can go to escape them,' Sebastien assured her. Or perhaps he was trying to assure himself? They were planning on fleeing together now, too? *Fools!* Leonardo thought. There was nowhere on God's earth that they could go that would be far enough. They would be hunted like dogs.

'We will speak more of it closer to the time. Goodnight for now,' the Queen said.

'Goodnight,' Sebastien replied and there was a pause before Leonardo heard two sets of footsteps, one making for the royal household and the other heading back into the city.

Leonardo lay in the mud, completely stunned. The idea was insane. They were insane! His mind whirred as he processed what he had just heard. How could this be happening? How could his oldest friend, Sebastien, have gotten himself into something so outlandish, so stupid!

He couldn't believe it, he couldn't! And yet, he had heard it. Sebastien was having an affair with Queen Eleanor and was about to forsake his vows to the Order. He would be a traitor.

Chapter 22

TWELVE YEARS AGO

They plodded on, dejected and sullen, their morale utterly destroyed. Leonardo felt a wave of emotions surging through him – hopelessness, frustration, betrayal and hate. *Those bastards*, he thought. *It wasn't fair!* They had done what had been asked of them. But to do it all over again, with no rest?

They hadn't any food or water left, either. They had consumed the last of it that very morning, thinking that they would soon be sat slurping a hot stew around the fire in the great hall. Yet, it wasn't so and, so far, none of them had bothered to address the issue of their lack of supplies. At least, not out loud.

What could they do? Up here, nothing lived, save for the odd hardy pine that, against all odds, had survived by bending themselves to the will of the wind, disfigured trunks a parody of their straight-arrowed cousins on the more hospitable slopes hundreds of yards below. The initiates had no time to deviate from the path.

The four of them walked in single file, placing one foot in front of the other. They moved faster than they had the first day, for they hadn't the yoke of the cross to bear, and yet they ought to have gone faster, regardless. Had they been fresher and more properly motivated, it would have taken them a fraction of the time.

No one counted the hours that went by, no one marked the distance. All they did was follow the tracks they had made earlier in the day, a bitter reminder of the feeling of success they had felt just that very morning. Every now and again, Sigbald or Sebastien would utter a string of foul curses, interjected with Magnus's name. Leonardo could never remember feeling so miserable. If it had been Magnus's desire to crush their spirit, it seemed he almost had his wish.

They had stopped several times, but only to rest for a moment. By now, none of them had a morsel of food to eat, or water to drink.

'By all the saints, I'm thirsty,' Ebel complained, smacking his dry, wind-cracked lips.

He scooped up a handful of brilliant-white powder and made to shovel it into his mouth, when Leonardo interjected.

'Wait! Do that and your body will fail twice as soon.'

Ebel paused, the snow halfway to his mouth, and shot Leonardo a look. 'You think I don't know that? It's either this, or succumb to thirst. I know which I prefer.' He then ate it, his warm mouth turning the snow to freezing water in moments before he swallowed, knowing that it would cost him valuable energy. Soon, they were all doing the same thing, resigned to it, though they knew better. For Ebel was right; there was no choice.

Leonardo felt that he and his companions were close to breaking point when they set up camp in silence that night. They hadn't got nearly as far as the first day, which only served to depress them further, for they knew that they would have their work cut out for them on the morrow.

As they dug their shelter, an argument broke out between Sigbald and Ebel as to whose turn it was to shovel and who was to compact the snow. Both Sebastien and Leonardo had to tear the pair away from each other, neither remembering seeing Ebel so infuriated. They feared that, had they not been present, Ebel and Sigbald would have been tearing chunks from one another.

Their shelter was filled with an atmosphere of quiet, cold tension as the argument had grated on everyone's nerves. Yet, other factors contributed to their misery, chief amongst which was their hunger. As they lay down, they were all painfully aware that they had not eaten since the morning, and their bodies were still in a deficit of energy since the arduous climb the day before.

Sleep that night came fitfully and Leonardo was plagued with nightmares and visions of howling wolves and winter storms. In the morning, he was the first to wake and sat up with a start, his eyes wide in panic as he thought he'd heard growling from outside their shelter, but it was just the wind.

The wind. That devil. As Leonardo shook the others awake and crawled from their hideout, he cursed it. It was incessant. Up here, it never stopped. It was so painfully cold and there was no protection against it. Even when he wrapped himself in his thickest cloak and furs, it always found a way through, pulling at him; a flying, swirling, broiling beast. He hated it.

Sebastien stumbled out behind him and cursed the cold air, stamping his feet and rubbing his pink fingers together. His breath came out in great clouds of steam, his hair thoroughly combed by the same wind that buffeted their clothes.

'We need to get moving,' he said seriously. 'We don't have much time.'

'I know,' Leonardo replied as he peered into the horizon in the dawn gloom. 'We don't. Look.' He pointed north and Sebastien followed his gaze.

There, they could see that the morning's wind was a precursor to something far worse. A black sky approached and a behemoth of a storm was gathering many miles away, a gigantic dark ghoul that threatened to engulf the world.

Sebastien cursed again. 'What are the odds that it will pass us by?'

'Slim,' Leonardo replied grimly. He called over his shoulder, 'Ebel, Sigbald! We have to move, now!'

The other two exited the shelter and saw what Leonardo and Sebastien were looking at. They, too, cursed, the argument the night before now quite forgotten in the face of this new development.

'Do you think it's possible to reach the Dove, climb it, retrieve the cross, climb down and make camp before that thing gets here?' Ebel asked them, his wide brown eyes fixed upon the haunting horizon.

'I don't know,' Sebastien muttered. 'But we have no choice. We have to try. Come on!'

They didn't need telling twice. The four of them gathered their things, strapped on their snowshoes, took up their walking sticks and set off at a pace, intending to close the last few miles to the base of the Dove as soon as was humanly possible.

They were imbued with a desperate vitality, despite their weariness. They knew that, to get caught in such a storm in the middle of winter, this high in the mountains, could very well spell their doom.

'Hurry!' Sebastien called to them all as soon as the slope up to the Dove began to climb steeply, and the thick blanket of snow soon gave way to the exposed ridges of ice and bedrock. They were panting from the effort as they picked their way over the uneven surface, slipping here and there on the ice.

They passed their old sled, none bothering to comment on its half-buried form as they filed past. Instead, their attention was split by the head of the Dove and the storm that had now doubled in size – or, at least it seemed that way to them, for it was much nearer. It had already been several hours since they'd broken camp, and they had significantly less time to make the climb than the last time. But at least now they were unburdened, and the approaching storm lit a fire of urgency under them.

'Quick!' Leonardo shouted. 'Climb any way you can!'

They scurried to the cliff face and, without ceremony, began to mount its surface, throwing their bags to the ground and taking with them only rope and blankets. They found their first handholds and began the climb, pushing themselves from the earth and gripping the rock face.

Minutes later, the ever-present wind stopped.

'Shit,' Leonardo said, for they all knew what that meant. It was the calm before the storm. 'We don't have much time!' he called to the others, who were now totally absorbed in their own battles with the Dove, knowing that one wrong move would see them fall to their deaths.

They paused to glance north and could see that their time was, indeed, almost up. Grey clouds swirled in a vortex that stretched from one end of the horizon to another, like a living wall that would churn everything to dust.

They climbed and climbed, tired, cold, hungry and desperate. It seemed that death and failure were pressing in from all sides, surrounding them and biting at their ankles. Had there been any observers, they would quickly have come to the conclusion that the end was nigh for the initiates of the monastery.

'We're almost halfway there!' Leonardo called down to the others. He had managed to break away from the rest of them and was resting on the same ledge they had reached the first time. Their dead companion had not moved, and stared up at him, the same look of surprise displayed on his frozen features.

Leonardo let his arms hang by his sides, shaking the blood back into them and felt himself floundering. He knew they didn't have much time – either before the storm engulfed them, or they dropped from fatigue.

Sebastien was there and Leonardo pulled him over, then the other two and they stood, hugging the cliff face in silence, their eyes drawn to the slowly approaching giant. It was almost as if it heard their thoughts, for, a moment later, a great rumbling boom split the sky as their ears were pounded with the sound of thunder, like the low growl of an angry God.

'How long do we have?' Ebel asked, a note of panic in his voice.

'Not long enough,' Sigbald replied and was already turning to continue their ascent. Leonardo took it up again, his freezing fingertips long since numb and scrabbling at the cold rock for purchase. Up and up they went, the escalade seeming to take forever. Each yard they went, the harder it got and, as his arms burnt, Leonardo wondered if they would ever reach the top.

'Come on!' he hissed, willing new life into his forearms. Then, the end was in sight. He glanced up to see the lip was a mere ten feet from him and spurred himself onward, gritting his teeth and finding the strength to climb. He was nearly there!

'Ebel!' a voice shouted from below. Leonardo looked down to see Ebel, a good twenty feet below the rest of them, hugging the rock, his toes planted in a small fissure and his arms in a spread-eagle position as his face pressed into the hard surface. He was unmoving.

'What are you doing?' Sebastien called down to him. 'Move!'

'I can't,' a tiny voice came back up to them.

'What do you mean, you can't?' Sigbald shot back.

'I… I just can't!' Even from where he hung, Leonardo could hear the desperation in Ebel's voice and he felt for the young man. It was all so much to bear, so much suffering. Wouldn't it be the easiest thing to just let go? The thought had crossed his mind once or twice. But they were so close!

'Ebel! We're almost at the top! Look! You can't stop now!' Leonardo shouted down, but Ebel wasn't moving.

'Move, damn you!' Sigbald shouted, his temper wearing thin. Ebel did not. Sebastien glanced up at Leonardo and they shared a worried look. If they couldn't get Ebel to move, he would die.

Sebastien tried a new tac. 'Ebel. We can't help you. You have to do this on your own, do you hear me? You have the strength, I know you do! You have to keep going. You owe it to yourself. You owe it to the rest of us!' He shouted the last words. Finally, after a short pause, they watched Ebel's thin fingers feel their way up the rock and grip the next handhold.

Leonardo breathed a sigh of relief as he watched his friend begin to pull himself slowly upward, and he somehow knew Ebel would make it. A minute later, Leonardo himself was at the top. A feeling of great relief washed over him as he was infinitely glad to be off the lethal cliff face. He pulled Sebastien up behind him, then Sigbald, and the trio waited for their last brother to reach them before hoisting him bodily over the lip and to safety.

This time, there was no time to celebrate their success, for the wind had begun to pick up again and all of them knew it would quickly get worse. They scrambled up the steep scree slope and, seconds later, reached the great gilded silver cross, their moods becoming bitter at the prospect of having to haul the thing down the mountain with them.

'I don't know if we can get back down before the storm is upon us.' Sigbald's voice sounded incredibly weary through the wind. He looked thin, tired and pale, as if on the brink of collapse. One look at Sebastien and Ebel told Leonardo that they were just as spent, and he imagined his appearance mirrored theirs. He certainly felt that way.

'We have no choice,' he said. 'If we stay up here, the storm will kill us.'

'Very well, then let's not waste any time.' Sebastien was already striding over to the cross and knelt to untie the first rope. The others joined him to help free it from the earth.

'We'll need to use the ropes again. Same pairs as last time?' Sebastien shouted to them. They all nodded a reply, as the last of the ropes was freed from the iron pegs. Then, they carried the cross to the edge of the scree slope and began to tie themselves to it and each other, just as snow began to blow into their faces with a howl of the wind. The storm would soon be upon them.

Leonardo tested the rope at his waist. This time, he was on the end, with a length running from his waist to Sebastien's, and from Sebastien to the silver crucifix. From there, it was coiled and knotted around Sigbald, before linking him to Ebel on the far end. Together, they made a long line, with the cumbersome cross dominating the centre. It was their intention to repeat the process they had used to climb with it, only in reverse; they would lower the thing between them, each pair bearing half its weight – though, this time, none of them were certain they had the strength to do so.

Leonardo doubted that, even with the plentiful burden of his own bodyweight, he would make it down alive. But now there was no choice. The four of them shuffled toward the edge of the scree slope, intending to lower themselves gently down to the lip of the cliff so as not to slip.

They all turned to take a last look at the approaching behemoth. Their hearts stopped in their chests as its hulking form loomed menacingly over them, blowing great gusts of wind that forced them to lean toward it just to remain upright.

'Let's go!' Sigbald shouted, making for the scree slope. But, as he did so, Leonardo noticed that, when he'd turned, his ankle had coiled itself in a length of the thick rope and Sigbald hadn't realised.

'Sigbald, wait! Your ankle!' But it was too late. Sigbald had already tripped, his feet caught up in the rope as he moved and he fell heavily with an 'Oof!' He slid down a patch of ice, taking Ebel's legs from under him where the smaller man stood. Ebel was knocked from his feet with a cry of alarm and the pair of them slid, their motion slowing only momentarily when the rope that linked Sigbald with the cross went taught, jerking it downward before Leonardo or Sebastien could stop it.

Leonardo watched in horror as his comrades scrabbled for purchase. The distance between them widened as the two men cascaded down the steep slope, dislodging pebbles and chunks of ice and snow as they went.

Then, the slack between the cross and Sebastien vanished and he, too, was jerked violently downhill with the combined weight of two men and the crucifix. Leonardo barely had time to dig in his heels before he was yanked forward, and any hope of halting their descent disappeared as the weight of his friends dragged him to the edge of the Dove.

Leonardo cried out in alarm and tried to fling out his arms, instinctively attempting to grab a hold of something solid, but to no avail, coming away instead with handfuls of snow or dirt. He was vaguely aware of the approaching lip and shouted a warning with a jolt of terror as he caught a glimpse of Ebel's slim, cloaked form slide over into the abyss.

Sigbald followed a moment later, coming to a jarring stop as he managed to plant his feet on a jagged rock that jutted from the cliff. However, it was too little too late, and his momentum carried him over and he disappeared.

There was a great *thunk* of silver and oak as the enormous cross thudded into a finger of protruding stone, wedging itself there for a moment before it, too, slid over the side of it, disappearing over the edge.

It was all happening as if in slow motion. Leonardo felt the ground slide beneath him as he was pulled headfirst down the slope. He looked down to see Sebastien reach up to him with an outstretched arm, his face a mask of shock and fear. It was too late; he went over and Leonardo followed a moment later, catching a glimpse of the ground hundreds of feet below as he fell over the lip of the cliff and began to tumble through the air.

This is it, he had time to think. *This is the end.* As the ground rushed up to meet him, a part of Leonardo was utterly petrified. Yet, there was another part that was filled with a calm sorrow. *So this is where I die,* he thought bitterly. It seemed incredibly unfair to him, even as he fell, the *whoosh* of air filling his world, that his life had been over before it had begun.

What had he done? What had he achieved? He had gone from being a babe in Sicily, the runaway son of a traitor executed for treason, to a beggar in the streets of Rome with his brothers and, finally, here, to whatever he was now, whatever he would die as. A man of God? Is that what he was?

Leonardo didn't have time to answer the question, for his freefall was brutally halted by the rope of his makeshift harness and, a fraction of a second later, his head smacked the side of the cliff, dazing him. Suddenly, his world became a pendulous wash of snow and mountains and, with a jolt of horror, he realised he was swinging in mid-air, the solid earth terrifyingly far below.

Blood poured from a deep gouge on his forehead and was blown across his face by the howling wind. He winced in pain as he felt a badly bruised shoulder and hip where he had impacted the rock, and the skin of his waist was ripped where the rope had halted his fall.

Leonardo reached out for the rock face to stop his gentle swinging and righted himself, instinctively planting his feet and finding a deep fissure to insert his right hand into for purchase. He looked up. Sebastien was fifteen feet above, straining against the rope that was trying to pull him upwards.

Leonardo followed the rope with his eyes and saw that it was looped around the jagged finger of rock the cross had thumped into, with the cross itself dangling on the other side facing Leonardo, less than an arm span from him; a shining counterweight that hung precariously from the cliff. A second rope looped around the junction of the crucifix, stretching out below to hold Sigbald and, further down still, Ebel.

Leonardo's eyes widened as he saw the state of his comrades. Ebel hung face down and unconscious, his arms and legs pointing to the ground, dangling into the nothingness as the rope tied around his waist folded his unmoving body in two. Leonardo could not see his face from where he hung and had no way of telling if he were alive or dead.

Sigbald, on the other hand, *was* alive. He was directly below Leonardo by some twelve feet, the rope that held him and Ebel pulled taught, and parallel to Leonardo's. Sigbald groaned. His eyes were closed and the knot of rope that held him seemed to protrude directly from his chest. The harnesses they had been taught to make had held, but Sigbald lay uselessly on his back, his legs dangling below with his chest pointed to the sky as the snowflakes fell intermittently onto his pale skin. The wind tugged at Sigbald and Ebel, causing them to sway gently, as if rocking them to sleep.

Meanwhile, Sebastien, who was fully conscious, hissed and seethed with effort as he braced his palm on the rock above. Leonardo could see that the only thing preventing the four of them from falling to their deaths was the length of rope that had mercifully caught on the protruding finger of rock upon the lip. And now, the cross, coupled with the combined weight of Sigbald and Ebel, was pulling Leonardo and Sebastien up and over the rock, and the only thing stopping that from happening was Sebastien's valiant effort as he pushed back against the massive weight.

'Sigbald!' Leonardo called. 'Can you hear me? Wake up!' But Sigbald could only groan as his eyes fluttered, but did not open.

'Aaargh!' Sebastien cried from the effort, baring his teeth and screwing his eyes shut as he fought against the weight on the other side.

Then, Leonardo heard a crunch and felt a great, violent jolt shoot through the rope as a large chunk of the rock above was dislodged and fell, causing Leonardo to lean into the mountain as it narrowly missed him on its plummet toward the earth below. He looked up to see that the rope had slipped down the jutting portion of rock by several inches, and the rock itself looked as though it might give at any moment.

'Sigbaaaald!' Leonardo bellowed at the top of his lungs. 'Sigbald!' He screamed his friend's name, hoping that, by shouting as loud as he was able, it might bring Sigbald to, and he could save himself and Ebel. By now, however, the epic snowstorm was minutes away from engulfing them and his cries were lost to it.

'Sigbald!' Sebastien took up the call, but it did no good, for he was even further away.

'Sebastien!' Leonardo shouted up. 'The rock won't hold much longer!' Leonardo looked from Sebastien to the rock and back to Sigbald in desperation, realising that they were perhaps seconds from death.

'If that rock breaks we'll all die!'

'I know!' Sebastien howled back, clutching at the handholds and digging his feet into a nook he had found with his toes. Leonardo's heart pounded with pure terror as he contemplated the length of time he would be freefalling until his body smacked into the ground. They were all about to die!

Ebel remained unconscious and unmoving, helplessly swaying and bobbing as the rope above him was agitated by Sigbald's incessant jerking of the limbs. Sigbald must have hit his head, too, but worse than Leonardo. It was clear he was in a bad way and seemed to display none of his cognisant faculties. He flailed and groaned and all Leonardo could do was watch, shielding his eyes from the snow and ice as it whipped around him.

Leonardo cried out in fear as he felt the finger of rock jerk again above him, and it seemed that, at any moment, it would break away from the cliff face and seal their doom.

Then, a terrible thought entered his head. The rock above would break, and when it did, the weight on the rope would rip them all from the sheer head of the Dove and they would all die.

Unless he cut away the weight.

The idea hit him as a punch of guilt. *Cut them away? The best friends he had ever had? No!*

He wanted to reject the idea and glanced up at Sebastien as he struggled with the rope. Sebastien would die, too, if he did not. They both would. Leonardo licked his cracked lips as he moved his left hand to his waist to check that his dagger was still sheathed there. It was.

Its blade was razor sharp, he knew. It could slice through a rope even as thick as this with ease. All he had to do was draw it and cut.

'Sebastien!' he called, looking up at his best friend. Sebastien did not hear; he writhed and bucked, doing his best to hold himself anchored to the rock.

'Sebastien!' Leonardo shouted louder.

'What is it?' Sebastien's eyes were still screwed shut from the effort. Even as he said it, the rock above him cracked and jerked again and he gave a cry of fear and surprise.

'I have to cut the rope!'

'What? No!' Sebastien shouted, looking down at Leonardo with a horror-stricken face. 'Leonardo, you can't!'

Cold tears began to run down Leonardo's cheeks as he pulled the dagger from his waist with his free hand. 'I have to!' he wept. 'It's the only way!'

'No! Don't you dare!' yelled Sebastien. 'Put that knife away, you bastard! Don't you put it anywhere near that damned rope, do you hear me?'

Leonardo sobbed as he was overcome with grief, guilt and shame. The horror of what he was about to do was making his wrist tremble, as he brought the blade to touch the rope to where it was tied just above the gleaming cross.

'Don't do it!' Sebastien screamed from above, though he was powerless to stop Leonardo. The storm was truly upon them then, and the visibility had shrunk to several yards in every direction. Ebel's limp body hung, barely visible, bumping into the stone below like a ragdoll, as Sigbald's moans were lost in the gale.

'Please, Leonardo! Stop, pleeeease!' Sebastien begged. The rock moved with another sudden jolt and another chunk flew from the top. They had seconds.

Leonardo sobbed mournfully as he stretched out his arm and began to saw gently at the twisted hemp fibres of the rope. The steel cut through them easily and they twanged apart gratefully as the enormous tension placed upon them suddenly disappeared.

Leonardo looked down at Sigbald's face as he cut the rope, just in time to see his friend's eyes open and a flash of consciousness pass over them. Horrified, he watched as a frown formed on Sigbald's face as two, intelligent blue eyes watched Leonardo saw away at his lifeline.

Leonardo's heart broke and all he could do was to shout, 'I'm sorry, Sigbald!' as his dagger split the last of the fibres that held him amongst the living and Sigbald began to fall. He reached out a hand to Leonardo as he went, a look of surprise and fear contorting his features as he fell silently.

'Noooo!' Sebastien roared as he was jerked back by the sudden release of tension, almost toppling from his perch.

But it was too late, they were falling. Ebel was the first to disappear. His body was engulfed in white fog and snow and, a fraction of a second later, Sigbald followed. He was reaching out to Leonardo with both arms, a desperate attempt to save his own life, his eyes filled with fear and wide as saucers, forming an image that seared itself into Leonardo's mind forevermore.

Then, he, too was gone and the cross followed, the burnished silver as magnificent as ever as the rubies twinkled in the dim, white light. Their friends disappeared from sight as Leonardo moaned in agony at what he had done.

In the same instance, the jutting finger of rock above them finally gave way and tumbled down, hurtling towards the earth at great speed. Then it vanished, swallowed by the tempest that spun around them.

'What have you done!' Sebastien cried through the billowing air. Leonardo did not reply. He could not. He shook from grief and the only thing he could do was climb down. What else was there to do?

Above him, Sebastien howled with sorrow. But he, too, saw that they had to reach the bottom of the cliff if they were to live.

The descent couldn't have taken them more than an hour, but it was the longest and most miserable hour of Leonardo's life. He was freezing, tossed around violently by ferocious winds, and it was a miracle he wasn't pulled from his holds. He was cold, so very cold, and hungry and tired. But, worst of all, he had just killed two brothers with a single slash of his dagger. The enormity of that awful truth weighed on his shoulders far more than the cross ever had, and it was all he could do to stop himself jumping to his own death in disgust.

I had to do it, Leonardo kept telling himself. *I had to*. It didn't help. Finally, after what seemed like an age, more level ground appeared beneath him and he jumped down to it, his body ready to succumb to the cold. Sebastien dropped down next to him, and Leonardo could see that he was crying. Without saying a word, they huddled down together in a cleft in the rock, tossing a blanket over themselves and squashing their bodies together to better retain the heat.

The cleft sheltered them from the worst of it, though the temperature was still well below freezing, and Leonardo's fingers and toes were white and numb. A memory of Njal's blackened digits the previous winter flashed across his mind and he tucked his hands deep under the folds of his robes and into his trousers beneath. Both he and Sebastien shivered themselves into what might have been sleep or death, neither of them knew. Their bodies were so incredibly worn and tired that it took them in a second, and the last thing Leonardo saw was the rough, brown fabric of the blanket pulled over him as the storm raged overhead.

Leonardo woke to realise he was stuck. Or was he? He tried to move, but couldn't. He opened his eyes to find that nothing covered him but the blanket. Why couldn't he move? Then it dawned on him that he was simply frozen.

With a great effort, Leonardo lifted up an arm to see that his hand was white as snow and winced. He couldn't feel his fingers and remembered the symptoms of the sickness Magnus called 'frostnip'. He glanced to his left; Sebastien was not there.

Leonardo remembered everything that had happened before the storm and groaned as he reached for the blanket and pulled it off him. He had never been so cold, and he thought how much easier it would have been to have stayed put and succumb to the mountain. But he had to know what became of Ebel and Sigbald.

He stood to find he was incredibly stiff and sore and squinted in the morning light. Had they slept through the storm and all of the night? They must have. He looked around. A set of footprints led away down the slope and, now that the air was clear and still, he could see perfectly fine.

The scene before him made his breath catch in his throat. The first thing Leonardo saw was the cross. It had broken clean in two, the halves lying pitifully amongst the rock and ice. Shards of pale, splintered oak stuck out like sharp teeth, whilst the gilded silver panels had sheared apart from the impact. Some of the rubies that had studded its surface lay on the snow, glittering in the sunlight.

And then, some yards further along and not a stone's throw from the bottom of the sheer cliff face, Sebastien knelt by two lifeless forms. They were linked by a rope, the end of which lay coiled, sliced clean through – a grim reminder of the deed that had been done. The bodies were covered in snow and, as Leonardo approached, he could see that the two men were dead.

The first was Ebel. His head was a barely recognisable mess, for it had split open like a melon. His body must have been long since frozen, because the snow had blown into his skull and crystalised there upon the exposed brain matter, half covering his face, so that he looked a part of the mountain as much as the bedrock that surrounded him. His brown eyes were half shut and haunting, and Leonardo felt a lump in his throat and had to look away.

Sigbald was opposite, spreadeagled on his back. He stared up at the sky with wide blue eyes, his mangled arms twisted at horrific angles at his sides. The rock that had fallen a moment after Sigbald had completely crushed his lower half, and long-since-frozen blood half covered by fresh snow pooled around his shattered hips.

It was a gruesome sight. Leonardo sobbed fresh tears as he stood in despair, not knowing what to do. Sebastien, who had been kneeling between the bodies with his back to Leonardo, turned and stood to face him. His face was pale as death, his skin pulled tight over his features and his lips awfully cracked. Sebastien's puffy red eyes glared a look of pure venom toward Leonardo, and he wore such a look of hatred that Leonardo had to step back in shock.

'You!' he hissed. Sebastien took two strides toward Leonardo and, without warning, had mustered all his remaining energy to punch him hard in the mouth, causing Leonardo's head to rock backward as he fell onto his bottom in surprise. He hit the ice with a thump and tasted blood a second later.

He looked up in horror as his best friend stood above him.

'You fucking killed them, you devil!' Sebastien roared as tears rolled down his cheeks. 'How could you? I should kill you for it!'

The pain Leonardo felt at those words was a knife to the heart and nothing had ever come so close to breaking him.

'No, Sebastien, I had to! I had to!' Leonardo wept, as he propped himself onto his elbows whilst his friend glared down at him. 'Don't you see? We would both have died!'

'No.' Sebastien's voice had never been so cold, and Leonardo choked as he thought that, in that moment, it could have extinguished any fire. 'You killed them. You did.'

Leonardo sobbed. 'Please, Sebastien, please don't say that...' was all he could whisper. But Sebastien had already turned away and returned to their dead comrades.

Leonardo pushed himself up off the ground gingerly and hobbled to stand several paces behind Sebastien. He stood there for a time, unspeaking, racked by the most appalling feeling of guilt and shame he had ever known, his friend's words seared into his mind.

You killed them. You killed them. You killed them.

They might have been standing that way for an hour. Leonardo could not say, but there came a point when he knew they would have to move or they, too, would die. He was certain that, if they didn't reach the monastery that night, they would perish.

'Sebastien,' he whispered. 'We have to go.' Sebastien did not reply at first. However, after a time, he gave a long, drawn-out sigh and turned, ignoring Leonardo and brushed past him, looking as though he were a hundred years old and not twenty. His gaze was fixed on the peaks to the west, where the monastery lay, and he made for them, not even bothering to collect his leather satchel.

'Wait,' Leonardo called to his back. 'The cross...'

Sebastien stopped and turned slowly, his face contorting into a hateful sneer. 'Is that all you care about? Finishing the mission? You always were the pious one, weren't you!' He spat the last words.

For a moment, Leonardo feared that Sebastien would leave the broken crucifix where it lay. But then he walked back over to it and cut, with his own dagger, the portion of the rope that linked one of the broken halves to Sigbald and looped it over his shoulder wordlessly, turning back towards the west a moment later and beginning his journey, leaving Leonardo alone with the other half.

Clearly, Sebastien didn't intend to wait for Leonardo, and Leonardo had to stop himself from crying again. He drew a long, shaky breath and steadied himself. Collecting the last of their spare rope and fixing it to the remaining half of the cross, Leonardo took one last, long look at Ebel and Sigbald and felt another wave of guilt that he hadn't the strength to bury them, before he tore his eyes away and followed Sebastien.

The journey back to the monastery was one of total misery. Neither Leonardo not Sebastien spoke for its entirety. Sebastien tried to put some distance between the two of them, though struggled – for, by then, they were both so weak that their march had devolved into a stumble and Sebastien was never more than a hundred yards away.

Leonardo watched as his weakened friend shuffled along. Every so often, he would fall into the snow as the weight of the broken cross became too much for him to bear, and each time Leonardo feared he would not rise.

But he did. A moment later, a robed arm would claw itself out of the snow and Sebastien's white fingers pressed themselves into it, sinking deep below the surface until it compacted enough to take his weight and he could push himself slowly to his feet. And then he would take a pitifully small step forward, pulling the rope tight, and Leonardo would fear again that, this time, the shattered crucifix would be too heavy for him to tug along. But then Sebastien would take another step, and then another and another.

They walked so slowly, almost delirious from fatigue, hunger and cold. It took them hours and hours. They walked for all of the new day, despite the fair conditions, and then the sun set, and they were still walking. The chill worsened, as it always did when night approached, and there came a point when Sebastien finally managed to pull away from Leonardo, disappearing over the endless hills and ridges. Leonardo could not say when it had happened, but he followed his friend's footprints blindly, dragging his half of the cross all the while as it made a rhythmical '*schoosh*' sound over the snow.

Nor could Leonardo say when he finally reached the familiar track that led up to the monastery, only that he found himself there. He groaned from the effort as he made the last climb, but then he tripped and hit the ground with a thud that knocked the air right out of him.

Leonardo tried to get up. He raised his arms to plant them on the snowy earth, so that he might push himself to his feet, but he found that he had not the strength to do so. Instead, he slumped back down into the snow, letting his face rest against its freezing surface as he thought, with bitter amusement, that he would die a mile from the monastery.

Perhaps it was all he deserved, for what a wretched thing he was. But then he felt two pairs of strong arms grip his own and haul him to his feet, catching a glimpse of an unkempt white beard before his eyes closed themselves, and he wondered if Magnus would be upset about the broken cross.

When Leonardo woke, he was lying on his cot in the bunkhouse. It was warm and he could hear the crackle of the fire in the hearth by his bed. A weight sat by him on the lumpy mattress and touched a damp cloth to his forehead. Leonardo opened his eyes to find Antonio peering down at him. Leonardo tried to sit up, but Antonio pushed him down, wagging his finger with his other hand.

He licked his lips thirstily and Antonio lowered a waterskin to them, letting Leonardo take small sips, and then wiping his mouth for him as he choked and spluttered, before replacing the waterskin with a spoonful of stew.

When Antonio had taken the bowl of stew away, Leonardo turned his head painfully to the right, feeling the fresh bandages that wrapped themselves around his forehead. He could see that Sebastien lay sleeping in his own cot, the hulking figure of Drogoradz watching over him.

Leonardo tried to sit up once more, but Antonio was there again to push him down and Leonardo did not have the strength to fight him. So, instead, he let himself drift off to sleep again.

When Leonardo woke the second time, there was no one to prevent him getting out of bed. The bunkhouse was empty, but the fire still crackled. He dressed himself groggily and stood, wincing in pain, as he saw that his foot was bandaged and wondered what had happened to it. He made his way to the door, pushing it open and headed out into the glaring sunshine, a stark contrast to the gloom of the bunkhouse, and he had to shield his eyes as he made his way to the great hall.

He pushed open the door gingerly, feeling the weakened and bruised muscles in his arms working twice as hard to do it. He entered, closing the door behind him, and let his eyes adjust to the gloom once more.

When they had, he could see that all his teachers were present. Antonio was running a whetstone down a blade on a table by the fire. Walter was stirring a pot of stew. Magnus studying a book, and Drogoradz was carving a spoon from a lump of wood. At the sound of his approach, they all stopped what they were doing and looked up.

There was a long silence as Leonardo walked to the centre of the cleared space in the great hall. He stood before his masters.

'They're dead,' he croaked.

Magnus sighed. 'We know, boy. We know.'

Leonardo couldn't help himself. He felt his body rack with fresh sobs as he wept for his friends again. 'I'm sorry....' he cried. Magnus rose and came to him, wrapping Leonardo up into a fatherly embrace that Leonardo gratefully returned, sobbing into the old man's shoulder.

'It's not your fault, boy,' Magnus whispered in a voice that was as soft as Leonardo had ever heard it. 'We brought them back yesterday, whilst you slept. They're in the chapel. I believe Sebastien prays there now.'

It took Leonardo a minute to recover, and he wiped his face before he told them exactly what had happened, and they all listened in silence. No one said a word when Leonardo choked as he came to the part when he made his fateful decision to cut Ebel and Sigbald away. When he had finished, there was a pause. Then Walter spoke.

'If you hadn't done it, you'd all be dead,' he said simply.

Leonardo sat there for most of the day, staring blankly into the flames. Walter brought him stew and goat's milk, for which he thanked him absent-mindedly. Magnus had explained that, the next day, they would bury Ebel and Sigbald and, the day after that, both Sebastien and Leonardo would be given the second baptism and be born again as agents of the Order of The Hand of God.

It was what Leonardo had been working tirelessly towards for a year and a half, for two brutal winters. Yet, now, ironically, it didn't feel like a victory. Leonardo had succeeded, but at great cost.

He avoided the chapel and Sebastien, instead returning to the bunkhouse to rest and inspect his foot. Walter had told him he'd had to remove a toe on the left foot that had been lost to the cold. But that, praise God, was all. Everything else had been recovering nicely; the blisters that burnt onto the skin of his fingers from the freezing air would heal, along with the gash in his forehead he had received when he'd collided with the rockface.

Leonardo grimaced as he unwound the bandages and inspected the neatly stitched lump of remaining toe. It would serve as a reminder, forevermore, of the fateful climb of the Dove that had claimed the lives of two more of his brothers.

Hours later, the door opened and Sebastien walked in, glancing over to where Leonardo sat on his bunk and quickly looking away, refusing even to acknowledge his presence and, instead, going straight to bed. Leonardo had tried to talk to his blanketed form, but had not received an answer. Sebastien, it seemed, was intent on ignoring him.

The next day, Leonardo made his way to the chapel after breakfast to look upon Ebel and Sigbald for the last time. They lay on two separate tables by the altar, their bodies washed and their broken limbs, or what remained of them, arranged by their sides. Someone had closed their eyes for them and, had it not been for the horrific wounds each had suffered, they could have been sleeping.

The two halves of the broken crucifix were piled in the corner. Somehow, it felt fitting that it, too, had not survived. It felt like an appropriate omen; a shattered cross to mark the passing of two good men.

Then, Leonardo watched as Antonio and Walter wrapped the two bodies in white cloth, before the donkey was readied to transport them down the mountain. It was a bizarre procession that made its way down the track that morning. Drogoradz led the ass with the two lifeless bodies roped to its back, while Leonardo followed behind Sebastien, who would not walk with him. Magnus, Antonio and Walter followed solemnly with picks and shovels. An hour later, they had made their way far enough down the mountainside that trees were able to grow, and the earth became deep enough to bury a man.

Drogoradz led them to a spot amongst the pines that was almost flat, and Leonardo could see several wooden crosses protruding from mounds in the earth marked by neat piles of rocks. Together, they hacked two fresh graves into the snow and soil, taking it in turns with the picks and shovels, whilst another collected as many large rocks as they could find.

The six men stopped to eat and drink at midday. The ass, tied to a nearby tree, snorted contentedly, picking its way through the snow with a hoof and sniffing at the forest floor next to where the two wrapped bodies lay.

After lunch, they continued and, soon, the graves were deep enough. Ebel and Sigbald were lowered in gently, before they were covered with earth and the stones were piled upon them. Drogoradz held out a fresh wooden cross to Leonardo and Sebastien each.

'We thought you might like to… carve the names yourselves,' he said awkwardly.

Leonardo took one gratefully and he sat some twenty paces from Sebastien as he carved into the wooden cross. Leonardo had to fight back the tears as his blade etched the letters 'E' 'B' 'E' 'L' into the cross, ensuring they were deep and clear. When it was done, they were handed back to Drogoradz, who used the head of the pick to hammer them into the earth.

They stood silently as Magnus performed the burial rights and spoke a prayer, before they joined in to sing a hymn for the deceased young men. Fresh grief racked Leonardo at the loss, and he remembered the men they had been. Boisterous Sigbald, always ready with a joke, and the intelligent, reserved Ebel, who would frown at their raucous behaviour in the bunkhouse.

They had been taken from this world before their lives had even begun, far too soon. Leonardo knew that, if anyone deserved passage to the garden of their Lord, it was Ebel and Sigbald.

Then, when the dead were buried and everything that needed to be said, had been, the six men made their way back up to the monastery. They ate together and, for the first time, Sebastien and Leonardo were welcomed onto the same table as their superiors.

Drogoradz had clapped them both on the shoulder and claimed, 'You're one of us now, gentlemen. Well done.' But neither of them had smiled. The conversation around them had been reserved, for their teachers had felt their grim mood and gave them time and space, for which Leonardo was grateful.

Sebastien still refused to speak to him when they climbed into bed that night, and Leonardo soon gave up trying to begin a conversation. The next day, they were summoned to the chapel once more and, when Antonio ushered them in before him, he barred the doors from the inside.

The chapel glowed. A thousand yellow candles had been lit, giving it a strange brightness. Before the altar, a great round copper tub had been placed. Leonardo could see that it was filled with water and chunks of ice, deep enough to submerge a man.

The ice bobbed up and down gently within it, as Antonio joined the three robed figures standing behind it. All their teachers wore pristine black robes, the hoods pulled over their heads so that their features were bathed in shadows.

Leonardo and Sebastien stood awkwardly, waiting for direction, until Magnus motioned them forward. The two young men stood facing the four instructors with the tub between them. Walter carried a smoking bauble on a chain that burnt incense and filled the room with a sickly sweet aroma.

'This is a sacred ritual,' Magnus barked in his usual harsh tone. 'It is given to only the most worthy and devout of the Order. Once passed, you will be humble men of God, with the power to be forgiven for your sins that you commit in His name. Serve Him in this way by doing whatever His will might demand, and you shall be absolved. Furthermore, you will be tied to the Order of The Hand of God for as long as you should draw breath, and there can be no going back. Do you understand?'

His blue eyes bore into those of the two young men and they replied, 'Yes, Teacher.'

Magnus fixed his eyes on Leonardo. 'Leonardo. Step forward,' he commanded.

Leonardo did as he was bid, swallowing nervously as he went to stand before the tub of icy water. Walter removed himself from the ranks of their watching superiors and drew a large, black bible from within the folds of his robes. He stopped next to Leonardo and, holding the book, nodded down at it, which Leonardo took to mean he should place his right hand upon it. He did so and felt the smooth surface of the warm leather.

'Leonardo of the Papal Finger, do you pledge your flesh and blood to the Order of The Hand of God?' Magnus's voice echoed eerily off the stone walls of the chapel, and Leonardo felt uncomfortable as five pairs of eyes watched him closely.

'I do,' he replied.

'Will you so swear, before God,' continued Magnus, 'to give your life in His service, and to do whatever is necessary to protect His kingdom, and to go to whichever corner of His earth you are required?'

'I swear.' Leonardo's heart hammered with the intensity of it all.

'Do you swear to put the needs of the holy Order of The Hand of God before your own and all others, and to respect the code that all who are encompassed by its ranks must follow?'

'I so swear.'

'Do you understand that to abandon its cause, or forsake its code henceforth, will result in your execution?'

There was an uncomfortable silence. Leonardo gulped. 'I do.'

'Then remove your garb and stand naked before Him, so that He might see through any guise of devilry, and allow yourself to be reborn!'

Leonardo stripped his cloak, then the furs he wore underneath and then his jacket, shirt and trousers and, finally, his hose, until he was completely bare. The hair on his skin stood on end as goosebumps covered its surface from the chill in the air.

Walter tucked his book away and he and Antonio moved to either side of the tub, the latter placing a thick wooden block in front of it to act as a step so that Leonardo might easier climb into it. He took a deep breath and stood on the block before swinging a leg into the water.

He gasped. It was freezing cold and he shivered as the water enveloped his leg. He touched the bottom with his toes and swung the other leg over and stood so that the water came to just above his groin. Leonardo watched Magnus, as Walter and Antonio placed their hands on his shoulders and began to push him slowly down into the water.

Leonardo allowed himself to be pushed down, keeping his eyes open until the last second, watching the unreadable expressions of Magnus and Drogoradz as he closed his eyes and became completely submerged.

It was cold under the water, but peaceful. The world faded away and his senses were dulled in the cocoon-like tub. Leonardo felt himself relax for the first time in a long time, letting everything above leave him, along with any feelings he had when he'd entered. In the water, there was no joy, nor fear, no love, hate or jealousy. No guilt. It was pleasant.

But then, Leonardo realised that he had been submerged for quite some time and needed air in his lungs. He tried to push up to the surface, but felt two strong pairs of hands clamp down on his shoulders as the weight of both Antonio and Walter pushed down upon him.

No, I need to breathe! Leonardo thought in panic. He pushed harder, but couldn't dislodge their weight and began to scrabble desperately, his arms flailing and sloshing at the water above, sending it cascading from the tub and onto the black robes of his masters, before splashing onto the stone-flagged floor of the chapel.

They're going to kill me, Leonardo thought as his lungs inhaled a mouthful of water and his chest began to convulse and jerk from lack of oxygen. *I'm going to die.*

But then he was pulled from the water and choked it from his lungs, before sucking an enormous breath of sweet air into his chest. Before he knew what was happening, Antonio and Walter were pulling him bodily from the tub and he was unceremoniously pushed onto one of the wooden pews by the altar and thrown a blanket to cover his modesty.

Magnus spread his arms wide and declared, 'You are born again as a son of the Order of The Hand of God! We welcome you, brother!'

'Hear hear!' Drogoradz clapped and stamped his feet, as Walter muttered, 'Welcome, brother.' Antonio squeezed his shoulder.

Then, it was Sebastien's turn, and Leonardo watched in fascination as he, too, was given the rights as Magnus spoke the words. Sebastien affirmed and then stripped naked before stepping into the tub. There, he was held, and a minute later he, too, was bucking violently as he fought for breath. The moment seemed to drag on forever and Leonardo was about to protest in panic, for he thought the masters really were about to drown him, before Sebastien was allowed to burst from the surface of the water and gulp down air in desperate breaths.

'Welcome, brother!' the others cried as they clapped him on the back, and Sebastien even managed a weak smile, the first Leonardo had seen him give since before the Dove. They were agents now, and Leonardo knew that the responsibility would weigh on their shoulders for the years to come. They were agents, and their lives had been pledged to something greater than themselves, Leonardo realised. That had to be worth something.

Once they were dressed and had all migrated to the great hall, Magnus explained that they were free to leave as soon as they liked.

However, he advised they wait a fortnight until mid-March, for it was still the last day of February, and they would struggle to travel the roads quickly once they were out of the Pyrenees.

Leonardo wanted to ask Sebastien when he planned to leave, but then remembered they weren't speaking, and that made him sullen all over again. Over the next few days, the laughter gradually returned to the great hall during mealtimes – though, now it came mostly from Drogoradz. He, Magnus and the others were clearly more accustomed to burying good men and had steeled their hearts against it, knowing that to mourn for an eternity would achieve nothing.

Leonardo's grief was still as fresh and present as ever, a dull ache in his chest that retuned anew each time he saw Ebel and Sigbald's empty cots. He had found, however, that it was best to keep his mind occupied. Though he and Sebastien were free to do as they pleased until the day of their departure came, he busied himself with the familiar daily chores of winter life at the monastery, from melting blocks of ice for drinking water, to shovelling paths in the yard when it snowed, to feeding the animals or cooking in the great hall.

He even practised his swordplay with Antonio and, on occasion, wrestled with Drogoradz, or revised his concoctions with Walter. They accepted him freely and called him brother. And, when he or Sebastien used the old title of 'Teacher', the older men corrected them and insisted on being called by their Christian names. It was a symbol that the barriers between them were now gone. Leonardo and Sebastien, as far as they were concerned, had proved themselves and they were, thus, treated accordingly.

Leonardo found a new comradeship with his old mentors, talking with them at length over meals to delve into their pasts, or quiz them about the missions they had completed in service to the Order. He found he rather liked them; even grumpy Walter didn't seem so bad, and Leonardo suspected there was probably a good deal more he could have learnt from the four men.

Over the next two weeks, Leonardo tried to do just that, and his skill with a blade was matched only by Antonio, the two men seeming to draw during most of their sessions in the cleared half of the great hall. On occasion, they took to the outdoors now that the weather was becoming clearer by the day, and spread salt over a patch of the yard so that they were not slipping on the ice. However, they could only do this a few times, and would have to wait until spring before they could continue outside.

Nevertheless, Leonardo took every opportunity his old teacher would give him to spar, relishing the chance to thrash himself into a sweaty frenzy with the wooden training swords, their familiar clatter ringing out against the squat stone buildings of the monastery.

Sebastien did much of the same, though he and Leonardo never sparred together, and it was not lost on the others that they were still not speaking. No one thought to push the subject, however, and Leonardo wondered if they could ever be friends again.

One morning, when spring seemed to be almost upon them, Leonardo woke to find that his friend's cot was empty and his belongings gone. The blankets were folded and placed in a neat pile at the foot of the straw mattress.

With a pang, Leonardo knew that Sebastien had gone and, without a second thought, he pulled on his boots, tugged his cloak around him and ran out of the door into the cool morning air. He made for the track and sprinted down, slipping and sliding on its surface, for he hadn't even bothered to strap on his snowshoes. He could see Sebastien's tracks there and followed at breakneck speed, scanning the terrain down the hill until he spotted a small, black figure with a sack of affairs slung over one shoulder upon the next ridge, several hundred yards away.

'Wait!' Leonardo cried as he ran toward him. 'Sebastien, wait!'

The figure turned to see who pursued him. He watched Leonardo's desperate descent for a moment, before turning wordlessly back and continuing on. A minute or two later and Leonardo had caught up to him.

'Sebastien!' he shouted, tugging on his comrade's arm and forcing him to stop and face him.

'What do you want?' Sebastien snapped, shrugging off Leonardo's grip.

'Why won't you speak to me?' Leonardo implored, not managing to disguise the hurt in his voice.

Sebastien shot him a look of daggers. 'You know why.'

Leonardo raised his hands in exasperation. 'Yes, it was my blade that cut the rope, and I will never forgive myself for that. But Sebastien, if I hadn't done it, we would both be dead, too.'

'No.' Sebastien's mouth twitched in anger. 'There would have been another way.'

'What?' Leonardo shouted. 'What other way?'

Sebastien did not give him an answer to that. Instead, he replied, 'You killed our brothers, and I never want to see your face again.' He said it with such quiet vehemence it almost made Leonardo shudder.

Sebastien turned and continued his march, leaving Leonardo standing alone in the snow. Leonardo bit his tongue to hold back the tears and felt anger bubble over and eclipse his sorrow. How could Sebastien not see that he had made the only choice? How could Sebastien hold him solely accountable? What right did he have to shun him for that decision? It wasn't fair!

Leonardo found his old strength and drew in a lungful of air and roared out to Sebastien. 'Well, damn you then, you bloody fool! I hope we never do cross paths!' At that, Sebastien paused for a second, but did not turn. He continued on without reply, following the track that would lead him down into the glacial plain below and eventually to Arreau. From there, he would take the northern road out of the Pyrenees and head back to his master in England.

It was the last time Leonardo would see him for another twelve years, and, as he watched his friend march away, he remarked that Sebastien was yet another brother he had lost since arriving at the monastery, the summer before last. Six good men had come and gone, and each of their losses was crushing to the point it made Leonardo seethe with anger.

He made a vow as he watched Sebastien's cloaked form disappear over the next hillock, to never allow himself to come too close to another person again, lest he lose them, too, or before they could hurt him. His face was a mask of bitterness as he nodded to himself, coming to the grim conclusion that he worked better alone, anyway.

And so, alone Leonardo would stay, with only his Lord God for company.

Gascony

Leonardo rubbed the short, blonde bristles on the top of his shorn head as he paced from one end of his room to the other. He had not slept a wink the night before, for his mind had been doing somersaults. All he could think about was the Queen and Sebastien. Sebastien and the Queen. The *Queen*. It still wasn't real. It couldn't be. Yet, it was.

Leonardo smacked himself on the side of the head, hoping that he would come to the realisation that it had all been a dream, just a fanciful dream. But his mind knew better. In an hour, he would have to face Sebastien when the parliament was called once more. He was not sure how Sebastien would react.

Leonardo wondered if there was some way for his friend to get out of this, and he racked his brains for how he might help him. Back and forth he strode, his boots thudding rhythmically over the wooden boards. It seemed like an impossible situation, and Leonardo wondered, for the thousandth time, how it had come to this. He rubbed his temples and shook his head incredulously, the awful reality of the situation still seeming illusory.

Finally, Leonardo thought he might have a solution. Firstly, Sebastien could not flee and nor could Queen Eleanor, that much was obvious, for it was suicide. Then, the Queen would have to claim that the child was her husband's and, if she hadn't lain with Henry for some time, she would have to seduce him as soon as possible; for, when the pregnancy began to show, there had to be no question that the baby belonged to anyone other than the King.

Lastly, Sebastien would have to return to his duties in serving the Nordic Finger and never see Eleanor again. That was the only way Leonardo could think to get his friend out of this mess, if it wasn't too late already. Yes, he decided, he would confront Sebastien after the parliament and stop him before he did something irreversible, as if what had already been done wasn't enough. Leonardo strode from the room, grim faced and determined.

He crossed the city, where the townsfolk went leisurely about their business, in blissful ignorance of the predicament Leonardo had to deal with. The square outside the massive judicial and parliamentary building was already filling with officials, high-ranking churchmen and nobles, knights and lords.

Their chatter echoed off the walls of the corridors as they filed in once a guard opened the doors to them, and Leonardo joined the hubbub, pressing himself forward with the crowd of men shuffling into the building.

'Bad business,' a portly man in his fifties was saying to his colleague. 'War with Castile would ruin us.'

'Aye.' His friend shook his head sadly. 'Don't know if we can afford that to happen.'

A younger noble overheard and scoffed, 'The pair of you sound like cowards! Let the Spanish King die on Gascony's shores, I say. We'll give him what for!'

'Don't be a fool, man!' replied the first man. 'Our numbers are low enough as it is. With the rebels on one side and the army of Castile on the other, we'll be crushed! Don't you remember the King sent much of his army home?' There was a muttering of affirmation at that, and the younger man held his tongue as they crowded through the double doors leading to the King's hall.

Leonardo took a seat silently and watched the people come through the door. Then, Sebastien appeared as one of the last. He stood on his tiptoes looking around, spotting Leonardo and acknowledging him with a wave, only to see that the seats around him were all full and sat elsewhere. Leonardo felt a grim sense of dread at the conversation he was soon to have with Sebastien, and chewed his lip, thinking about the best way to broach the subject with him, as the great lords, including John de Gray, Roger Bigod and Drogo de Barentin, entered, taking the seats that had been reserved for them on the front row before the dais.

A minute later, Peter Bonefans entered the hall. 'All kneel for the King and Queen!' he cried. There was a great shuffling and scraping in reply as the men bowed their heads and knelt, as King Henry and Queen Eleanor made their entrance.

'Sit, please,' the King ordered brusquely. 'There is much to discuss and little time.' Everyone sat.

'Now,' the King began. 'The situation is delicate. We have to decide whether to—' The King had stopped, freezing mid-speech on the dais, as the sounds of hooves clattering on a stone floor and shouting were heard coming from the corridor. There was a murmur of confusion from those gathered, followed by a gasp of surprise as Peter of Savoy burst in through the double doors upon his mount, a desperate look on his features as the red-faced guards tumbled through in his wake, clearly having been unable to stop him.

'Peter?' the King said incredulously. 'What is the meaning of this? You come to my parliament, armed, horsed and late to boot? Explain yourself!'

A hush fell over the watching crowd as all heads turned to Peter of Savoy, as the sweating noble caught his breath, clearly having been riding at speed for some time.

'Your Highness… it's Gaston de Bearn…' he panted desperately.

'What about him?' the King asked, his brow furrowing.

'He… he rides west, with an entire army from Pau this morning. He means to attack Bayonne!' Peter's voice rang out clear in the hall and there was a collective gasp from everyone who heard it.

'What!' the King snapped, a stricken expression forming on his face. 'But… but…' he spluttered, 'the last information we had promised that the rebels were disorganised and spread closer to Toulouse!' His face turned from a shade of bright red to white in a second. 'How is this possible?'

'I don't know, Your Highness, but it is happening! And he might have even set off yesterday!' At Peter's words, there was a great cry of outrage and anguish. Shocked faces could be seen everywhere, on the King, the Queen and all of the lords.

'We've been played!' Peter cried as the noise rose to a din as the hundred or so men moaned amongst one another at this awful news. At that moment, Leonardo wondered if the whole charade with Cristoval del Soria and the threat of war was merely a distraction, whilst Gaston rallied his men in the south.

Recently, all reports had suggested that the rebels were hemmed into the south-east by a good chunk of Henry's knights and men-art-arms, who prevented them from regrouping, and all it would take would be a final hammer blow to crush them, once and for all. But now it seemed that they had underestimated the rebels, if what Peter said was to be believed, and that Gaston had somehow amassed an army and slipped past his enemies.

If that was true, there would be nothing between him and Bayonne and, as this awful truth dawned on everyone present, the clamour in the hall rose another pitch. Gaston could not be allowed to take Bayonne, for, if he did, he could hold the city for months, forcing Henry's coffers to tip themselves dry to oust him. More worryingly, it would provide the perfect landing pad for King Alfonso of Castile to safely position his army on the mainland, if and when he did invade.

The King was clever enough to see it. However, as all looked to him for orders, he could only splutter incoherently on the dais, balled fists shaking by his sides with emotion, though whether that was fear or anger Leonardo could not say. The nobles waited for their King to speak, but he did not – or could not, as he was seemingly paralysed by the development.

Finally, Queen Eleanor stood from her throne and shouted, 'Drogo! You know what to do!'

The bald, bearded knight leapt to his feet. 'Aye, Your Highness,' he replied. He nodded, then turned to the rest of the fretting nobility. 'The King's army will follow me!' he roared in his best parade ground voice, its strength echoing from the stone walls.

Without further ado, Drogo was striding from the hall, followed closely by his knights. Then John de Gray was on his feet and Roger Bigod, too. Peter of Savoy was wheeling his horse around as the great lords of England were followed by the rest of the nobles, leaving King Henry to splutter in horror on the dais.

Leonardo caught sight of Sebastien following the rest of them, and made to go himself, wincing at the deafening cries of anger as the men called each other to action. There was only one option for them now: they had to intercept Gaston before he reached Bayonne. Fortunately for the King, he had amassed a good deal of competent commanders about him, and they organised themselves into detachments, and the spearhead of elite knights that would decide whether Gaston could be stopped would be led by Drogo.

Unfortunately, a good deal of them were already out in the countryside and it would be too late to recall them. Drogo would just have to work with whomever was in Bordeaux. Leonardo jogged down the steps of the parliamentary building and observed Drogo in the square, surrounded by men and barking out orders as each asked what they should do.

'You will all rendezvous on the southern road, as quickly as you can,' he shouted out. 'Travel light. Only weapons and a little water. I ride in an hour and if you're not there, I will leave you behind!'

Roger Bigod, John de Gray and Peter of Savoy were giving instructions to their own men, ordering them to gather at the point Drogo had instructed. The square was a hive of activity as men ran this way and that, shoving aside perplexed townsfolk who had been unfortunate enough to be in the wrong place at the wrong time.

Just then, Leonardo felt a hand on his shoulder and turned to see Sebastien standing by his side.

'I say they could use our help, eh?' he said with a smile and a wink. Before Leonardo could even reply, Sebastien was striding away toward Drogo, and Leonardo had no choice but to follow.

'Drogo!' Sebastien called as he jogged up to the knight. 'How does an extra pair of hands sound?'

Drogo looked up from the roster sheet he was scanning and grinned, his eyes lighting up as he saw who'd called for him. 'Aye! I need every pair of hands I can get, especially the pair of you! Ride with me today and I shall be in your debt, gentlemen.'

'Ha! I won't forget it!' Sebastien smiled, turning to Leonardo. 'What say you, Leo? Are you in?' Both Drogo and Sebastien looked hopefully at him.

Leonardo looked from one to the other and sighed. He could hardly stay behind. 'I'm in,' he said.

'Excellent,' Drogo said gruffly. 'Prepare yourselves, then. There is little time.'

Sebastien slapped Leonardo's shoulder and jogged away with an excited whoop at the prospect of some action, leaving Leonardo to curse under his breath. The matter of the affair would have to wait,

Leonardo decided. For now, the fate of Gascony hung in the balance and his friends needed him at their side.

'Eighty-five miles!' Drogo shouted back to John de Gray, when asked what the distance was from Bordeaux to Bayonne. The knights were about to depart, all three hundred and fifty-nine of them, plus Leonardo and Sebastien. It was not a great number by any stretch, especially since more information on Gaston's force had put it at almost two thousand. But more would join them on the road, Drogo had assured the men.

It was already mid-morning when the last of Drogo's men galloped from the stables to join the braying, stamping column of warhorses, arrayed four abreast on the road, snaking back toward Bordeaux like some gigantic thorny snake. Lance tips bristled, and a weak winter sun peeked out from an overcast sky to reflect off the knights' helms.

Drogo waited at the vanguard with the other lords, joined by Leonardo and Sebastien, for Drogo had insisted they ride together.

'Then Gaston will have a head start,' John de Gray said grimly.

'How far from Pau to Bayonne?' Sebastien queried.

'Only forty miles,' Drogo said scowling. 'Gaston will get there this evening, if he set off the day before.'

Sebastien cursed. 'Can it be done?' he asked. 'Can we get to him before he gets to Bayonne?'

Drogo looked around furtively, making sure none of the knights heard him. 'Honestly, I don't know. But we have to try. If we should fail, then it is likely that Gascony is lost.'

Sebastien nodded seriously, chewing his lip as he fiddled with his horse's reins. All of them were mounted and armoured. Leonardo wore maille and gambeson, and had scavenged a shield and a lance from Drogo's armoury. The knight had also donated him a great helm, which hung from his saddle pommel by its straps. *Leonardo the knight,* he thought to himself, and would have been amused had the circumstances been different.

'I take it we will not be waiting for the rest of the King's army?' he asked Drogo.

'No,' came the gruff reply. 'They will be too slow. The King and his men-at-arms will follow on foot. We take mounted men only, and we strike before they even know we're there.' Drogo scratched his bushy beard thoughtfully. 'There won't be much to do in the way of tactics when we get there, just hit 'em hard.'

'Understood.' Leonardo nodded and he wondered if he would get to experience what it was like to be part of a heavy cavalry charge, the most devastating weapon of war on the face of the earth.

Drogo stood in his stirrups and craned his neck, looking down the line as the last of the stragglers arrived and a banner was flown to signal that they were all present. He looked around at his captains. 'Are we ready?' he shouted. They nodded in response.

Drogo turned to the other lords. John de Gray, Peter of Savoy and Roger Bigod gave the knight a nod and Drogo signalled to one of his men. The knight took a horn from his belt, sucked in a deep lungful of air and blew a long, piercing note that rang out into the cold morning.

All along the line, the cream of the English knights cheered in exultation, for they knew they were going to war. The horses whinnied and brayed, infected by the moods of their riders, as the front of the column broke into a trot. For anyone watching, it must have been a magnificent sight; hundreds of neat lines moved in disciplined ranks, their banners fluttering in the breeze, with the colours of whomever they served displayed proudly on their surcoats, whilst the horses themselves were adorned with fine cuts of cloth, with coats of arms mirrored on each breast.

Leonardo felt his horse lurch into action beneath him, without him even having to coax it forward. It seemed the beast was as eager as the rest of the men for rebel blood. He settled in for the ride and the first hour went by steadily, perhaps even pleasantly. The commanders at the vanguard were able to ride abreast and discuss the plan of action, each matching their horse's rhythm in the saddle.

After a while, however, the horses began to sweat and their riders followed suit soon after, for riding in full armour was no easy task.

By the second hour, the quick pace had caused Leonardo to chafe between the thighs and he found himself panting. He glanced back to see that the orderly column that had set out from Bordeaux had devolved into a hundred smaller clusters of men as they tried to stay with the vanguard.

Drogo pushed them on for another hour until he allowed them to rest for lunch, though Leonardo suspected it was more for the horses' benefit than the riders. He was grateful nonetheless and slid from the saddle to pat his weary steed, uncorking a waterskin that hung from his belt.

He watched as Sebastien stretched his back out with a grimace, taking comfort in knowing that he wasn't the only one that suffered. Leonardo's heart sank when he heard one of Drogo's knights estimate that they had only gone twenty miles and were not even a quarter of the way.

Drogo gave them a minute more, allowing some of those who had fallen behind to catch up, before climbing back up into his saddle and gesturing for the others to do the same. Half reluctantly, Leonardo gave his horse a final pat before climbing onto its back once more.

A moment later, they were away again, though this time there was no idle chatter, for both man and horse were focused on the ride. The steady trot they maintained would have been acceptable for a few hours, but by the time five hours had slid by Leonardo was in agony. The skin of his thighs had been all but chafed away and his lower back ached painfully from holding his weight upright all day. Worse, his horse was white with sweat, and he could see it struggled to breathe, the breaths coming out in short, laboured snorts.

They were big, muscular war horses, bred to smash into a line of infantry with devastating force. Their strong suit was the battlefield, certainly not a long, arduous slog better suited to horses bred for endurance, like the ones a professional messenger service might have ridden. Though their mounts were fit and trained, Leonardo feared they would be too exhausted to make the long journey, let alone fight.

After several more miles, they came to a great crossroads. The front rank of the vanguard skidded to a halt when other riders appeared from the trees. After a brief moment of panic, when the captains began to call the men present into fighting formation, Drogo waved to them with a sigh of relief, seeing that they bore the colours of the King.

'My lords!' the lead knight shouted. 'We have received the orders to meet you on the southern road and here we are. Tell us what to do!'

'Good!' Drogo shouted back. 'Fall in behind us. But first, what news of Gaston de Bearn?'

'He will be at Bayonne by evening, if he is not there already!'

Drogo cursed and, without another word, spurred his mount on. The rest of the men followed, as the newcomers wedged themselves into a gap in the column, matching the trot. As the English knights hammered down the road, more appeared from the trees, arriving from the cordon that had been put in place to prevent the disaster that had now come to pass. They trickled in in small clusters, adding their weight to the mass of elite troops.

Leonardo could only guess at how many they numbered now, but it must have been over four hundred. The sun was well past its highest point and had begun its downward trajectory, taking them into late afternoon. Drogo paused once more, declaring it would be the last stop of the day. Leonardo supressed a groan as he slid from the saddle again, and almost collapsed in a heap of metal on the ground. His body had long since drawn upon its last reserves of energy and all he wanted to do was lie down onto a bed roll. But it was not to be.

'We ride until nightfall!' Drogo called out, receiving a collective groan from all who heard, and Leonardo knew they felt just as spent as he did. Then, word came up the column that some of the mounts had dropped from exhaustion and were dead.

'Are there no spares?' John de Gray asked. The reply was in the negative. 'Then they'll just have to follow on foot!'

Sebastien, sitting near to Leonardo on the grass, prodded the flesh of his inner thighs gingerly and winced. 'By Mary and Joseph, I don't think I've ever ridden so hard for so long!'

'Nor I,' Leonardo put in.

Sebastien looked around furtively and dropped his voice. 'Look at the men, look at the horses! I don't know what kind of shape we'll be in by the time we reach the rebels, but it won't be an optimal one, that's for sure.'

'No, you're right,' said Leonardo. 'But if we don't get to Gaston before he gets into the city, we will lose hundreds more trying to take it.' The pair of them fell silent at that, knowing that riding the horses half to death was the better of two poor options.

'I've never been in a cavalry charge,' Sebastien grinned after a moment.

Leonardo shook his head and smiled. 'Come on, there won't be a cavalry charge if we don't get there. Look, they're mounting up already!' Around them, the other knights were reluctantly hauling themselves into their saddles for the last time that day, their horses whinnying in displeasure at the thought of more riding.

They were underway again and Leonardo was almost grateful that the winter days were shorter, and the light faded quicker, for, after another two agonising hours, Drogo gave the order to stop. The river Adour lay before them, snaking its way westwards towards the ocean, and they would have to cross it in the morning. It was a landmark, a testimony of its own that they had managed to travel so far in a single day. It was an incredible feat of stamina, though no one had the energy to celebrate it – and, more importantly, they knew that the real test was yet to come.

There was a moan of relief from all who heard the order, and a hasty camp was set up and sentries placed. The men who were not on guard duty collapsed under a blanket on the damp forest floor by the road. No one had bothered to unsaddle their horses, for they knew that, in just a few short hours, they would have to be in them again before the sun had risen.

Before Leonardo lay his weary body down to sleep, he learnt from reports that they were eight miles from Bayonne. They could only hope that Gaston was slow in his attack, for, had he wanted to try to scale the walls, there was little the skeletal garrison left in the city could do to defend it against so many.

Early the next morning, Leonardo was woken by one of the sentries, and pulled the blanket from his face, sitting up groggily and rubbing his eyes. He shivered. It had been cold in the night and he stood, shaking the life into his limbs. Sebastien squatted next to him, tearing chunks from a block of cheese he had secreted somewhere on his person the day before. Sebastien glanced over to him and offered the cheese out silently. Leonardo broke a piece off with a nod of thanks and handed it back, grateful for whatever sustenance he could get.

He looked around to see the rest of the men stirring, and it wasn't long before the captains and commanders were bellowing at their men to get on their feet and prepare their horses. It seemed that none of them would be given the chance to properly wake up before having to clamber once more onto their mounts.

'Come on, you lazy bastards!' someone shouted. 'On your feet!' The knights grumbled, but collected their weapons and were soon leading the horses back onto the road.

Drogo and Peter of Savoy stood tensely, discussing in low tones what the course of action would be when they finally found the rebels. Both of them seemed agitated, as though they knew that Gascony could be won or lost by a margin of hours.

The sense of urgency had spread to the other men, too, for Leonardo did not hear the usual chatter and laughter of a military camp waking for the day. Orders were barked and the men were horsed within minutes. Sebastien and Leonardo leapt back up onto their protesting mounts and, though they could see the poor animals were not at their best, the night's rest had at least done them some good.

Then, the horn was blown once more, but that morning there was no great cheer, just a weary determination to plough on. The pace this time was quicker than the previous day, for they had but eight miles left to cover. The day before, they had passed the road that led east to Peyrehorade, and Leonardo had spotted the spires of its churches in the distance. From there, they had turned west to trace the banks of the Adour before they made camp.

Villagers screeched in terror as the knights thundered past, paying no heed to the peasants as they barrelled them out of the road. There was a much greater sense of urgency to reach their destination. However, there was yet one more great obstacle to overcome. The river Adour itself.

It flowed deep and wide and there were scant few bridges that spanned its great girth. As Drogo ordered his men to find them a fording point, Leonardo gazed into the muddy waters from the northern bank.

'God help us,' Sebastien said as he pulled on his horse's reins next to Leonardo, a lance resting on his right shoulder. 'This will not be easy.'

Shouts came from further down river and they turned to see one of the knights standing in his stirrups, beckoning the others to him with his lance. 'Over here!' he shouted. 'There is a ford here!'

'Come on!' Leonardo cried, and kicked his horse into action, galloping over with a swarm of other mounted men. Drogo fought his way to the fore and inspected the crossing point with a frown. Leonardo watched the man's mind work and saw him glance briefly up and down the river, as if wondering if there were somewhere safer to cross, but finally deciding that there was no time.

'This will do,' Drogo nodded and waved his men forward. Soon, the first of the English knights were trotting down the bank and many hooves were splashing into the shallows as the horses whinnied with nerves. Their riders did their best to calm them and ushered them on. Leonardo watched as the first of the knights' mounts were soon submerged up to their necks, as the horses struggled to cross the great distance.

By his side, Sebastien kicked his own horse into action and was soon knee deep in the water, the great power of the Adour threatening to pluck the horses away downriver. Fortunately, their mounts were strong and Leonardo was grateful for his horse's resilience, patting its side as it carried him deeper into the river.

Even here, at a relatively narrow stretch of the Adour, the river was easily more than a hundred yards in width and the knights were slow in crossing it. Leonardo felt incredibly vulnerable as he reached its centre and had an awful vision of a band of enemy archers appearing from behind the trees on the far bank. He squinted, scanning the tree line quickly, but seeing nothing. The water splashed around him as the other horses half swam to solid ground.

Then, the first of the knights had reached the far bank and trotted up the shallow slope, holding his lance high as a rally point for the others to head to. Fortunately, it was low tide; Drogo had timed the crossing well. Even so, it was not a speedy affair, and they wasted valuable time that they did not have. It took Leonardo a good ten minutes of travel through the murky water to reach the southern bank and he was grateful to do so, for the strong currents had made him anxious of being swept away.

Others were not as lucky, however. When Leonardo turned, he could see that there was still a bottleneck on the far bank where the knights splashed into the ford. Upriver, a group of Roger Bigod's men had taken the initiative and decided to try to ford a little way up from the rest of them. But, even as Leonardo watched, one of the knights stumbled into the water with his horse, only to find it was much deeper and the horse fell, throwing its rider off.

There was much shouting and pointing as the man splashed around desperately as the current dragged him downstream, his panicked flailing limbs making a parody of the King's finest soldiers as his armour threatened to drag him to his death. Luckily for the knight, a group of his fellows, already in the process of fording the river downstream, formed a barrier from their mounts, and managed to catch the spluttering knight before the current carried him to his death.

There were other delays, too. Some horses refused to enter the water, braying and lashing out on the opposite bank as their riders desperately clung onto their reins, while other horses simply collapsed by the water's edge, too exhausted to go on.

Drogo sat upon the high ground next to Leonardo, rallying his men to him. He cursed as he turned back to see the great, unorganised mass of men and horses splashing their way through the Adour. He tapped his fingers on the saddle in front of him impatiently, his gaze torn between his knights in the Adour and the western road leading to Bayonne. His men milled about him in a swarm, awaiting instruction.

'John!' Drogo called finally, once the majority of his men were present. 'Where is Sir John?' His knights looked around, searching the hundreds of faces for the esteemed household knight.

'Here!' a voice shouted from somewhere at the back of the throng and the knights parted to allow John de Gray to pass through. 'What do you need?'

'John, would you stay here and rally the men who have yet to cross? I fear we do not have the time to wait for them.'

'Aye, I can do that,' John de Gray nodded.

'Good, then meet us on the road as soon as you are able,' Drogo ordered, and John de Gray nodded. 'As for the rest of you, with me!'

The legions of knights were soon galloping away along the road behind their lords, the column stretching into a thin snake. The terrain around the Adour was flat, and the leafless trees of the woods blocked their view of the city of Bayonne for a time. However, a half hour later, a knight shouted and pointed at the tip of the cathedral that could be seen peeking out from behind the branches, and they knew that they were close.

Leonardo's mind raced as he imagined what they would find there. Had Gaston even begun the assault on the city? Were his men even now scaling its walls? Or perhaps the garrison had seen Gaston's force arriving and had already capitulated, knowing there was no hope of victory? If that was the case, then they were too late, and their near hundred-mile dash had been for naught.

Here and there, hovels appeared. Their inhabitants, who had been tending to their animals or tilling the earth, shrieked in fear, running back inside and barring the doors at the sight of so many armed men. Drogo ignored them, his eyes fixed firmly ahead.

Soon, there were more buildings, and then, after a dog's leg in the road, they had their first sight of rebel soldiers. A mounted sentry was leaning against a tree trunk, looking bored, with his mount tied next to him. Leonardo watched as the man looked up and had the shock of his life.

'Cut him down!' Drogo roared as the sentry fumbled with his reins and hopped up onto his horse, galloping away. One bold knight urged his mount on, expertly steering it through a field and over a fence. The horse jumped gracefully and, as the knight bore down on the sentry, he brought his lance up and launched it as if it were a spear.

It struck the sentry in the back and the man cried out in pain, falling from his horse. Seconds later, more of Drogo's men were circling the fallen man, and he was put from his misery as several more lance tips skewered his flesh and the screaming ceased.

Drogo knew that the likelihood of them going much further without alerting the rebels was next to nothing, and now it was a case of attacking them before the rebels could form up against them.

'Quickly now!' Drogo shouted, his voice reaching new levels of urgency. 'To the city walls!'

Leonardo was caught up in the fervour and spurred his horse onwards with the mass of other knights, Sebastien sticking to his side. They pressed onwards, and the trees gave way to more fields and small shacks and huts in which the farmers lived. Moments later, Leonardo had his first glimpse of the stone walls of Bayonne. There, in the distance, he could see thousands of men swarming around a great military camp at the base of the walls, and his breath caught in his throat at the sheer number of them.

Gaston had an entire army – knights, men-at-arms, archers and more. Leonardo scanned their mass, even as the first of them pointed in alarm to the rear. Open meadows provided ample space for their encampment; but, beyond, the tributary river of the Nive fed into the Adour from the south, meaning that there was no good way to encircle the rebels. Equally, the rebels would have nowhere to retreat to.

Leonardo could see breaching ladders carried in their ranks, which were quickly dropped at the sight of the new threat of mounted warriors that had appeared at their rear. Already, Gaston's captains were calling for them to form up in response.

Drogo rode before his men. 'Don't give them time!' he shouted. 'Don't give them time to regroup! Form a line here, quickly!'

The other lords relayed his orders efficiently, and soon there was a neat file of English knights, two ranks deep, arrayed on the opposite side of the meadow, some three hundred yards from the rebels.

'My God,' Sebastien said, gazing in wonder at the swarming sea of men before them. 'We are going to attack that?' he asked under his breath, almost in disbelief.

Leonardo crossed himself and gripped his lance where it had been resting on his stirrup. 'You wanted a cavalry charge, you've got one.'

'Helmets on!' someone cried, and there was a clattering of metal as the knights pulled their great helms over their heads, and their worlds were reduced to thin slits.

Suddenly, Leonardo could hear his own breathing as all the noises outside of the hardened steel were dulled. He surveyed what he was sure was about to become a bloody battlefield and whispered yet another prayer, as enemy spearmen began to form hasty ranks, their bristling metal points aimed menacingly at him.

'Ready?' Drogo shouted to his commanders. They nodded in response as Drogo galloped up and down the line, knowing that every second they wasted was a second more their enemy had to prepare.

Hooves stamped the ground in anticipation as Leonardo took long, deep breaths to calm himself. A man to his left quickly lifted off his helmet and vomited over his horse's neck.

Gaston's army was vast, larger than they had initially been led to believe, and yet more men were turning and sprinting to form up the new line at their rear. Leonardo glanced around him to see that they were near the centre of the English line. Peter of Savoy took command of the left, and Roger Bigod the right. Drogo held the centre and took the lance that was offered to him by one of his knights, pulling on his helmet a moment later as his thick, bushy beard and bald head disappeared.

'God save us, Leo,' Sebastien muttered through the vent holes on his helm, as Leonardo realised he'd been tensing every muscle in his body.

There was a brief moment when time itself seemed to come to a standstill, and the world froze. The two armies faced one another, the sobering reality of the battle mirrored on every face. Even the most battle-hardened veterans amongst them felt a great knot of fear in their guts.

Some trembled, others fidgeted, and all wondered if they would live to see another day. Only a fool would believe they would all come out of it unscathed. However, they were knights, after all. They were the fighting elite and the best the English crown had to offer. Reputation was at stake, and none of them could baulk at the thought of attacking a few disloyal subjects, even if the rebels did outnumber them four to one.

'Right then!' Drogo roared to his men into the silence that followed. 'Let's kill the bastards, shall we?' His knights erupted in a mighty cheer, jabbing their lances into the grey, overcast sky. Leonardo and Sebastien could not help but cheer with them, so taken up were they in the moment as excitement, fear and anger swirled in equal measure behind their eyes, and their hearts pounded in anticipation.

'Show them what English steel tastes like, boys!' Drogo cried. 'Attaaack!' The cheer that followed was deafening, even from behind the great helms. Horns blew and the line of knights advanced slowly in a walk. *What a sight to see!* Leonardo thought. It must have been terrifyingly magnificent for the rebels opposite.

Two great ranks of heavy horse advanced upon them, bright red surcoats and banners displaying the livery of the lords fluttering in the wind – and, of course, the lions of England, which were stitched into a permanent snarl. The horses tossed their heads in agitation and countless armoured men wore dispassionate masks of steel, the slits, where hard eyes peered through, the only hint that they were mortal at all and not some sort of demon of war.

The walk shifted to a trot, as the expert riders glanced left and right to ensure a strict cohesion was maintained until the last second. Leonardo covered the flat ground of the meadow on his own mount, feeling the horse stiffen in preparation of what was to come. With his left hand, he held the reins, his forearm looped through the straps of a shield, whilst his right gripped the shaft of a ten-foot lance, the unfamiliar weapon heavy under his arm.

Thousands of hooves thudded into the earth at once, and the noise filled Leonardo's world. *This is it,* he thought. *This is it!* The trot became a canter at the bark of another order that was repeated down the line. Leonardo saw, from the corner of the slit in his helm, the other riders begin to couch their lances, taking aim at the enemy line of rebel men-at-arms, who were a mere hundred yards away, the distance shrinking rapidly with every second that passed.

He watched as an enemy captain gave an order, and the line of men-at-arms made way for countless crossbowmen to aim their weapons between their ranks. The captain chopped downwards through the air with his sword and the air was filled with a thousand '*clacks*' as the crossbows discharged their bolts and the men stepped back.

Leonardo instinctively dipped his head, screwing his eyes tightly shut and bracing himself for the impact. A fraction of a second later it came. Two bolts glanced off the top of his great helm, their impact rocking his head to one side as, in the same moment, his right shoulder was jerked sharply backward as another bolt smacked into it, bursting links of maille apart. Leonardo cried out in pain, along with his horse, which had taken one of the nasty iron barbs to the breast.

The horse did not slow, however, nor buck, and its momentum carried Leonardo onward as the rest of the bolts missed their mark, disrupting the air beside his head with a '*whoosh!*' as they sped past. Leonardo hissed with pain, barely having time to look down at the bolt protruding from his shoulder, and was immediately grateful for the armour he wore. From what he could tell, the maille and gambeson had sapped most of the projectile's energy before it had broken his flesh, and the head of the bolt had dug only a relatively shallow wound.

Other men had not been so lucky, and here and there they toppled from their horses as the bolts found their mark, piercing the soft flesh of their jugulars through gaps in their armour. Knights fell, only to be trampled under the hooves of their own horses, their comrades having no option but to leave them where they lay and ride on.

341

When the final order came, hundreds of English knights broke into a gallop, charging across the remaining fifty yards of ground at tremendous speed, all notion of coherency thrown to the wind with a mighty cry of rage. Leonardo kicked his horse's sides as hard as he could, but it wasn't necessary, for the beast was champing at the bit and already bore him along at a frightening speed.

'Aaargh!' Sebastien yelled beside him. And then Leonardo was yelling, too, as each knight reached a sprint, now close enough for them to select individual targets for their lances.

The noise of the battle was incredible! Leonardo knew he would never forget it as long as he lived. It was like thunder, drowning out everything else. A storm of man, horse and steel thundered along the meadow, thousands of hammering hooves gouging out great chunks of earth from the ground and tossing them into the air like leaves. Riders bared their teeth as the lances were lowered, the wielders ready to thrust needle-like tips of hardened steel that carried a ton of weight behind them.

Leonardo's eyes widened behind his slits; he could see the individual faces of the men in the line before him now. They looked as terrified as he was. It was said that a heavy cavalry charge was the deadliest military weapon on the face of the earth, and Leonardo believed it.

The last twenty yards passed in the fraction of a second, or the amount of time it took a man to blink. Before Leonardo knew it, there was a thunderous *crash* as the first English heavy horse collided with the rebel soldiers.

The charge was devastating. Leonardo's lance speared clean through the chest of a man, its momentum taking the man momentarily off his feet as the tip burst through his back, shattering links of maille as it went.

All along the line, a similar story of carnage unfolded, the worst being where the enemy had not yet had the chance to properly regroup. Their ranks exploded as King Henry's knights hurtled through, decimating the rebels with a single, terrible sweep. Blood gushed from the sickening wounds caused by the lances, as they pinned their victims to the soft earth in horrified cries of anguish and pain. The lucky ones died instantly, and they were plenty, for the sheer impetus of the charge smashed them with an unparalleled ram of energy, snapping spines like twigs where men had gotten too close.

Leonardo ducked a spear thrust as his horse continued to cannon through the ranks of enemy soldiers. Eventually, however, the densely packed formation of Gaston's army brought the cavalry charge to a grinding halt, and, though many rebels had died, countless more still stood in defiance of the crown.

Leonardo's lance was long gone, and he barely had time to draw his sword before a man was jabbing up at him with his spear. Someone charged from behind him and hacked the man down, and Leonardo recognised the plain surcoat of Sebastien as he wheeled his mount around to fight, side by side, with Leonardo.

There was no time to thank him, for the press of bodies that surrounded them were dense and eager to strike back at their enemy. Leonardo leant back and parried, thrusting his sword down into a man's neck, causing him to scream and drop into the mud as blood squirted out in jets of crimson.

Another took his place, and they was joined by yet more. Leonardo glanced around in panic to see that they had gone too far, as the other English troops were some yards behind them. Hemmed in, even Leonardo could not parry so many points and he tried desperately, crying out as a sword was thrust into the maille of his left leg.

Then, one of his attackers had thought to spear his poor horse in the eye, whilst another hacked at its snout with a falchion. The beast screeched, jumping, kicking and bucking wildly as it lashed out at the enemy soldiers, forcing them back in a ring as an iron-shod hoof shattered a rebel's face.

Warily, they gave the animal space and, as it seemed determined to do the fighting for Leonardo, it was all he could do to stay mounted as it thrashed desperately. From the edge of the narrow slit of his helm, Leonardo could see Sebastien struggling with his own foes, only vaguely aware of the rest of the battle raging around him.

Then the spearmen were advancing once more and Leonardo's horse tried to retreat, but stumbled on a corpse. It was the only chance the enemy needed. A dozen spears were thrust into the horse's breast and the animal fell backwards and died with an awful scream of agony. Leonardo's world span as he was tossed rearwards like a doll, and he crashed to the earth with a jarring thud that took the wind from his lungs.

Dazed, he pushed himself to his knees, scrabbling for his sword where it had fallen next to him, only to look up in horror to see several men charging toward him.

Leonardo brought the sword up to parry, his shield blocking another blow and he hauled himself to his feet, desperate to regain some control of the situation. He thrust into a helm and slashed at the less-armoured legs of the men-at-arms, causing a spurt of blood to erupt from a severed artery, his foe howling in pain as he fell.

Leonardo took the brief respite to assess what was happening around him. A loose fighting line had churned the soggy meadow into a mud pit, where the King's men fought the rebels desperately. Though their charge had been horrifically successful, they were yet outnumbered and fought hard against Gaston de Bearn's rallying army. Some remained mounted and fought from horseback, but most were now on foot, the air filled with their defiant cries, yells and insults as they refused to give any ground to the rebels.

Not fifteen feet from him, Sebastien's armoured form could be seen upon his horse, surrounded by men-at-arms as they butchered the animal beneath him. As Leonardo watched, his heart stopped with a pang of shock as the rebels gripped the maille skirt that protected Sebastien's lower half and, as if in slow motion, pulled him from the saddle. Flailing desperately with his sword, Sebastien fell amongst them and disappeared from Leonardo's view.

Leonardo gave a roar of rage, hacking down the men that stood before him and charging the group of men-at-arms that surged, like a pack of hungry wolves, upon the prone, armoured man that was his friend. Leonardo brought his shield up as he ran and smashed into the nearest of them with all his weight, causing the man to fall directly onto Sebastien's outstretched blade.

He was impaled, screamed, then died. As Sebastien tried desperately to free his sword from the corpse, Leonardo slashed away at the other foes, winning them both some space to fight. The others backed off warily, until one of the soldiers lunged with a spear. Leonardo caught it on his shield, the tip burying itself in the wood. He had to yank his arm backward to free it, thrusting at the man whilst he was unbalanced and scoring a minor wound.

Sebastien had given up trying to free his sword and had, instead, pried a falchion from the fingers of a dead soldier, using the machete-like blade in angry, chopping blows, one of which struck true and nearly lopped a man's hand clean off. The extremity hung on by a scrap of flesh as the soldier gazed at the spurting stump in silent horror, before stumbling back between the ranks of the advancing men.

'There are too many of them!' Sebastien said in the lull as he backed away, with Leonardo at his side.

'I know!' Leonardo shouted back. 'We need to get back to our own line!' They edged backwards, risking a glance behind them to see that the 'line' was quickly dissolving into an unorganised mess of scrapping groups of men, and resembled more the winding curves of an estuary than the neat formation it had once been. *Still, there was more safety there than here*, Leonardo thought.

They backed away, parrying blows as they went, careful not to trip on the dead or wounded that already littered the ground as they retreated. Just then, Leonardo looked up as the enemy line bristled and Gaston's elite knights pushed their way through to the fore. The knights presented themselves eagerly, brandishing swords and shields, ready to get stuck into their enemy.

They were heavily armoured, with only scant few gaps between maille or plate to exploit – and, worse, they were well trained and fit.

'Come forward then, you dogs!' Sebastien cried defiantly toward them, but they were already marching steadily onward. Leonardo braced as two of them singled him out, advancing upon him in high guard.

They attacked, lunging with well-practised motions that might have caught out a lesser man. But this was what Leonardo excelled at; even weighed down with armour, he was more than a match for any of Gaston's men.

They learnt, but too late. Leonardo had a fraction of a second to brace himself in his guard position, anticipating the moves the knights made before even they did. He knew the lunge was coming and, instead of leaning back, ducked under it, bringing his sword around at the same time in a perfect strike to puncture a deadly diamond-shaped hole in a jugular, as he sidestepped away from the other.

The first fell and was dead within moments. The second knight looked down at his comrade in alarm and Leonardo pressed his advantage, arcing his blade downward in what appeared to be a mighty slash, which the man quickly blocked with his shield, only to realise it was a feint. Leonardo deftly changed the trajectory of the sword mid-strike and redirected it to the man's ankle, where the hem of the maille trousers ended and a small portion of the skin was protected by naught but a thin layer of fabric.

Predictably, it did little to halt the lightning-fast strike, and Leonardo's sword tore through muscles and tendons alike, felling the knight with the blow.

Suddenly, someone cannoned bodily into him and he crashed to the ground, wet mud seeping in through the slits of the helm and blinding him as he choked on it. Leonardo scrabbled blindly at his attacker, desperately trying to buck him off, but to no avail. His arms were being forced to his sides and he was terrified that the killing blow would be delivered at any moment. But then, all the force left his attacker's arms, and the weight slid from Leonardo's body to fall beside him.

Leonardo sat up, spitting mud and scooping it quickly from the slits of his helm. Sebastien stood above him, his dagger planted in the temple of the corpse lying at Leonardo's side. Leonardo leapt to his feet, found his sword and thrust at a man over Sebastien's shoulder, skewering him neatly through the mouth. He died with an awful gurgle, just as Leonardo and Sebastien found themselves standing back to back, their weapons at the ready, preparing to defend against their now wary foes.

'Thanks for that,' came Sebastien's muffled voice. 'I was about to say I'd returned the favour, but you one-upped me again!'

'It's nothing,' Leonardo replied as he eyed the enemy. 'Someone's got to have your back!'

'This doesn't look good, Leo! I don't fancy our chances against so many!'

Leonardo said nothing, but watched grimly as more of the rebel men-at-arms began to rally around the knot of knights in the centre. He was vaguely aware of a mounted figure at their rear, a large bulky shape atop a horse that surveyed the battlefield. Was that Gaston de Bearn? Leonardo had no time to make up his mind and switched his attention to the immediate threat.

Just then, more armed warriors appeared at their sides, and Leonardo recognised the helmet of Drogo de Barentin.

'Need a hand?' came the gruff voice through the mud-spattered steel of Drogo's helm.

'The more the merrier,' Leonardo grinned as he allowed the knights to fall into step beside him.

Together, they advanced and met the enemy with a clash of steel. In the chaos that followed, Leonardo somehow lost his sword and resorted to drawing his dagger, trapping the sword arm of an enemy knight in the deadly melee and headbutting him with all his might, the blow dazing the man for a second, which was all the time Leonardo needed to thrust upwards through the man's chin. The knight gurgled and spluttered in shock, beads of blood splattering from the ventilation holes of the helm and trickling down in carnal rivulets of deep crimson.

There they fought, the elite of each army hacking away at the other, neither willing to yield. Around them, men fell and died brutally, joining the mass of corpses so churned with mud and gore that it had become impossible to distinguish friend from foe.

The battle raged, and Leonardo fought side by side with Sebastien, each saving the other from the countless blows. They fought fiercely, each the equal of a half dozen men, a blurring dash of limbs and steel as their attacks felled foe after foe. But, even then, they were being pushed back, for the enemy were many.

'Hold!' Drogo roared as he felt it, too. 'Hold here, damn you!' The men held, but they wouldn't for long, for the throng of bodies before them would soon overwhelm them. Leonardo panted, for, fit as he was, they had been fighting for some time, and he was close to burning out.

'Hold!' Drogo shouted again, a note of desperation in his voice this time. If they broke, the enemy would cut them down to a man, Leonardo was sure. 'Hold, for the love of God!'

Leonardo gritted his teeth, slashing wildly, his attacks no longer the embodiment of finesse and precision. It was all he could do to hold the enemy back. With a jolt of panic, he realised they were going to break at any second and it would all be over. Leonardo shut his eyes and whispered a final prayer.

He opened them. Was that thunder? A rumbling sound was coming from behind him. What was it? Leonardo could not turn; the enemy were too close. The rumbling grew louder and louder. It was thunder, it had to be. A storm was approaching!

Leonardo watched as the rebel soldiers turned toward their left flank. He followed their gaze, just in time to see a fresh wave of perfect, pristine loyalist knights blitz over the meadow and smash into the rebels on the left. Within seconds, the left flank had been completely obliterated, and John de Gray could be seen hacking down with his sword in mighty strokes, cutting down rebels as they fled before him.

Sebastien cheered, and hurled himself forward with new vigour, his falchion wreaking havoc upon the distracted enemy. As the first of them fled, those remaining in the fray faltered, just as the English pressed up against them, their reinforcements invigorating them with a new energy as the two units merged into one. Leonardo capitalised on the enemy's sudden loss of will and, within moments, it had all become too much for them. Their resolve broke.

First was the left flank, where the fresh wave of English knights had struck. Then the mood spread to the rest of the rebel army and their grit became panic as they turned and ran, sprinting toward the walls of Bayonne to avoid the bloodthirsty wrath of their pursuers.

Some threw down their arms and fell to their knees before the walls, pleading up to the garrison to open the gates and let them inside, anything to save them from the slaughter that was sure to come. Predictably, the garrison were deaf to their pleas, for why should they help the men whom, an hour earlier, meant to storm their city.

Then the English caught up with them, and the butchery began. Animalistic screams rang out and the sandstone walls of Bayonne were spattered with blood, as the final remnants of Gascony's rebels were brutally dismembered beneath them.

'After him!' Drogo was shouting, pointing towards the pack of mounted riders that had used the chaos as an opportunity to flee. Leonardo turned to see the plump figure of Gaston de Bearn and a handful of his knights galloping away across the meadow and watched, in helpless dismay, for there was nothing he could do without a horse.

Drogo's remaining mounted men would not let the rebellion's instigator escape, however. They circled around, shouting and directing one another, pointing to the pack of riders. Leonardo watched, with the slaughter unfolding behind him, as Gaston and his last men were cut off and surrounded. Then, they had surrendered, and the battle was over.

'We've won!' someone cried, and the cheering was taken up by all the loyalist knights when they finally tired of the butchery, and their enemy knelt in surrender before them. Leonardo threw his sword into the mud, unbuckled the strap of his great helm and tossed that aside, too, before falling to his knees in exhaustion.

When he stood a minute later, he looked around him. The scene of the battle was a bloody mess. It was worst where the two lines had met; there, entrails slid from rendered flesh, curling into the grass among the gory horror of severed limbs and shattered bones. Muddy corpses lay motionless, while countless other bodies stirred, moaning pitifully as the wounded clutched at their broken bodies. They crawled deliriously here and there, the first men of Drogo's force already rushing to help them.

What a grim affair battles are, Leonardo thought. Even to one for whom killing was an occupation, the carnage was almost unbelievable. He wrinkled his nose in distaste, for the odour that reached him stank strongly of blood and shit. He looked down to see that he was caked in mud and gore; he tried to brush it off his surcoat, but gave up after a moment, realising it was futile.

Orders were being shouted, and the surviving rebels were being roughly apprehended as the English knights manhandled them at the tips of their swords, the garrison cheering them from the walls. Bundles of ropes were tossed down so that the loyalists could secure their captives' wrists as more of their comrades went to help the wounded.

Leonardo remembered his own wound with a stab of pain, and put a hand up to his right shoulder where his maille shirt had been pierced by the bolt. He winced as his fingers came away with blood, moving the shoulder around gingerly. Fortunately, the wound seemed to be superficial.

'Hey!' came a familiar voice. Leonardo turned to see Sebastien grinning, standing behind him and looking as messy as he did. 'You're alive!'

'Only just,' Leonardo grinned back.

Sebastien laughed. 'That's good enough, I'd say.' His expression became serious as he continued. 'You saved my arse a few times back there. Thank you.'

Leonardo felt awkward for a moment at his sincerity. 'And you saved mine. That's what brothers do, isn't it?' He stuck out a grubby hand between them and Sebastien looked down at it, before grasping it with his own and pulling Leonardo into a fraternal embrace.

'Aye,' he croaked when they broke apart. 'That's what brothers do.'

Leonardo felt pride swell in his breast at being able to call Sebastien his brother again, and a lump built in his throat at the thought of having someone as high a calibre as Sebastien as his friend. He was no longer alone, at last.

Just then, shouting was heard coming from the far side of the meadow, and both Leonardo and Sebastien looked up, together with the other knights around them, at the source of the noise. Four loyal knights were dragging an overweight, middle-aged man thought the mud. The man protested indignantly, his expensive clothes becoming spattered with filth as they watched.

'Get your damn hands off me!' he protested. 'Don't you know who I am, you low-born scum! Unhand me!' Then, the knights did just that. They tossed Gaston de Bearn into the mud and blood of his dead soldiers, his rotund body falling with a mighty splash.

He let out an 'Oof!' and scrabbled around to right himself. When he looked up, Leonardo saw mud covering a plump, moustachioed face, his balding scalp lined with long, thin rat tails of dark hair. Two, beady black eyes looked up to see a pair of thick, mailed legs standing over him. As Gaston's eyes looked slowly up the stocky figure, they settled on a face that had a slab of a nose, and a scar running from one cheek over the lips, finishing in a thick, bushy beard, the only hair upon the wizened head.

'Gaston de Bearn,' Drogo de Barentin said with a nasty smile. 'I've got you.'

A flicker of fear passed across Gaston's face as he looked up at Drogo. 'You can't treat me like this!' he exclaimed. 'I'm a noble. I ought to be awarded the proper respect of my rank!'

'Quiet!' Drogo barked and snapped his fingers. 'Take him away. And gag the fat oaf. I don't want to hear another bloody word from his treacherous mouth.'

'Yes, sir!' his knights said with a smile, relishing their orders as they dragged the rebel leader through the battlefield for all to see. The rest of the loyalists cheered and applauded, laughing at the sight of the struggling Gaston.

Then, Drogo turned to Leonardo and Sebastien with a smile. 'I saw the pair of you fight back there. I thought you were done for, for a moment. It seems you're hard men to kill.' Drogo clutched at a bloody wound on his forearm that had been hastily bandaged. Other than that, he looked unharmed.

'I thought we were done for, too!' Sebastien replied as he offered his hand to Drogo, who shook it willingly. 'By God, that was some fight.'

'Yes, it was,' Drogo agreed, shaking Leonardo's hand in turn. 'Maybe I am getting too old for this,' he said with a rueful smile. 'Join us tonight. I'm told the King will be here with the rest of the army by tomorrow.'

'Just in time,' Sebastien said with a wink and Drogo laughed.

'Thank you, both of you,' he said sincerely. 'You did me a great service fighting for me today.'

'The honour is ours,' Leonardo replied, smiling fondly at the older man.

'Now!' Drogo clapped his hands together. 'I've work to do. But tonight, we celebrate! Join us!'

Later, Leonardo and Sebastien wandered down to the Adour to wash the filth from their skin, before joining Drogo and the rest of the victors for strong wine in the encampment the rebels had vacated. The garrison of Bayonne had accepted hundreds of prisoners into their jails, filling them to the brim, until makeshift cages had to be lashed together from timber to house the rest.

The English knights were free to drink and revel in their victory, toasting their fallen comrades around the campfire. Hundreds of gruesome wounds were being tended to by surgeons from the city, the men working up a sweat as they performed operation after operation on makeshift wooden benches, set up under tents erected in the main streets of Bayonne.

Leonardo and Sebastien joined Drogo and drank, grateful to have lived through the carnage relatively unscathed. The evening passed in a swirl for Leonardo and, for a time, the rest of the world was forgotten as he and Sebastien discussed what a close-run thing it had been, each fuelled by the victory and the miracle it was that they were not dead.

For Leonardo, it was surreal. He had never known anything to be both sombre and joyous in equal measures. While some celebrated, others wept for the dead, reminding them all of the price paid to win the King his lands. When Leonardo finally laid his weary body down upon his bed roll that night, however, sobering thoughts haunted him, and the events of the previous days flooded back in a rush.

Sebastien had already made a grave error, and he was about to make a worse one. Leonardo knew he would have to confront his friend to try to stop the madness he planned. The grim thoughts plagued Leonardo into his dreams, and he wondered if, despite having survived a harrowing event as the battle at Bayonne, Sebastien would come to a far stickier end sooner than he anticipated.

Chapter 23

GASCONY

'Oh, forgive me, forgive me, Lord King!' Gaston de Bearn sank to his knees on the ground, the movement causing his enormous bulk to wobble beneath his mud-spattered finery. King Henry stood above him, his lips pursed. 'I was so wrong, Your Highness. I was wrong to fight against the crown!'

'Yes, Gaston, you were,' King Henry said in his most disappointed voice, as if scolding an unruly child.

'But you must understand,' Gaston pleaded, 'I only resisted because de Montfort's rule was so unjust! Had I known that you no longer heeded that evil man's council, I would have lain down my arms in an instant, for you are a wonderful and fair King!'

The main square of Bayonne was lined with hundreds of people, from peasant to lord, all to witness the spectacle before them. A great, wooden structure lined one side of the square. Gallows had been erected, upon which bound men were being led in rags, and marched up the wooden steps in a grim procession of the condemned.

They were minor rebel leaders and Gaston's staunchest supporters. Leonardo watched, along with the waiting crowd, as an executioner stopped each man before a beam hanging above them, from which a noose dangled before their eyes.

The King stood in the centre of the square, flanked by his royal guard, the cowering bulk of Gaston de Bearn lying prostrate before him in a snivelling display of subservience.

'The man has no shame,' Sebastien muttered in revulsion, as the executioner fixed each noose in turn around the necks of Gaston's captains. Some trembled with fear, flinching at the executioner's touch. Others stood proudly, the rope tightening around their lifted chins. A hush fell over the crowd as an official began to read their crimes aloud from an official document.

The King sighed, looking down at Gaston thoughtfully. 'What am I to do with you, Gaston?' he asked, stroking his short beard.

'Spare me, Lord King!' Gaston wailed, shuffling forward to kiss the King's boots, before being thwacked by the butt of a spear as the King's guard stepped forward to remove him. 'Spare me and I swear, on everything that is holy, that I shall be your most loyal servant until I take my last breath!' Gaston shielded his head with his arms.

In the background, there was a collective gasp from the watching crowd as the executioner kicked the first of the condemned from the gallows. The man fell several feet, before the slack in the rope around his neck was pulled taught and his body jerked violently, his neck snapping with a sickening crunch.

'Hmm, are you sure I can trust you this time, Gaston?' the King asked, his eyebrows raised pointedly as the dead rebel swayed behind him.

'Oh yes!' Gaston beamed, sensing the King's indecision. 'I swear it, here and now, Your Highness, King of Kings, ordained of God. I am your man!' Another captain was kicked from the gallows and another brutal 'crunch' rang out in the square, as a little girl began to cry.

King Henry allowed himself a smile. 'Very well, Gaston, but I mean it this time. This is your last chance. Understood?' Henry said, wagging his finger in warning.

'Of course, Your Highness, of course! You are so generous, so magnanimous, so merciful!' Gaston pushed himself to his knees and flung his arms out wide in relief, a broad smile spreading across his face as another of his men plummeted from the gallows. This time, the fall did not break the man's neck, and he choked and jerked at the end of the rope in a sickening dance of death.

Leonardo's gaze flitted to where Drogo de Barentin stood behind the King, a poorly disguised look of disgust displayed on his face at the King's leniency, as Gaston stood swaying, before attempting to walk forward and embrace King Henry. The King's guard swatted him away once more as the King placed his hands on his hips, a fond expression on his face as he looked upon the fat, dirty Gaston.

'Return to your estates, Gaston. And remember what you promised me here!'

Gaston couldn't believe his luck. 'Never has there been a more deserving King! A thousand thanks, Your Highness!' He bowed as deeply as his gut would allow before the guards escorted him away, much to the confusion of the rest of the nobility present.

'Unbelievable!' Sebastien spat. 'Come on, let's get out of here.' He turned, pushing his way through the watching crowd. Leonardo took one last look at the gallows as the last of the captains was pushed from them and died, swaying gently in the February breeze along with the rest of them, as the child continued to weep loudly into the silence that followed.

'Drogo's given me a couple of horses,' Sebastien said as Leonardo caught up with him. 'I say we leave for Bordeaux now and we can get there by tomorrow night if we're quick.'

As they strode down the street to the stables, Leonardo was deep in thought, the knowledge of his friend's affair with the Queen weighing heavily on his mind. It still seemed such an outlandish idea, that Leonardo struggled to imagine it, though he had heard the words come from Sebastien's very lips.

Marriage. Baby. It was too much.

'Alright,' Leonardo said eventually, deciding he would confront Sebastien on the road. 'Let's go.'

They were soon riding upon fresh mounts, and Leonardo winced as he felt the still-raw skin of his inner thighs rub uncomfortably on the saddle, the blisters having not yet healed from the rapid dash south. It seemed like a month had passed, but it had only been several days.

The King had arrived with the rest of the army the evening after the battle to find, to his pleasure, that it had been won for him already. It seemed the rush to intercept Gaston before he reached Bayonne had paid off and the rebellion was at a close. Drogo had prepared the captives for the King's justice and, that morning, had witnessed the execution of some of the rebellion's leaders, while many more had been imprisoned.

There was still the threat of Castilian invasion, though at least the crown could divert all of its focus to that problem now that Gascony had been pacified. As for Leonardo, his work was almost done; for, on the matter of diplomacy between the crowns of England and Castile, he could not be of much use.

For the time being, they would return to Bordeaux and wait to see how the politics unfolded from the King's seat of power. The army would follow them once affairs in Bayonne and the south had been seen to, and the King had ensured that the lords of Gascony were once again loyal.

Leonardo and Sebastien had ample time to enjoy the journey north this time. At least, Sebastien at seemed to, despite the drizzle of rain that fell upon them as they rode along.

Leonardo could not, however. He brooded in the silence, broken only by the clop of their horses' hooves, thinking of how best to bring up the subject that consumed him.

As the journey wore on, Leonardo knew that Sebastien could sense something was up, though he said nothing. They stopped to eat lunch and Sebastien broke out a leg of salted pork he had bought before they left and they shared the meat, sitting together on the log of a fallen tree.

'It's a bit grey today,' Sebastien muttered through a mouthful of pork as he looked up at the sky.

'Hmm,' was all Leonardo could manage, his mind churning at the thought of Sebastien's stupidity. Anger and exasperation mingled within him as he wondered how Sebastien could have been so foolish as to lie with Queen Eleanor. What had he been thinking? And his vows to the Order! Leonardo fumed silently, doing his best to mask it by glowering into the dirt.

'Right then!' Sebastien said cheerfully after a time. 'Onwards we go.'

They stood and saddled up once more, pulling their horses reluctantly from the patch of grass they had been grazing on and continuing north in silence. Finally, when the sun began to dip in the sky after a few more hours, Sebastien suggested they set up camp for the night, and Leonardo was grateful to do so.

'I'll get a fire going,' Sebastien declared once they had unsaddled the horses and secured them. They had chosen a site off the beaten track, some hundred yards in the woods where they were less likely to be disturbed by passers-by, and camouflaged their presence, just like they had been trained to at the monastery.

The monastery. There was another thing that had yet gone unsaid. The passage of time had since blurred the faces of Ebel and Sigbald in Leonardo's mind, though their spirits were with him as much as they had ever been. He still felt the weight of their deaths upon his shoulders after all these years, and he remembered the last words Sebastien had said to him before they parted ways. *You killed our brothers.*

They had cut Leonardo deep, though the years that had passed had dulled the pain and he realised that, since he had reconnected with Sebastien during this time in Gascony, he had appeared to have forgiven him. Though, whether Leonardo had forgiven himself was another matter entirely.

Leonardo sat on a rock and rubbed his shorn head with his hands, wondering for the thousandth time if there had been anything he could have done differently that day on the Dove. Sebastien, meanwhile, had come back to the clearing with an armful of branches, tossing them to the ground with a thud once he had cleared a patch of earth of leaves and moss.

'What's up with you?' he asked Leonardo as he knelt with flint and steel to light the fire. 'You've been quiet all day.' The noise of the steel striking the flint filled the clearing as Leonardo took a deep breath and began.

'Sebastien, there is something I need to speak with you about,' Leonardo said slowly.

Sebastien stopped hitting the steel against the flint and he looked up into Leonardo's bright green eyes, suspicious of Leonardo's grave tone.

'What is it?' he asked warily, pushing a lock of his light brown hair from his face.

Leonardo bit his tongue. He had rehearsed a hundred different ways of saying it, none of which seemed quite right. But he knew that it had to be said.

'I… I know about you. And *her.*' The sentence hung in the air like a ghost and the two men looked at one another from across the clearing. The silence that followed was deathly still, and Leonardo waited for Sebastien to say something, anything.

Finally, Sebastien stood, discarding the flint and steel. 'And?' he said simply. Leonardo's heart sank. With just one syllable, Sebastien's voice had conveyed a challenge, the single word brought from his lips with a cool edge that cut through the air, and his brown eyes hardened.

'I can't let you do it,' Leonardo replied, his voice barely a whisper.

'You can't let me do it,' Sebastien repeated, his face twisting into a sneer. 'And what is it you think I'm going to do exactly, brother?' He spat the last word like an insult and it stung Leonardo, as if Sebastien had hurled a rock at him.

'You're going to run away with her. I overheard you talking.' Leonardo stood, facing Sebastien defiantly. 'It's madness, Sebastien. Madness!'

Sebastien had frozen, his eyes wide. 'You overheard us talking?' he asked incredulously, his eyes flitting back and forth as his mind raced. 'You've been spying on me?' Sebastien looked at Leonardo as if he had just slapped him. He took a single step forward, planting his boots firmly on the forest floor beneath him.

Leonardo held up his hands in a pacifying gesture. 'Yes, but only because I wanted to h—'

'I should have known!' Sebastien interrupted, cutting through Leonardo's hasty explanation with a shout. 'I should have known they'd send you to spy on me! Tell me, how long has the Order suspected? Months? A year?' Sebastien took another step, his upper lip gurling into a grimace, his brown eyes dark with rage.

'What? No!' Leonardo tried. 'Not for the Order, Sebastien. Not for—'

But Sebastien was hearing none of it. His voice lowered to a menacing croak. 'You can't let me do it,' he said again, taking another step toward Leonardo.

'No!' Leonardo roared in response. 'I can't! It's madness, Sebastien! It's death! I won't let you! The Order would never let you get away with it, you fool!' His voice echoed around the nearby trees, their branches swaying nonchalantly, oblivious to the tension that surrounded the two men.

Sebastien's eyes widened. 'So that's why you're here,' he whispered, his voice suddenly laden with sorrow. 'You're here to kill me.' His dark eyes bore into Leonardo's and Leonardo was stunned.

'What...? No!' he protested, but Sebastien had taken another step forward, his right hand dropping slowly to his belt, the fingers curling around the hilt of the dagger that hung there.

'Of course they sent *you*. They would have known they could use you to get closer to me.' Sebastien's nostrils flared dangerously. 'You've finally come to cut my rope,' he uttered, his voice still low, though now the words were heavy with a cold anger that was a hundred times worse. 'You vile worm!' he hissed, drawing the dagger from its sheath with a rapid motion, holding it up before him and taking another step forward.

'Wait, Sebastien!' Leonardo implored, his wide eyes fixed on the dagger his friend was brandishing, as it dawned on him that Sebastien had gravely misunderstood his purpose. 'Let me explain!' He took an instinctive step back, holding his hands in the air as if the gesture might calm Sebastien somehow, but his friend was having none of it.

'No!' Sebastien cried. 'Let *me* explain! I knew this day would come. I knew the Order would send someone after me eventually, I just didn't think it would be you! No matter,' he sneered, a cold rage gripping him. 'Let me tell you what I would have told them, Leonardo. That woman and that baby are the only things in my life that have given me any real meaning. I've been searching for that something as long as I can remember, and I have never been more sure about anything! I would die a thousand times to protect them, do you hear me! A thousand fucking times!' Sebastien's voice hit Leonardo in a wave of fury and Leonardo staggered back, appalled at the sheer force of rage that was directed toward him.

'Damn you, Sebastien, let me speak!' Leonardo pleaded as his friend took yet another step closer.

'I'm done with speaking to you, you snake! Just as I was beginning to trust you again, after all this time. I should have known better!' Sebastien's eyes were ablaze with energy, and he brought his dagger up into a familiar striking poise, ready to leap forward and attack at any second. 'I won't let you take them from me, and I don't care if I have to kill you for it.' He growled like a feral dog, teeth bared, and body tensed for action.

Leonardo was half frozen in shock, still reeling from the fact that Sebastien could believe the Order had sent Leonardo to kill him. 'Please!' he begged Sebastien one last time. 'Hear me!'

But it was too late. With a snarl of pure fury, Sebastien lunged, jabbing his dagger into the space where Leonardo's chest had been, a fraction of a second before, with a blow that would have easily slain a slower man. Leonardo leapt back, stumbling over a rock as the apoplectic Sebastien stalked toward him, hatred in his eyes.

'See reason, man!' Leonardo cried, but Sebastien was too far gone. So consumed was he with defending what he had, that Leonardo's pleas fell on deaf ears.

Sebastien darted forwards once more with a thrust that Leonardo was only barely able to twist away from, the tip of the blade scraping the woollen fabric of his black robes. He recovered, just in time to leap aside from a sweeping slash that would have split his face in two.

Sebastien bellowed in fury, advancing, always advancing, as Leonardo did all he could to avoid each killing blow. Back he went, stumbling here and there as his enraged brother blazed toward him with an almighty, unstoppable wrath.

'Sebastien!' Leonardo shouted. And forward Sebastien came. The dagger thrust once more and Leonardo felt it pierce the skin of his chest, raking the flesh and easily splitting it apart in a stab of pain. Leonardo watched as he saw Sebastien draw the blade back once more, its tip dripping the crimson of his life's blood and he knew that Sebastien was about to kill him.

Then, the part of Leonardo's spirit that fought to keep him alive took over, and he was victim to his instincts. He watched helplessly, as Sebastien readied himself to trike the final blow and felt his body shift its weight, steadying itself.

Sebastien's dagger was coming forward again, but Leonardo's left hand moved to block it, and his forearm collided with Sebastien's outstretched wrist, redirecting the dagger harmlessly into the air by his shoulder, the momentum bringing Sebastien forward.

In the very same moment, Leonardo had countered with one awful but perfect movement. Sebastien stopped dead in his tracks, the snarl fading slowly from his face and the anger in his eyes flickering out as he looked down slowly, his mouth forming a ring of surprise.

There, just below his sternum, Leonardo's own dagger was planted to the hilt in his flesh. Leonardo had drawn it instinctively as he parried Sebastien's thrust, and Sebastien had thrown himself onto it. The pair stood, frozen in a deadly embrace of combat, as each looked as horrified as the other.

'Leonardo,' Sebastien managed, his voice no longer full of anger, but surprise. 'I forgot how fast you were.' Then he fell back, tumbling to the forest floor with a thud, his dagger flying from his hand. He lay, spreadeagled, his eyes staring up at the canopy of bare trees in shock.

Leonardo was stunned. His hand was still frozen in mid-air, where it had gripped the hilt of his dagger that was still buried deep in Sebastien's torso, and a look of horror twisted his features at what he had just done.

Laboured breathing jerked him from his inertia and he fell to his knees beside Sebastien. His hands trembled as he stretched them toward the dagger as it rose and fell with each agonising breath Sebastien drew in.

'No!' Sebastien choked, looking up at him. 'Leave it!'

'What have I done?' Leonardo muttered disbelievingly. 'God, what have I done!'

Sebastien groaned with pain as he lifted his head to look down his body, his face twisting with fear and agony as he saw the fatal wound in his breast. He sighed and let his head fall back down to the forest floor, a small trickle of blood forming at one corner of his mouth.

'No no no no!' Leonardo cried, rocking on his heels. 'Why did you make me do that, Sebastien?' he asked, gripping his friend's shoulders and shaking him. His eyes welled with tears, his voice almost a sob. 'Why did you make me do that? I was trying to help you!'

Sebastien winced, and a look of confusion flitted across his pale, freckled face. 'You were?' he asked weakly, his head turning to face Leonardo.

'Yes, of course I was! I just wanted to help you, that's why I followed you. I wanted to *help* you!' Leonardo's voice broke and the tears fell from his eyes and rolled down his cheeks.

'The Order didn't send you to kill me?' Sebastien's voice was weak and laboured now, as if every word cost him great effort and pain, for his face twisted into a grimace as he spoke.

'No! I would never, I swear!' replied Leonardo. 'I just couldn't let you run away with Queen Eleanor, not a *Queen* for heaven's sake! It would have been suicide for the both of you. I just wanted to make you see reason!'

At that, another flicker of confusion crossed over Sebastien's features. 'Queen?' he asked, his eyes searching Leonardo's. 'What do you mean?'

'I… I overheard you speaking with her, about your baby, about marriage!'

Sebastien's lips curled into an amused smile and he began to laugh. However, the action devolved into a horrible gurgle and more blood bubbled around his mouth, a fresh stream of it staining his deathly white skin. Sebastien choked on it, coughing it up from his throat and it flew up in a shower, speckling his face like a smattering of red freckles.

'Not the Queen,' he gurgled, half amused. 'I'm not *that* stupid! It was the girl with the auburn hair, a lady-in-waiting!' Sebastien coughed up more blood, taking a laboured breath, his lungs fighting to take in oxygen and not the thick, red fluid. He went on. 'Her name is Olivia. She's a Savoyard, but a cousin twice removed. She is an orphan set to inherit nothing. She is no one...' Sebastien's eyes shifted their gaze from Leonardo's own and up to the canopy as a distant longing filled them.

'We were going to be married,' Sebastien whispered, the hint of a weak smile forming on his lips. 'I love her, and she carries our child. We were going to be married!' As his features melted into a blissful daydream, his eyes began to lose focus and it was clear he did not have long.

Leonardo felt the words hit him like a hammer blow. It hadn't been the Queen that Sebastien was planning on escaping with, but her maid! He had been mistaken.

He wailed in sorrow, his body racked with uncontrollable sobs as his tears flooded down his cheeks, falling onto Sebastien's face to mingle with the blood.

Taking his friend's head gently in his lap, he kissed the cool skin of his forehead. 'I'm so sorry, Sebastien!' he wept, sniffing back the mucus as he looked down into his friend's face. 'I was wrong! I'm so, *so* sorry!'

'It's alright,' Sebastien replied with a sad smile. 'It was just a dream. That's all men like us can really do, isn't it?' His lips barely moved, the words escaping in a whisper that faded into the air. 'But it was a good dream.' Leonardo looked down to see Sebastien's robes stained with a dark mass spreading outwards in a ring from the dagger's hilt. His face was white as snow and his breathing had slowed, so much so that his chest barely moved.

Leonardo's heart broke as he realised what he had just taken from the only friend he had in the world.

Sebastien turned his brown eyes back to focus on Leonardo and his hand gripped Leonardo's arm. 'I'm sorry, too,' he said, looking up at him.

'You?' Leonardo snivelled. 'What are you sorry for?'

'What I said to you at the...' Sebastien choked and gurgled again and he fought for breath. 'At the monastery,' he managed, managing to control himself. 'It wasn't fair. It wasn't your fault. I... I was just angry. I needed someone to blame.'

'Shh, don't you worry about that,' Leonardo said, his jaw quivering as he wept. He used his free hand to stroke Sebastien's thick brown hair, as though he were a father rocking a son to sleep.

'No,' Sebastien said, strengthening his grip on Leonardo's arm, an echo of urgency in his eyes. 'I am sorry. You were a good friend. You saved my life that day.' Sebastien's smile returned as he looked up into the bright green eyes that were oceans of sorrow.

'And now I've taken it from you!' Leonardo moaned, wiping away the mucus on his sleeve.

'Don't say that, Leo. For men like us, every day is a gift.' Sebastien spluttered and another gush of blood poured over his chin as he gasped for breath, and he bucked, his eyes wide with fear. A second later it had passed, but his breathing was coming in short bursts now, for his lungs were full of blood and he was not long for the world.

'There is something else...' Sebastien hissed desperately. 'I was going to tell you, I just needed to know I could trust you again.'

'What is it, brother?' Leonardo asked.

'The Order. It is not what it was when we were recruited. It hasn't been for years.'

'What do you mean?'

Sebastien's eyes bore into Leonardo's. 'I thought you would have known. It no longer serves the greater good, but has instead become *infected.*'

'Infected? With what?'

'Corruption...' Sebastien coughed. 'Spreading from the top. You need to get out, Leo. You... need... to...' Sebastien tried to speak, but with every word more blood spilled from his lips and poured over the short hairs of his beard, dying them red.

'Don't speak,' Leonardo said as he wept. 'Don't speak.' He adjusted Sebastien's head in his lap, laying it back so that his brown eyes stared up at the canopy once again. Leonardo stroked Sebastien's hair as he bucked gently, his body still clinging on and fighting for air.

'It... it's peaceful here,' he gurgled.

'Shh,' Leonardo whispered as he stroked his friend's head. 'It is.' He began to rock him gently, tears pouring from his eyes like a torrent to fall onto Sebastien's brown locks. 'Do you remember the mountains?' he whispered to his friend and all Sebastien could do was nod gently. 'They were so beautiful. I'm honoured I got to know you there.' Leonardo looked up into the trees, imagining the magnificent snowy peaks of the Pyrenees, where he and Sebastien had shared so many memories together with the others that they had called brothers.

He smiled at the memory, and thanked God for giving it to him. That golden age of youth that they had spent together, laughing and joking, a time when the world was full of possibility and had not yet been sullied with the cynicism of age.

'The mountains,' Leonardo said, his voice a wistful whisper. But when he looked down into Sebastien's brown eyes, they were glassy and unfocused, fixed upon the branches that swayed gently above them, the last thing he had ever seen. He was dead.

Leonardo wailed and sobbed uncontrollably, still stroking Sebastien's hair with his hand. His heart felt like it had shattered into a hundred pieces, the pain of Sebastien's loss so great he thought it would kill him, there and then, made all the worse by the sight of his own dagger that remained buried in his brother's body. Leonardo was alone once more, and there he wept with the corpse, until the moon was bright in the sky and his eyes had no tears left to shed.

Leonardo curled up next to Sebastien on the forest floor, lying dumbly, his body feeling like it had become suddenly hollow, and a dreamless sleep took him.

When he woke, he gasped in the chilly morning air, turning to Sebastien in the hopes that he would wake, too, push himself to his feet and crack a joke, as he had when they had shared a hundred campfires before. But Sebastien remained where he lay, still and unblinking.

Leonardo sat there, looking into his friend's face for a long time, wondering why he hadn't let Sebastien kill him. He thought of the girl, Olivia, and her unborn child. Sebastien's child. Tears filled his eyes once more as he imagined a priest marrying them in secret as they giggled and held hands by the altar, staring lovingly into one another's eyes, filled with excitement at the thought of the new life they were about to begin together as a family.

But it would never come to pass, for Sebastien was dead and Leonardo had killed him and the dream had been so cruelly stripped away. Leonardo thought about what Sebastien had said the day before. *You've finally come to cut my rope.*

Leonardo felt wretched. He didn't want to go on anymore. There seemed little to go on for. He glanced back at Sebastien's corpse and knew he had to bury it.

Leonardo finally stood and searched the clearing until he'd found a suitable stick. Then, he began to hack away at the earth, letting the work consume him. The stick broke, and he fetched a new one, not pausing for breath. Every now and again, he would glance over at Sebastien's lifeless body and a lump would well in his throat.

It took him most of the morning to hack a deep enough grave into the hard ground and, by the end of it, he looked down to see that he was caked in mud, but he didn't care. Leonardo silently amassed a pile of large stones beside it and then moved to stand over Sebastien's body. He looked peaceful, his face still displaying the hint of a smile. Leonardo smiled back. *Even in death, he is defiant,* Leonardo thought.

He did his best to clean the body, and closed Sebastien's eyes for him before he gently removed the fatal blade and wrapped his friend in a cloak, covering him before lowering him into the grave as gently as he could. Leonardo gazed down upon Sebastien's face for the last time, before covering it with the cloak and tucking it around his body.

Leonardo clambered out and looked down at the swaddled figure. He took a shaky breath and thought that he had buried too many friends over the years. Silently, he began to scoop the fresh earth back into the grave with his bare hands until Sebastien disappeared to the world forever. Then, he piled the rocks on the grave so that they formed a protective mound.

Leonardo found a suitable stick and cleaved it in two with his dagger, lashing one half to the other with chord, before sitting on a rock to carve his friend's name into the green wood. It was the best he could do for him, and a tear came to his eye as he remembered that they had once done the same for Ebel and Sigbald.

Now it was Sebastien's turn. As Leonardo carved the name, he wondered if anyone would be there to carve his own when death eventually came for him. He sighed. Who was left? Who would do so for him? Everyone he had ever known or loved was dead and gone. He was alone.

Leonardo finished carving the cross before hammering it into the earth at the head of the grave, and he stood back to administer the final rights. He mumbled the prayer, making the sign of the cross and hoping that Sebastien's soul would find a place in heaven.

He finished and it was done. Leonardo stood motionless, staring down at the fresh mound of earth. He stood for a long time, not knowing what to do with the knowledge that he had just killed his last friend and buried him. He realised that he didn't feel himself, then wondered when the last time he had even been himself was. Certainly not that year. The year before that?

No. Longer. Somewhere along the line, he had become a shell of a man, his actions mechanical, with little original thought that might breathe meaning into his existence. Now, he was even less than that, he knew, as his eyes flickered to the makeshift cross with the name 'Sebastien' carved upon it. It was the only thing that suggested Sebastien had even existed, a meagre memorial for such a good man. *He deserved more*, Leonardo thought.

A temple ought to be build there... no, a cathedral. Even a monument of obsidian, a mile high, would not have been enough. Leonardo sighed as his bottom lip quivered again.

How can I ever come back from this? he thought.

Chapter 24

◆·◆

GASCONY

Cristoval del Soria was a happy man. He strode from the parliamentary building in Bordeaux with a smirk on his face, flanked by the flamboyant bodyguard befitting a messenger of the King of Castile. He knew he looked resplendent in a tunic of pale blue, cuffed with white silk. Another splendid hat rested at an angle upon his head as per the Castilian fashion, a feather protruding from it.

He hummed to himself as he strolled back to the lavish lodgings the English king had granted to him and his men when he had arrived in the city by boat, a little over a fortnight before. The next day, he was set to sail home bearing good news.

The defeat of Gaston de Bearn had been a minor setback, but no matter. Henry was wise to yet be wary of King Alfonso's threat to invade. The threat still stood, and Cristoval knew his master was serious, and had done an excellent job of declaring as much to the English parliament once most of its members had returned from Bayonne.

He chuckled at the memory of the livid King Henry as he stalked back and forth once Cristoval had read aloud his King's list of demands, finishing that, if they were not met, a Castilian army would invade Gascony within the month.

Henry had had no choice but to concede, agreeing to meet the full list. Cristoval relished the moment that he personally would stand before King Alfonso to proudly announce that the English king had pledged to declare war on Castile's sworn enemy, the kingdom of Navarre, to change the destination of his promised crusade from the Holy Land to North Africa and Morocco. And, lastly and most importantly, Henry had agreed that his young son, Edward, would marry Alfonso's sister, bringing an endowment worthy of the marriage.

The words sounded sweet in his mind, and Cristoval thought they would sound even sweeter on his lips. Castile had won a great victory without ever losing a man. He hummed to himself contentedly as he and his guards rounded the corner and arrived at the impressive building of his lodgings, constructed from carved stone blocks and elegant archways, making a two-storey house that sat in the wealthy district of Bordeaux, just within the walls. It was, no doubt, Henry's way of trying to impress the dignitary.

Cristoval had yet more guards at the gate, and they opened it for him on his approach, bowing their heads respectfully. Cristoval puffed out his chest and grinned. Life was good.

'Have the servants cook up a feast tonight!' he declared to one of his guards as he searched for a cup of wine. 'Tomorrow, we go home bearing good news!'

'Yes, sir,' one of the guards said mutely, trotting off toward the kitchen.

'I'll just use the privy!' Cristoval called, as he exited into the private walled garden at the back of the house. He hummed to himself and chuckled. Even the privy was impressive! A well-constructed building, placed at the back of the garden, more of an outhouse than a privy, and made from thick beams of timber. Cristoval made his way over, deciding with a grin that he would get drunk that night.

He pushed open the door, turned and locked it behind him. But then Cristoval froze, staring at the wooden door. An awful feeling crept over him and the hairs on the back of his neck stood up. He had seen something out of the corner of his eye.

His heart pounded, and his breathing became shallow. Slowly, he turned to look over his shoulder, into the corner of the room. A dark, robed figure stood there silently, a pair of green eyes shining out from under a hood that bathed the features below in shadow.

Cristoval's eyes widened in panic and as he turned back to fumble with the latch on the door. In a fraction of a second, the dark figure leapt across the room at a speed that was not human and Cristoval felt the cold steel of a blade press threateningly into his jugular as the man spun him, slamming him into the door.

'Please don't kill me!' Cristoval cried, holding his hands up in terror. Looking through his fingers, he found, to his surprise, that he recognised the face below the hood. 'You!' he said. It was the man that had approached him in the square asking about King Alfonso.

'Me,' the voice said.

'W-what do you want from me?' Cristoval asked.

'The same thing I wanted last time,' the voice said coolly. 'Information.' The steel bit deeper into Cristoval's neck.

'Aargh! Alright, alright!' Cristoval squirmed. 'What was it? You wanted to know if King Alfonso was directed by someone, yes? If he was steered toward disrupting the English king by another?'

The man nodded and Cristoval gulped. He looked anywhere but into those green eyes, for they were the most terrifying thing about the man.

'And don't lie to me,' the voice said calmly. 'I will know.'

'Very well!' Cristoval held up his hands. 'You win!' He licked his lips and racked his brain, trying to think clearly. 'The King has many counsellors, as Kings do. Some are his lords, some his judiciaries, and some are of the Church. But there is one he meets with in private council. I don't know why. Often, the King seems to come to a decision based not what is discussed in court, but during those private sessions.'

Cristoval felt the blade shift upon his skin and he cried out in pain.

'Who?' demanded the man.

'I... I don't know him. I've only seen him in passing and never met him. I—'

'A name. Give me a name.' The green eyes burnt with fire and Cristoval realised that, with a jolt of terror, if he did not give this man a name, he would die.

'Solomon!' he cried, squirming under his captor's grip. 'His name is Solomon! He is a bishop! I swear, that's all I know! I swear!' Cristoval sobbed, pitifully, hoping that his attacker would realise that he was but a harmless man and that ending his life was not worth the trouble.

Cristoval opened his mouth to beg some more, but the blade had already left his throat and he was shoved toward the privy, landing heavily upon it with both hands on the rim. He found himself staring down into the pit of faeces below, choking for breath.

He whipped around in terror, already bringing his arm up to shield himself from the blow that was sure to come. However, the door to the privy had already banged shut and he was alone again.

Queen Eleanor and her entourage strolled around the King's Garden, admiring its beauty, even though it was still winter, imagining how pretty it must be in spring. The gardens bordered the King's home in Bordeaux and were kept in good order, along with his house in his absence, by an army of servants.

They did an excellent job of maintaining the neat pathways, and wonderfully designed niches were constructed here and there, creating little alcoves where there were benches placed to sit upon. Even here, in the heart of the city, the Queen's guard were never far away, and a quick glance would tell Eleanor that they mirrored her movements from twenty paces.

She was surrounded by her ladies-in-waiting and servants, all of whom she was very fond of and was loath to go anywhere without them. They chatted happily amongst each other, as they often did, whiling away another day in her service. That was, all but one.

Olivia was quiet. She had been ever since the King's army had returned from Bayonne. The battle had claimed many lives, and Eleanor had feared that Olivia's lover, Sebastien, had been one of

371

them. Eleanor had enquired of Drogo when she had seen him, and he had been happy to report that, yes, he had indeed laid eyes upon Sebastien after the battle and even drank with the man.

Sebastien had been fit and well then, Drogo had said, well able to carry himself upon his own two feet and displaying no sign of significant injury. Drogo had given him two horses, and had seen him leave Bayonne for the northern road to Bordeaux with the green-eyed man, named Leonardo.

However, ten days had gone by and Sebastien had not reported back to the Queen. It was odd, Eleanor thought, as Sebastien was such a reliable man. Though he kept odd hours and often saw to other tasks than the ones she had for him, he was not one to leave for any length of time without first letting her know.

As the days wore on, and Sebastien had not appeared, Eleanor had grown increasingly worried. She glanced at the desolate Olivia to her left. The poor girl had been so full of excitement and relief when she'd heard that Sebastien had, indeed, survived and would surely be returning to her as soon as he was able.

Eleanor had made all the preparations for the couple's marriage, discreetly paying off a local priest to perform the rights in the chapel of a small church in the city. She had even prepared a wedding gift of a sack of gold to present to the married couple that would help them begin their new lives, wherever they ended up. For their future, she was not worried, for Sebastien was perhaps the most resourceful man she had ever known, and she knew he would protect Olivia and their unborn child with his life. There was always work for a man like him, and Eleanor did not doubt that he and Olivia would find a quiet corner of the world to be happy in.

But a day had passed, then two and then three, and Sebastien had not appeared. Olivia began to worry, her bubbling excitement suffocated by a blanket of doubt. Olivia had voiced her concerns to Eleanor at night, as she snivelled herself to sleep. Perhaps Sebastien had been robbed along the road?

'Don't be silly,' Eleanor had reassured her, for who could rob Sebastien and live to tell the tale?

'But what if he's found another woman?' Olivia pressed.

'Don't be a fool!' Eleanor had cooed. 'Sebastien is in love with you, my dear. He'd move heaven and earth for you!'

And yet, Sebastien had not come back. Eleanor felt a knot of apprehension build in her gut and could not even imagine what poor Olivia felt. Days had turned into a week, and Eleanor had sensed that something was wrong.

She sent her men out to look for the priest named Leonardo, but they came back with nothing; the man was a ghost. Eleanor chewed her nails as she walked along, thinking about what else might be done to find Sebastien, but coming up with no better ideas. But then, a few days later, the mysterious man she sought appeared.

'Your Highness!' shouted a voice. Eleanor looked up to see Sir Derek striding toward her with none other than Father Leonardo. 'A visitor,' the knight barked gruffly as he bowed.

'Thank you, Sir Derek. You may leave us,' she said, her eyes never leaving the tall, handsome priest clad in robes of black.

Olivia came to stand beside the Queen. She looked up at Father Leonardo expectantly, knowing he was a colleague of her lover's and praying that he had good news for her.

'Your Highness,' he said in a level voice and gave a deep bow. Eleanor searched his face as he straightened, but he was annoyingly good at keeping his expression blank. He stared back with a pair of piercing green eyes.

'I've been looking for you,' she said tetchily.

'I know,' came the simple reply.

'Well? Where have you been? Where is my man, Sebastien?' the Queen asked impatiently, doing away with the pleasantries.

'My colleague, Father Sebastien, has been called away on urgent business for the Order, Your Highness,' Father Leonardo said impassively.

'Urgent business?' Eleanor asked, a look of confusion crossing her pretty features. 'When will he be returning?'

The green eyes flickered from the Queen to the face of Olivia, and then, for the briefest of moments, down to the girl's belly.

'Not for quite some time, Your Highness,' Leonardo replied, and Eleanor's heart sank. Suddenly, she knew what had happened.

Olivia's eyes brimmed with disappointment as she looked from Father Leonardo to her mistress and back. 'But he must have said *something*,' she protested. 'How could he just leave like that?'

Queen Eleanor's jaw clenched. 'Leave us, would you, Olivia? I would speak with Father Leonardo alone.'

Olivia turned unwillingly, a slouch to her gait a result of the unfavourable news, and she walked to join the rest of the Queen's ladies.

Once she was out of earshot, Eleanor turned back to Father Leonardo, her eyes hard.

'What happened?' she demanded, a steely tone to her voice.

However, Leonardo did not baulk. Instead, those piercing green eyes seemed to burn, the only source of emotion on his noble face. 'He happened to have the misfortune to work for a mistress, so naïve, she thought a man like him could grow close to another without consequence.' The voice was laced with a quiet anger and the green eyes were ablaze.

Eleanor took an involuntary step back. 'Did you kill him?' she whispered, her hands trembling.

'Yes,' whispered the green eyes. 'And so did you.'

'Me?' she said, the accusation stinging her like a slap.

Father Leonardo gestured to the pregnant girl behind her. 'You should have known that the Order would never have allowed this.'

Eleanor was taken aback. *Her* fault? He had said it was her fault! She paused. Was he right? She gulped and gazed into the green eyes once more. They stared back defiantly, giving no ground. Bile rose in her throat.

'You're a monster!' she stammered, her hands clenching into fists.

'Yes,' the man agreed simply. 'And you are a fool.' He turned and left the Queen there, shaking, striding away down the path and turning to head through the gate, disappearing forever.

Eleanor could not decide if she was more angry or sad as she turned back to look at Olivia. She looked at the sweet features of the young woman, her round eyes full of worry. Her gaze was drawn to the protective hand Olivia had begun to place instinctively over her bump, feeling the growing foetus within.

That child would never know its father.

Epilogue

Leonardo watched as a mason chipped away at a lump of stone, expertly facing off one portion of it, pausing every so often with a set square to check for flatness. He was absorbed in his work, oblivious of Leonardo's watchful eyes. Tiny chunks of masonry blew apart where the chisel struck the stone face.

The air was filled with the metallic tapping and, glancing around, Leonardo could see a dozen other masons working away on their own wooden worktops, each with a different slab of limestone placed before them. Past the masons' lodge, workmen milled around a site, standing in deep trenches and hacking away with picks or shovelling out the already loosened earth, where yet more men scooped it up into wicker baskets, filing away over well-beaten tracks to where an enormous cart waited, already half full.

There, they deposited their payload, arriving from several different points on the site, creating a vein-like workflow that reminded Leonardo distinctly of ants returning to a nest along many different routes.

In the centre of it all, a master builder directed the heads of each team, poring over a set of detailed plans drawn up onto a large piece of parchment paper. Leonardo watched as the man pointed to a low stone wall in the process of being erected, instructing a younger man, with complex hand gestures, as he went. The young man was nodding vigorously, before appearing to interject with a suggestion and began making his own hand gestures to emphasise his ideas.

All in all, there must have been around seventy workmen on the site, each engrossed in their different tasks. Leonardo surveyed the footprint of the foundations and could plainly see that the building being constructed there would be enormous.

'Magnificent, isn't it?' Emilio Di Volterra said with a smile. 'Come,' he touched Leonardo's arm. 'Let's walk some.' They turned away from the new site and headed down the track toward Emilio's villa, in the rolling hills some miles outside the city of Rome.

'What will be built there?' Leonardo asked his adoptive father, glancing back at the hive of activity they were leaving behind them.

'A new villa, a chapel, stables, a bath house and two new barracks for you and your comrades. Servants' quarters, as well as several other outhouses,' Emilio said proudly.

'*Two* new barracks?' Leonardo frowned. 'I did not know there were so many of us.' He had just arrived at Emilio's estate in Italy, which seemed to have grown significantly since he was last there. Now, the lands of the cardinal of the Vatican stretched over two shallow valleys and made up many hundreds of acres. Leonardo did not doubt, either, that there were other estates besides.

'Yes,' Emilio replied, 'the old villa is so full at the moment, I suspect we'll need more space.'

'Full? Of whom, Father?'

'I have been hiring more men, my boy.' Emilio waved his hand dismissively. 'A little more protection wouldn't go amiss.'

Leonardo said nothing, but wondered why Emilio's villa, of all places, needed more protection. First, its very existence was kept a secret to Emilio's political adversaries – that is, if there were any of those remaining. And, second, there were usually at least several of the Order's agents based there at any one time – trained killers and versatile super-elite soldiers, just like Leonardo, that should have been able to deal with almost any threat. Why was it that Emilio had felt it necessary to hire several dozen mercenaries to boot? Or, did their presence serve another purpose?

Leonardo glanced at Emilio. He had shed his cardinal's robes for the day and looked resplendent in a tunic of black trimmed with white and gold, intricate stitching forming patterns in the expensive cloth around the hem and cuffs. He wore a thick cloak that matched his outfit, along with the Order's signet ring. His fingers and wrists were adorned with bejewelled rings and bracelets, marking him out as a very wealthy man.

Emilio's hair and neatly trimmed beard had more flecks of white in them, though his lined face had lost none of its sharpness, and one look in his eyes told Leonardo he was as dangerous as ever.

'So,' Emilio said, 'what have you learnt, Leonardo? Tell me everything.' As they walked, Leonardo began to recount the chain of events that had occurred in Gascony, giving the account in a matter-of-fact tone as though it had all happened to someone else. Though, there were certain parts he left out.

When he finished, Emilio nodded thoughtfully. 'I see. And Gascony remains in the hands of the English king. Good, that should keep the Franks from becoming too powerful and upsetting things. At least, for the time being. And what of the other thing, Leonardo? Did you find anything out?' He shot a questioning look in Leonardo's direction.

'I did, Father. It seems that the Castilian king leans heavily upon the council of a churchman, a man named Solomon.'

Leonardo watched Emilio's face carefully. He knew the older man well enough to detect a hint of recognition flicker across his face.

'Interesting,' Emilio mused as a sly smile began to spread across his lips. 'That is *very* interesting.' It was almost as if Leonardo had told him something he wanted to hear.

'Who is this man Solomon, Father?' asked Leonardo. 'Is he the Iberian Finger? If so, why would he be acting against you and the others?'

At that, Emilio chuckled and patted Leonardo's arm reassuringly. 'Don't you worry about that, my boy. Leave the politicking to me for now!'

Leonardo clenched his jaw. Whatever was going on, Emilio didn't want him to know about it. If this man Solomon was indeed one of the other Fingers, then he was acting against the rest of the hand, an organisation that worked via mutual cooperation of the different branches to achieve their goals. They had to agree for it to function. Yet, Emilio did not seem perturbed by this; indeed, he was glad.

Leonardo's eyes darkened as he remembered what Sebastien had said before he'd died. The Order, it seemed, was changing.

'And what of the other?' asked Emilio 'The agent of the Nordic Finger you linked up with? Sebastien, I believe his name was. Did everything go well? Has he now returned to his master?'

Leonardo paused before answering. 'Yes, Father, everything went well. I believe he is on his way home as we speak.'

Emilio nodded contentedly. 'Good, that's good, Leonardo. You have excelled yet again.'

Leonardo gave a false smile as he looked briefly at his adoptive father. It was the first time he had ever lied to Emilio.

Historical note

First of all, if you've made it this far, thank you very much for reading! Now, what can we say about this period in time? Well, I'll start by saying that the Gascony rebellion was not the most pivotal point in the English crown's history, nor the most interesting, but hopefully I've done a decent job of keeping you engaged.

Why, then, did I choose to write about it? The answer is simply because it fitted in with Leonardo's time frame. There were lots of interesting things happening during this century and, as much as I'd love for Leonardo to be involved with all of them, it simply wouldn't be credible to have him gallivanting around as an eighty-year-old, for example.

Where our present-day story takes place, in Gascony 1253, we see the meagre remnants of the once-great Angevin Empire. The extent of these lands in France was quite impressive in their heyday; in the late 12th century, the Plantagenets (the English monarchical dynasty) controlled around half of what is modern-day France, splitting the country north-south down the middle and holding the western portion of it.

This was established by King Henry II, who inherited Normandy and Anjou at birth and expanded the Angevin Empire during the latter half of the 12th century. Unfortunately for England, he was succeeded by King John, who was arguably the worst king in English history to ever sit upon its throne. John managed to lose the vast majority of English territory on the continent through a series of military failures and the alienation of his nobility.

Today, John is seen as the archetypal villainous king due to his cruel, petty and lacklustre personality traits. His reign is one of those 'what if' moments in history, where one has to wonder what might have been had England maintained and expanded the Angevin Empire at that time.

In any case, when Henry III becomes king in 1207, the early years of his rule were overshadowed by civil war and Magna Carta, a mandate that restricted the power of the monarch that Henry had to abide by, lest he suffer the wrath of his nobles. Remember, though medieval kings were thought to be ordained by God himself and were undoubtedly the 'top dog', they still had to be mindful of appeasing powerful lords. For, in feudal society, should such a lord take umbridge to the king's rule, they had the power to raise an army of their own.

Henry tried to reconquer the lands on the continent that had once belonged to his father, but without much success. One of his more famous failures was the Battle of Taillebourg in 1242, which marked the end of his military campaigning to expand. Instead, he was plagued by rebellion, both in Gascony, as we have seen, and in England.

The rebellion in Gascony happened much like I have described, with a few small embellishments that I'll get to. The characters are mostly real, such as Queen Eleanor of Provence, whom I describe in this book as a quite capable woman. From the books I have read on the period, historians seem to confirm this, noting her as a competent queen and a force to be wrestled with. Though she loved her husband Henry, there were several times during his reign that she 'wrestled' with him over matters of the state, such as who would become the next Bishop of Flamstead.

Simon de Montfort was a very real character too, and quite an interesting one; it's a shame I wasn't able to weave him into the narrative a little more. He was a very capable military commander and did everything Henry asked of him, though he did so a little too effectively for the likes of the Gascon nobility. They revolted against him (it seems the French reputation for revolution was strong even a thousand years ago) and Simon, as a result, imprisoned Rostand Solers – who did, in fact, die in his custody, being one of the chief gripes the rebels raised against Simon at parliament, where he stood trial before the king.

This ultimately led nowhere and Simon was dismissed from Gascony, leaving Henry to clean up his mess, as we see in the book. De Montfort would later go on to rebel against King Henry himself in England and was killed in the battle of Evesham in 1265.

Drogo de Barentin was real and a trusted household knight. He, along with John de Gray, were installed as seneschals whilst they waited for Henry to arrive with the rest of the army. While I do not believe that Drogo would have held a lofty enough position as a household knight as to command an entire army, I do think that he was at least a trusted and capable man for the king to have installed him in such a position in the first place.

The 'battle of Bayonne' is, unfortunately, completely fictional. The history books I have studied simply mention that Gaston de Bearn was 'intercepted'. Maybe I missed something. Regardless, I decided I would embellish his interception just a tad, leading into the climactic event of the book.

As for the crown of Castile, it is absolutely true that King Henry had to concede an unfavourable treaty to Alfonso under the threat of invasion. Henry certainly couldn't afford a ward like that and he was very upset at having to redirect his beloved crusade from the Levant to North Africa; he had very much been inspired by Louis IX of France, despite the disastrous outcome of the seventh crusade.

Now, moving on to the second narrative in the book, there isn't a whole lot to say. The Order of The Hand of God is an entirely fictional holy order (as far as I know…). As someone who has done quite a bit of military training in both the Alpine mountains and the Pyrenees, I know just how breathtaking they can be. I am also well aware of how dangerous they are, too.

Several of my military comrades were killed in avalanches and countless more injured while in the mountains. They are an incredibly dangerous place to be and, of all the hostile environments on the planet, they can kill you the quickest. That was why I thought it would be a perfect place for Leonardo and his brethren to train. The mountains would have weeded out the incompetent fairly quickly and the harshness of the environment would have toughened them up fast.

I do not think that medieval people would have ventured into the mountains in winter if they didn't have to. Unlike us, they did not have the technology to survive there. Even for folk on the plains thousands of metres below, the winter cold would have claimed victims every year. But, high up in the mountains, that cold would have been greatly magnified and the chances of survival without shelter in January would have been very slim.

I describe the way we used to build shelters in the military, hollowing out the snow from a snowdrift whilst packing it down and then squeezing ourselves into it like a tin of sardines. That would probably have been the only way to do it back then as well – as, in the 13th century, they didn't have sleeping bags. Therefore, only the most reckless folk of the Middle Ages would have travelled the mountains in winter.

Lastly, I'd like to point out that this is 'historical fiction' after all. If you are a bigger history nerd than me and you realise that I have made a few mistakes, of which I'm sure there are a couple, please don't get too upset! This was never meant to be a definitive historical account of the time, it's just for fun! If you want something a little more factual, I can recommend *Henry III: The Rise to Power and Personal Rule* by David Carpenter. It is an incredibly in-depth book and should serve you well on all things Henry III.

If you enjoyed this and would like to read more of my books, you can find out more on:

www.harrydobson.co.uk.